LAKEHOUSE
INFERNAL

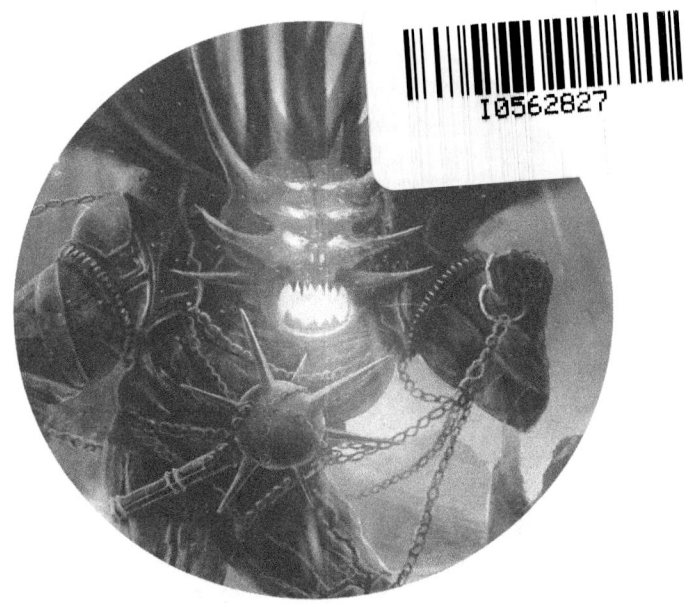

CHRISTINE
MORGAN

deadite
press

DEADITE PRESS
P.O. BOX 10065
PORTLAND, OR 97296
www.DEADITEPRESS.com

AN ERASERHEAD PRESS COMPANY
www.ERASERHEADPRESS.com

ISBN: 978-1-62105-300-2

Lakehouse Infernal copyright © 2019 by Christine Morgan

Cover design by Deadite Press

Printed in the USA.

For Lee, who is living proof some of the sweetest people write the sickest shit...with eternal (and infernal!) thanks!

INTRODUCTION BY EDWARD LEE

What makes a book a "great" book? Many camps have their own criteria which they apply to the definition. The Critical Camp, the Popular Fiction Camp, the Fringe Camp, the Art House Camp, the Speculative Camp, etc. We're told, for example, that Hawthorne's *House of Seven Gables* is a great book, and also Thomas Pynchon's *V.*, and also Gabriel García Márquez' *One Hundred Years of Solitude*.

Why are these called great books? Because of the allegorical relevancy their themes and characterizations purvey to our inquisitive and knowledge-hungry minds, and because of the light they shine on history, past eras, and social dynamics foreign to us modern folk. Indeed, they make us aware of "our existential position in this oblivious and often hostile universe," of "man's inhumanity to man," and of—ah, yes!—"Symbolism."

Is the cigar really a cigar? Is Hemingway's reference to "felled trees" in *In Our Time* really a suggestion of a man's fears of encroaching erectile dysfunction? And if it *is*, then what's the big deal? Why is that an "important" suggestion or observation? Is Hawthorne's famous story "Young Goodman Brown" really a symbol of the innocence of youth and the worldly temptations that seek to lead the chaste into corruption? Do I really *believe* that Hawthorne, scribbling away by lamplight in the *Customs House*, wrote the story with this symbolism consciously in mind, or that he gave Brown's wife pretty pink ribbons in her bonnet to symbolize her purity? No, ladies and gentlemen, I do *not* believe that. But, my point?

The Critical Camp tells us that great books fulfill the goals of literature...but we're never really told straight up what those goals are. I won't dispute the literary importance of *House of Seven Gables*, *One Hundred Years of Solitude*, and *V*.

But...

Have you ever *read* those boat anchors? The *only* people who've read these books in our time are students ordered to read them for their literature classes. Oh, yes, they're important but—seriously—they're *boring as fuck*.

It's not my intention to discuss the why's and wherefore's of the other "camps" because that, too, would be just as boring, more boring even than–I hate to say it–Michener's *Chesapeake* or anything by Anthony Trollope. I won't dispute the many many entertaining novels that also demonstrate literary merit. But let's face it, in this day and age—the age of the internet, digitalization, Starbucks, Ubereats, and more fuckin' apps than there are people, I think it's honest to say that a reasonable definition of a great book is a book that is *entertaining*. The more consistently entertaining, the greater the book.

To me, this is the perfect Litmus Test for horror fiction. And I'm here to tell you that Christine Morgan's *Lakehouse Infernal* is a *great* book.

I received it with some excitement. Let me explain. Some time ago, Ms. Morgan asked my permission to use a smidgen of the occult science in my novel *Lucifer's Lottery*, so I said sure. Her premise sounded diverse and intriguing: a lakehouse in Hell. I couldn't wait to see what she did with this idea. Then the manuscript arrives but I'm real busy, see, I've got deadlines, see, plus I'm fuckin' OLD now, see, so I don't get as much work done each day as I used to, but I told myself I'd read the first ten pages to check it out, then get back to my novel in progress for a week or so and try to make some headway. Then I would read Lakehouse Infernal in its entirety.

After one page, all those great reviewer cliches rang true: "unputdownable," "relentless," "page-turner," "rollercoaster ride," "you can't stop till you've read the last page," etc. To hell with my deadlines—this book left me no choice but to read it from start to finish. It was unacceptable to put it down at the end of a chapter, and see what happens later. I had to know what happens *now*.

Of course, I'm *not* into going to tell you what happens. You'll want to know yourself after you've read a few pages. *Lakehouse Infernal* is the most entertaining novel I've read in years. It's about a Grand Adventure, just as many great novels involve a grand adventure: *Huckleberry Finn*, for example, *Alice in Wonderland*, and *Red Badge of Courage*—literary classics, yes, and while Morgan's book is by no means "important" the way those books are, it's a hell of a lot more entertaining. That's the key: entertainment.

And you ain't gonna find anything else I'm aware of more entertaining than this. Think Spring Break, only instead of a beach house, it's a lakehouse, but the lakehouse *is in fuckin' hell*, that's right, a chunk of Hell that's been upheaved and pushed up into our pretty little world—sunny Florida, no less! And just wait until you're introduced to the shit that's in the lake. And when multiple parties of characters converge on our lakehouse—including holy rollers!—here's another reviewer cliche: "It spells a recipe for trouble," lemme tell you!

Seriously, *Lakehouse Infernal* is the coolest, ball-bustingest, most outrageous, and most *entertaining* horror novel you're likely to find in a long time. And lemme tell ya, if you like the gross-out thing like I do, this story's a veritable Whitman's Sampler. Morgan gets it, she knows the market, and she's not writing Little Bo Peep, she's writing a gross-out party about a lake full of sewage from Hell!

So, fuck you, Mr. Hawthorne, fuck you Mr. Pynchon and Mr. Marquez, and eat my shorts, Mr. Hemingway *this* book is a blast! Yours *aren't*!

Edward Lee
July 27, 2018
Largo, Florida

PROLOGUE

And then all Hell broke loose.

Such a common cliché. Trite. Overused. A lazy shortcut. Not to mention, highly inaccurate.

Even in this case.

All Hell broke loose?

Not hardly.

What happened that day at Lake Misquamicus was nowhere near all Hell breaking loose. Wasn't even 66.6%, which would have been thematically and numerologically appropriate.

All Hell, now, *all* Hell breaking loose would have consumed the entire Earth. Probably the Moon. Maybe more. Maybe a good chunk of the solar system. Like those dramatizations they show of what will happen when the Sun eventually bloats out into a red giant, expanding through one orbital planetary belt after another, the way rapid weight gain goes through the pants sizes.

Hell, as with space in another famous literary work, is big. Really, really, mind-bogglingly big. We aren't talking only your basic Biblical Hell here, either. About every underworld or realm of the punished dead you can imagine, from every mythology our cultures have ever known, is represented. Tartarus? Xibalba? Gehenna? Hel? They've got the complete set.

Nor is it just some vast cave with lakes of fire, cauldrons of boiling shit, and medieval torture devices. Not *just*. To be sure, those *are* available, but eternal torment has gotten much more sophisticated over the millennia. Hell's a city, the ultimate city, a sprawling collection of districts and provinces, upscale neighborhoods and dismal tenements, colossal factories and elaborate pleasure-palaces.

It's the Mephistopolis, baby, and it is beyond anything those ol'-time religions could imagine. Makes Milton look like a piker and Dante a little bitch.

The Mephistopolis. Expansive, encompassing, devious and sinister. Think New York plus Vegas plus Washington D.C., multiplied by the most decadent eras of Paris and Rome...the wealth of Dubai and Tokyo, the slums of Mumbai, South Africa, Haiti...from beyond the ultimate in opulence and luxury to below the most wretched nadirs of poverty and despair...the Mephistopolis has got it all and then some.

Magic has kept pace with mortal-world science, thaumaturgy with technology, alchemy with chemistry. Instead of coal or oil or natural gas, power is generated by the suffering of damned souls; how's *that* for a renewable resource? No energy crisis going on there!

Hell's also a growth industry. Sin is big business, always has been. Heaven may be harder to get into than one of those exclusive fancy-ass restaurants most people can't afford, but it's a cakewalk to end up in the Mephistopolis. The admission's free...anything else will cost you. An arm and a leg is getting off easy.

Speaking of free admission, there's also been a population explosion. Mirroring the one on Earth, with a diabolical twist—not much attrition happening among the damned. A soul is immortal; the initial spirit-body it inhabits upon arrival is identical to the person in life, but able to endure and 'survive' much more damage. Which, by the way, is definitely going to occur.

Pain isn't quite currency in Hell—they mint their own official stuff, and of course there's plenty of barter—but it might as well be. Mutilation, amputation, and various forms of maiming are commonplace. Assaults of infinite varieties are everyday hazards, not that 'day' means much there. Cannibalism, or whatever you'd call it given the diversity of species from ghouls to demons to mythic monsters, is always popular.

With all that, you might think the damned get burned through fairly quickly, but that's where the immortal soul fine-print catch comes in. Once the initial spirit-body is destroyed, the soul is incarnated into something else. If you're lucky, you might trade up. Very few, however, are lucky. The odds of coming back as a Copro-Leech, Pus-Aphid, or Ghor-Hound are much higher.

Then there's the aforementioned diversity of species. Imps, Trolls, Vampires, Werewolves, Gargoyles, Golems, you name it...again, the Mephistopolis has got them all and then some. Baby booms of Hellborn, Broodren, and Hybrids, the results of constant infernal couplings and rapes, further increase the numbers.

***

So, yeah. Hell is big. Hell is bustling and crowded. For *all* Hell to break loose would mean the end of the world, the apocalypse to end all apocalypses.

Part of Hell, though...

That's another matter.

A rather small part in the Mephistopelian scheme of things, really.

Say, about six billion gallons' worth.

The size of a modest lake. Florida's Lake Misquamicus, for instance. Which, on the day in question, contained about six billion gallons of fresh water. Plus assorted aquatic plant life, fish, crawdads, and one unsuspecting guy in a rowboat...his story is told elsewhere.

11

Fresh water, in a realm where the seas are blood and bile and pus and filth, would be more than worth its weight in gold.

It wasn't stealing, not exactly. They took the lake, oh yes. But, as said, this wasn't a theft. More like a trade. Even-steven swapsies, a permanent Spatial Merge, exchanging the contents of the lake for the contents of a reservoir filled from the Gulf of Cagliostro.

Six billion gallons. Of blood and bile and pus and filth. Plus, again, assorted…things. Creatures. Debris. Flotsam and jetsam. Detritus. Severed limbs and heads. Drums with damned prisoners sealed up inside. The usual kind of stuff you'd expect to find in an infernal ocean.

A problem, to be sure. Still, considering the staggering size and scope of the Mephistopolis, a relatively small one.

And then all Hell broke loose.

Since the first half of the trite cliché is therefore debunked, how about the second?

Broke loose.

Suggests chaos and carnage and mass destruction, sweeping epic fight scenes, big-budget blockbuster movie action, doesn't it?

Again, not quite what happened.

Lake Misquamicus was no major vacation destination, no tourist attraction. Just another Florida lake, quaint and quiet, almost obscure. A few campgrounds and cabins surrounded it, a lakehouse or two.

There were places to rent rowboats and Jet Skis or go parasailing. There were a couple of little general-type stores for ice and firewood and picnic supplies, a couple of bait shops, a clam shack, a seedy bar where the handful of resident regulars and the occasional adventuresome camper might go for a few beers. The local celebrity was a horror writer/filmmaker who seemed to spend an inordinate amount of time squirting presumably fake bodily fluids on busty models.

Quaint, quiet, almost obscure.

Ground Zero for six billion gallons of blood and bile, pus and filth.

Without warning, out of nowhere, all at once, whoomp-there-it-is.

The stink of it, the abattoir *stench!* Rotting meat and raw sewage—and not just *any* raw sewage, this was raw sewage from Hell! The unholiest of excrements! Quite possibly the shit of Satan Himself!

The humid, fuming *heat* of it! No more cool clear refreshing lake temperatures here, but somewhere between bathtub and hot spring, almost sickly-steaming.

The *color*, no bright special-effects corn-syrup red, but churning maroon and crimson streaked with the vilest greens, yellows, and browns. The slopping wet fleshy *sound* of it lapping the shore, lapping like mouthfuls of tongues, sometimes lapping *with* mouthfuls of tongues!

Oh, it was disgusting, it was a violation of every sense, a violation of *sanity*, a nightmare made real. It was fundamental beliefs turned inside out, knowledge shattered, a forced re-examination of science and natural laws.

But it still was just one lake, one obscure and fairly small lake. Yes, there were...things...in it. Living things, for want of a better word. Fishlike things, and sharklike things, and a serpentine abomination so huge it put Nessie to shame. Other things, such as relics from shipwrecks clearly of no human or earthly construction, or those sealed drums with their shrieking contents.

Hardly a breaking-loose, though, is the point. Those fishlike or sharklike or serpentine whatevers were, again for want of a better word, aquatic. They weren't going to get far.

It wasn't as if Hell's whole demon army had crossed over.

Nope. Even-stevens, it was only one guy.

* * *

Well, one guy plus three hulking Golems under his command.

One guy who, in life, had served in the legions of glorious Rome, bringing conquest and slaughter to barbaric lands. Civilization at the sharp point of gladius or spear, civilization with extreme prejudice. In death, damned to Hell where he belonged, he'd followed a similar career path, rising through the ranks of Grand Duke Cyamel's Exalted Security Brigade.

His name was Favius, and onto nearly every inch of his powerful frame had been magically grafted the face of a victim. Demonic and Damned, Hellborn and Hybrid, they covered his skin in a gruesome patchwork mosaic.

He also wore Hell-forged Roman-style armor, and no doubt made quite an impression when he'd first waded onto the banks of what had once been Lake Misquamicus, emerging blood-drenched into the living mortal world.

Pity there was only one person there to witness the dramatic moment.

A person Favius even, surprisingly, spared. Was it just not worth the bother? Or was it *mercy*? Was he a man— or whatever—of his *word*? He had, after all, always been unflagging in his obedience, loyal perhaps to a fault.

Well, loyal *definitely* to a fault…it was his loyalty that had landed him splash in the Reservoir, attempting to save a superior officer. Anyone else might have done it with thoughts of potential gratitude, indebtedness.

But, not Favius. He had dived into the vile muck without thinking of his own gain. Thinking only of his duty, his loyalty.

Loyalty to the point, even, of selflessness? Self-sacrifice? Nobility? Honor? Was this Favius…soldier of Rome, soldier of Hell…at the core of what remained of his soul…a *hero*?

14

Let's not get carried away, here.

Though, carried away was, in effect, precisely what happened to Favius, when the Spatial Merge kicked in. Carried away, crossed over, imported, exported, swapsies... the result was the same. Centuries after his original death and damnation, here he was, returned to God's green Earth.

Along with three Golems, and six billion gallons of creature-infested blood, bile, pus, and filth.

So, maybe not *all* Hell, and maybe not much of a breaking loose, but what happened that day at Lake Misquamicus did not go unnoticed.

In no time, it was all over the news, all over the internet. Local authorities were quick to respond, and quicker to retreat—this was rural *Florida;* they were used to drug-runners and moonshiners, prostitution, domestic violence, occasional sex-trafficking. Not something like this!

What even *was* it?

Natural disaster? Hardly...supernatural disaster, more like. A toxic spill? A terrorist attack? An invasion?

Next came the government, the National Guard and the military, a dozen alphabet-soup agencies stepping on and tripping over each others' dicks. FEMA, NSA, CDC, CIA, FBI, EPA; nobody knew whose purview an unprecedented event of this kind might fall under.

After an initial whose-line-is-it-anyway clusterfuck, though, there was no lollygagging. No BP Oil blame-gaming or post-Katrina buck-passing, no bipartisan finger-pointing or other such bullshit.

Of course, faced with the overt and undeniable theological implications—this was some act-of-God wrath-of-God end-of-days Biblical stuff—the paranormal and religious and occult aspects also had to be considered.

Clean-up was impossible. Clean-up *how*? Six billion gallons? Drain the lake? Into *what*? Dispose of it *where*? It might not be nuclear waste, but what about biohazards?

Contaminants? Infection? Ebola and AIDS and hitherto-unknown diseases?

What if it seeped into the groundwater? What would it do to the surrounding ecosystem? The flora and fauna? What about invasive species? What about the things *in* the hellish blood-lake? And the things—the *people*, if that's what they were?—that had come *out* of it?

Too many questions. Not enough answers.

This was mobilization time, action time. Something had to be done and it had to be done *fast*. Containment, and quarantine.

Whatever political fuckwittery the future might hold, this time on one thing the entire country—indeed, the world—was agreed.

Build the wall.

1

When got his first car, Gregory Nachtwald also got a metric fuckton of advice and input from various family members.

Dad—tire pressure, oil changes, antifreeze, wiper fluid, always carry jumper cables, regular tune-ups, cans of fix-a-flat, always keep current on license/insurance/registration.

Mom—seat belt, air bags, mirrors, blind spot, alarm system, put your phone away, don't pick up hitchhikers, park somewhere safe and lighted, beware carjackings.

Uncle—how to spot a speed trap, how far above the posted speed limit is generally let slide, how to talk your way out of a ticket, how to contest a ticket if the talking-out-of fails.

Cousin #1—dude get a muscle car if you wanna get laid, don't go the hybrid shit, nothing dries up a puss faster than some stupid electric wind-up toy, need a classic Mustang, 'stang for 'tang, guaranteed!

Aunt—wait half an hour after drinking before you get behind the wheel (often soused herself, she may have gotten that mixed up with her pool-rules).

Cousin #2—how come *Greg* gets a car when he's only *sixteen* and *I* have to wait until I'm *eighteen*?

Grandpa, maternal—you just try driving a Jeep through the jungle with poison snakes dripping down from the trees and them narrow-eyed sons of bitches lurking in the green waiting for you to hit a pit trap or a land mine, and we came to this village once, bunch of huts in the middle of nowhere, made out of mud and straw, and…

Cousin #3—now you can take me to the mall every day!

Grandma, paternal—hang this medallion from your rearview, Gregory; it'll keep you safe.

The medallion she gave him was a sterling silver disk on a chain kind of like a string of rosary beads, the beads polished mother-of-pearl and petrified wood. On one face of the silver disk was an engraved design, some sort of ornate symbol of lines and curlicues within an irregular seven-sided shape...a septagon, Greg supposed, though uneven. On the other face: *Never drive faster than your Guardian Angel can fly.*

Greg had dutifully hung it from his rearview, as much to placate the old lady as anything else.

He loved her, of course, respected her as was her matriarch elder's due. He didn't even mind spending time at her house, helping with yardwork—admittedly, her garden was weird, not much in the way of nice normal roses or geraniums there. She also made the best apple-cinnamon snickerdoodles he'd ever tasted.

But, even as a kid, he'd never been much of a one for religion of any stripe. Church seemed to him a waste of a perfectly good part of the weekend. Holidays were about presents and food. As for angels, guardian or otherwise? He'd stopped believing in those right around the same time he'd given up on Santa and the Tooth Fairy. Still, hanging the medallion was a small gesture to him that meant a lot to her, so, he did it.

Once he got used to the dangling sway in his field of vision, he barely noticed anymore...except when the silver pendant caught the flash of an errant sunbeam or oncoming headlights, or when a passenger remarked on it.

He did have to admit, over the years he might have developed a sentimental half-superstitious attachment. He knew he was a good driver, alert and conscientious, heeding the laws of the road. That, really, was why he'd

18

never had so much as a fender-bender or parking citation...
or a flat tire, or overheated radiator, or even a turn blinker
go on the fritz.

Good driving. Alertness and conscientiousness. Not
any guardian angel good-luck-charm.

And yet, whenever he sold one car to upgrade to another,
transferring the medallion was one of the first things he
always did.

It became a ritual, almost talismanic.

So, when he learned to fly and bought his own plane,
the decision of cockpit adornment was a no-brainer.

***

Never drive faster than your Guardian Angel can fly.

It must have worked. Unblemished record, excellent
condition trade-ins, not even so much as a dead battery or
running out of gas.

Which wasn't to say Greg's automotive life was
supernaturally charmed; he did still need to put gas in the
tank, for example. The odometer didn't spin backwards to
erase depreciation, none of his cars went spontaneously
cruising to make roadkill out of his enemies, and the radio
stayed tuned to whatever station he'd set. No *Christine*-
level tricks there, in other words.

He'd just been lucky. Lucky, alert, conscientious, and
skilled. Kept his rides clean, too, free of gum wrappers and
empty Starbucks cups and receipts, the usual accumulations
of road-litter. Regular trips through the car wash, regular
detailings and waxings. His angel, if he had one, shouldn't
have had much to complain about in those regards.

A further bit of coincidence contributing to his
superstition, however...often, when driving, he'd get
sudden hunches, sudden urges or impulses. To take a
different route than usual, to stop off for a soda or snack

even if he wasn't feeling particularly hungry or thirsty, to roll up his window. He'd heed these, then later learn his usual route had been traffic jam city backed up for miles, or a tanker truck overturned in a colossal fireball right about where he otherwise would have been, or the homeless panhandler who staggered up to the car at an intersection would've vomited down the glass instead of into Greg's face and lap.

The one and only time he'd driven without his grandmother's gift, having hired a rental car on a vacation, he'd experienced no major calamities…but no end of annoying pains in the ass, from a defective headlight to a wrong turn to not being able to switch off the damn heater. Normal hassles, things people had to deal with every damn day, but it had thrown him for such a stress-loop he'd barely been able to function.

With all that, it became hard not to believe someone or something was looking out for him. He took to touching the medallion, pressing its cool silver surfaces between foreknuckle and thumb, or running his fingertips along the string of beads. He wouldn't want to ride a bike or a skateboard without it, and public transit was right the fuck out of the question.

Never drive faster than your Guardian Angel can fly.

How fast, exactly, was that? he'd wondered, in his younger years. Fast enough, he supposed. He'd never been pulled over, not that he was a total scofflaw speed-demon.

But when he decided to get his pilot's license, he found himself wondering again.

Never drive faster, okay, point seemingly proved. Never *fly* faster? Might be another story.

Grandma Nachtwald had long since shuffled off ye olde mortal coil by then, so he hadn't even been able to ask her. Instead, he just looped that strand of beads where it wouldn't be too in the way in the cockpit, and hoped for the best.

It made him grin, though, envisioning his guardian angel—some white-robed, feather-winged, rosy-cheeked, beatific blonde, the plastic statue from a front yard Nativity Scene brought to life—windblown and harried and flapping like mad to keep up with his Cessna.

On this particular sunny spring day, his Cessna was a buzz-humming blur in the blemishless blue. Below, Florida sprawled humidly green, glittering here and there with waterways and condo complexes and amusement parks. He was bound for a small airfield near Ocala, feeling a little bit like Robin Hood or some other daring, dashing outlaw.

He skimmed the medallion's beads through his fingers. Their texture always pleased him, slightly rough despite having been polished. Mother-of-pearl and petrified wood, parts of once-living things, not just cold inert gemstones from deep in the earth.

If he *did* have an angel, if there was luck to be had, he knew he could use it.

Drug-running was dangerous work.

***

All at once, out of nowhere, things felt bad. Really bad. Like, full-scale DEA operation at the airfield bad.

Greg twitched as if agents with guns drawn were already surrounding him, shouting orders. Show us your hands, down on your belly, no sudden moves!

Bad.

Go to jail, go directly to jail, do not pass GO, do not collect $200, that kind of bad.

What was he supposed to do now? While there were plenty of other places to land, most of those handled business far more illicit than his, and were run by people just as well-armed and a lot scarier than the DEA.

Go to jail was one thing.

Gut-shot and dumped for the 'gators was another.

Change course, his mind urged. *Divert, go around.*

Change course to where? Go around what?

Checking his flight path, he saw he'd already drifted somewhat off-course. Not much, not enough to be a problem with fuel, but he'd caught a stealthy side-wind—

Before he could correct, the plane juddered. The controls jerked in his hands. The engines cut out and the instruments went haywire, dials spinning.

For a moment, the Cessna hung suspended mid-air, silent and serene. Then it tipped and dipped into a long, swooping arc.

Greg did what he could. Did everything he could think of, including some creative and effusive swearing. All to equal avail, which is to say, bupkus. He was going down. Down, down, down.

On the display, he glimpsed a red-marked zone, a no-fly-zone, an oblong outlined in dot-dashes, not a military base but some other sort of restricted area out here in the boonies, and didn't he remember...hadn't there been...a few years ago, yeah...a lake, something about a lake, something had happened to a lake...

Would a water landing be better? Better than plowing through trees and into the ground, maybe, but still no picnic, except a picnic for the 'gators, oh sure they might say Florida's lakes had good fishing, were great for boating and swimming, but Greg was pretty sure anything larger than a bathtub out here was going to be chock full of 'gators and water-snakes...

The plane veered and yawed and plunged as he fought the controls. Every loose item in the cockpit caromed around like buttons in a clothes dryer. His medallion whipped this way and that, beads clickety-clicking.

He saw a narrow black line cutting through the humid

green tangles, a road, and indulged a brief fantasy of using it for a runway, landing safely despite it all.

Then he saw the lake.

It was...

It was red.

Not red like the zone marked on his display, but a dark and awful *red*, a muddy maroon, a blood-shit kind of red as if a giant had squatted and offloaded a million gallons of hemorrhagic diarrhea.

More like six billion gallons, but Greg was in no state to be pedantic.

A lake of blood-shit, and *now* he remembered...the news coverage, the panic, evacuations, reports...a hoax, some said, a government cover-up of another industrial accident...terrorism, said others...monsters and aliens... the uproar over the churches...the wall...

He saw the wall, too, as it passed far beneath him. From up here it looked flimsy and stupid, a wall that wouldn't stop a runaway shopping cart, topped with ludicrous curls of barbed wire.

Oh, and the stench! He gagged, his gorge helplessly lurching. Never mind 'gators or water-snakes; he would sooner plow the Cessna straight into solid rock than into that reeking blood-shit stew!

Greg yanked one last time, desperately, on the controls. The world reeled and spun. Light flashed, a bright magnesium flare against silver, the medallion swinging wildly, its weird septagon-symbol lit up in white fire.

He both felt and heard a bacon-like sizzle as it smacked him square in the middle of the forehead.

Next came a thunderous, apocalyptic crash.

And then...nothing.

"All the places we could go for Spring Break and you

2

drag us way the hell out here." Trevor looked through the windshield at an empty stretch of two-lane blacktop unspooling between close ranks of dense foliage, and laughed.

Chelsea smiled thinly and spoke with a sugar-sweet venomous edge. "If you had better ideas, brother-dear, the time to suggest them was a week ago when we were making plans."

"I suggested some," Andy said from the back seat, where he sat semi-squashed but uncomplaining between Madison and Kayla.

The big sleek luxury SUV did feature a third row, but it was packed to capacity with luggage, supplies, and essentials. Mostly essentials. Essentials of the fermented and alcoholic variety. Meaning, a lot of beer, plus some stronger stuff.

Andy, of course, had his own stash of essentials, some in his backpack, some in the not-a-man-purse satchel he carried with him everywhere. He was well aware that, in the formulaic scheme of things, his role was that of the Stoner, the lovable burnout, the goof, the occasional comic relief.

Except that, in defiance of the usual pattern, he had a girlfriend. Sort of. Kayla used to be with Trevor, but now she was with Andy. He wondered if that made her, in the aforementioned formulaic scheme of things, the Slut. What he did know, without wondering, was she'd drop him like a hot beat if she thought she had a snowball's chance of

24

getting back with Trevor.

What he also knew was, the role of Slut was one for which Chelsea could throw down a decent audition. Not that she slutted in Andy's direction or ever would; he knew that, too. Lovable burnout goof or not, Chelsea made no bones about the fact she considered him a Grade-A loser, and funny-looking to boot.

Yeah, well, fair enough, he kind of was. Her type was more the dudebro fuckboi underwear-model type anyway, all abs and waxed chests and hair gel. If Trevor hadn't been her brother, she probably would've been all over him.

Then there was Madison, sitting on the other side of Andy from Kayla. The Good Girl, the Sandra Dee, the Betty to Chelsea's Veronica. Wholesome fresh-faced innocent beauty without realizing it; she might admit, under duress, that okay she was maybe kind of *cute*, but sure no movie star. Who often seemed less Chelsea's friend than Chelsea's pet project, the goal being to get her to let go, loosen up, and do the corruption boogie with the rest of the sinners.

He frowned at that, which was an odd thought even for his smoke-mellowed brain. Then again, given their destination, was it really such an odd thought?

"You suggested Disney World," Chelsea said.

"Well, yeah. You ever get wrecked and go on Space Mountain?"

Trevor laughed again. "Hey, these days, security there's tighter than our dad's ass. You try getting through while holding."

"So, instead," ventured Madison, raising her eyebrows, "we're going someplace with military checkpoints, someplace we're not supposed to be, someplace you can't just pay admission."

Chelsea shook her head. "Would you quit worrying? We have every goddamn *right* to be there. It's our *property*. We *own* it."

25

"As for the military," added Trevor, "chill, okay? I told you, we've got it covered. My buddy Jason is stationed at Checkpoint Jericho. He'll let us through, no problemo." He twisted around to offer a grin and a wink.

Neither of which worked much magic on Madison, who only pursed her cutely kissable lips into a skeptical moue. "Will he let us out again?" she asked.

"Damn well better," said Chelsea. She slowed the SUV and pointed. "Hey, look. We must finally be almost there."

Once upon a time, the billboard had depicted a bikini babe with a fish, and the words *Visit Scenic Lake Misquamicus*! Ghosts of the old sign still showed through, but it had been painted over with a mural of pitchfork-wielding cartoon devils.

And, in big violent brush-slashes of red:
Area 666.

***

Madison Jones did not care for the look of Area 666, or whatever this former townlet had decided to call itself.

A single stretch of main street was visible, lined with ticky-tacky little businesses; all the residential areas would be well hidden where rundown trailers and decrepit shacks wouldn't prove eyesores. At one time it must've wanted to look like sleepy bayou, but hadn't been able to get past 'do you hear banjos?' territory.

It was a total tourist trap, of course—this *was* Florida; she couldn't count the number of swamp tours and alligator farms they'd passed on the drive—with the requisite souvenir shops hawking overpriced junk, deep-fried-everything food stands, and the like. But, following the event, the locals had evidently mustered to try and capitalize on their hellish misfortune, and given the place a hasty makeover.

Signs boasted Satan's Spicy Hot Wings, Gates of Hell Gifts, the Red Devil Saloon, Lucky Lucifer's Lottery, the Deadly Sins Buffet, and so on. Their storefronts and windows had undergone similar artistic treatment as the billboard, with comical demons, lakes of fire, succubus pin-up girls, and so on. There was an ad for "Hellshine Homebrew: made with authentic lake water!" and another for "Damnation Dan's Veggie Stand."

The others in the car whooped and mocked each kitschy new discovery, but Madison, wedged in the corner by weed-smelling Andy, just shook her head. Maybe it had been a good idea at the time, something to kick a little life and commerce into just one more struggling community... maybe it had even worked, for a while.

Now, though, Area 666 looked deserted, a ghost town of fading paint, disrepaired buildings, cracked or broken glass, graffiti, and mold. Nothing appeared open. Nobody was in sight. Not even a stray dog or adventuresome rat.

She opened her mouth to ask if they were really sure about this, then closed it again before a single word got out. This was Chelsea they were talking about, Chelsea Carmichael, who got what she wanted come hell or high water.

Glancing at another shop—Little Devils Toys and Treats—Madison wished her brain hadn't phrased it quite that way. Hell and high water were apparently all too real around here. Assuming it *was* legit, not some government scheme or scam to cover up a toxic spill or who knows what...they had to be serious, though, didn't they? They'd built the wall...taxed the *churches*, for the first time in forever, and yowza had *that* gone over well with the evangies...

Then Area 666 was behind them, and up ahead was indeed the wall itself, like something out of a post-apocalyptic prison zombie movie.

"Let me do the talking," Trevor said. Evidently, 'talking' meant more than words; he hauled out his wallet for good measure.

Chelsea snorted but didn't object. Kayla was messing with her phone, while Andy leaned forward to peer between the front seats. Madison did likewise, squinting through the windshield.

"Dude," Andy said. "That's the checkpoint?"

"What were you expecting?" asked Trevor.

"I dunno, man, chickenwire, chain-link, a couple guys in a shed, maybe with walkie-talkies and one of those gates like you see at a parking garage."

Instead, what greeted them was a set of concrete towers that reminded Madison of where firefighters trained, topped with swively gun turrets. Gun turrets, she noted, that pointed not outward toward Area 666 but inward toward the lake. As for the gate, it was a massive metal affair, no chain-link on rollers but huge heavy bank vault style slabs on railroad tracks.

"Ummmm," she ventured.

"No," Chelsea said. "We're not turning around. We came all this way, that house is our property, and we are going to spend Spring Break here. Got it?"

Madison turned the rest of her *ummmm* into a meek little *umkay* and slouched deep into her corner as a door at the base of one of the towers clunked open and an armed guard stepped out.

***

For an 'armed guard,' he was hardly the body-armored stormtrooper Trevor expected…although he had a Batman-style utility belt worn gunslinger low on his hips, and carried an evil-looking gun, he'd zipped away the lower legs of his camo cargo pants, wore sneakers without socks, and his uniform shirt hung open to reveal a snug black tank top beneath.

The tan was new, the abs and pecs were sure as hell new, but even with a pair of dead black sunglasses covering his eyes, Trevor had no trouble recognizing him.

He rolled down the window. Hot humidity rolled in, quickly overpowering the SUV's air conditioner. The heavy, swampy smell of it was far from pleasant, eliciting mutters of disgust and dismay from the back seat.

"That is dank, yo," said Andy, "and not in the good way."

Ignoring him, Trevor leaned out and waved, put on his best smile, and called, "Jason?"

The guard stopped, shoved the shades up atop his slightly-shaggier-than-regulation hair, and squinted. "Trev? Holy shit, Trevor Carmichael, is that you?"

"Hey man, long time no see." He hopped from the car, taking a quick check of his reflection in the side-view as he did so.

"You really came? I thought you were talking from your ass." Jason laughed and shook his head.

They high-fived and bro-hugged and damn those really *were* some new pecs and abs! The Jason he remembered hadn't been pudgy, but he hadn't been buff either, and this Jason with his kind of a commando vibe going on made Trevor wish he'd been better about keeping in touch.

"Spring Break, hey, why not?"

"Yeah, but Spring Break, here? In *there*? You gotta be kidding me."

"Oh, come on, you don't have to give us the act," Trevor said. "We just want to check out our folks' lakehouse, hang a few days, drink a few beers, party, have a good time."

"Not in there you won't have a good time, sonny-boyo," a gruff smokes-and-whiskey voice cut in.

Another guard had emerged from the tower, and he was

no Sarge straight from Central Casting with the jaw and the greying buzz cut. His hair was shorter than Jason's, thinner, greasier, receding, and topped with one of those stupid red ballcaps. A belly of the sort Trevor believed in these parts was called a 'dunlap' led the way, encased in a flag-eagle-pickup 'MERICA tee shirt. The shirt's collar was lost in chins, above which were stubbled jowls, and he didn't need to turn around for Trevor to know the back of his neck would look like a package of sweaty hot dogs.

"Russ, this is Trevor, an old school buddy of mine," Jason said. "His parents own a place on the lake and he's wanting to check it out. Hasn't seen it since AllHell, am I right?"

"Right," Trevor said. "Kind of curious to know if it's still standing, what shape it's in. I mean, my dad says there's a caretaker and housekeeper who look after it, but..."

Russ nodded. "But who's to know? Might have let it slide. Might be squatting there. Might be worse. The people—if you wanna call 'em people—on that side of the wall, there's no telling."

"Technically," began Jason, sounding apologetic but hinty, "we're not supposed to let anybody through..."

Trevor flipped open his wallet. "I totally understand."

The dandruffy caterpillars Russ used for eyebrows arched with interest. They arched further as, behind Trevor, a car door opened and closed.

"Christ on a yo-yo, what's the damn hold-up?" Chelsea called. "Cash not good enough? Do I have to flash them my tits?"

"Well since you mention it..." Russ leered, slicking a wet tongue across broad, fleshy lips.

"Oh, for fuck's sake." She strode around the hood of the car, the dangly diamond in her pierced navel winking in the hazy sun. Already bare-midriffed with a loose crop top covering a skimpy bikini, it wouldn't take much to put the girls on display.

***

Oh god here we go again, thought Kayla as Chelsea strutted toward the gate guards. Time for the tit-show.

Then again, could you blame her? Chelsea did have great ones. Kayla—veteran of many a wet tee-shirt contest and drunken frat party—could attest to that. Besides, it worked. The tactic had gotten them into more bars and clubs, even when they'd still been underage, than she cared to count.

As the fat guard leered and the younger one turned to look, she could tell it was about to work again. Between Trevor's wallet and Chelsea's tits, the Carmichael twins were able to get pretty much anything they wanted.

Kayla herself might've been able to pull it off, being no slouch in the boob department either, but she knew her best feature was at the rear. "You got a black-girl booty," a boyfriend had once told her admiringly. "Guy could just motorboat those peach-globes all day long."

She shifted position on the booty in question, which by now was more than ready to be out of the car. It'd been a long drive in cramped quarters, and she still wasn't a hundred percent sure what she was doing here. Was she along as Chelsea's friend? Andy's girl? Was Trevor thinking to take her back?

Who knew? Who cared? They had booze and weed. And, if Chelsea's insistence was to be believed, a luxurious lakehouse with hot tub and all the amenities waiting for them.

Waiting for them in Hell.

If any of it was true.

Why build a wall with military checkpoints if not, though?

Again, who knew and who cared?

Outside, Chelsea had lifted shirt and bikini top and

was doing her patented sexy wiggle. The fat guard nearly drooled down his chins. The other, Trevor's hunky pal, gave a slow blink and appreciative nod.

Trevor, she noticed, didn't bother to glance at his sister's display. His attention seemed much more fixed on the younger guard. When the cash changed hands, his touch might've lingered a little longer than was bro-approved. Kayla hid a smirk. She'd often suspected Trev swung both ways, and today he was swinging thataway for sure.

The deal was done. The fat guard returned to the tower while Trev and his buddy said goodbye. Chelsea slid behind the wheel, adjusting her top. "Piece of cake," she said.

"Cheesecake," added Andy, snickering.

The big metal gate began grinding open, without any ominous music or anything. The humid tangle of shitwood on the other side looked just like the humid tangle of shitwood on this side.

Trevor got back in the SUV. "Told you it'd work. Two hundred bucks and a peek at my sister's rack. Not a bad deal."

"Um..." said Megan from her corner, as they drove through and the gate rumble-clashed shut behind them.

"Um what?" Chelsea's eyeroll wasn't visible and didn't need to be.

"What about getting back out again?"

"What about it?"

"What will they want for *that*?"

A sharp retort started to form on Chelsea's lips, but stalled there, her brow furrowing. Andy made a thoughtful 'hunh' noise. Kayla figured meek little Mads might have a point...what if an eyeful wasn't enough next time? What if the guards, that fat old fuck in particular, wanted something more?

Only Trevor blew it off. "It'll be fine," he said. "You think they'd leave us in here? It'd be their jobs, or their asses, when anybody found out they let us in in the first place."

"If we make it out," Megan said.

"This better not be about demons and shit again," said Chelsea. "When we get to the house, we'll probably find those so-called caretaker freeloaders squatting there like Frogface at the gate said. Then our dad will sue them down to the ground."

"If nobody's there?" Andy asked. "If the place is a rundown wreck?"

"Then we rough it or head for the coast," Trevor said. "Chill, man. Seriously. There's nothing to be worried about."

***

The further they went along a road that clearly hadn't seen much traffic or maintenance lately, the quieter and more tense the mood got in the SUV. When the silence started to piss Chelsea off, she tried for some music, but her gadgets were on the fritz and the best she could do was turn on the radio.

Most of the stations sounded like protracted farting or hissing sessions. She found a clear one, but after it played "Highway to Hell" followed by "Devil Inside," annoyance made her choose the silence after all.

What was it going to take to convince her brother and friends that the whole thing was a hoax? A government cover-up of some toxic spill or military experiment, a land-grab because valuable resources had been discovered in or around Lake Misquamicus...okay. Sneaky, shitty, but fair enough.

That actual demons had busted through from actual literal Hell? Please. Though whoever had the idea to use it as an excuse to tax the bejeezus out of those leechy money-grubbing mega-church bastards was a genius.

And if the lake was red, big deal, the lake was red. People dumped green dye into rivers in Boston and Chicago for St. Patrick's Day every year. As far as Chelsea was concerned, it just meant no swimming would be on the agenda. They'd still have the deck and the beach and the hot tub. Assuming, of course, the caretaker and housekeeper really had been doing their goddamn jobs.

Low-hanging boughs scraped the roof, while lower-hanging mossy vines slapped along the side windows like those flappy things going through a car wash. Some of them left slimy wet trails on the glass. Occasional bugs and ugly little wiggly things plopped onto the windshield from above, but she smeared them to goo with the wipers.

Then a great big ugly wiggly thing plopped onto the windshield from above, and everybody cried out. Chelsea stomped the brakes and hit the wipers at the same time. The brakes worked. The wipers didn't, just smacking at the thing, which coil-writhed around faster than a striking snake to attack, sinking what looked like pinchers into the black automotive rubber.

"Dude, what *is* it?" Andy said from the back. Both Kayla and Madison, trying to shy away from their own windows, were nearly in his lap.

"A millipede or something," Trevor replied.

"Oh like you're some kind of bug expert," Chelsea said.

The thing *did* have a sinuous, segmented body and a whole lot of legs…but it also had an upcurled barb-hook of scorpion tail, and its head was some sort of cross between a cobra and a crab…and as she leaned forward to get a closer look, a row of slitted yellow eyeballs opened all down its side to stare directly at her.

"What the *fuck*?!" Trevor didn't scream, but it was close.

Chelsea, on instinct, hit the horn. The sudden loud blare made the creature twitch and curl into a watermelon-sized pillbug ball. Not about to miss the opportunity, she floored the gas. The SUV lunged ahead, tires jolting over fallen branches, throwing everybody around in their seats. The scorpi-milli-whatever rolled off the side, and when she felt a hefty thump-crunch, she could only hope the rear wheel had gooshed the fucker flat.

Far faster than prudent, she roared them down the road, but the further they went, the weirder shit got. Were those faces, huge human *faces*, staring in contorted agony from the treetrunks? Was that a hunched bearish figure with an alligator's ridged back and tail bounding alongside them?

Behind her, Madison and Kayla and Andy were all gabbling at once. Beside her, Trevor was doing the same. Chelsea tuned them out, gritting her teeth. She had come too damn far to—

Then they crested a rise, the underbrush giving way to a panoramic view, and there sprawled what used to be scenic Lake Misquamicus, putrefying under the hazy sun in its full unholy glory.

3

She'd been on the phone when it happened, fighting with Bill but trying to keep her voice down so the kids wouldn't hear.

They were upset enough already, not understanding why Daddy wasn't at the lake with them, why Mommy had angry-cried for most of the drive, why they'd rushed through the packing so haphazardly that key items—Billy's GameBoy, Sherri's favorite inflatable dolphin floatie—got left behind.

The babysitter. The goddamn *babysitter*, how cliché was that? How goddamn fucking midlife crisis cliché was that?

Somehow, despite the earliness of the hour, she'd gotten them fed and to bed. They were exhausted, tired and confused, hadn't even argued much. A slapdash dinner of hot dogs and boxed mac and cheese, followed by ice cream sandwiches for dessert, had helped. Fortunately, Sharon followed the family tradition of keeping the lakehouse's larder and freezers well-stocked, so they'd only needed a quick market stop for perishables on the way.

The goddamn perky-titted, firm-assed, giggle-headed, nineteen-year-old *babysitter*!

The phone conversation—or, rather, the fight—had followed the usual course of such things. *Honey let me explain, it was stupid, a one-time mistake, give me another chance, for the sake of the kids, you know I love you, we can work this out.*

Well, fuck that noise. Fuck it all right in the ear-hole.

"I want a divorce," she'd said, pacing the long screened-in porch where she had her cousins used to spend many a summer night.

The sun had been setting, a building bank of clouds threatening at a possible evening thunderstorm. The air felt electric somehow, making the fine hairs prickle and stand up on her arms and the nape of her neck. A hush hung in the trees. Out on the lake's glimmering quicksilver surface, a lone figure sat in a rowboat.

"Sharon, look, I know you're upset, I know you're mad, and you've got every right to be—"

"Oh, thank you *so* much for telling me how I'm allowed to feel! God, Bill!"

How she, in that moment, envied the boat's occupant! Out there on the serene water, surrounded by peace and quiet, maybe pulling up crawdad traps for a dinner far more delicious than store-bought hot dogs. Out there, not having the Big Divorce Bitch-Out with some lying, cheating, babysitter-fucking bastard.

"I'm sorry, okay? How many times do I have to apologize?"

In that moment, hearing the whiny-sulky tone in his voice—yeah, he was sorry, all right, sorry he got caught—she wanted to go down to the shore and see how far she could skip her phone like a stone.

"I'm just saying, we've built a nice life together, let's not throw it away over one little slip—"

"One little slip? Is that what you're calling it? It's been going on for six months!"

From the corner of her eye, she'd noticed the dark clouds really roiling, the trees bending, the lake's ripples turning choppy. As if the weather itself were responding to her emotions.

"Well, hey, can you blame me? You know how things have been with us—"

"Don't you dare say this is my fault!"

"Damn it, Sharon, I don't want a divorce!"

A blast of wind hit the house, shuddering the windows. The lights flickered.

"Tough shit. I do. I've decided."

"You can't just—"

"And I'm keeping custody of Billy and Sherri," she'd said, noting the boater on the lake rowing like crazy for the shore, the oars churning up great splashes. Whoever it was had some strong arms.

"What? No. No. Sharon, please."

"Look on the bright side, you won't need a pretense to invite your little cherry tart over anymore." Her smile had felt wicked, a cruel and vindictive curve.

"I won't let you take my kids!" Bill yelled. "I'll see you in Hell first, you bitch!"

And then...

FWOOMP.

He'd said he would see her in Hell first, but Hell came to her.

***

I'll see you in Hell first, you bitch.

Sharon laughed, looking out on the lake. Laughed as she had done, years ago, after Bill uttered his famous last words.

It was laugh then or scream, laugh or go insane.

How about laugh, scream, *and* go insane?

But, so what? Who cared?

She had Billy and Sherri, didn't she? Without any legalese, without courts and lawyers, child support, custody battles. Without any of the shitty playing off against one another divorcing parents often did. The bickering, the backstabbing and undercutting, buying affections.

Like her own parents had done. Like her various sets of aunts and uncles had done. The entire extended family, fractured and torn apart...as if Gran and Pop-Pop had been the linchpin holding them all together.

Gran and Pop-Pop and this lakehouse.

An A-frame originally, various extra rooms had been tacked on over the years, the better to accommodate expanding generations. Most of those additions had happened in the 1970s, so it was lots of fake wood paneling, lots of the avocado/mustard/burnt orange color palette, lots of macrame hangings and post-hippie kitsch.

She vividly remembered the adults...lounging around in caftans, drinking Mai-tais, eating Swedish meatballs and gelatin molded concoctions...skinny-dipping in the lake or smoking weed out by the hot tub when they thought the kids were asleep.

She remembered Fourths of July, barbecues and fireworks, further-flung relatives parking campers in the yard, the annual ping-pong tournament, Pop-Pop in his ridiculous red-white-blue trunks, Gran with her huge floppy flowered sunhats.

Those seemed like the good old days. Back when she'd been too young to understand grown-up problems, before the apocalyptic shitstorm following Gran and Pop-Pop's deaths.

Oh, and hadn't *that* exposed secrets and scandals and dragged every skeleton from its closet? Much more than skinny-dipping and weed-smoking had gone on during those long weekends and lazy summers. Swinging, yes... wife-swapping and free love...but when called by those names, they generally required all the involved parties to be in the know. Otherwise, it was regular old adultery.

Adultery.

Cuckoldry.

Fooling around.

Possibly even accidental incest.

Illegitimacy, too. Were her cousins only cousins? Suddenly, nobody knew.

And clandestine abortions.

Along with alcohol and marijuana, there'd sometimes been harder stuff. Cocaine, LSD.

Not to mention the deaths. Tragedies—a car wreck, a drowning, a heart attack—revealed in new lights. Was it an overdose? Suicide? Even murder?

Throw in some amnesia and an evil twin, and they would've had their very own dynastic soap opera. If it hadn't been canceled. If the funeral planning blowouts and inheritance squabbles hadn't resulted in the entire family fracturing. From then on, it had been bitter divorces, estranged children. Most had never spoken to or seen each other again. A few kept in nominal touch with greeting cards, but that was the extent of it.

Farewell, big family gatherings at the lakehouse.

When the smoke had cleared and the dust had settled, somehow ownership of it had passed to Sharon's father. Who hadn't wanted anything to do with it, but neither could he bring himself to sell it. And so, when he'd dropped dead with his liver rotted to mush, lo and behold, it had come to Sharon.

Now it was hers. Hers, and Billy's, and Sherri's. Bill had no hold on it, no claim legal or otherwise.

It was hers, just as the children were hers.

A little different, maybe. A little changed, since Hell had come to Lake Misquamicus. Everything around here was different, was changed. Including Sharon herself.

In some ways, the changes were good.

For instance, she hadn't aged a day.

Neither had Billy or Sherri.

Every mother's chief dread and sorrow was the knowledge that her babies would grow up and leave her, but Sharon no longer had to worry about that.

She did sometimes wonder, though, what Bill would think. If he would even recognize them, provided he ever saw them again.

***

When the whole of Lake Misquamicus had vanished with an ear-popping pressure change, only to be replaced a heartbeat later by an equal measure of unspeakable filth, Sharon somehow held onto her wits.

Through terror and revulsion...through chaos and panic...mayhem and madness...through the abominable warping of reality and natural laws...against sanity-shattering assaults on mind and senses and soul...she'd held on.

She had to.

Maternal instinct. She had her children to think of. Billy and Sherri. She'd brought them here, and by God or whatever, she intended to take care of them.

They'd hunker down, she'd told herself. Ride it out the way they'd ridden out hurricanes and tropical storms. This would pass.

There were tears and tantrums, of course. They didn't want to *be* here, they didn't *like* it, they wanted to go *home*, they wanted *Daddy!*

What were they supposed to *do* with the power out? The fridge and freezers wouldn't work, or the stove; it was just canned stuff and cupboard stuff; she'd promised them all the ice cream and popsicles they could eat!

Billy couldn't watch TV or play video games or *anything;* he was so *bored* and this was the worst vacation *ever*! Sherri wanted to swim but the lake was all gross and ucky!

She soothed them, did her best to keep them entertained with books and board games and crafts. They had a radio, flashlights, plenty of candles. The taps still ran and the

41

toilets still flushed, thankfully; even more thankfully, the water supply wasn't piped from the lake.

Most of the other locals—and yes, Sharon considered herself such; her family had owned the property for decades, regardless of whether they lived here full-time or not—opted to do the same. They were just too damn proud, too damn stubborn.

Or too damn scared and too damn stupid. Not that it mattered much either way.

Hunker down. Ride it out. Wait and see.

It would pass. It would blow over.

Help would come. They didn't *need* help, no, of course not, but surely the government owed them something for their troubles. Surely there'd prove to be someone to sue.

Meanwhile, early-season campers packed up in a hurried exodus. Some must have made it out in time; others were turned back by roadblocks.

A *quarantine*, the entire area was under government quarantine, military lockdown, media blackouts! There would be no evacuations. No one allowed in or out. Rumors ran rampant of soldiers shooting those who tried to cross over.

It was crazy. It didn't seem possible.

Then again, neither did what had happened to the lake. Neither did what was *in* the lake, or emerged *from* the lake.

Still, people adapted. A person could get used to anything, it was said.

After a while, it wasn't so bad. They got by. They made do. Nobody was very neighborly, but news got exchanged, along with occasional goods and services. It reminded Sharon of pioneer days, homesteads where folks mostly kept to themselves, minded their own business, and only rarely interacted with each other as a community.

There was, of course, no little one-room schoolhouse. The very idea of a church was absurd, though some self-styled preachers of the new infernal world order wandered about. There were no general stores, either; both of those, which had only been campground quickie-marts in the first place, got looted to bare walls early on. Likewise the bait shops and clam shacks.

The places for renting Jet-Skis and speedboats stood abandoned, their sleek water-toys useless and decaying under layers of blood-rust. Rafts and rowboats were another matter...those worked fine, if sluggishly in the warm semi-coagulated stew...fine, until something capsized them from below...the fishing, though, who knew what might come up on the line?

The bar, a seedy and disreputable redneck roadhouse long before any of this, continued going strong.

Plus ça change, as they said. *Plus ça change.*

***

"Billy," Sharon said, hands on hips in the universal gesture of parental exasperation. "How many times do I have to tell you? *No* using your sister as a pain-battery!"

"But Mo-o-o-m!"

"Don't 'but mo-o-o-m' me, mister. Unhook her from that."

"She *likes* it!"

Sherri, strapped upside-down onto a *cross-saltire*, giggled. Her reddish complexion had gone redder than usual, almost maroon, from blood flow to the head. Alligator clips pinched the arch of each nostril and her septum. Others clamped her upper and lower lips, her earlobes, and the tapered tip of her tongue. The silvery, serrated metal teeth dug into tender bruise-purple flesh.

From the ends of the clips snaked thin wires, connecting into the guts of a circuit board from what used to be part of one of Billy's science-kit experiments. The device now bore little resemblance to what had originally come out of the box, since what had originally come out of the box was not etched with occult symbols, inset with chunks of carved bone, and topped with a glass dome inside which eldritch yellow sparks shot through whorls of scarlet vapor.

"Hi, Mommy!" chirped Sherri, as well as she was able under the circumstances. "Billy's agonocizing me!"

"See?" Billy, from beneath the hood of his dark blue bathrobe, gave Sharon the sort of look children reserved for particularly dense adults. "I told you, she *likes* it!"

"If she likes it," said Sharon, "then it's not going to work very well, is it?"

This evidently had not occurred to her little warlock, whose face screwed up into a ponderous frown. "Can I cut some of her fingers off?"

"Hey!" Sherri clenched her fists below the heavy wrist-cuffs.

"*May*," Sharon corrected. "And, no, you may not cut off her fingers."

"Aww. You never let me do nothin'."

"*Anything.*"

He heaved a monumental sigh, rolling black gold-pupiled eyes.

"Now," she continued, "unhook her, then both of you wash up for lunch. I'm making meat-splats."

That cheered him up, and Sharon smiled as she walked back to the kitchen. It was in many ways the same as it had always been, the same seventies kitsch from her own childhood, though the ubiquitous sunburst clock no longer kept reliable time, and the appliances had been modified to let them more or less function on a different power source.

Human suffering was the latest in renewable energy, and after some fiddling around, most of the homes around Lake Misquamicus were fitted with agonicity adapters. The main generator station was run by the Riggerses, who had been local caretakers, housekeepers, and handymen since ages immemorial. Or at least as long as Sharon's family had owned property here.

It bothered her now and then to think that she had working lights because some hapless unhappy campers existed in a state of endless torture, crucified or pressed between beds of nails or systematically mutilated and burned...so, she just tried not to think about it.

She checked the meat-splats, which were sizzling in a cast-iron pan, oozing bilious grease. She flipped them to sear the other side, though she'd leave them raw and gooey in the middle the way the kids preferred. Then she cut some thick slices from a loaf of mixed cornmeal/bonemeal bread, and spooned canned carrot slices over a bed of black-veined garden greens. Not that they'd eat their vegetables, but, a mother had to try.

That done, she stepped out on the side deck. The wind was in her favor today; the lake-stench almost pleasant, the gurgling shrieks of banshee-fish a distant discordance.

Distant enough for her to hear the burr-choke-sputter of what sounded like an engine faltering overhead.

She looked up. Her brows, or the thin ridges of fine scales that had replaced them at some point within the last few years, drew together as she watched a small plane corkscrew crazily across the sky.

It went down with a terrific crash, behind a sickly strand of trees on the far side of the lake.

***

Sharon watched the smoke rise for a few seconds, then realized she'd better get back to the meat-splats before plumes of smoke rose in her own kitchen.

Once she'd removed them from the heat, she leaned to the window over the sink and peered in the direction of

45

the plane crash. Would this be it? The start of a wildfire? Not like they could count on the fire department or forest rangers for help.

They'd been lucky so far in avoiding any such further disasters. The lack of campers was a plus; the steamy humidity, moister and danker than when it'd been water, was another.

And, like the residents, the local flora and fauna had undergone their own changes. Become...acclimated, as it were. The nearer the shore, the more pronounced the effects.

The children, washed up, scampered in and took their places at the table. Billy had shed his junior-warlock robe, the desiccated fang-turtle head he wore on a string around his neck looking incongruous against his faded Ninja Turtles tee-shirt. Or perhaps it was the other way around, perhaps it was the cartoon faces that looked incongruous.

"What was that noise, Mom?" he asked, reaching for the pitcher of sulfur-laced instant milk. It foamed yellowish-white as he poured it into his cup, smelling of rotten eggs.

"Was it a dragon?" added Sherri, who, once righted from her upside-down position, had done her wild-curly hair into six uneven pigtails. Small bruises and scabs marked where the clips had been.

"An airplane," Sharon said. "It crashed in the woods."

Billy's onyx eyes widened. "Did anybody die? For-real-die? *Die*-die?"

"I don't know, sweetie. Pour some milk for your sister, please."

"Can we go see?"

"I wanna see!" Sherri bounced up and down in her chair. "I bet there's parts all over!"

"Yeah! Parts and blood! A real *big* meat-splat!"

"Maybe later," she told them, putting plates in front of each.

"Eew gross, carrots!"

"Just eat them, Billy." She sat down and forked a carrot slice into her own mouth to set a good example.

As they ate, the kids speculated about the plane crash, how many people had been on it, if they'd been cut in half or 'decapernated,' if their heads would still be alive, and what would become of any survivors.

The answer to that last one, Sharon had a pretty good idea. Despite the quarantine and the wall, outsiders still occasionally got in. Scientists, military, occultists, reporters, thrillseekers...and it didn't often go so great for them.

No matter how well-prepared or well-equipped they thought they were, they weren't. Who ever *was*? How could *anyone* be?

As for coming in by way of a plane crash?

Assuming any such survivors weren't driven immediately insane, assuming they managed to avoid being mauled and eaten by something from the lake— the fanged-turtle skull Billy wore was from a hatchling; the adults averaged the size of a Volkswagen—or a Hell-touched predator on land, assuming they didn't run afoul of toxic thorns or poison plants...assuming *all* that, which was fairly fucking unlikely...

Well, then there were the people.

Fortunately for Sharon and the kids, just as she considered herself one of the locals, so did her neighbors. They'd known her family for three generations; four now, counting Billy and Sherri.

Others, though...the tourists and day-trippers, the campers, the cabin-renters, the passers-through...the strangers who'd just happened to be here when Lake Misquamicus underwent its unholy conversion, who hadn't escaped before the roadblocks and lockdown...

"Can I have another meat-splat, Mom?"

"Finish your carrots first."

He complained but he complied. As Sharon got up to serve him another juice-dripping portion, she glanced out the window again.

Aside from the smoke-plume, nothing seemed to have changed. Yet, the edges of her consciousness prickled, as if in premonition. Something was different. Something was happening, or going to happen.

Whatever it was, she supposed they'd better prepare and be ready.

4

On that day, oh that day, that most glorious day...

His initial reaction had been disappointment, to be sure; a cheated dismay. After all his hard work, his pain and toil, his unfailing obedience, to be denied the very fruits of his labor had indeed seemed a cruel twist of fate.

When, with an immense implosion and expulsion of infernal energies, the Merge had been effected...when the contents of the six-billion-gallon Reservoir crossed over, contents including by accident of happenstance Favius himself...when he'd felt the wrenching transference, seen the skies warp above him...

Yes, his first thought had been how he would now never have the chance to drink of the precious fresh water being brought to the Mephistopolis, all because he had in selfless loyalty leaped in to save his superior officer. Not that Favius held it against him; he had been a dedicated soldier of Rome and then of Hell, and considered it the ultimate honor to have so done his duty.

Missing out on the fresh water, though, after untold centuries among the Damned...

Then he had realized, as he'd struggled to keep his head above the seething displaced surface, what it meant... and any sense of disappointment or dismay vanished in a savage rush of euphoria.

What was a missed chance at a few cupfuls, doled out no doubt stingily by Lucifer's quartermasters, when here he was with the whole mortal realm at his disposal?

His for the taking, to seize and to plunder! To claim, not in his own name but in that of his Emperor Eternal! To be vanguard, advance scout, for Hell's mighty armies!

True, he had at his command only three Golems. Hardly a legion, but it was a start. He'd waded ashore, the blood-filth streaming from every crevice of his armor, and stood with them upon the very skin of God's own green earth.

Breathing the clean air, hearing the wind in the trees, early stars glinting above him in a natural twilight, Favius knew he would partake of much more here than just fresh water. The delicacies of the living world were a feast laid before him, praise Satan!

But those were for later.

Duty foremost.

Business before pleasure.

And so he had spared the woman who'd been upon the beach, who'd witnessed his emergence and answered his questions.

Dorris, her name had been. A Greek name by the sound, though she did not much appear so. Buxom, if aged...a crone but a busty one...he could have thrown her to the ground, torn her flimsy garments from her, raped her half to death without a second thought, and then given her to the Golems to dismember at their whim...but he hadn't.

Again, duty foremost, business before pleasure. His drive, his purpose here, was service. Not lust, not even ambition. Those, too, were for later.

Summoning the Golems to follow, leaving Dorris to run for her life like a madwoman, Favius had begun his march of conquest.

Behind him, the lake still seethed and churned as it settled into its new confines. Its denizens flapped and splashed, unable to comprehend what had transpired; one moment they'd been swimming around the Gulf of Cagliostro...then the great pipeworks had siphoned them into the Reservoir, and then they were here. Along with garbage, wreckage of derelict ships, sealed prison-casks, and other detritus.

Shrieks arose as mortals came rushing from cabins and campgrounds, wondering what had disturbed the evening's tranquility. Immediately upon finding out, many went insane, or fainted, or collapsed wracked with violent convulsions of vomiting. Some fled, as Dorris had done. A foolish few ventured closer, only to be snapped up by hungry jaws.

All of these, Favius had likewise spared, or ignored. He strode on, making for the largest structure within sight, which seemed to be some sort of public house.

As good a place as any to resume his ungodly work.

***

Yes, that glorious, glorious day!

The public house, or bar, or whatever it was, sported a weathered sign painted with the word "Crawdaddy's," along with a comical caricature of some crustacean-looking long-bearded creature holding a foaming mug in one claw and a smoking pipe in the other.

Favius had marched toward it, the Golems in formation behind him.

Outside were parked an arrangement of vehicles, most of them battered heaps of rust. A door stood chocked open, emitting the dim flicker of firelight and a gabble of argumentative voices.

"...watch the game with the blammed power out?"

"...wye-fye don't work neither..."

"Nor my phone, the hail?"

"...kind of place you runnin' here, Crawdy?"

"Now listen here, you all are welcome to quit your bellyachin' or take your business elsewheres! This is none of my doin'. I don't own the 'lectric company."

Favius strode into their midst.

Favius, in his Hell-forged Roman armor, nail-studded war-sandals slapping the floorboards, the weighted leather strips of his battle-apron swinging against his thighs.

There followed a moment of gape-mouthed silence.

He used it to survey his surroundings—rickety furniture, grubby patrons, sputtering mismatched candles, sour beer. The pride of the place seemed to be a strange sunken-topped table upon which were strewn small balls of polished stone, the men around it holding long thin sticks like staves or spear-shafts.

Then the largest of the men present, whose fat-slabbed but thick-muscled arms displayed crude tattoos, spoke. "What's with *this* faggotry? Fella's wearin' a *skirt*!"

"Uh, Zeke?" said another, closer and of clearer eye. "Fella's got other folks' *faces* sewed all into his skin."

"I am Favius, Conscript First-Class and Vanguard of Satan's Legions!" he declared, voice ringing. "Surrender and suffer; resist and suffer more!"

The Golems clomped in one by one, the size of the door forcing them single-file, and another jaw-dropped silence greeted their hulking immensity.

"Break those who fight or run," Favius told them. "Take the rest slaves."

Three huge heads nodded.

"Slaves?" someone repeated. "Look, mister, this is America—"

Favius, in a lightning-fast maneuver, snatched the long stick from another man's slack, whirled it, and forcefully threw. For all it lacked a spear-head, it flew straight and true well enough, the blunt nub at the end punching through the protester's throat. He crashed over backwards, blood gurgling, choking, scrabbling at his skewered larynx.

A third silence held, broken as the grizzled elder behind

the bar—Crawdy, presumably; the owner—raised empty, quavering hands. "Here now, just a minute," he said. "We don't want no trouble."

"No trouble?" bellowed the large man called Zeke. "This skirt-wearin' faggot just done kilt Emmit, and you say no trouble?"

With that, the bullish fool rushed at Favius, swinging big fists. Favius met him square on, broke both his elbows with crackling wet snaps, heel-kicked his left knee sideways for good measure, and before Zeke could so much as begin to register the pain, Favius slammed him face-down bent over the strange table.

Several of the others made as if to dash for the door, only to be duly caught and broken by the Golems, broken at spine or neck, femur or pelvis, swiftly broken with crushed and pulverized bones, and flung to the dirty floor where they twitched like crippled insects among spilled beer and cigarette butts.

"Where I come from," said Favius, as Zeke howled and swore, "this faggotry of which you speak is a matter of perspective."

He tore away the man's trousers, exposing large hairy buttocks. Zeke's howls of fury turned to panic-tinged outrage.

"To penetrate..." Favius went on, spreading those buttocks and sluicing an unfinished mug of beer into the crevice between them.

"Holeee shit!" screeched the bar's only female patron, a crone even more aged but less buxom than Dorris had been. "He's fixin' ter put a cornholin' on Zeke Bodean!"

"And," Favius continued, hiking his tunica and battle-apron, "to be penetrated."

Which he then, most forcefully, demonstrated.

***

A day, indeed, of glorious conquest.

Favius thought back on it often, thought back on it fondly.

How, at his first brutal thrust, the man bled like a child bride...how Zeke's shrill screams had soon turned to blubbering, begging sobs and mewling whimpers...how the other patrons, there in the bar, had looked on in shocked horror...how, by the end of it, the sound was a visceral squelching...the satisfaction beyond sexual he'd felt as he pumped his seed deep into the man's ravaged innards...and how, when he withdrew with nearly as much violence as he'd entered, the clinging prolapse of Zeke's bowel had extruded in a kind of birthing...a fleshy, intestinal, vestigial tail plopping wetly against the backs of the man's bloodied, shit-streaked legs.

Of the onlookers, Favius had noticed only one whose attention showed as much sadistic fascination as horror, a gangly gingerish youth, all pock-marks and freckles. Several times during the rapacious proceedings, he'd slicked a tongue over thin lips, his breath quick, his eyes bright. This, too, seemed beyond sexual, more derived from witnessing such humiliation and pain.

And it was he who'd dared approach, with posture of proper deference, once Favius stepped back from the splayed ruins. He'd held out a scrap of toweling cloth, saying, "'Scuse me, there, sir, but you got some mess on your pecker; thought you might want to give it a wipe-down."

Still covered as he was with the coagulated, tacky contents of the Reservoir, Favius was hardly much concerned for cleanliness—which was, after all, next to godliness and therefore anathema—but he found the youth's attitude intriguing.

"Who are you?" he asked, taking the towel for use as suggested.

"Name's Ritchie, though most folks call me Spot."

"The fuck you doin', boy, talkin' to this maniac?" cried Crawdy from behind the bar. "Git 'way from him or I'll blow a hole through you, too!"

Crawdy had, it seemed, forsaken his earlier don't-want-no-trouble philosophy. His formerly empty—if still quavering—hands were empty no longer, burdened by some sort of weapon. A 'sawed-off shotgun,' as Favius would later learn.

It spat iron pellets in a thunderous belch of fire, but the nearest Golem had already placed itself in front of Favius, so that the pellets thwacked into its dense, claylike skin with no more effect than a fistful of pebbles flung into thick mud.

A second Golem reached one massive arm over the bar, gripped Crawdy by the neck, and squeezed. The old man's head popped off like an olive from the stem, landing nose-first on the bar's surface amid ashtrays and beer glasses.

The sole woman uttered a piercing screech—a Harpy of the Underworld could have done no better!—and tried to run. The third Golem swung an arm, catching her mid-chest, staving in her ribcage as if it were a brittle wicker basket.

Any further attempts at flight or resistance proved equally short-lived. So did the people who came running from the road, shouting that there was some serious crazy fuckery afoot down t' the lake, phones gone screwy too, sheriff and county-mounties on the way.

Favius had then turned to Spot, who'd watched all the carnage with evident excitement.

"You," he said. "Do you pledge servitude? Not to me as your master, but to mine, to the Master of masters, the Master of us all? To Lucifer, the Morning-Star, in His Unholy Name, praise Hell ever-after?"

Wide-eyed, even exalted, the pock-faced youth nodded. "Whatever you say. Whatever you want."

"So be it." He raised the wadded towel, sodden with semen, shit, and blood, and swiped three inverted crosses, one onto Spot's forehead and one on each cheek. "Be anointed, and serve. Keep this place, tend it, await further instructions."

"But...you heard what they said, the cops're comin'!"

"Yes," said Favius, signaling to the Golems to follow. "And we will be ready for them."

***

They'd waited, Favius and his Golems, on the road Spot had told them would be the most likely for the 'cops' to use. A delightful cacophony arose from the surrounding woods. Mortals in terror, mortals in madness, mortals in pain…could any sounds ring sweeter to the ear?

It was chaos, Hell's own glorious chaos. The residual power from the Merge spread in ripples, expanding from shore to land, altering the very soul and substance of any living things it touched. Diminishing, yes, diffusing as it went; mighty though the spell had been, a single lake however large was but a portion of God's cherished Earth.

Yet, here was the foothold. Here was the indelible Mark.

Here, overwhelmed with purpose and pride, was Favius. Honored. Humbled. Whether accident or destiny, he was here. And would, in Lucifer's unholy name, serve.

Whispers seemed to reach him, whispers not in his ears but in his mind. Information. Advice. Not orders, not even instructions, but suggestions. Helpful hints. Favius heeded those whispers intently. He knew all too well that he knew all too little of this world. Much had changed since the era of eternal Rome. He had witnessed those changes reflected in the Mephistopolis, mimicking in twisted mockery the advances in technology, architecture, communication, and culture. No longer were ballistae and Greek fire the most potent weapons of war, no longer did the phalanx and chariot rule the battlefield.

He had a great deal to learn, and the best way to do so...

It did gall him a bit, did rankle his gullet and stick in his craw. It smacked of cowardice and dishonor—not that honor was his concern; loyalty and obedience were his concerns. Deceit was sometimes necessary. Deceit in the service of the Prince of Lies was a privilege.

Sirens warbling, lights flashing, the 'cops' in their vehicles approached as Spot had predicted. Favius knew immediately these were no elite troops. These were barely better than a village militia, half-disciplined peasants armed beyond their worth. Some time in the Legions would have soon set them right. Or killed them. Either way.

The Golems stood shoulder to shoulder to shoulder, huge and impassive, clay slabs roughly formed like men but twice the size, effectively blocking the narrow lane. Favius stood before them, chin high, gladius in hand, his Hell-forged armor glinting and the tormented faces sewn into his skin expressing their silent suffering.

Three 'cop cars' screeched to dust-flinging halts, askew every which-way. Men spilled out, men with more 'guns.' Babbling and shouting, already pushed near the brink of insanity just by what they'd seen thus far, they seemed to have scant idea what to do.

Upon beholding Favius in his war-glory, and the hulking Golems, scant idea became no idea. Or several conflicting ideas acted on at once.

One demanded, "You with the sword, drop it!" Another threw himself in the dirt, curled in the fetal position, and began praying. A third took aim; a flash burst from the end of her little 'gun' and a fast-moving projectile pinged off Favius's breastplate with the sensation of a fairly solid punch to the chest. A fourth ran. A fifth jumped back into the 'cop car.' A sixth brandished a 'shotgun' superior to the one Crawdy had used, yelling something about 'take down this ugly motherfucker!'

As with his quite reasoned and rational response to the Zeke-bitch's remark about faggotry, Favius would have been glad to fuck this man's mother…or, indeed, his own, though his memories of her were millennia old and their paths had, to his knowledge, not yet crossed in Hell. However, no such mother presented for the fucking, unless the woman who'd shot him had children at home. He considered it.

But, no.

"Crush them," he said to the Golems. "Kill them all."

Which they dutifully did. And, as the whispers in his mind told him, courtesy of something called 'dash-cams,' the entire mortal world would witness them do it.

5

The way the bus bounced along the old gravel back-road proved quite a something for giving June...feelings...well, feelings down *there*.

She squirmed in her seat, squeezing her thin thighs together. She really wanted—*really* wanted!—to angle her pelvis so that down *there* pressed firm and direct into the bouncing vibration.

If she did, though...if she did...

It already felt so good, too good, getting her all in a dither, a warm and slippery dither.

Any further...stimulation...

Why, she would go off like an alarm clock!

Right here in the church bus. Right here packed in the third row like sardines with her mother and Mr. and Mrs. Shinn.

As if she didn't have distractions enough already. Brother Lucas behind the wheel, for instance, his bald ebony head gleaming and his deep voice as he hymn-sang delivering its own thrilling vibrations. Or Crusader Markane, sitting up front beside him, lean and tough Crusader Markane, who wasn't handsome, not exactly, but *intense*, a man with his checkered past, ex-con turned preacher.

Or, in the row just ahead of June, Ramon and David, the college youth-group boys...one dark and sultry, Puerto Rican ex-Catholic, almost as exotic as Brother Lucas...the other a former Mormon golden-child, clean-cut, blond and beautiful.

And so what if she was nearly twice their age? Wasn't that what all the cougar fuss was about?

Not, June knew, that she could by any stretch of the imagination rightly be called a cougar. She was, as her own mother never failed to remind her, an old maid, a spinster.

"Even when you were a little girl, I could tell," Margaret Goldsmith would say. "Scrawny thing, plain as the last slice of bread. Any wonder you never saw so much as a kiss?"

Wasn't for lack of trying. June always inwardly cringed to remember.

Chasing boys around the monkey bars at recess, desperate wallflower hope at middle-school dances or parties, hanging out at the bowling alley and pizza arcade Friday nights as a teen...nothing.

She'd attempted the online dating, she'd asked friends to play matchmaker, she'd even gone in secret to a succession of sleazier and sleazier out-of-town bars. Getting more and more careless, more and more desperate. Taking stupid risks. Being foolish. Damn near looking for trouble.

And still, nothing.

Nothing, at best. Laughter, mocking, and revulsion more often than not. Sometimes anger, offended outrage. "Not with my worst enemy's dick!"

Honest to God, she couldn't *give* it away.

Once, at a truck stop, it had almost happened; a beer-gutted ball-capped drunk-off-his-ass long-hauler had pawed her nearly-nonexistent breasts through her blouse and slobbered on the side of her neck before passing out in the parking lot on their way to his rig.

By now, June had just about given up. It was romance novels late at night in her narrow spinster's bed, steamy movies or cyber chat rooms when Mother was at Bingo, long baths, quickies with the shower massager. She wished she were brave enough to buy or order some of those 'toys,' but would die of embarrassment if anyone found out.

Oh, but the sensations this bus ride was causing!

Since Brother Lucas was driving, was it such a far stretch to say *he* was causing them? She most certainly would not mind Brother Lucas doing things to her, things to elicit sensations like this. The very thought made her weak in the knees. Made her warmer and slipperier, down *there*.

Or, the entire trip *had* been Crusader Markane's idea... he'd planned their route, rented this bus they'd jokingly named the Holy Roller...and Crusader Markane, as he often reminded them in his sermons, was a man who'd known sin. A man who'd done sinful deeds. Many, many sinful deeds.

Then they reached a rough patch of road, bumping over gravel and ruts and potholes, and it was all she could do not to scream.

***

In the middle of Mr. Shinn regaling them for the umpteenth time with tales from the front lines in the war on godless baby-killing—he and his wife had picketed no less than fifty abortion clinics over the years, flung paint-soaked baby dolls, made untold teenage girls and single women cry, set a murdering butcher's car on fire, and got arrested twice after run-ins with "liberals and lesbians"—Mrs. Shinn's shrill, nasal busybody bray interrupted.

"My heavens, Junie, are you all right? You look so flushed, dear! And sweating, sorry to say such an indelicate thing; I know we ladies don't sweat, we glisten, but goodness me! Are you sick? Margaret, I think your daughter's sick!"

"I'm fine!" June said, trying to sound normal while quivering on the edge of a boneshaking orgasm.

She gritted her teeth in what was meant to be a smile. Everyone was looking at her. Even Brother Lucas in the rearview mirror, his broad handsome mahogany features furrowed with concern. Even Crusader Markane, twisting in the passenger seat.

"Fine," she repeated, though just meeting the Crusader's gaze caused another surging spike of heat from her loins. "A little…oh…carsick maybe…the…ah!…bumps."

"Road is mighty rough," Brother Lucas said. "Sorry 'bout that. Doing the best I can."

Mrs. Gabelman leaned forward from the very back seat, where she rode—lucky bitch!—sandwiched between her corporate cutie husband and Brother William, who had kind of a careworn silvering George Clooney thing going on. She tapped June on the shoulder with a cool water bottle.

"Here you go, hon. This'll help."

Only if June unscrewed the top and dumped its contents over her own head in a makeshift cold shower, but, she accepted it anyway, mumbled something in gratitude, fumbled a sip, and gripped it in both hands. Her knees pressed together. Her thighs shook. Her clitoris throbbed, sending pangs reverberating through her lower body.

"If you need us to pull over, Sister June—" began Crusader Markane.

"No!"

"She's fine," her mother said. "Aren't you, June? Not going to whoopsie?"

If she'd been flushed before—which she had been, no doubt—she was firetruck scarlet now. The sweat (ladies glisten!) on her brow and dampening her armpits had gone clammy.

"I'm not going to whoopsie!"

She was going to something, all right, but not whoopsie.

"Whoa, hold on," called Brother Lucas, as the front tires rolled onto a bumpy log bridge.

And that was it. With Crusader Markane's dark, intense eyes still fixed on hers, a cascading crash of climactic sensations supernovaed out from June's *down-there*. Her back arched. She couldn't restrain a gasp. As her muscles convulsed, her fists clenched and she squeezed the water bottle hard enough to make the cap pop off in a sudden ejaculatory geyser.

Ka-sploosh!

Half the occupants exclaimed aloud. Her mother and Mrs. Shinn were caught in the splash zone. June got that cold shower after all, too little too late, soaking her chest and lap and legs.

One of the most powerful she'd ever had, and she couldn't even enjoy it! Couldn't ride the wave and prolong the quaking pleasure as the bus crossed the bridge with further rumbling bounces. Mortified, drenched, she wished a giant sinkhole would open in the earth and plunge them to a fiery cataclysmic doom.

No such luck. Brother Lucas stopped on the side of the road, and the next several minutes were full of sliding doors, fresh but humid and unpleasantly fragrant outside air, blotting paper towels, and general milling about as people took the opportunity to stretch their legs.

June just wanted to die. Was being smote down on the spot too much to ask? Did she have to have Mrs. Gabelman fussing over her so much that her mother felt compelled to join in or look bad?

And something in Crusader Markane's gaze...oh, God, could he tell what had really happened? Oh, God, did he *know*?

***

If the Crusader did know, he wasn't saying. Not to June, anyway, though he went over to Brother Lucas and drew him aside. They conversed in low tones, darting glances in her direction.

If they *both* knew...

The very idea made her weak in the knees. Embarrassed, yes, ashamed to the point of craving oblivion, but some not-so-secret inner part of her was lewdly delighted.

"I do believe our dear Sister June just came her brains out," the Crusader might be murmuring.

"Yeah, I could tell she was getting turned on back there, jouncing over those bumps."

"It's always the prim-looking ones, Brother. Wildcats in the sack."

"Preach that. And the plain ones try harder, do anything you want."

"Maybe, before this trip is done, I'll get her down on her knees for some personal salvation."

"Anoint her up good, praise the Lord."

June shook herself. They were not discussing any such thing! They weren't glancing only at *her*, but at the bus, and all the passengers!

David and Ramon, however, the golden-boy Mormon and sultry Puerto Rican, *had* been glancing at her...or at least glancing at Mrs. Gabelman dabbing at June's wet blouse with handfuls of paper towels. Probably the latter.

Wasn't it just her luck, too? The closest anyone else had come to touching her breasts—such as they were—in years, and it had to be this fussing, solicitous, sympathetic pretty little porcelain doll. With her big blue eyes, flaxen silk hair, velvety lashes, rosy cheeks, and perfect smile...she and her husband could have been in travel agency brochures or real estate advertisements.

"Thank you, Sister," June said, taking the damp wad of paper towels. "I can take care of it. Thank you."

"Yes, no need to baby her," June's mother added, stepping back from her own token helpful ministrations. "She's a grown woman."

"Oh, I know, only lending a charitable hand." Perfect smile, perfect dimple. Perfect unwrinkled clothes and perfect modest makeup despite the long ride and cramped conditions. Probably had 'Made in Stepford' stamped on the nape of her neck.

"We must be getting close by now," Mr. Shinn said, consulting a folding gas-station map.

His busybody wife, a dumpling on legs, nodded. "Why, you can smell it on the very air, can't you? The scent of evil and corruption."

It was true. Or, if not evil and corruption, slaughterhouses and open sewers. They'd been warned, they'd read testimonials and seen videos in preparation, but—as with anything else in life—experiencing the real thing in person was bound to be different.

"Another few miles." Brother William, who didn't speak up often, looked wan but determined. All June knew about him was that he'd lost his family in some tragic event, wandered a lost soul for a while, and finally found his way to their congregation.

Well, okay, she also knew the combination of 'careworn George Clooney' and 'painful past' made most women want to comfort him until comfort and loving solace turned into something else...

"If everyone's ready?" asked Crusader Markane. "Sister June?"

"Yes, fine, ready," she said.

His intense gaze took them all in. "Soon, we'll arrive at our destination. I'm honored and humbled by your faith in following me this far, in keeping to our cause. However, I would be remiss in not making sure, one last time—"

"No need." Brother Lucas' deep voice tolled like a bell. "We're with you."

"We are," David and Ramon said together, doing a high-five for the Lord.

"With you and with God and the holy angels," added Mrs. Shinn.

"We'll give Satan's army what-for!" Mr. Gabelman sounded like he was delivering a pep talk at the company picnic, his simpering Stepford-doll beaming adoringly with every word.

Brother William only exhaled, looking more determined than ever. Careworn George Clooney heading with purpose and resignation toward his almost-certain death.

They piled back into the bus, and, singing hymns, resumed their journey to the Devil's Lake.

***

The temperature didn't rise. The skies didn't turn to ashes, nor the sun to blood. But none of that was necessary. They could tell. They could *feel* it. They *knew*. It didn't even have to be about faith or belief.

It simply *was*. It was truth. God's own irrefutable truth. The Devil's Lake.

Hell was real. Hell was real, and part of it was here.

Actual Hell on Earth.

The ultimate test, the ultimate proof.

June had heard plenty of crackpot theories about hoaxes, conspiracies, and special effects. Most of it came from the logical scientific types, the atheists and evolutionists, who couldn't accept they'd been wrong. Some, admittedly, had come from various other religions…until further information revealed aspects of them *all* were valid.

There was no point anymore arguing whose was the One True Faith. No more need to squabble amongst themselves. Never mind bickering between Catholic and Protestant; it encompassed far broader strokes. Christian or Jew, Muslim or Buddhist or Hindi, even the old-time mythologies like the Aztecs and Egyptians were represented.

Every faith, every church and temple and synagogue, had seen drastic upswings in membership and new converts.

It wasn't a matter of mega-churches anymore; it was meta-churches, welcoming all, assimilating, blending. As long as you worshiped a benevolent god—any benevolent god, or goddess, or whatever—against the forces of sin, wickedness, and evil...you were okay in the eyes of the great consolidated meta-religion.

The only division left these days was between the believers and the deniers, and the deniers were seriously outnumbered. For the believers, what mattered was how *much* you believed, and how you demonstrated it.

Including fanaticism and zealotry, which, June supposed, was what this pilgrimage had become.

As for herself, her own status and standing, well...she *did* have her sinful thoughts and urges, they *did* consume a large portion of her waking thoughts and *had* led her toward some dubious decisions or courses of action, even *if* those decisions and courses of action had never really panned out. But she'd never faltered in her faith. She'd recognized her guilt, admitted her flaws and her weaknesses.

If it took walking into the very presence of Hell to face literal demons, if it required sacrifice or suffering, or martyrdom, was that so much to ask?

Or...if something happened to happen in there...being surrounded by sin, depravity and temptation...where even the strongest of men might be overcome by lustful urges... where even innocent women risked being ravished...well, wasn't it worth the risk?

Her mother, of course, was in it for bragging rights. A casual "oh yes we've been to Devil's Lake" would carry Margaret Goldsmith's church social and bingo parlor cred for *years*. The Shinns probably wanted enemies they could confront without risking arrest; enough people still cared about liberals and lesbians, but who was going to protest fighting the possessed and the damned?

She suspected several of her companions aboard the

Holy Roller had similar motives, not that any of them would admit it. No, it was serving the Lord, making a stand, providing an example, showing that those of true faith wouldn't sit idly by tolerating evil in their midst.

Besides, with the new taxation policies no longer exempting them, the meta-churches were paying through the nose. "Taxed up the ying-yang," as Mr. Shinn put it, usually adding that at least the money was going to a good cause instead of bums, druggies, runaways, homosexuals, illegal immigrants, and welfare queens, like the libtard snowflakes wanted.

A good cause, as evidenced by the wall directly ahead of them. It was hardly majestic; though she'd seen pictures, she'd still been hoping for something impressive and monumental. But it was a wall, *their* wall, *God's* wall, holding Satan's forces at bay and defending the righteous.

Until, that was, the righteous could clean, cleanse, and reclaim this land.

Starting today. With them, with this bus, and Crusader Markane.

***

Checkpoint Gabriel might have been the smallest and most remote of the infamous six, little more than a pair of kiosks to either side of a wire-topped steel gate, but its guards responded with prompt alertness as the Holy Roller approached.

Maybe they were glad for the change in pace, something to break up the monotony. June had read how they did rotations for weeks or months at a time, like forest rangers stationed in the wilderness. Sleeping on cots, eating pre-packaged meals, as cut off from the outside world as the poor damned and doomed inhabitants.

The first to emerge was a woman, low-slung fatigues

and a sports bra showing off a rock-hard bronze physique. Her dark hair was cropped short, a bandanna twisted into a rope tied like a sweatband. She reminded June of someone from a movie. Give her a big-ass gun, and she'd be the tough chick from Aliens. Sanchez? Instead, a brutal-looking sidearm rode on one hip, a sheathed machete on the other, and a knife-hilt protruded from one combat boot.

She waved the bus to a halt as her partner appeared. He, in faded jeans and a tie-dyed tee shirt, was tall and toned-but-lanky, with a grey ponytail and goatee, round sunglasses, and a peace sign pendant worn on the same chain as his dog tags. As if to add to the incongruity, he *did* have a big-ass gun, handling it in a way declaring he knew how to use it.

"That's some firepower," Brother Lucas said, breaking a rather nervous silence.

"Have faith," replied Crusader Markane. "We're all on the same side here, soldiers for God."

Mr. Shinn stirred in his seat, grumbling under his breath about hippies and feminazis, but his wife nudged him and he shut up.

Sanchez, or whoever, motioned for Brother Lucas to roll down his window. Before he could do so, Crusader Markane swung open his door and stepped out. He held up both hands, relaxed and unthreatening. The hazy sunlight struck indigo highlights from his hair and made his crisp white shirt seem to glow.

Not exactly handsome, perhaps, but intense, as June knew. The visible scars and tattoos only added to the effect. Even from here, she could see Sanchez do a slight head tilt of appreciation.

"Greetings, Sister," he said. "May the Lord's love be with you on this blessed day."

Sanchez kept her cool. "State your name and business, sir."

He introduced himself and cited the name of their meta-church. "My flock and I—"

"Oh, man, let me guess," sighed the hippie. "You want to go in and pray the Sa' away."

"We have come, yes, to confront the very forces of Hell."

"It's a bad idea," said Sanchez. "Really bad. I suggest you turn around and head home."

"I do value your concern," Markane said, "but we are resolute. I have the necessary paperwork, although if I did not, I would still expect you to permit us to pass. We are—"

"On a mission from God, yeah, Elwood, I can dig it," the hippie cut in.

Markane grinned. "You joke, Brother, and I like your humor. However, for my flock, this is no joking matter. Beyond this wall, Evil has set its abominable red stain upon the Earth, and we mean to show the dark forces and their unholy masters we will *not* allow it, we will *not* stand by and tolerate this affront—"

He was cranking up the fire and brimstone with his usual charismatic fervor, which got June tingling all over again. Such intensity, such *passion*!

"Enough!" barked Sanchez. "Okay, fine. You want to go in, we'll let you go in. Trust me, though, you'll be back in a hell of a hurry—no pun intended. You may think you're prepared for what's in there, but you're not."

"I assure you, Sister, we are. We come armed and armored with our true faith."

"Yeah." Sanchez nodded. "Yeah, good luck with that."

6

Something smelled like a tire-fire, a burning landfill, scorched metal and melting plastic.

An improvement, in other words.

Groaning, Greg dragged open reluctant eyelids. He peered, through smoke and disbelief, at a landscape tilted sideways, partially obscured on the right by a curved line of rounded shadows.

Eclipses. Planetary occlusions all in a row.

No. It was a strand of beads, petrified wood and mother-of-pearl, draped loosely over his right eye. He groped up and found the silver medallion stuck to his brow.

Stuck?

Adhered.

As if glued, as if seared into place.

The bright white-hot glare, the magnesium flash, the sizzle…it *was* seared there, seared into his skin like a brand, and he thought of whichever of the Indiana Jones movies it had been where the guy goes to grab the metal artifact from the flames, only to get its design burned onto his palm as a result.

Had he been branded by his own good-luck charm? How absurd was that? Was he going to go through the rest of his life with *Never drive faster than your Guardian Angel can fly* printed backward across his forehead?

Maybe it wasn't the smartest move, but he dug his fingernails under the medallion's edges and pulled.

Peel-*riiip*. The sensation of tearing off a Band-Aid, only

71

worse. Greg yelped, his eyes both crossing and watering. He clenched his free hand into a fist. As the stinging pain faded, he unclenched it, and dabbed gingerly with his palm, expecting it to come away bloodied.

It didn't. Nor did it hurt to touch the spot, after that initial sting. He poked and prodded, and traced what felt like thin raised ridges of scar tissue in some kind of design…

Okay, so, he *wasn't* going to go through the rest of his life with *Never drive faster than your Guardian Angel can fly* printed backward across his forehead…he was going to go through the rest of his life with some weird seven-sided symbol embossed there instead.

Wait.

He had a 'rest of his life'?

He was alive?

He was! He *was* alive!

Strapped in his seat, held half-upsidedown with the ruined cockpit a smoldering broken eggshell around him, the wreckage of his Cessna—still not fully paid for—likewise smoldering, canted at a crazy-skew angle…but, alive.

For now. If he didn't unhook himself and get out soon, he might very well char-broil on the spot…damn near a miracle the fuel hadn't gone up already…

Greg clawed for the releases, found them, and probably should have considered the logistics of his position before dumping himself headfirst in an unceremonious heap. Only then did the prospect of other injuries occur to him; he could have fractures, shards impaling his kidneys, arteries only tourniqueted by the pressure of his harness…

Too late now, and no matter. He sprawled and then crawled, mucky soil and slick damp greenery under him.

Once he'd cleared what he hoped was a safe distance from the crash, he flopped over onto his back and just lay there, chest heaving for breath. Which, since he'd also cleared some of the smoke-zone, was breath filled with an ungodly rotten-meat/raw-sewage reek.

The lake, he remembered. That awful, red, blood-shit lake.

"What the hell?" he gasped. "Seriously, what the hell? And where the hell am I?"

"Well put," someone said, in a voice like delicate wind-chimes. "Not entirely accurate, perhaps, but, close enough."

Uttering a startled and fairly embarrassing unmanly squeal, Greg scrambled to sit up. At first, he didn't see anybody—great, now he was hearing things; probably had a concussion, brain damage.

"What the Hell, seriously, and where the Hell, indeed." The wind-chimes voice spoke again and this time he was able to track it to its source.

Probably had a concussion, brain damage?

Strike the *probably*.

He *definitely* had brain damage. Wasn't just hearing things, but seeing things as well.

Things like that naked angel, perched on a branch.

***

The angel didn't look anything like the white-robed, feather-winged Nativity Scene beatific blonde of Greg's imaginings, yet he knew that's what he was seeing.

She—he presumed, based on the lissome shape and flowing hair—stood maybe all of two feet tall, had skin as smooth and subtly rainbow-whorled and opalescent as mother-of-pearl, and seemed haloed in a diffuse silvery glow like mist and moonlight.

And yes, she was naked, though somehow in a not-naked way. She reminded him of the fairies from Disney's *Fantasia*: slim sylphlike build, long legs, pert but nippleless nubs of breasts, no hint of genitalia. Her eyes were enormous, anime-eyes taking up most of her face, pools of innocence and purity—

"What we *are*, in fact," said the angel in her delicate wind-chime voice, "is fucked, my friend. Well and truly fucked."

Greg blinked. The crash really must have rattled his brains, making him hallucinate like whoa. Maybe he was going into shock. Maybe he was bleeding out from his injuries. Maybe he was dying and this, of all things, was his final vision.

Most people got the glorious welcoming tunnel of light...he got a pint-sized naked angel who said 'fuck'?

He groaned and leaned over, elbows on knees, head in his hands. The stench of his surroundings—burnt oil and plastic and rubber, the sewagey slaughterhouse reek from the lake—washed over him again and he struggled not to puke up his guts.

His fingertips found the medallion's sigil flash-branded on his brow. The silver medallion itself, with charred bits stuck to it but entirely cool, rested against his chest. He'd looped the strand of beads around his neck without being aware of it.

Once he got a temporary handle on the urge to hurl, he managed to look back up, squinting, expecting the angelic apparition to be gone.

Nope, there she was. She'd pushed off from the branch upon which she'd been perching, and hovered in mid-air on a shimmering iridescent dragonfly-wing blur.

"Still with me, sport?" she asked. "Not much I can do if you go and die now."

"You're...you're my guardian angel?"

"Sort of. And, until today, I thought I was doing a pretty decent job of it."

"This is crazy." He sunk his head into his hands again. "Am I really having this conversation?"

"Yes, and you need to pull it together if we're going to get out of this mess. Save any existential crises for later, huh?"

Nodding was a mistake. He groaned again. "How bad am I hurt?"

The angel shrugged. "However bad it is, you're going to have to walk it off."

"No magic healing? No divine intervention?" Greg, moving with the slow care of an invalid or old person, levered himself more or less to his feet.

"I'm not that kind of angel."

"What kind are you?"

"I am of the *Custos Viatorem*, the servants of Saint Menas."

"Uhh..."

"An Egyptian precursor to the one you might know as Saint Christopher."

"Oh, sure, patron saint of travelers."

Leaning on a tree trunk, he looked around at the crash site from his new upright perspective. His plane was a loss, but it hadn't exploded, and the smoldering wreckage didn't appear immediately likely to start a forest fire. He supposed his luggage and other personal effects were a loss as well, not to mention his cargo.

But, he was alive. A check of his pockets told him he still had his wallet, and—

His cell phone!

Greg whipped it out faster than a quick-draw gunslinger. He uttered a quick mental prayer—under the circumstances, what with an angel right here in front of him, praying didn't sound so far-fetched—as his thumbs tapped at the screen.

The angel in front of him, however, shook her head. "Yeah, good luck with *that*," she said. "Technology won't work so well here. Remember what I told you before? Not entirely Hell, but close enough."

***

Her name, she said—or, at least, the name she went by in the earthly realm—was Ethriel. She also told him that, no matter how bruised and confused he might be, he needed to get on his feet and get moving.

"Where?" Greg asked.

"Anywhere. Doesn't matter. Out of here would be good. Pronto."

"Well, yeah, but, what's the rush?"

"Trust me."

He heaved a sigh. "Okay, okay. Why not, right? I'm probably concussed and hallucinating. May as well play along."

"Tell yourself whatever you have to."

"Should I bring anything?" Then he looked again at the plane and decided not to bother. He'd escaped with his life already. No sense trying to rummage in the debris. His luck today, *then* it would explode. "Never mind. Lead on."

"I can't."

"Huh?"

"I can't lead. I can only guide as you go."

Greg rubbed his aching temples, then skimmed his fingertips again over the medallion's sigil seared into his brow. "Can you also explain as we go?"

Ethriel didn't answer until he actually chose a direction and began walking. "That, I can do." She fell in beside and slightly behind him, flitting along on her buzz-shimmer wings by his right shoulder, at the edge of his peripheral vision. "Or try to. It's not easy. I haven't really interacted with mortals directly very much."

"Yeah, what's the deal? Why haven't I seen you before? Why now?"

"Circumstances are a little out of the playbook."

"Fucked, you mean."

"Fucked. This area, around the lake, holds residual

magic from the Spatial Merge. It's kind of a between-place, bordering your normal world and Hell. Enough to allow me to manifest in physical form. Well, not 'allow' per se. I don't have a choice. I'm on enemy turf."

"Hell," Greg said, pausing and turning toward her. "As in, literal Hell?"

"Keep walking," she urged.

"Where am I going?"

"I told you, it doesn't matter."

He resumed his random course through the blighted wilderness, if more at an aching ramble than a normal stride. It seemed to be sufficient for Ethriel, who gave him a quick overview of what had happened to this part of Florida. It sounded far-fetched, even considering what he remembered from the news...but he also had a 'fuck'-saying angel at his shoulder, so, who was he to judge?

"So, there are, what? Demons here?"

"Hopefully not many."

"Uh..."

"Damned, for sure," she said. "Denizens and beasts, corrupted creations, but hopefully not many true demons. We'd be doubly-fucked then. I sure would be, anyway. A demon or devil would love to get its hands on an angel, low-ranking or not."

"What would they do to you?"

"Chain me, rape me to madness for a thousand years, breed unholy spawn upon me. You know, the usual."

Greg shot her an awkward glance. "Uh...how? I mean, you don't have...you aren't...uh..."

"Pff. You don't know demons. They can't find a hole, they'll make one."

He grimaced. "Thanks for the visual."

"You need to understand the stakes here. The danger. Whatever we run into, it's not going to be a picnic for you, either."

Don't ask, don't ask, do not ask.

"But, wait." He touched the sigil scar again, and the medallion itself where it rested on his chest. "What about this? What about you? You're my guardian angel—thank you, Grandma, by the way; sorry for being an ungrateful shit. Aren't you supposed to protect me?"

"Correct on all counts. I am and I will, but there are catches. Fine print."

"Fine print?"

"Look, the *Custos Viatorum,* we aren't that high on the heavenly totem pole. We're protectors of travelers, yes. Travelers. Which means our influence is limited."

"To when I *travel*," he said, in a flash of understanding. "That's why you were so eager to get me up and moving. I have to be going somewhere for your powers to be at their full effect."

"Good boy. Celestial star for you."

***

Greg walked a while, mulling things over. They were headed away from the lake, which suited him fine. If Ethriel was right and the magic got stronger closer to it, then the further the better as far as he was concerned. Though...

"What happens to you when we reach the wall?" he asked. "Will you disappear?"

"I'll lose this physical manifestation at some point," she said. "Disappear, though? No. Not altogether. Not as long as you bear the sigil."

He touched his forehead again. "Yeah, about that..."

"Yeah. Looks like you're stuck with me, sport."

"It's not the medallion?"

"It was, but there's been a transference. The medallion's still a potent charm. It's pure silver, if nothing else, and the beads have their own protective properties because—"

"—because they used to be part of living things?" he guessed, remembering his earlier thought.

"Another celestial star for you!" She patted him on the head, her little hand light as the buffeting of a butterfly wing. "Also doesn't hurt that it was an oath-gift."

"From my grandmother. But you knew that, didn't you? Were you her guardian angel, too?"

"How else do you think she hitchhiked across the country and backpacked through Europe when she was nineteen?"

"She did what?"

"She never told you those stories?"

"She was my *grandma*!"

"People had lives before you came along. People will have lives after you're dead. In the grand scheme of things, you're an eyeblink."

"Why protect me, then?"

"Even a single eyeblink can make a difference."

Greg nodded. "Okay, fair enough. Now, since your powers only work when I'm traveling—"

"Oh, here it comes."

"What?"

"Go ahead."

"Well, really, aren't we all, constantly, traveling in one sense or another?"

"Rotation of the Earth, orbital path around the Sun, spinning of the galaxy, expanding universe, the relentless passage of time? Who are you, Neil DeGrasse Tyson all of a sudden?"

"I didn't necessarily mean astrophysics," he protested, experiencing another of those surreal 'am I honestly having this conversation?' moments. "Isn't life itself a journey? A spiritual journey?"

"I knew it," Ethriel said, not un-smugly. Instead of patting him on the head, she flicked the rim of his ear. "You're one of *those*."

"Those whats?"

"Loophole-lookers. Rules lawyers. Creative interpreters. Every genie I've met says the same thing: there's always someone who wants to wish for more wishes. Cheat the house. Game the system."

"Hey, you were the one who brought up fine print and catches in the first place. I was only curious."

"Traveling." She pointed at his walking feet, mimed driving a car, swooped her hand in an airplane gesture. "Planes, trains, automobiles, horses, bikes, skateboards, boats, etc. Crawl, if you have to. What counts is that you're going somewhere."

"Treadmill? Exercise bike?"

"Are you done?"

"Okay, okay." Greg laughed. "So, you can guide me, protect me. Those times I'd feel this weird urge to take a different route, or the way I never had a breakdown on the side of the road...you?"

"Me."

"Thank you."

"You're welcome."

"Shouldn't I get a better rate on my insurance, then?"

"Suuure, that'll go over great."

"Just asking." He pictured himself pleading his case to Flo and the Gecko and J. Jonah Jameson. Safe driver discount, indeed. "What else can you do?"

"Uriel's pinfeathers, it's never enough for you mortals, is it?"

"I didn't mean...I do appreciate..."

"Teasing," she said, and did the head-pat again. "It's a fair question. Trouble is, I don't really know. Ward off harm, alleviate discomfort; kind of vague. You're not as bothered by your injuries anymore, are you? Or the Hell-stench from the lake?"

"I..." He paused. "Now that you mention it...that is,

80

I still feel them, I still smell it, but…only when I think about…when I focus on…"

"That was probably the wrong thing to say," fretted Ethriel.

Too late; he'd thought about and focused on.

7

So much for democracy, so much for majority rule. Not when Chelsea Carmichael was in the driver's seat. Andy was first to give up arguing; he saw where this was headed and wanted no further part of it. Instead, he slumped down, shut his eyes, and tried to zone out as the others continued their useless efforts to get her to turn back.

Not happening. Never mind trees with faces, centipede monsters on the windshield, hulking shaggy shadows, or whatever dog-sized winged what-the-fuck had gone flapping across the road. Never mind the lake—Chelsea had said something about green rivers on St. Paddy's Day, but if that was dye out there, Andy was a giraffe—or the way their phones and iPods kept glitching.

She had her teeth in it now, her pride on the line. They were going to that lakehouse no matter what. Even Trevor, pouring on the brotherly charm, couldn't sway her.

The lake, though…man…dude…the lake. Andy had never been here before, but he was pretty sure no lake on the planet was supposed to look like that. He was deffo sure no lake on the planet, except maybe that one in Scotland, had enormous spinosaurus finny humps rising and submerging.

He was the only one who'd seen that particular spectacle, and decided to keep his mouth shut. Kayla and Madison were freaked enough already. And maybe he'd imagined it. Yeah, why not? Whose imagination *wouldn't* run wild in a bad scene like this?

Up front, Trevor made the mistake of saying, "Come

on, Sis, quit being such a stubborn bitch. The rest of us just want to get out of here."

Screech and oof, thrown against their seatbelts by the abrupt deceleration as Chelsea stomped the brakes.

She whirled, eyes wild, to examine her passengers. "Oh, yeah? That what you want? You all want to get out of here? You all want to go back?"

Everyone nodded, even Andy, though he did so warily.

"If that's what you really want," she went on, "I can't stop you." She pressed the control for the automatic door unlocks, which clunked obligingly. "Go for it. Hop on out."

"What?" Madison sounded ready to cry. "You mean... walk?"

"Goddamnit, Chels," Trevor said. "It's miles."

"And with those...those..." Kayla couldn't even finish, only shuddering and pressing so hard to Andy's side he felt not just her boobs but the rapid whumping of her heartbeat.

"Hey," said Chelsea with a casual hair-toss. "I'm going to the house. The rest of you, make up your own minds."

Talk about a no-brainer. Get out and walk? After what they'd already seen? A quartet of mute headshakes were their answer.

"Didn't think so." Smugly, Chelsea re-locked the doors and started driving again.

They passed the remains of what once had been campgrounds, tattered scraps of tent drooping from skeletal frameworks interspersed amid the rusted-out hulks of RVs. They passed an abandoned boat-rental/bait-shop place, and a gas station still appearing mostly intact—

"Don't stop," Andy said. "Or else some toothless old coot will tell us we shouldn't be here."

"We *shouldn't* be here," Kayla muttered.

The road followed the shoreline awhile, and this time there was no not-seeing the surface and submerge of finny humps. Or the way what Trevor said used to be a pleasant sandy beach now looked strewn with driftwood piles of bone. Or the way some gnarled trees by the lake's edge seemed laden not with fruit but with pulsating membranous cocoons. Not that anybody dared say anything.

Andy caught a glimpse of Chelsea's tight-drawn expression in the rearview mirror. Even she was finally having second thoughts, but that pride wasn't about to let her back down.

Then the road made a turn, and ahead of them...like a vision...like the princess castle at Disney World...there stood a huge, ritzy lakehouse straight from a vacation brochure...intact and perfect...and waiting.

***

As soon as she saw the house, Madison relaxed. Not totally, but some. She'd picked up on Andy's cabin-in-the-woods vibes and was expecting...well...a cabin in the woods. Rustic. Without power or running water, an outhouse in the yard.

This, though, this was every bit as posh as Chelsea had promised. Picture windows glittered like sheets of diamond. A shining barbecue grill and luxurious hot tub graced the deck. They would each have their own rooms, and there were bound to be plenty of cozy nooks where she could curl up and read while the others caroused.

Oh, she'd have a drink or two; she wasn't a total prude. But if Andy's cabin-in-the-woods scenario also extended to the girls getting wasted and making out, well, she'd leave that to Chelsea and Kayla. Sure wouldn't be the first time.

Despite her earlier misgivings, she found herself looking forward to the stay, thinking maybe it wouldn't be so bad after all.

Then someone opened a door, and the lake-stench hit,

and the next Madison knew, she was out of the SUV barfing into the bushes. The worst stink ever! Worse than when she'd been a kid and the septic tank exploded. Worse than discovering the hard way a fridge hadn't been plugged in all week.

It was shit and rot and slaughterhouses, and with each gasping breath she got another wallop of it, which made her barf again, a cycle lasting until she sank to her hands and knees, shaking and weak, wondering if she'd literally barfed her guts out.

Normally, mortification would have taken over then, but she was far from the only one to have such a reaction. Weird that the sounds of her friends also vigorously vomiting should be comforting somehow, but, there it was.

Even with her stomach on empty, her gorge kept hitching. She spat the vile taste from her mouth, thinking in the back of her brain that, as awful as the smell of puke was, it still beat the unspeakable reek of the lake.

Thinking, also, that those were some strange-looking bushes she'd offloaded her last several meals onto. Thinking that bushes didn't usually rustle and move when there wasn't any wind.

"Inside," she heard Trevor say, with an urping hiccup. "Get inside."

Chelsea stumbled past, gag-horking, a keyring clinking in her grasp. A sobbing Kayla was right behind her, the front of her shirt plastered to her chest by a wet and chunky bib.

"Madison, you okay?" asked Andy from somewhere nearby.

Well, of course she wasn't! None of them were! Who the hell *could* be?

Instead of saying any of that, she just nodded, vaguely glad she'd decided to go with a ponytail.

She heard Chelsea's cry of victory; one of the keys must've done the trick. She felt Andy's hesitant hand on her back, and felt something warm yet clammy slide across her knuckles.

A worm please be a worm only a worm not one of those pinchy scorpion millipede bugs—

Her first glance said it was nothing more than a vine or a root.

Her second glance said vines or roots didn't move on their own, weren't sickeningly fibrous and flesh-colored, like a raw length of twisted tendons. With…with long, curved, yellow fingernails.

Pure white-hot terror blotted out the lake stench, Andy's concerned voice, and everything else. Madison reared back, screaming fit to split her throat. As she tried to yank her arm away, several more tendon-fingers whipped from under the bushes to ensnare her at wrists and ankles.

"Andy, help!"

But Andy was shrieking and running for the house.

The puke-splattered bushes themselves rose up, strange growths on the grimy carapace of what looked like a land-bound crawdad made from flayed cadavers. The finger-things bristled from where claws would have been, it had stubby legs, and…

…and…

…and a hideous, demented, evilly grinning human face…

Madison managed one more scream before it ripped her to pieces.

***

Even with everything else going on, even with the horrible screams from outside and Kayla doubling over to vomit again, even with Chelsea shouting at him to shut the fucking door and Andy shrieking for him to wait, Trevor noticed that the lakehouse was exactly as he remembered.

The side entryway—their mother had never allowed it to be called a 'mudroom'—led through into the spacious chef's kitchen, beyond which an open floorplan flowed into a combination dining/living room, boasting large river-rock fireplace and floor-to-ceiling picture windows, and why was there a chirpy real estate agent in his head?

Trevor glanced out, ready to slam the door in hopes of cutting off that ungodly smell from the lake. Andy was almost there, running like a cartoon character, legs pistoning crazily, his arms waving pool noodles, his eyes and mouth comical round O's. If he did shut the door, Andy might burst right through it, leaving a cutout of himself in the wood.

But where the hell was Madison?

He yelled this very question at Andy, as the latter barreled past him full-tilt gonzo.

"She's gone it got her close it close it close it!"

With no sign of her, and the stench rolling in like a physical fog, Trevor did, and the inner door too as he and Andy joined Chelsea and Kayla in the kitchen.

It helped. It helped a lot. In here, away from that blood-rot-shit miasma, the air was clean if slightly musty, tinged with the aromas of Pine-Sol and bleach.

Where the hell is Madison? continued as the clamoring question of the hour, while Andy's garbled explanation made no sane kind of sense.

"It *got* her!" he shrieked. "I *told* you, it *got* her, she's *gone!*" Then he threw himself into the breakfast nook for a total bawling hysterical breakdown.

Trevor looked at Chelsea, who looked back at him. They'd never had the full twin telepathy people talked about, but they clicked in sync often enough. Drawing lungsful and holding their breath, they went into the mudroom—side entryway, if you please—to peer through the narrow windows.

There was the SUV, parked askew with all its doors flung wide open. Various items—someone's phone, someone's purse, someone's sunglasses—lay scattered where they'd been dropped in the abrupt exodus. Puddles of puke made colorful blotches, a few with footprints leading away—and wouldn't their mother have a fit if anybody tracked that inside!

But no Madison. The last Trevor remembered of seeing her, she'd been running for the bushes flanking the driveway. She clearly hadn't jumped back in the SUV, and she clearly hadn't followed the rest of them to the house, so, yeah…

Where the hell *was* she?

"Fine, screw it," said Chelsea. "She's a big girl."

The four of them regrouped and cleaned up as well as they were able—the water worked, though it turned out the power didn't—then did a quick exploration of the house.

It was still exactly as Trevor remembered, the furniture present and accounted for, the knickknacks in the same place. The fridges and freezers were empty, but a good supply of dry and canned goods stocked the pantry.

Nobody else was here; clearly the caretaker and housekeeper had been doing their jobs, but there was no indication of any squatting, break-ins or misuse.

Well, okay, one thing wasn't as he remembered…the view. By unspoken mutual agreement, he and Chelsea drew blinds that had hardly ever been used, casting them into shadow and closing off the panoramic, nightmarish spectacle of the lake.

They sat on the couches, Kayla pulling one of the requisite plaid throws around her shoulders despite the heat. Nobody spoke for a long time. Then everybody tried speaking at once.

"Whoa, whoa, whoa." Trevor raised his hands. "One

at a time, huh? We've got to stay cool, get our heads on straight, figure this out. Starting with you, Andy…*what* did you say happened to Madison?"

***

Kayla let them talk without really listening. Anything they had to say about the lake, or crawdad-monsters eating Madison, or what they should do next…yeah, let them talk, let them argue.

It didn't matter. It wouldn't matter.

All she cared about was, when she'd taken a shower, it had been water instead of blood or worse. Not hot water, just tepid, but no maggots had come squirming out of the showerhead to plop onto her naked body. No clawed fingers had reached up through the drain.

Maybe the quickest shower of her life anyway. This was hardly the occasion for languid steamy lathering as if for an audience. In, scrub off the puke, rinse, wring out her clothes as much as possible, and out.

Over the years, it seemed various odds and ends and spare articles of clothing had been left behind in the lakehouse's closets. She'd been able to find a floral-patterned sundress that fit and was almost kind of cute, though with nothing to wear beneath it, she was sway-jiggle city up top and around back, and her nipples showed through the thin fabric like sleepy round eyes.

She sat on one of the couches with her legs tucked under and a throw blanket over her shoulders while Andy broke down crying again after repeating his description of what happened to Madison. It sounded crazyass bullshit…but… Madison still had not appeared…and crazyass bullshit was seeming more and more plausible all the time.

"Okay," Chelsea said. "Maybe coming here wasn't the best idea."

"Gee, ya think?" Trevor rolled his eyes and she beaned him with a souvenir pillow shaped like a seashell.

"But that's not important," she went on. "The thing is, what do we do now? Guessing we don't want to stay here all week."

"Fuck, no," came a sniffly voice from Andy's direction. "I say bail."

"Bail is sounding pretty good to me," said Trevor.

Chelsea hooked a thumb at the covered windows. "Go back out there?"

Kayla shuddered, the memory of the lake's stench still fresh in her mind. She was in no hurry to get another whiff of that, but what else could they do?

Trevor made an indifferent kind of shrug. "We'd have to anyway, sooner or later. All our stuff's still in the back of the—"

SKREEEEE-ONNNK!

Even indoors, the half-screech/half-bellow was a deafening earsplitter wallop, sending them bent double with hands clapped to ears. That last ONNNK was a bass vibration felt in the bones.

It was followed by a series of slow but purposeful humongous ground-shaking thuds, then a noise like a wrecking ball smashing into a tank. Metal crunched and squealed, and then a car alarm was going off in a spate of wailing whoops.

"Shit!" Chelsea sprang up, rushing to the window.

Against their better judgment, they all followed, peeking around the edges of the blinds. All four of them stood jawdropped at the sight of a...

Giant turtle?

Dinosaur, one of those ankly-o-somethings?

It was as big as a UPS truck, its heavy shell a greenish-black color edged with six-foot reddish-black spikes, its four trunklike legs greenly armor-plated, its clubbish feet thumping deep divots. A trail of prints led back to the lake, along with rivulets and runoff still dripping from the huge form. Tendrils of plants hung like seaweed from its spikes, upon one of which was impaled the rotting carcass of a man-sized fish.

Its head, also armor-plated, was the wrecking ball, sweeping around on a stoutly muscular neck to wham into the SUV again. More metal crunched. The roof crumpled like a beer can crushed in a fratboy's fist. The alarm ended in a shrill blurt.

Triumphant, the turtle-dinosaur-whatever SKREEEEE -ONNNKed to the sky. Its jaw was a bulldozer bucket crammed with tusks and fangs, its eyes yellow-orange orbs.

Then it heaved its bulk up, revealing an enormous armor-plated two-pronged reptilian dick, and proceeded to violently violate the stricken vehicle.

***

Chelsea could not believe she was standing here watching some monster-movie reject hump their SUV to death.

But, no denying, that's what was happening.

The SUV, already looking like it had been through a demolition derby and car-crusher combined, buckled beneath the immense weight. The double-dicker battering ram punched through the rear window and into the packed cargo compartment. Beer and tequila gushed from flattened cans and broken bottles. A cooler went spinning blue and white, lid coming off, packages of bratwursts flying in all directions. Suitcases and duffle bags spilled from the open doors, shedding shirts and shorts and swimsuits.

SKREEEEE-ONNNK and stomp and thrust! Another walloping clang as the underside of the beast's bulldozer jaw caved in the SUV's hood. Oil and assorted engine fluids puddled with the booze. And gas? Had the tank ruptured?

Was it going to explode?

She kind of hoped so. Kaboom, whoosh, fire. Take *that*, you prehistoric rapey fuck!

Until, of course, the flames spread and the house burned down and they all died; not much satisfying revenge to be had then.

"Are we really seeing this?" Andy asked no one in particular.

"I wish I *wasn't* seeing it," Kayla said.

"Gamera going to town on our ride?" Trevor sounded detached, almost amused.

Chelsea grimaced as the devil-turtle picked up its not-exactly-glacial pace, its tusks and fangs gnashing, a series of glottal grunts issuing from its slobbering maw. "I'm just glad we're not in it."

The commotion had drawn a lot of notice, and now there could definitely be no denying what they were seeing. Even she was unable to hold onto her hoax theories about chemical spills and government conspiracies.

This was real. This was real and right before their eyes.

Hell on Earth, it really was. Shambling half-skeletal bodies clawed up from shallow shoreside graves to watch, while bat-winged imps with horns and pointy tails settled onto the deck railing like a flock of curious birds. Out in the lake itself, the heads and shells of other fanged turtles poked from the bilious crimson surface, while further out past them churned something both blobbish and seething with tentacles.

With a final colossal heave and bellow, the dinosaur-turtle-whatever spewed its load. Gushers of stuff the color and consistency of rancid cottage cheese splattered the remains of the SUV's windshield and side-splashed through the gaps where the doors used to be.

All four of them went "Eyyuuuugh!" in unison, retreating from the windows and letting the blinds drop back into place. They stared at each other. Nobody seemed to know what to say.

Trevor found his voice and/or his wits first. "So much for our fast getaway. We may be stuck here a while."

"Oh dude please fuck no," Andy moaned.

"We can't be stuck here, we just can't," Kayla said. She was wringing her hands. Literally wringing her hands. Chelsea had never seen anyone in real life do that before. "There has to be something we can do. Call for help?"

"You were the one griping about our phones not working," Trevor said. "Can't get service, no internet, no signal, nada. I checked the landline when we first came in and it's dead too."

"Dead," said Chelsea. She glanced at Andy. "Madison *is*, isn't she? Dead, I mean. You weren't making that up."

"I didn't see, but I heard her screaming, and this noise like a dog tearing into a turkey carcass, and..." His eyes welled, he sniffled, and he turned away for another crying fit.

Kayla sat down, putting her well-wrung hands over her face. Her breath was hitching, her shoulders shaking—her unfettered boobs were Jello in an earthquake—and she'd no doubt be commencing full waterworks soon as well.

"And then there were two," said Trevor. "Well, Sis? Any bright ideas?"

"Shit, I don't know…break into Dad's liquor cabinet and get seriously fucking bombed?"

He laughed. A strained laugh, maybe, but still a laugh. "I think that is a good goddamn plan."

***

Getting seriously fucking bombed may have sounded good to the others, but it wasn't Andy's thing. He liked a few beers, sure; he'd just never cared for the harder stuff. Let alone the top-shelf stuff that Trevor and Chelsea found when they broke into their father's liquor cabinet.

What he wanted, what he needed—wasn't that a song?—was a nice relaxing mellow. Booze amped him up, made him hyper. Weed was what the situation called for. A few deep tokes, and maybe the chaos in his brain would settle down enough to let him start trying to make heads or tails of this mess.

Problem being, the rest of his stash had been in his luggage. And his luggage, along with everyone else's, was strewn across the yard, smashed, trampled, and covered in turtle cum.

Even if he could get it, he doubted he'd be able to bring himself to smoke it.

No, that was crap. He would. After a while, he'd say screw it and light on up. He'd had it baggied, wrapped, and tucked in the middle of his spare underwear. It'd probably still be fine.

Fine and green, promising comfort, promising relaxation.

Exactly how far from the house *was* his battered old backpack?

Downstairs, raucous laughter and bad singing told him the makeshift drunken non-karaoke karaoke party continued going strong. Chelsea, for all her other many talents, was butchering 'Bad Romance' so badly it was a wonder Lady Gaga herself didn't show up to slap her.

Now, that, that would be a sight. Andy would rejoin the party for that.

He'd excused himself and come upstairs, choosing one of the lakehouse's guest bedrooms at random. It had a sliding glass door onto a smaller balcony, overlooking the main deck below and the bloody cesspool of a lake beyond, and the first thing he'd done was yank the drapes shut. No view, thank you very much.

Without kicking off his sneaks—if an emergency evac opportunity appeared, he'd be ready—he flopped sideways onto the bed. A vague puff of stale dust wafted up. Been a while since anyone changed the linen, but who cared? The fact the place was in as good a shape as it was seemed miraculous enough.

Miraculous and more than a little weird. It'd been how long? This dusty staleness spoke of a few weeks neglected, not years. The caretaker and housekeeper had been doing their jobs. So, where were they? What did they know about what had happened? More importantly, could they help them get the fuck out of here?

The longer he lay there, the more he wished for a smoke. Just a couple of puffs to steady him, take the edge off.

The longer he lay there, also, the less the walls and ceiling above him seemed like normal walls and ceiling. Instead of wood, paint, paneling and plaster, the room looked…

He couldn't put his finger on it. Weird, somehow. Fake, somehow. CGI. Good CGI, but CGI nonetheless.

Or, and this being by far the more likely, his brain was fucking with him. And why not? It should be, after what he'd seen today. After the drive, and the lake, and Madison, and Gamera…

She'd screamed at him for help. "Andy, help!" rang in his ears' memory with vivid clarity.

"Andy, help!" but he hadn't. "Andy, help!" but he'd run.

More tears trickled hot from the corners of his eyes.

He hauled himself upright, squared his shoulders as much as they'd square, and faced the sliding glass door to the balcony. Maybe, from there, he could see the bushes where she'd vanished. Maybe he'd been wrong, and she was only tangled up or unconscious.

Yeah, and maybe Lady Gaga *would* drop in for karaoke…

Okay, okay, maybe he was also hoping to catch a glimpse of his backpack. It might be undamaged. It might be not too far to attempt a salvage operation.

Holding his breath, he slid open the door.

***

She sees him, sees him up there, sniveling and sobbing and trying not to retch, the smell of the lake still strong in his nose but the influence of the house already working on him.

She sees him, Andy the fuckwit chickenshit coward, Andy who ran as she screamed for help, as she was torn to pieces.

Oh, and how it had hurt! The yank and rip, the gristle-pop of joints leaving their sockets! Skin stretching to unbearable lengths before tearing loose in raggedy flaps! Arteries whipping around like a kid's summer water toy, spraying blood, spouting blood, pumping blood!

I'll die and it'll stop hurting, *she'd thought.* ***I'll die any second, any second now...***

An arm and an arm and a leg and a leg, not quite drawn and quartered but close enough, wrenched from her torso, the agony tremendous, seeing the spasms of nerves make her feet helplessly kick, make her very own hands seem to be waving goodbye.

Dead I'm dead I must be dead I have to be...

Into each gory hole by shoulder and hip, the crawdad-thing's tendony fingers digging and gouging, burrowing through meat and muscle, hooking into the arches of her pelvis, hooking the top of her ribcage...and yanking again!

She'd felt it all. Felt it all though she should have bled out, gone into shock, something. Felt it all though she should have died.

Unendurable pain! Unendurable except she had to endure it because there was nothing else, no escape into sweet empty blackness of death!

She'd felt it all, just as she now saw it all.

With new eyes, of course. Her old ones were gone, plucked and eaten, tasty orb-morsels followed by the puke-slimed length of her uprooted tongue. A delicacy!

Instead of oblivion's welcome embrace, there'd been a jarring, a burning, a sizzling transition, and suddenly she was...she was...whatever she was.

Something small, the world grown huge around her. Something with a twitching whiskery nose to which the lake-stink was the aroma of bacon sizzling on the grill, something with a thick coat of oily fur and a naked tail, something with webbed feet and a butt-heavy waddle, and an overbite the words 'buck tooth' couldn't come close to describing.

I'm one of those what do you call thems, *she'd thought.* ***A Florida swamp-rat, a nutria...but not...but more...but other...but else.***

Because a normal Florida swamp-rat, a natural and ordinary nutria, wouldn't also have a long thin hornet's stinger jutting from the end of its tail. The waterproofing oils of its fur wouldn't be a gummy-slick contact poison. The bite of its oversized front teeth wouldn't cause living flesh to instantly rot.

Mmm, rot, rotted flesh, soft and spongy, sloughing leprous from the bone!

She looks, with her new eyes, her yellow hell-rodent eyes, at Andy. Andy, up there on what he believes is the balcony of what he believes is a lakehouse. He's leaning over, peering at the wreckage of the SUV.

Probably wondering if he dares make a dash for his stash; if anything can overcome his chickenshit cowardice, it'll be the need for weed.

Yes, she sees him, she sees everything, sees the 'house' as it truly is, and he'd better move soon if he's going to.

Do it, Andy, *she thinks.* ***Do it, go for it, that's your backpack there, isn't it, the blue one? You can reach it and get back if you're quick, sure you can!***

He stares longingly at the backpack, battered but uncrushed amid broken suitcases and beer cans. A few scarlet imps still investigate the SUV's ravished carcass, but most of the spectators by now have moved on. The lake may smell like crisp frying bacon; a Fang-Turtle's ejaculate mixed with gasoline and antifreeze is another matter.

It makes her whiskery nose wrinkle, but she creeps carefully closer through the safer underbrush. When Andy makes his attempt, she will be ready.

8

After the 'cops' had come the true military, and Favius couldn't help but be impressed. These were proper troops, disciplined and trained. Their flying machines buzzed sleek and black, dragon-wasp marvels of invention. Their 'guns' proved potent indeed; unleashed in their full fury upon the largest of the Golems, they perforated the dense clay almost to the point of causing harm.

So, yes, heeding those whispers, heeding the wisdom of deceit, he'd surrendered. He'd bidden the Golems stand down, their instant compliance with his command not going unnoticed by his wary captors...according to plan.

For it was that some aspects of war and warriors never did or would change. Be they mortal or Damned, Roman or modern, certain truths remained universal and undeniable. Show men a new way to kill, a way potent and powerful, and they would want it. Covet it. Do anything to obtain and control it.

Show them nigh-invulnerable, nigh-unstoppable, mindlessly obedient super-soldiers? The prospect and potential of an army of Golems?

Oh, such raw, naked greed-lust, Favius had never beheld. And he had, in his time, seen a *lot* of raw, naked greed-lust.

Having duly 'surrendered,' he was taken 'prisoner.' That the Golems would answer only to Favius, that no amount of earthly tests could explain them, that he let it be implied he knew the secrets of their construction and operation...

his 'captors' fell all over themselves to be accommodating. Generals, senators, and scientists alike were so overtaken by covetous desires, their salivations could have filled in equal measure another Reservoir.

Even now, in this laughable 'captivity,' Favius enjoyed luxuries and indulgences beyond any he'd known in life or in Hell. To think, he'd felt that initial pang of disappointment at missing his chance to drink the fresh lake water!

He had all the water he wanted, now, in abundance! Hot or cold, his at the turn of a tap! The mighty aqueducts of Rome could have done no better. Water to drink, to wash in, to spill his piss and drop his shit...the most powerful Demon Lords knew no such extravagance!

And food, food like nothing he'd tasted or dared to imagine! Some familiar from before death and damnation, yes...bread and salt, olive oil, eggs and fish, wine...and others all but beyond comprehension. Chocolate, sugar, fruits, coffee, ice cream in a plethora of flavors, a thousand kinds of cheese! He did miss the unique tang and texture of well-prepared human flesh, harvested from the spirit-bodies of the Damned, but he was served various animal meats at every meal and found them tasty.

His 'captors' provided him also with palatial comfort, which they seemed to think of as a detention cell. Clearly, none of them had so much as an inkling of what dungeons were like where he had come from. Heaven's clouds, pillows stuffed with angel-down, and linens woven from the hair of virginal saints could have been no softer.

Entertainment of all sorts was his at a whim, day or night. Less than ideal entertainment, perhaps...'movies' were still not the thrill of being at the great gladiatorial arenas, close enough to feel and smell the sweat and the blood and the death...nor were the women they provided him particularly exciting, being for the most part lowly, disposable, or drugged...and the stakes for which these soldiers gambled were ludicrous.

The books, though, and this 'internet,' limited though his access to it may be, gave him a veritable wealth of information. So did the regular 'interrogation sessions.' Their avid questioning taught Favius far more than he divulged, and what he did divulge wasn't likely to be of any practical use.

It soon occurred to him, to his amusement, that the highest commanders entertained grandiose notions of an actual war with Hell. Not only of having one, but of *winning*.

"We'll nuke the bastards," they said. "That'll show 'em. You don't mess with the U.S. of A."

***

Sometimes, they brought in priests to see him, clergy of various denominations. From the more intellectual and scholarly Jesuits and rabbis, to the utter lunatic snake-handlers and speakers-in-tongues...shamans, druids, wiccans...televangelists...even the occasional Satanist. They brought in doctors, scholars, occultists, paranormalists, historians, linguists. Psychics and psychiatrists. Atheists. Stage magicians.

Favius humored them. He found it amusing. No matter how they tried, they could not debunk him. They could not exorcise or banish him. They couldn't medically explain the suffering faces sewn into his skin, or his ability to shrug off minor wounds. They couldn't explain him, or the Golems, or any of it, without first having to accept and acknowledge the reality of magic.

Strange stumbling block. A surprising number of mortals seemed fine with the concepts of Heaven and Hell, angels and demons, their Lord God above, Lucifer and the dark gods of the underworlds below. But, bring magic into

101

the mix, and suddenly it was all nonsense, fakery, and fairy tales?

Many of the atheists and rational scientific types seemed deeply, personally offended by the entire matter. The believers, of whatever faiths, all at least shared a common vindication—they might be off a little in the precise details, but *their side was right!* Here was proof! Irrefutable *proof*!

It didn't take long for smugness to set in. Nor did it take long for hatred from the opposite camp to set in; once, so-called 'experts' famous for exposing so-called 'frauds' tried to assassinate Favius. Which, he had to admit, had been an impressive effort. To smuggle weapons past that much top-tier military security? By mere sleight of hand? They almost could have been dangerous. If not so blinded and stubborn, they might have become powerful warlocks or arch-wizards.

And if Favius hadn't killed them, of course.

He'd had little choice. The taller of the two had been all bravado and bluster, cocksure, holding a pistol while offering Favius one last chance to reveal the 'trick'…one last chance Favius instead had used to drive the heel of his hand up under the man's chin, lifting his feet off the floor and smashing his skull against the ceiling. The other turned out to be a quick and dexterous little pain in the nethers, silent, but fighting like a cornered weasel. He'd made Favius wreck half the room in the process of dragging him down, both of them bloodied and messy by the end.

Fortunately, his 'captors' had been understanding. He, Favius, was the big prize. Damnation in the flesh, a soldier in Hell's infernal army. Their key to creating and controlling legions of Golems of their own, which would certainly give the Chinese or Koreans or ISIS or whoever reason to think twice before messing again with this great nation.

Compared to that, what were a couple of overpaid Las

Vegas hucksters who, as one general put it, "pulled rabbits out of their asses"?

Yes, they really wanted Golems. Each new round of tests and trials only further convinced them. Favius, curious himself, cooperated. He'd always wondered about the extent of a Golem's capabilities, its limits. The technicians—what this military called their warlocks—were, if anything, even more in love with the Golems than the generals and senators.

They'd even given them names. Thing, Hulk, and Juggernaut. Who needed no food, no sleep, no wages. Who existed only to perform brute labor, and to kill. Each with tireless strength, unburdened by morals and emotions, unable to be swayed by threats or by bribes.

Favius enjoyed watching the tests. He enjoyed the expressions of other onlookers as Hulk hammered a cinderblock wall into rubble, as Juggernaut plodded stolidly through flamethrowers and over land mines, as Thing picked up a suspected terrorist by the ankles and split him like a wishbone. Stealth and agility were another story, but the time the trio had been turned loose against an armored column was something no one who saw it would ever forget.

***

He had been a 'model prisoner,' had he not? He'd learned much and luxuriated more. Had killed many and struck terror into the hearts of others. He had witnessed before his very eyes the faith of devout believers crumble, and ushered non-believers into the glorious service of Satan.

A few—a deranged few, to be sure—had even come to consider him, in some strange way, a friend.

A friend. Because they'd on occasion taken meals together, thrown dice together, conversed of matters beyond those pertaining to the Golems, shared jokes…because they'd become accustomed enough to his appearance to no longer recoil with horror and revulsion…

A *friend.*

He, Favius, formerly of the most esteemed Grand Duke Cyamel's Exalted Security Brigade, and eternal Rome before that. Loyal soldier, loyal unto utter damnation, Lucifer be with all soul's suffering praised! Loyal, perhaps, to a fault…yet a serendipitous fault which had brought him here, the better to do his fearful master's bidding.

A friend. An ally. A co-conspirator. They viewed him through the warped lenses of themselves, and why not? Why wouldn't Favius be as eager as they were for power and profit? Why *not* help them raise up the unstoppable army they so coveted? He'd be well and amply rewarded.

If war was his purpose, whether on Hell or on Earth, well, as they said, go big or go home! Let it be not just war but WAR, that most ultimate end-of-days battle long prophesized, by whatever name he preferred. Armageddon or Ragnarok, no matter, so long as the land burned and the seas boiled, the skies smoked. So long as the sun turned to night and the moon turned to blood. So long as the cities fell, the living died, the dead walked, beasts of olde were unleashed, and a thousand years of agony ruled the world!

How short-sighted, these generals and senators. Short-sighted, greed-blinded, prideful, naive. They honestly expected not only to direct and control the destruction, but survive and thrive, and emerge from the wreckage as rich phoenix kings.

When Favius had pointed out what might seem to be some obvious flaws with this goal, they loftily assured him they had plans in place. Contingencies. Bunkers and shelters. Strongholds. To these remarks, he'd only nodded. Hubris had been the downfall of far greater than they, but it was not for Favius to say so.

He'd eventually agreed. Of course he had! And they well-congratulated themselves for it, for having swayed him, won him over. Or even tricked him; he supposed plenty of them were smugly confident of that, those who deemed him an archaic antiquity, a mere grunt, cannon-fodder from ages past. They didn't care, as long as they got what they wanted.

Neither did he. Let them think as they would.

Now, he rode in the midst of a heavy military convoy, the tank-transport an armored vault on immense treaded wheels. Under diligent guard, of course—friend, ally, or co-conspirator did only go so far—but unshackled as a token gesture of trust. They'd even returned his sturdy gladius, though the hilt had been peace-bonded because token gestures of trust also only went so far.

Along a low central bench sat Juggernaut, Thing, and Hulk. Silent. Immobile. Waiting. Obedient. Their eye-slits black and empty, their huge fists curled placidly on their slablike clay thighs. The vehicle, despite its titanic build, had groaned and settled when they stepped in.

Six soldiers surrounded them, while Favius was flanked by a scientist and a specialist. His 'handlers.' Far more than their jobs or reputations were on the line. In truth, they were hostages...though *whose* remained less than clear.

The military convoy rumbled onward, toward the lake. Enclosed in this windowless compartment, Favius could see nothing else, but knew the cars ahead held officers, the trucks at the rear were laden with troops and munitions, and directly behind this tank-transport was another, carrying the top-secret result of several months' work.

9

They'd chosen the campground from those listed on the map partly because it was close to Checkpoint Gabriel and partly for its name—Bible Creek. If that wasn't some sort of an omen, nothing was.

On the way, witnessing the vile changes of the landscape growing progressively worse the further toward the lake they went, an anxious apprehension filled the bus.

Filled the menthol-scented bus, that was. The whole interior smelled like Vicks, and for good reason. Each of them carried a small container and had, at Crusader Markane's urging, swiped a thick glob of the jellied goo under their noses. It would, he assured them, help mask the unholy reek emanating from the cursed Devil's Lake.

Which it did, but at the cost of sending June's mind back to childhood illnesses when she'd been stuck in bed with it slathered over her little chest. The wild-cherry flavor of cough syrup always had a similar effect. Suddenly, she'd be eight years old again, watching Price is Right on the portable television while her mother sat in the other room, smoking and clipping coupons and chatting on the phone.

Still, it was better than the lake-stink, which was the awfulest (and offalest) thing June had ever sniffed in her life. Her mind kept trying to come up with comparisons and falling short, so she finally just huffed deep of the Vicks and tried not to think about it.

Bible Creek Campground proved to have seen better days. Once, it would've been neatly marked campsites,

106

each with picnic table, parking space, and firepit. Now, it was long-abandoned, overgrown and weedy. Most of the numbered posts were gone or tipped over. In the rough center was a hexagonal open-sided shelter, the roof half-collapsed. The bathrooms weren't flush potties. Corroded faucets on pipes jutted out of the ground here and there like disinterred bones.

The sign at the entrance had been vandalized, some of the letters gouged and scratched out so it appeared to read "**BI LE REEK**," and the historical marker—a plaque set into a concrete slab—was covered with a flyblown pile of rotting animal corpses.

"We must be strong," Crusader Markane reminded them. "We knew there'd be atrocities."

Pretty little Mrs. Gabelman had gone pale as milk. Her husband kept patting at and reassuring her, calling her his stalwart angel. Ramon and David went to work unloading tents, sleeping bags, and camping gear from the back of the bus. Everyone pitched in, helping set up. Even June's mother, if with something of an air of long-suffering woe. Margaret Goldsmith had never been one for camping. Her idea of roughing it was a motel without complimentary continental breakfasts.

The Shinns tested the faucets and found some still working; they'd have clean water at least, praise the Lord! And, by the half-collapsed hexagonal shelter, a good-sized stack of old firewood covered with a grimy tarp meant they didn't have to go gathering sticks.

As for the lake, they'd seen it in all its hideousness on the drive, but from here it was visible only as festering maroon swatches through the trees. A trail led toward it, the sign broken and askew but legible. Another sign warned to watch for dangerous wildlife, presumably alligators and snakes, but aside from the flies buzzing the piled carcasses, Bible Creek Campground seemed inhabited by nothing larger than mosquitoes. Huge, ugly, dragonfly-sized mosquitoes, but still just mosquitoes. For which, they had packed several cans of bug spray and plenty of citronella candles.

Soon, half a dozen two-person tents clustered near a larger communal firepit. June wasn't thrilled about sharing close quarters with her mother, but what else could she do?

Though, with Brother Lucas saying he'd sleep in the bus to make sure no one came along and tried to mess with it, he'd be alone…and also meant Brother William and Crusader Markane would each have a tent to himself…

Dream on, Junie-June, she inwardly scoffed. *Just dream on.*

***

Duties were assigned and carried out with reasonable efficiency, the older men in charge of building the fire, the women in charge of organizing meals, the younger men— David and Ramon—posted to keep watch. Nobody was to go anywhere outside the camp on their own, even to the bathrooms. Always in pairs or teams.

Then Crusader Markane called Brother Lucas over to the bus and asked him to help unload the rest of the gear. June watched, amazed, as they lifted away some carpeted panels in the rear compartment and hauled out a footlocker, several duffle bags, and a wooden crate.

Heavy, too…Brother Lucas's muscles bulged so as to strain the seams of his sleeves as he manfully lugged the footlocker over to one of the picnic tables. As soon as he set it down—the table creaked—he stripped off his shirt. An undershirt, so thin it was nearly see-through and so tight it might've been airbrushed on, clung to his chest. The sight gave June another rush of tingles and palpitations.

"Not the heat, but the humidity," he said, mopping his

smooth ebony pate with the wadded-up shirt. "Am I right?"

"Right as rain, Brother," Crusader Markane said, slinging two duffle bags onto another table.

"Too bad about the lake. I could do with a dip." Lucas stretched, broad chest expanding, powerful arms flexing, before going to fetch the crate.

June had to sit down and feign being dizzy. Well, feign the reason for being dizzy. It *was* hot, there *was* heat, and not all of it by a long chalk came from the environment. She accepted another water bottle from the solicitous Stepford-bitch, rubbing it across her forehead and taking a long drink.

"What's all this?" asked Brother William. Mr. Gabelman hadn't been any good at starting the fire, and Mr. Shinn hadn't been much better, but once he took over, it blazed up nice and vigorous.

"The rest of the gear." Crusader Markane dropped two more duffle bags near the others, then unlatched and opened the footlocker. Removing some layers of pan-denominational prayer books, meta-church hymnals, and assorted literature, he stepped back and beckoned for them to have a look.

Now revealed was an arsenal of shotguns, hand-guns, and sleek black wicked-looking military-type weapons. June was no expert, couldn't have distinguished an Uzi from an AR-15, but whatever these were, they looked like the kind any dedicated maniac might pick to shoot up a school. And boxes of ammunition. And an egg-carton-looking foam thing cradling what had to be grenades. And a bundle of either road flares or sticks of dynamite.

They all stared, gape-mouthed. David let out a low whistle. Ramon crossed himself. Mrs. Gabelman pressed her palm to the base of her throat, where she wore a charm bracelet cluster of religious symbols on a fine gold chain. The Shinns, so hardcore when it came to yelling at women outside abortion clinics, took simultaneous steps backward and looked shocked.

"Are those paintball guns?" asked Mr. Gabelman, then flinched as the shocked looks and gape-mouthed stares shifted to him.

"Don't be a numpty," Margaret Goldsmith said, in the absent-minded dismissive tone she usually used on June. She gulped, as if it was only now occurring to her that all the 'holy war' stuff hadn't been mere pulpit rhetoric, and those coveted bragging rights might bring actual risk.

Brother Lucas crowbarred the lid from the crate, taking out one of a dozen police-style riot helmets, with clear plexiglas visors in front and their meta-church logo decals pasted on both sides. He held it like Hamlet with the skull, nodding his approval.

In the duffle bags were Kevlar vests, padded gloves of the type used in training attack dogs, and…were those gas-masks? First-aid kits?

Brother William cleared his throat. "Armed and armored with our 'faith,' you said?"

Markane shrugged, the corner of his mouth slyly crooking. "Can't have too much faith, Brother. Can never have too much faith."

***

Their late lunch consisted of classic camp-out fare: hot dogs, baked beans, potato salad, lemonade, cans of soda, bakery cookies. It almost could have been an ordinary group picnic.

Except for every bite of food tasting like menthol. Except for the whiffs of the lake that the menthol couldn't fully mask, and the distant but unnatural animal—maybe animal—noises. Except for the guns, and the vests they'd all been buckled into at Crusader Markane's insistence.

The helmets and gloves, he said, could wait until they were ready for actual battle, but he wanted everyone prepared. There was no telling what might emerge from the woods without warning, what horrors might slither and splash up the shore.

Some of them—her mother and the Shinns in particular—looked downright absurd. June suspected she did as well, cinched into padded Kevlar, a loaded shotgun resting by her side as she balanced a paper plate on her knee.

But, Brother Lucas had helped her into the garment, and she didn't think she'd only imagined his strong fingers lingering, taking extra time, being sure it was nice and snug. He'd also instructed her in the weapon's use and basics, including folding his massive body around hers, covering her hand as they gripped the weapon's hard length. Ooh, and the way his deep voice reverberated in her bones, every word seeming loaded with suggestiveness! Having his entire attention, for those few moments, fixed just on her, sent delicious shivers thrilling through her from head to toe. His musky male scent was far preferable to menthol, bug-spray, and woodsmoke. Feeling the warmth of his skin against hers, his breath stirring some loose strands of her hair…

She could hardly remember a thing about the shotgun instructions, and no wonder. But it couldn't be that tricky. Point, shoot, ka-blam. She'd get the hang of it quick enough, she was sure. If and when she had to.

The Gabelmans looked like they'd been drafted into a gated-community homeowner's association militia, while David and Ramon both resembled fresh young cadets. Brother William was now careworn George Clooney with a gun.

The dragonfly-sized mosquitoes made a few strafing runs despite the campfire smoke and bug-spray, but mostly kept their distance. Something skittered and chittered in the branches overhead, but all anyone could glimpse of it was a long mongoose-like shape.

After eating, golden-boy David asked if he and Ramon could scout the area, so Mr. Shinn and Brother William agreed to stand watch. Mrs. Gabelman expressed an interest in seeing if there was still a creek at Bible Creek—one of the askew trail signs indicated there'd been one at some point. Her husband was reluctant until Crusader Markane suggested Brother Lucas go with them, at which point June spoke up.

"I wouldn't mind having a look around." She patted her shotgun as if she knew how to use it.

"I thought you were going to help us with the dishes," her mother said, drawstring lips pursing.

June picked up a stack of used paper plates and dropped them into the fire, where they flared brilliant orange amid ashes and embers. "Done."

Her mother huffed, but June was sure she saw Brother Lucas hide a grin, and that made her little act of defiance worth whatever cattiness and snark would be headed her way later.

"Eyes and ears open, hands steady, hearts strong," Crusader Markane told them. "Trust God, but stay alert. Watch out for each other, and be safe."

"You know it," Brother Lucas replied.

Everyone else nodded. David and Ramon snapped off little salutes; they seemed eager to get going. Mr. Gabelman still seemed dubious. June had a flash of hope he'd change his mind, convince his wifey-poo, and leave her to go off alone with Brother Lucas…but, no such luck.

"If you run into trouble," Markane went on, then paused, gesturing at their hardware with a half-beatific, half-savage smile. "Well, I'm sure we'll hear you give it holy what-for."

***

They followed the marked trail toward Bible Creek, Brother Lucas in the lead with June behind him and the Gabelmans bringing up the rear.

June still felt kind of silly, buckled into body armor and toting a shotgun through the woods, while at the same time feeling excited and more than a little badass, too. She was no Sanchez from the checkpoint, to be sure, but she had to be more competent than either the corporate yuppie or his porcelain-doll wife.

Maybe she'd even have the chance to impress Brother Lucas. Anything could happen.

There did turn out to be a creek, or at least a creekbed with a trickle down the middle. The rest was dead plants, the small bones of fish and frogs, and more mosquitoes. The trail continued upstream, so they did the same, until they reached a spot where the reason for the low water level became apparent.

Someone or something had built a dam, a high mound of sticks and branches, mud, rocks, leaves, and twigs. Past it, half-flooded trees and mossy hummocks protruded from a wide-spreading pool. Fleshy-looking pinkish lily pads floated like large flattened ears. Bugs skated the surface. Sleek silvery shapes flitted in the depths.

"Beavers?" asked Mr. Gabelman.

"Maybe," Brother Lucas said.

"Or maybe not," June added, pointing to a series of nets and wicker crawdad-traps, secured to stakes spaced along the shore.

"I see a boat over in those reeds," Mrs. Gabelman said. "Does someone *live* here?"

"What poor soul would want to live in a place like this?" Her husband set a comforting hand on her shoulder.

"No one too friendly, I'd guess." Brother Lucas drew his

gun, more as a precautionary measure than for immediate use.

June fumbled with the shotgun. Mere moments ago, she'd felt excited and kind of badass; now a nervous lump had formed in her throat and her fingers were clumsy and she only hoped she didn't blow off her own foot by mistake.

"Hello?" Mrs. Gabelman called, voice high and slightly shaky. "We're good people, church people. We're here to help." Opening her purse, she brought out a stack of tracts. "We'd like to talk with you about the Lord God."

Lucas and June stared at her in disbelief. Even her husband seemed taken aback.

The lack of response from the surrounding wilderness didn't deter her, having instead an emboldening effect. "Let us pray with you, pray for you," she went on. "Let us guide you to seek repentance and salvation. Through the Lord God, all things are possible."

The tall reeds rustled. The boat rocked, sending ripples fanning across the pool. A faint noise, a whimper or plaintive little cry, reached their ears.

"Hello?" Mrs. Gabelman called again. "Please. We *are* good people. We come in peace."

What next, June wondered? 'Take us to your leader'?

Brother Lucas shook his head. "I don't like this."

"Someone is there," the Stepford-ninny insisted. "You heard it too, I know you did. Someone hurt or helpless. What if it's a child? A baby?"

"A baby?" June echoed. "Are you serious? What would a baby be doing in a rowboat?"

"A basket among the bulrushes served for Moses, didn't it?"

"You aren't going to find Baby Moses out here!"

"Where is your faith, Sister?"

"I keep it right next to my common sense! Don't you?"

A muffled snort of laughter from Brother Lucas sent a

flush suffusing her cheeks.

Those big china-blue eyes brimmed with tearful reproach. "Will you be one who turns aside and passes by? Will you spurn a person in need?"

"I'll go," Mr. Gabelman said, less in conviction and more as if just wanting to fend off the waterworks. "I'll look, all right, honey?"

She beamed at him, clasping her hands all oh-my-hero to her bosom, then shot June an arch glance.

"Careful," Brother Lucas said. "I'll cover you."

"Yeah." He swallowed, steeled himself. "Yeah, good, thanks. Teamwork."

He made it six steps.

Six whole steps.

June counted.

***

Mr. Gabelman made it six whole steps toward the rowboat in the reeds, where his ninny wife no doubt expected him to find a darling abandoned baby they could raise as their own.

As he was about to take the seventh step, a crazed naked man with black hair and red eyes burst from the surrounding undergrowth and plunged a spear into his chest.

"Shit!" bellowed Brother Lucas, opening fire. His first shot obliterated the man's face. Boom, and it was ketchup and raw meatloaf His second shot tore a ragged furrow in the man's side—just above a stunted twist of what appeared to be a misshapen third arm—as he dropped.

Mrs. Gabelman screamed like a horror movie audition. June managed not to do the same, though a sharp breath caught in her throat.

"Ow," said Mr. Gabelman, with more surprise than pain. He looked at the spear—a crude weapon apparently made from a bunch of steak knives lashed to an old broom handle—and said it again. "Ow." The blades had gone through his Kevlar vest as if it were nothing, a crimson stain already blossoming on his button-down shirt.

Other screams, these ones maniacal and raging, erupted from the trees. More crazed naked people, men and women with wild black hair and furious red eyes, rushed to attack. They had their own makeshift weapons, as well as their own grotesque deformities: club feet, cleft palates, extra-jointed limbs, a teenage girl with clusters of tiny fingers where nipples should have been, an old man who had a third red eyeball bulging from his forehead like a goiter.

The shotgun, with which June had been clumsily fumbling not a minute earlier, swung up sure in her grip. It bucked and roared. The shock knocked her backwards onto her behind, but even as she fell, she saw the nearest of the freakish creek-people's stomach go blasting wide open.

Another of them, a hag whose features seemed twisted Picasso-style, leaped at June, snaggle-toothed and screeching. She rolled, jabbed upward with the hot double-barrel, and pulled the trigger again, all in one motion. The hag's neck exploded in a chunky spray, leaving nothing above the collarbones as her head tumbled ker-plunk into the pond.

Nearby, Brother Lucas kept firing as the creek-freaks hurled stones and waved clubs. A group of kids—no, conjoined triplets with three upper torsos sprouting from a central five-legged trunk—tackled him and took him down in a flailing flurry of too many arms.

Mrs. Gabelman, still screaming, bolted for her husband as he sagged to his knees. "No, no, no, no!" Grabbing the spear, she yanked the half-dozen embedded knife-blades from his chest. Blood burst from the holes like a showerhead. She got it full in the face, in the wide-open mouth.

"Ow," said Mr. Gabelman for the third time, weakly. Then the old man with the bulging forehead-eyeball hooked him in the throat with a fishing gaff and pulled out his larynx in a tangle of vocal cords and veins.

June didn't know when or how she'd made it to her feet, but the teenage girl was upon her, fingers—all of them, stubby revolting tiny chest-fingers included!—clutching and clawing, snagging her vest. The girl's wild laugh screeched in June's ears. The shotgun was wedged crossways between their bodies, at a useless angle. On instinct, June hiked her knee, hitting Little Miss Fingers square in the naked, filthy, black-tufted crotch.

From whence *more* fingers scrabbled, digging at June's leg! She slammed her heel down, onto the creek-girl's freaky monkey foot—fingers *there*, too!—with a hard crunch. The girl squealed in pain. A shove sent her sprawling. And, again displaying innate ability out of nowhere, the butt of June's shotgun hammered Little Miss Fingers dead-center between those rabid red eyes, folding her like a cheap lawn chair.

Panting, June looked around for the others, just in time to see the remaining creekers, carrying the Gabelmans, vanish into the woods.

10

No power meant no ice in the freezer, so he couldn't have his scotch on the rocks like a classy-fucking-gentleman the way Dad would have insisted.

Trevor snorted and took another swig straight from the bottle. Dad was going to have plenty to be pissed about already; one more wouldn't hurt.

Across from him, Chelsea mixed her eleventeenth martini and downed it like a pro. Kayla had rum and Coke, the Coke lukewarm from a stack of cases in the pantry. She made a face each time she took a sip, but kept on steadily sipping.

The singing and laughing had tapered off somewhere in there. Now they just sat and drank, as if maybe, if they got drunk enough, this would all go away.

What else was there to do? Just drink and wait it out. Wait for rescue. For Jason to come check on them...

...his imagination obligingly unfolded a shirtless sweaty action movie scene, and Trevor forgot the rest of whatever he'd been thinking.

"Does anything about this seem weird to you guys?" asked Kayla.

Chelsea side-eyed her. "Are you fucking joking?"

"I don't mean the lake or the turtle. I mean, here in the house. It's like the rooms aren't as big as they look."

"How would you know? You've never been here before."

"Yeah, but—"

"Yeah but nothing." Chelsea gulped what was pretty

118

much raw vodka by that point. "Tell you what, though... that dead bitch Madison was right...gonna take more than a tit-flash to get us out of this shitstorm."

"Probably have to suck some dick," Trevor said.

"Yeah, right, probably starting with your buddy at the checkpoint."

He leaned back, regarding the rustic roofbeams criss-crossing the living room and the unlit chandeliers hanging among them. Grinning, he thought, *Well, hey, if you don't want to...*

"Never mind *him*," Kayla said, tipsily stirring her glass. "The *other* guy, though—"

"So what?" said Chelsea. "I'd suck a whole battalion of dicks if it meant we never had to see this damn place again, and don't tell me you wouldn't."

As they fell to arguing over which of them had sucked the most dick, or the worst dick, or who was the best at dick-sucking, Trevor kept gazing at the roofbeams, a slow frown seeping over his face.

They *did* seem lower than he remembered, as if the room wasn't as big as it looked, or whatever Kayla had said. But then, wasn't that what happened when you went back as an adult to somewhere you hadn't been since you were a kid? Perspective and perception changed, and—

"Whoa, whoa, what?" he said, reverie breaking to the realization that he was no longer alone on the central sofa. Both girls had joined him there, one on each side, bickering and doing catty hand-smacks at each other over his lap.

"—settle this right here and now," Chelsea said.

"Settle what?" Trevor asked, attempting to shake some booze-fog from his head but failing.

"Which of us is better," Kayla said, "though obviously it's me."

"In your dreams!"

"In every guy's dreams!"

They reached for his groin and Trevor did a quick, defensive arm-cross…except, drunk as he was, he spilled the scotch and almost punched himself in the nuts. "Whoa!" he said again. "The hell are you doing?"

"Sucking your dick," Chelsea said, as if he were an idiot. "Then you decide who's best."

He blinked. Various objections and protestations blundered through his head—Kayla was his ex, and Andy's girl…and, oh, right, Chelsea was his *sister*!—but he'd already been packing a semi thanks to thoughts of Jason. When Kayla eluded Chelsea's cat-slaps to grasp him, his body responded without further input from his brain.

Moments later, they had him bared to the air, each with a hand curled around his shaft, arguing over who'd go first.

Which was when some damn asshole had to knock on the door.

***

The knock sobered them up the way a dash from a bucket of cold water would—a gasping shock temporarily smacking them to their senses. Kayla scrambled to a different couch, Trevor hastily stuffed himself back into his pants, and Chelsea, looking more mad than guilty, jumped up and headed for the door.

"Wait!" Kayla cried. "You're not going to open it, are you?"

"Well, duh!"

"But the stink, and the monsters, and—"

"And maybe some answers or our ticket out of here." Chelsea pulled the front door open.

The lake-smell did roll in, though somehow less utterly vile and repugnant than before. Whiffs of other scents drifted with it, gasoline and beer and a pungent spoiled-milk/rotten-egg/dead-fish odor the origin of which Kayla didn't want to think about.

Chelsea, meanwhile, took half a step back in surprise. Whatever she or any of them might have been expecting to see, a big hairy guy barefoot and bare-chested in faded overalls was far down the list.

He had muscles on his muscles, a broad flattish nose, a jutting jaw, and mismatched eyes—one bloodshot brown, the other an almost luminous silver. He blinked, then a wide smile revealed teeth that would've given an orthodontist a hard-on.

"Ho-leee shit!" the guy said. "Chelsea goddamn Carmichael, izzat you?"

"...yeah...?"

"And your brother?" he went on, looking past her at Trevor, who stood uncertainly as well as unsteadily in the middle of the living room. "Why, baptize me sideways, I cain't hardly believe it! The Carmichael kids themselves!" His gaze returned to Chelsea, the silver eye piercing as a drill bit, the brown one salacious. "All growed up, too!"

"Who the fuck are you?" Chelsea asked, diplomatic as ever.

"Don't'choo recognize me? Lester Riggers! My ma and pa been lookin' after this place for your ma and pa since long as I can remember."

Trevor moved up behind Chelsea. "*You're* Beanpole Lester?"

With an absurd aw-shucks gesture involving a head dip and a twisting of one foot, he replied, "I guess I filled out some from those days, yeah. Been no shortage of hard work since the AllHell."

"You were, like, ten years older than us," Chelsea said.

"Well, you know how 'tis. But never mind that; I see you had a spot of trouble." Lester jerked a thumb over his shoulder at the sad remains of the SUV. "Were it Ol' Hornyshell? He got a real thing for vee-hicles. Went after Heck Bodean's truck once. Now, I ain't no friend of Heck's, but I got to hand it to him, that day he drove like Dukes-a-Hazzard."

"What's going on?" Andy had appeared at the top of the stairs; Lester's gaze shifted to him. And then to Kayla, where it lingered, silver piercing and brown salacious.

"Brought some friends with you, as well, I see," he said. "Sorry I couldn't drop by sooner, but it's been a real nun's twat around here today. Plane crashes and shoot-em-ups and devil knows what all else. But I promised Ma and Pa that I'd look in, make sure no strangers was up t' mischief. They don't get around so well lately. But they are gonna be fit t' pop when they hear it's you!"

"They…uh..." Trevor cleared his throat and ran distracted fingers through his hair. "They've been taking pretty good care of things for folks who don't get around so well."

"It's mostly me and Ronny as what does the heavy liftin'. Now, you must remember Ronny. You and some of your friends threw him off the end of the dock one summer. Poor dumbass near to drownt!" He slapped his thigh and laughed.

Trevor joined in with a weak chuckle. "Oh…yeah… that was, uh..."

"Don' let it worry you none. Ronny ain't the grudge-holdin' kind."

"Good to know—"

Lester's huge grimy mitt shot past Chelsea to seize Trevor by the neck. "Me, though," he growled, "that's another story, rich boy."

***

Trevor made a *glaaack* noise and Chelsea was ready to go for the backwoods bastard's balls, when Lester released his grip, stepped back, and laughed.

"Just messin' with you is all," he said. "Saints, Ronny was a real boogersnot back then; I threw him in the lake more'n once myself. You're aces in my book." His two-tone gaze crawled over Chelsea again. "Aces, yes indeed."

With a shaky laugh of his own, Trevor said, "Glad to hear it." He probed gingerly at the red marks on his throat.

"Thought you was about t' piss yourself for a minute there."

"So did I."

For that matter, he looked like he still might. Chelsea didn't think she'd ever seen actual fear from him before, even when they'd been kids. Trevor had always been untouchable, all confidence and cockiness and arrogance. But getting neck-grabbed by this hulking brute had changed that.

"We square?" Lester asked.

"Sure."

Grinning, Lester gave Trev one of those companionable bro-punches to the upper arm, almost knocking him over. Trevor's own grin was more a tight rictus of pain as a fist-sized bruise immediately began to blossom.

"Hey, listen, Lester," Chelsea said, hoping to distract him before he decided a playful rassle was in order and her twin ended up a human pretzel. "We only just got here and we don't know what the fuck's going on. Can you tell us anything that might help?"

"Hunh." He looped his thumbs in the overall straps, rocking back and forth on the dirty heels of his bare feet. Feet which, she noticed, had such thick and leathery callused soles they might as well have been shoes. "Well, 'taint so bad once you get used to it…still plenty of people around, and we make do. Got us a barter system worked out and ever'thing. Crawdaddy's is still open, you know, over by the old boat launch. Heck Bodean, he runs the mail, not that there's as much of it as used t' be; think most the outside world would as soon forget 'bout us. Mostly his business is with that hotshot writer fella, deliverin' mannerscrips an' such."

"Why won't our phones work?" Kayla butted in. "Don't you have internet?"

Lester slid her another lascivious once-over, too. "Them fancy phones and com-pooters? Nah, closer y'are t' the lake, they's no good. But if you're fixin' as to stay on a while, me and Ronny can getcha hooked up fer power."

"Uh yeah no," Chelsea said. "We weren't planning on staying. We'd be gone already if not for..." She waved in the general direction of the demolished SUV.

"Yeah, hey!" Andy ventured another step down the stairs. "You mentioned that one dude had a truck...can he, or you, or anybody, give us a lift?"

"Yeah!" Kayla started to bounce, thought better of it, and folded her arms across her chest. "Andy, you're brilliant!"

"What, you mean like drive you somewheres?" Lester scratched his chin, pondering.

"To one of the checkpoints," Chelsea said. "Don't care which; any will do."

"So you don't wanna stay on a while, then?"

Her temper spiked. "No, we don't wanna stay on a while, you ignorant yee-haw!"

"Chels!" Trevor hissed, nudging her with an elbow.

"Sorry." She drew a breath. "It was a mistake to come here, okay, that's on me, I admit it, I own it, my-fucking-bad, but all we want now is to get out before anything else happens."

"Well, that's too bad you feel that way," said Lester, slowly, his disappointment evident. "We always like us some new blood."

Chelsea decided to skip right over the many possible creepy implications of his phrasing. "Can you find someone who'll give us a ride, or not?"

"I reckon as I can ask around. Cost ya, though."

Trevor patted at his pockets. "Sure. Let me grab my wallet—"

"Weren't you payin' attention, rich boy? Got us a *barter system*, I said. Your outside money ain't no good in here."

***

"Can't believe that worked," Trevor said later.

Chelsea shot him an arch look. "Has it ever *not*?"

She'd shown Lester her tits, of course. No mere flash this time; she'd bared them for what must've been a full thirty seconds, doing her little shimmy-shimmy-shake, cupping them, dandling them, and even tweaking her own pert pink nipples to boot.

It was the first time Andy had gotten the full view himself, and he had to admit, they were fantastic. Not as big as Kayla's, but firmer and flawlessly shaped. Dream tits. No airbrushing, no Photoshopping, no augmentation of any kind, just nature's own homegrown perfection. No wonder she was so proud of them.

"Okay, but now what?" Kayla asked, still hugging herself.

Good question.

Lester was gone, having agreed to ask around about getting them a ride to one of the checkpoints in exchange for the gander at Chelsea's chestworks. But, even with the door shut and locked behind him, nobody relaxed. He'd have keys anyway, and if those failed, the dude was built like a locomotive and could probably bash down a wall without breaking a sweat.

"Now we wait?" Trevor suggested. "Hope he does find someone, and hope whoever he finds isn't going to want too much more on their barter system exchange rate?"

Chelsea didn't look thrilled. "Yeah, about that, I know I said I'd suck a battalion of dicks to never see this place again, but...I have *some* goddamn standards."

"And he said it might take a while anyway." Kayla wrung her hands—funny, Andy had thought people only did that in old melodramas. "A day or three, wasn't that what he said?"

"Yeah, and that in the meantime he'd be sure to stop back in and check on us." Trevor surveyed the remains of their raid-the-liquor-cabinet party, and put on a hillbilly drawl. "Mebbe have us'n a few *dranks* like ol' *fraands*, her-yuk-her-yuk."

Chelsea smacked him in the already-bruised arm and he quit.

"This is messed up, man," Andy said.

"Majorly messed up," agreed Kayla. "I don't want to stay here! This house gives me the creeps. It's like it's watching us and closing in and you can feel it breathing."

They all looked at her.

"What?" she said. "It *is*!"

"Yeah," Andy said. "I don't think it's a real house."

"Okay, stop," said Trevor, rubbing his arm. "It's a real house, of course it is. We're standing in it, aren't we?"

"Don't pretend you don't feel it too," Kayla told him. "Maybe it *was* a real house, but not anymore. It's changed."

"Can we not?" said Chelsea. "Can we just fucking *not*? Things are bad enough without freaking ourselves out over spooky house bullshit."

"We're going to go legit bananas if we have to stay cooped up in here more than a couple days," Trevor said. "If we haven't already."

"So, let's do something." Chelsea turned on them with sudden purpose. "Let's not wait on Lester. There are other people. There's the guy who does the mail run; let's find him and make our own arrangements."

"Find him how?" asked Kayla.

Trevor snapped his fingers. "The writer Lester was talking about. I remember him. Edgely or Edley or something like that. Wrote some sick horror shit; Mom always thought he must be a serial killer."

"Oh, *that* guy!" Chelsea snapped her fingers too. "The property just past Bighead Rock?"

"Yeah. It isn't very far. We could probably—"

Kayla gulped. "You're not suggesting we go on foot, are you?"

"What choice do we have?" Trevor shrugged. "Beats spending the night here, waiting for Lester to come back."

Andy wasn't too sure about that...hiking through twisted hell-woods and along the nightmare lakeshore... looking for someone who probably hadn't really been a serial killer despite what Mrs. Carmichael said...but who *had* been messed up enough to write 'sick horror shit' even before all this happened...

Still, Trevor was right.

What choice did they have?

***

She waits after the stranger leaves—he passes near her hiding place and she catches his scent, and knows he is of here, not as changed as she is, but solidly adapted.

She waits and watches the 'house,' wondering what her former so-called 'friends' will do next. Rot-flies buzz in a lazy cloud above her. They're also waiting, waiting for what she might do next.

After a while, the front door opens again. A head peeks out. Trevor. Handsome, handsome Trevor. To whom she was always part of the scenery, his sister's funny little pet. Would Chelsea want her for a funny little pet now? She doesn't think so.

127

Trevor peeks, then emerges. Kayla and Chelsea follow. Then Andy, fucking chickenshit coward Andy who ran as she screamed for his help. They carry grocery bags and weapons—a butcher knife, a claw hammer, some sort of fireplace tool.

As they stand in a tense cluster, staring at the scenery and the SUV debris, her rodent-keen ears pick up part of their conversation. Their plan sounds stupid. Even after all they've seen, they still don't fully believe how bad it might get.

Well, they will. Soon enough. Sooner yet, if Andy does what she expects him to —

He does. He goes for his battered old backpack, largely unscathed and not drenched in coagulating ejaculate. He goes for it as she knew he would, his need for weed stronger than common sense.

And she goes for him. Her new low-slung bottom-heavy waddling body is surprisingly fast on its webbed feet. She's almost there by the time the others see her and start shouting warnings.

Andy, who'd just been bending to reach for the backpack's strap, is awkwardly posed and off balance, and trips over himself as he tries to turn. He lands with an "oof!" on his scrawny ass, then gapes as he sees what rushes toward him.

His bony legs are bare from the ragged hem of his cutoffs to the tops of his sneakers. He tries in an ungainly flail to kick her and misses by miles.

His skin is so thin and tender, so defenseless! Her prominent front teeth sink into it like biting a soft piece of fruit. Beneath is the lean, juicy flesh of his calf muscle.

How he squeals and hollers! He smacks at her with his hands. A twitch of her hindquarters whips her tail around, its stinger piercing his palm. He squeals again as his arm goes numb to the elbow, but numbness should be the least of his worries. Numbness should be a blessing, because everywhere his skin has made contact with her oily fur is already discoloring, and inside his leg that juicy calf muscle loosens, the tissue breaking down.

Trevor runs toward them, yelling, brandishing the hammer. Withdrawing her front teeth with a wet slurp, leaving a squarish hole in Andy's leg, she scurries for cover under the mangled chassis of the SUV.

***Now** Andy becomes aware of his slime-burning skin and the loosening dissolve in his leg. His cries hit a new pitch. He grabs his calf and it gooshes under his hand. Pink-tinged serum and pus squirt from the hole.*

She can smell it, the breakdown, the delicious spreading decay. The rot-flies smell it too, their buzzing growing louder, more eager.

Chelsea and Kayla rush to help as Trevor hauls Andy upright. They're all yelling, panicked, freaking out. Andy hop-totters on one foot with an arm slung around Trevor's shoulders. Their stumbling quartet makes it a few steps before everything below the knee on Andy's other leg sags and droops and sloughs off the bone in a liquefying cascade.

*Oh, and if they'd been panicking and freaked out **before**...*

But, to their credit, they don't drop Andy like a hot beat. They stick with him, half-carrying him toward the road, exposed tibia and fibula and all.

When they are gone, she trundles out and starts stuffing her cheek-pouches with moist, soupy, plum-black rotting flesh.

***

Maybe they should have gone back in the house. Maybe that would have been the smart thing.

Well, really, the smart thing would've been not to have come here at all, but too late for that now, wasn't it?

As for the house, it had taken them so much psyching up of themselves to leave it in the first place, going back in didn't even cross Trevor's mind until they were a good ways along the lakeshore road.

Just then, Andy passed out and went from being the gimpy wheel on their clumsy four-person wagon to being a slackness of utter deadweight. A lot of deadweight for such a skinny dude, not to mention a skinny dude missing a hefty portion of his leg.

But yeah, deadweight was deadweight, which Andy suddenly was.

The girls lost their holds. Trevor tried to manage the burden alone, couldn't, and let go before he went sprawling. Andy flopped face-first onto gravelly asphalt and didn't move.

"Jesus fuck," panted Chelsea. "This is nuts."

"Is he dead?" asked Kayla. "His leg, did you see—"

"We all saw," Trevor said. Crouching, he rolled Andy over and poked at his neck, checking for a pulse. "He's not dead."

"But his leg—"

"Yeah, I know."

"We have to *do* something!"

Do something? Do *what*? None of them even wanted to look at it! Still, she was right, so Trev forced himself to examine the...wound? Could you call it a wound? Holy shit, the guy was mostly naked legbones from knee to shoe; whether he still had an intact foot or not was a toss-up.

The way the skin had gone all runny-stretchy...the loose sponginess of tissue...the sounds...

No. No, dude, don't think about it, don't go there.

"It was that mutant devil-rat-thing," Chelsea said. "When it bit him, it poisoned him or some shit."

Clearly, that poison wasn't done yet. The discoloration had spread to Andy's lower thigh, turning it a suppurating pus-oozing red shot with skeins of purple-green. His flesh was melting and rotting before their very eyes. The smell was...wow, it was bad.

"He's going to die, then, if we don't—"

"Don't what?" Trevor looked up at Kayla. "What do you want me to do, cut his leg off?"

"If you have to!"

They had gathered some supplies from the lakehouse's pantry—water bottles, granola bars and packages of beef jerky and fruit snacks—before setting out. They'd also grabbed a few makeshift weapons, though Trevor had lost his hammer when he threw it at the mutant devil-rat-thing. Their remaining arsenal consisted of Kayla's fireplace poker and Chelsea's butcher knife.

"Chels, give me the knife."

"Are you fucking serious?"

"And see if you can start a fire. We'll need to cauterize."

"Are you fucking *serious*!?"

"Hey, we have to try! He's falling apart to sludge here!"

She handed over the knife and joined Kayla in gathering what bits of wood were nearby. Trevor was no med student and doubted they could build a blaze hot enough to matter, doubted Andy's survival even if they did, but yeah...they had to try.

He pushed the hem of Andy's cutoffs higher, revealing as-yet-undamaged flesh. Had to get ahead of the corruption...though wasn't the femur the thickest bone in the body? How was he supposed to cut through that with a kitchen butcher knife? Plus, the femoral artery...

But he could see it spreading, and there wasn't time to dick around.

Besides, how often did opportunities like this come along?

"Try not to hurt him!" Kayla begged.

"Hurt him?" Chelsea dumped a pile of sticks on the

ground. "Probably going to kill him."

Which might be better, really…there was going to be no hospital, no air-ambulance helicopter and trauma team, no medical miracle.

The blade was sharp, the meat like butter—*filet mignon,* Trev thought—and Andy's blood leaped in a spouting red geyser.

***

"What's *wrong* with you?" Kayla cried at Trevor. "You have to tie it off with a belt or something first!"

"Oh…yeah."

She snatched the bloodied knife from him, used it to slice at the hem of her sundress until she could tear off a long strip, then handed it back. Kneeling beside the mercifully unconscious Andy, she looped the length of cloth around his thigh and used one of the sticks she'd gathered to twist the ends and cinch it tight. Super tight, tight as she could.

"Smooth move, brother-dear," said Chelsea, using Andy's lighter on the rest of the piled sticks.

"At least I remembered the cauterize bit."

Kayla wracked her brains for other tips from a long-ago first aid course. Something about pressure points, right? And shock? Should they put another stick between his jaws so he didn't bite his tongue off, or was that for seizures?

She was surprised and gratified to see that the tourniquet slowed that red geyser to a pumping wellspring…and dismayed to see that the discoloration, sloughing, and nasty loose sponginess were still spreading.

"Hurry," she said to Trevor.

"You really want me to cut his leg off?"

"What else can we do?"

Trevor shrugged as if to say, 'not much,' and dove back in with the butcher knife. No finesse, just hack and slash, blood spatter everywhere, the steel edge grinding and grating and scraping on bone. When he'd carved away as much muscle and tendon as he could, he set the knife's point against the exposed femur and banged a rock on the end of the handle, hammering it.

"This is bullshit stupid," Chelsea said, fanning the fire. "We couldn't roast a marshmallow on this, let alone sear a stump."

CRACK! went the femur, suddenly partway unhinged at an angle. Trevor swore as he wrenched and twisted, trying to break through the rest of the bone. The splintery-snapping sounds were worse than the initial crack. But then it was off, a crazy-jointed jumble like part of a broken Halloween decoration, a gory and glistening skeleton leg ending in a slime-drenched sneaker.

"Bullshit stupid," repeated Chelsea. She held up a stout branch, its end a sputtering torch. "Here you go."

"Great, thanks." Trevor sounded less than enthused, but he took the crude torch and jammed its flame with decisive savagery against mangled, blood-seeping flesh.

The sizzle and smoky whiff brought to mind hamburgers hitting a grill. Whether it was the smell or the pain, Andy picked a bad time to revive. Not that there was a good time, all considered. He came up thrashing and screaming. His stung hand flopped uselessly on his wrist, a puffy coin-sized welt dead-white in his palm.

"Hey, Andy, my man, easy there dude—" Trevor began.

Andy looked down at himself. At what was left of himself, at what was being done and what was happening to the rest of himself. At Trevor pressing the torch to a blackened ring of charred meat with a jagged end of bone jutting out. At his sneaker, amid that jumble of other bones.

"You asshole!" he shrieked at Trevor, and went for him with his good hand, a wild swing that shouldn't have connected in a million years but did, breaking Trev's nose with a brittle crunch.

"Mother-*fuck*!" Eyes gushing water, nose gushing blood, Trevor dropped the burning branch and covered his face. "Son of a—!"

"The hell are you doing?" Chelsea ran at Andy. She scored a kick to the sternum that knocked him flat. "He's trying to save your dumb ass!"

But, as Andy fell back, his shirt rode up to reveal more seeping, suppurating blisters fanning out in a tree-shape across his stomach. His stung hand bloomed with them, too, the swollen blemish in his palm seeming to bubble.

Kayla realized any attempts at saving his dumb ass were too little, too late...so she snatched up the fireplace poker and caved in his skull.

11

The aches and pains he'd stopped noticing came flooding back anew, his body reminding him none too gently that HEY STUPID you were in a PLANE CRASH! At the same moment, the blood-shit-rot stink, though more distant than it had been, made his gorge rise in a sickly hiccup.

Dimly, Greg was aware of Ethriel fluttering around him, saying sorry, telling him to get moving again and it'd go away, apologizing for being such a fuck-up of a guardian angel.

"I'm okay," he said, steeling himself against a wave of vomiting. He dragged a foot forward a step, when what he really wanted to do was curl up in a ball and whimper until a nice nurse brought him painkillers.

That reminded him of his cargo. Maybe he should have poked through the wreckage after all. Some Oxy or Vicodin would be just the thing. Not because he was one of those drug-runners who sampled the goods, no. Because he was a drug-runner who had just been in a PLANE CRASH.

His stomach lurched again. Even if he'd had something to take, he couldn't have kept it down, not now. Not when the whole world smelled like roadkill.

He urped a little, spat, wiped his mouth with the back of his hand, and staggered another few steps. It did help; the pained old-man hobble eased into a more normal limping. The ungodly reek receded somewhat from his awareness.

"I'd about sell my soul for a gl—"

Ethriel did another ear-flick, no mere sassy chiding but a sharp *zing* that smarted like a bastard.

"Ow!"

"Don't say shit like that. Especially here."

"Okay, okay." He rubbed his ear.

"Someone might take you up on it."

"I get it already."

"I'm not sure you do. After what you've seen so far, you still go around being cavalier about souls? They are *far* from casual currency, and here you are, ready to throw yours away for a glass of water?"

"It was only a figure of speech!"

"Not around here. Around here, you barter for your right arm, or your left nut, or whatever, it could happen." She hovered in front of him so they were nose-to-nose, her iridescent wings a whirr-blur, her enormous anime-eyes serious as an undertaker's. "It. Could. Happen."

"I got it. I told you. I got it."

"See that you do."

She resumed her spot by his shoulder, as if tethered there by an invisible bungee cord, as he oriented himself away from the lake and continued his non-recreational hike. His nature walk, or un-nature walk…Greg was no botanist, and no Florida native, but he didn't have to be to know it wasn't supposed to look like this.

There he'd been, worried about quicksand marshes and 'gators. Those would be a nice normal change of pace compared to the trees with curling claws and horribly pendulous 'fruit,' or the sulfur-yellow piss-pond with a spiny frog the size of an ottoman squatting in it, or—

"Reeee-deeeep," gurgled the frog, and its tongue shot out, unspooling eighteen feet of nasty mucus-glistening pink.

"Nuh-unh!" said Ethriel. A flash of pearly light flared, accompanied by a brief many-voiced harmony—*heavenly choir*, Greg thought.

The frog's tongue shunted aside as if it had hit a curved

glass wall, stickily adhering to one of the pendulous 'fruits' instead and plucking it loose with a moist sucking sound. The tree writhed, clawed boughs flailing, the other fruits wobbling gelatinously. A shower of goo trailed through the air as the frog, maybe not realizing the missed target, reeled in its prize with a yank like a tape measure retracting.

For a creature the size of an ottoman to have a mouth the size of an industrial clothes dryer didn't seem possible, but, there it was. The revealed maw, also nasty-pink and glistening with mucus, was lined with inward-curving rows of hook-teeth, Into these, the unripe fruit flew.

Glomp! went the frog. Woodchipper puree went the fruit.

"Uh-oh," went Ethriel. "Run."

***

Run? *Run*, she wanted?

The frog began to swell. Not just its throat-pouch; its entire body. Inflating like a balloon. Like that little girl at the chocolate factory, the one obsessed with chewing gum. Bloating like a blister, like a big wet burgeoning zit. Bubble-bursts of noxious fluid erupted from its mouth. Pulp and juice, mucus, other stuff. As if the frog were trying to puke out its unexpected meal, with no luck. Those hook-teeth made for a one-way trip. Down the gullet. Do not back up, severe tire damage.

Run, she wanted, and Greg decided he was good with that. Before the whole frog popped, spraying showers of ick in all directions.

He ran.

With Ethriel close at his shoulder, he dodged this way and that through a veritable grove of the writhing, laden trees. Branch-claws swiped at him, but his guardian angel deflected each strike, and he somehow chose the safest—

137

or, least deadly—route on impulse.

Riper fruits jiggled in a way that might've been un-nature's attempt to appear enticing. *See how plump we are, how succulent, how juicy!* They oozed syrupy nectar, thickening the air with a cloying fragrance like cherry compote and raw steak. Their soft, malleable rinds rippled, shapes moving and pressing from within, reminding Greg of pregnant bellies.

Oh, and he did not want to see what would birth squelchily out of them!

Nor did he feel any desire to turn and look when, from behind, there came a flatulent blorping splurt and subsequent irregular patter-plops.

He ran, avoiding the—

"What *are* these?"

"Utero-melons."

"I'm sorry I asked."

—avoiding any contact with the fruit as assiduously as he avoided asking any of the other dozen or so questions that sprang illogically to mind.

Then he did ask one.

"What happened to the frog?"

"Whatever was incubating in the melon wasn't ripe yet. Before they're ripe...don't you mortals have some ritual involving Mentos and soda?"

"Sorry I asked, part two."

They left the grove, or it petered out into more ordinary-abnormal wilderness again. A sort of path, possibly the remains of an old hiking trail, wended through thinner trees and denser brush. Fleshy trumpet-shaped 'flowers' on gnarled green stalks waggled lewd stamens as they passed. Other 'flowers' unfolded petals in a blooming of overlapped eyelids, revealing hexagonal multifaceted fly-eyes as big as ping-pong balls.

Then the trail reached a place where the land sloped

away into a shallow bowl of a small valley, a crazy half-wild vineyard sprawling in leafy profusion along rows of bone-stick trellises. Figures wearing broad-brimmed sunhats gathered clusters of jet-black grapes into wicker baskets. At the center of the vineyard was a large wooden structure like a silo or roofless water tower. Surrounding it were presses and stomping vats, and pallets of clay jugs.

A moonshine operation, Greg could have expected. A winery, though? A winery that sent his mind immediately to Disney's *Fantasia* again…not fairies this time but the mythology pastoral…

…only, the workers weren't pretty centaur fillies and hunky centaur stallions…the workers were scarred and mutilated almost beyond recognition…

…and no chubby little cherubs flitted around, but bat-winged goblin-imps…

…and, presiding over the revelries from a lounging couch by a feast-table, was not some cheerfully soused, bumbling Bacchus…

…though he did resemble, kind of, a character from another Disney animated feature…a devil-version of the wisecracking satyr voiced by Danny DeVito…dusky-skinned, corpulent, and shaggily goat-legged…

Greg didn't realize he'd stopped—peering with stunned and befuddled amazement at the scene—until Ethriel cried a warning.

He spun, just as an upended empty wicker grape-basket slammed down over his guardian angel, catching her like a bee in a jar. Two of the workers held the basket pinned to the ground, while two more advanced on Greg with scary harvesting shears.

"Run!" Ethriel shrieked, tiny fists battering at her impromptu prison. "Go, Greg! Keep moving! I'll find you! *Run!*"

***

Run, she wanted.

Yeah, no. Not happening.

Before the effects of Ethriel's buffering spell, or whatever it was, wore off and let his injuries remind him yet again of their presence, Greg surprised even himself by doing a deft Jason Statham spin kick that took one of the workers oof in the ribs.

That one doubled over with a grunt, scary harvesting shears whickering off into the weeds. The second worker snarled and slashed.

Greg's attempt at a Jason Statham dodge wasn't quite as deft, the nasty blades tearing his already-torn shirt and scoring a shallow but hissing-hot slice to his upper arm. But, better the arm than the neck, better shallow than deep. He rushed the mutilated man, crowding him, getting inside his reach, throwing a fist into the bastard's jaw.

Which turned out to be a mistake…

The worker's head was wrapped from the neck up in tight loops of barbed wire, the barbs digging in, turning his face into a mask of crusted scabs and seeping wounds. His lips were dry and shredded, his mouth barely able to move. One deranged eye squinted through taut crisscrosses. The other was lost in a gored nestle of scar tissue.

Punching him felt like driving his knuckles into a cheese grater. Greg bit back a yelp. Talk about "this'll hurt me more than it'll hurt you." In grappling distance, seeing up-close the evidence of deliberate cutting and burns, the whip-weals, the abraded nipples, he wasn't sure if he *could* hurt this guy.

They had a quick, struggling stand-off, the worker with Greg in a half-hold while trying to bring in the shears for the kill, and Greg doing his best to fend them off with blocking arms. Blocking arms that shook, strength flagging rapidly, the wicked points pressing steadily nearer and nearer his chest.

Long thin porcupine-quills of pearly-white light streamed through every gap in the wicker-weave, Ethriel fighting to escape from the upended basket as the other two workers fought just as hard to hold it down. They winced and flinched from the angelic radiance, but it didn't seem to be harming them.

Still more workers came dashing up from the vineyard. The demonic satyr had propped himself up on an elbow, watching the proceedings with idle spectator-sport amusement while imps cavorted and capered above.

The one Greg had kicked in the ribs was recovered now. And annoyed. He, too, had been wrapped about the head and face with barbed wire, ragged flaps of dried skin hanging from his cheekbones, both ears crudely bisected along the diagonal. Having lost his shears, he went for Greg with his bare hands...upon which, several finger joints had been amputated.

Greg's captor snarled again, twisting away in a defensive 'mine!' body gesture and reversing the shears to level the blades' business ends as a further 'fuck you' and 'or else.' Stubby-Fingers McSplitEar hesitated, snarling back what sounded like a 'you and what army' challenge. No-Nipples One-Eye scissored the shears, snicky-snick, in reply.

"Bring them...to me," called the satyr, much more William Shatner than Danny DeVito. Pauses and all.

Although he made the command lazily, even languidly, the worker showdown over who'd get the privilege of gutting Greg alive was just-like-that over. Each of them snared him in an armlock, hefting him suspended between them with the toes of his shoes just able to scrabble at the ground. However emaciated and carved-up they might be, they possessed plenty of wiry field-labor muscle.

The other workers had scrounged up a piece of plywood

from somewhere, sliding this underneath the upended basket with Ethriel caught inside, the way Greg's mom would use a cup and a sheet of paper to humanely catch a spider to release outdoors.

He didn't think 'humanely' or 'release' were going to factor very far into this equation...

The workers finally got their angel-trap secured, and began an ungainly but triumphant procession through the grape-trellises, toting Greg and Ethriel toward certain doom.

12

"I had to do it," said Kayla. "I had to."

She kept muttering it like a mantra, which was a slight improvement on the previous drawn-out low moaning. And the drawn-out low moaning had been an improvement on the hysterical wailing.

Still, if she didn't knock that shit off soon, Chelsea was going to pop her one right in the mouth.

"I had to do it. I had to."

That's what I'll say after I shut her up, Chelsea thought.

Okay, sure, it was tragic they'd lost another friend. In such an awful, gory, disgusting way, too…Andy, rotting alive, decaying and dissolving from the inside out… smelling like an overstuffed dumpster behind a chicken restaurant in the heat of high summer…the matter of the amputation/cauterization…Kayla bashing in his brains with a fireplace poker…

And there was nothing exactly noble in the way the rest of them had fled the scene, leaving him for whatever scavengers might get there before he totally melted…but what were they going to do, bury him?

"Screw it, he's gone," Trevor had said, none too buddy-buddy with Andy anymore. His voice was muffled and nasal. He'd torn more pieces of cloth from Kayla's sundress to plug his leaking nostrils, was already getting a raccoon mask around his eyes, and his squashed nose would never be the same.

So, yeah, they'd left Andy. Andy, and most of what they'd brought with them from the lakehouse, none of them

143

exactly having clear presence of mind.

"I had to do it," Kayla said.

Now, here they were, no longer running but sticking close together, following the road as it curved to follow the shoreline.

Not too close, thankfully—basking along the redbrown shitmuddy banks were dozens of 'gators, or what might've been 'gators at one point. The largest held its long jaws open as several tiny imp-things picked leftover morsels from between serrated teeth. A bunch of smaller ones, recently hatched judging by a half-buried nest of eggshell fragments, hissed and fought and bit at each other. It was no kittenish play-fighting; they were in it to win it, going for the kill. When an injured combatant tried to seek refuge by an adult, presumably mommy, the adult snapped it up in a lightning-fast bite.

"I had to do it. I had to."

"We know!" Trevor sounded as aggravated as Chelsea felt. This hand-wringing bloodied Lady Macbeth routine was getting beyond old.

They'd passed a couple of derelict cabins, roofs sagging, walls askew, being reclaimed by spiderlike vines. They'd passed a rusted-out, flattened camper that must've met the same fate as their SUV. They'd passed a four-person tent that looked clean and brand-new, but the way its sides heaved in and out made it appear to be breathing...and when one of its zippered flaps unzipped itself invitingly, they'd picked up their pace without comment.

Ahead, a rocky promontory jutted into the lake, culminating in the huge misshapen boulder known as Bighead Rock.

Chelsea had never known why; it barely resembled a head, or if it did, the head must've belonged to some hideous circus freak. Still, Bighead Rock had been a destination when they were kids, a place for climbing, a place where the boldest would jump from the height. She and Trevor had only done it once, their last visit here, daring each other and ending up jumping together, holding hands.

"Hey," he said, "remember when we—?"

"Yeah. You were so scared!"

"*I* was scared?"

"Come on." Chelsea veered from the road. "Let's see what we can see."

"Are you insane?"

She paused, thinking about it. "Probably. Aren't you?"

"Well..."

"After what we've been through, it'd be a surprise if we weren't."

"I had to do it. I had to," Kayla said.

"*She* sure is," Chelsea added. "She killed Andy."

"Yeah, but I cut off his leg and burned him with a torch."

"What do you want, a fucking medal?"

***

The hike to Bighead Rock proved rougher than Trevor remembered, the old path up the promontory overgrown and obscured by matted snarls of wiry grass—not green grass, but every shade of human hair from white to blonde to curly black, like fields of unkempt pubes. Itchy, clinging, burr-laden unkempt pubes.

"Wish I'd worn boots," he said, earning dirty looks from the girls because Chels wore sexy sandals and Kayla had on flip-flops. Fucking *flip-flops!*

Well, but tough for them…Chels and Kayla hadn't had their noses broken. His whole face throbbed in time with his heartbeat, each step was a seismic impact, and it hurt like hell just to blink.

Who'd've thought mellow stoner Andy packed such a punch?

145

Scraggle-feathered bird-things nested in the denser thickets, ready to charge out in a flurry of squawking, and pecking should anyone tread too close. The anthills weren't ordinary anthills anymore but shin-high mounds teeming with tiny buzzsaw spider-beetles, their shiny carapaces emblazoned with occult-looking patterns.

They reached the flattish plateau atop Bighead Rock, Trev and Chelsea in the lead with Kayla, muttering how she had to do it she just had to, bringing up the rear.

It used to be a prime spot for watching fireworks on the Fourth. There hadn't been enough of a town to put on an official show, but people all around the lake would start lighting off their own as soon as the sun went down. From the regular roadside-stand purchases to full-on illegal explosives, the sky would be lit up with bursts of color and the echoes would roll back and forth from shore to shore.

Sights and sounds of freedom. Alcohol-fueled freedom. What better way to celebrate than by chugging jugs of moonshine and blowing a few fingers off?

Some of the benches and picnic tables were even still in place, while others had been demolished, burned, or repurposed into items of medieval-looking torture and execution.

"Is that a guillotine?" asked Chelsea.

"I think so," Trevor replied. "Want to go see if there's a head in the basket?"

"No, thanks."

The view was still impressive, if in a drastically different and far less picturesque way. Lake Misquamicus had been blue and scenic, clouds reflected on its surface, occasionally etched by wakes from Jet Skis. It had been quiet and serene.

Not so much anymore.

Below them to the left was what had been a sandy cove,

the mild shallows marked off by floating rope-buoys for safe family swimming. On any given summer day, colorful inflatables would've crowded the water, kids playing while adults relaxed on towels or folding beach chairs.

Now, the cove had become Gamera Central, a real dino-turtle bay. None were as big as the one who'd raped the SUV, most falling size-wise somewhere between 'manhole cover' and 'compact car,' but the spikes and the *skreee-onk*ing were the same.

To their right was what the kids used to call The Plunge, a long drop into deep water, terrifying but exhilarating. A glance over the edge now showed a long drop into a whirlpool of blood.

"Hey, there's the hippie house," Chelsea said, pointing across the lake at an A-frame with a hodgepodge of additions. "Mom always thought they were having orgies over there."

"They probably were, and she was pissy because she never got invited." Trevor pointed another direction. "And there's the shithole bar our buddy Lester mentioned, and I bet that cabin's where the author lives. Looks like they've all still got power."

"Lester did say he could hook us up."

"Uh-huh." He smirked at her chest. "For a price, no doubt."

"I'm not sucking his dick. Told you, I have standards."

"Weren't you gonna suck *mine*? Some standards...Sis."

"I wasn't really going to."

"You had it in your hand, working it like a gearshift," he said.

"I was drunk. We all were. So what. Shut up." Huffily, she spun from him, then froze. "What the...Trevor, look... look at our house."

147

***

She'd killed him.

She had to do it. *Had* to.

He was dying anyway, dying already, dying in such slow, awful, melting pain!

Poor Andy. Not such a bad guy. Low-maintenance as a boyfriend, that was for sure. Didn't demand to know where she'd been, who she'd been with, what she was doing. Didn't spy into her phone or messages. If not the most exciting in terms of going out, preferring to zone and stone and binge-watch, neither was he a fuckboi cheater flirt, like Trevor. Poor, decent, mellow Andy.

Whom she'd killed.

The poker, cracking into his head, reminding her of the way her grandpa used to whack the top of a soft-boiled egg with a spoon to get at the gooey goodness within. Only this hadn't been goodness. Gooey, yes. Goodness, no.

The sensation of skullbone-give into thick mush, overdone oatmeal, lumpy chowder! Blood and gobbets. Brain-giblets. The sound of it! The feel!

Sobbing, she wrung her hands and stared at the lake. The red, red lake.

Kayla was peripherally aware of Chelsea and Trever's conversation—oh, Chelsea so totally would have sucked his dick; she'd probably wanted to suck his dick since they hit puberty; only surprising she hadn't done it already. When they'd started pointing out various landmarks, Kayla hadn't really been interested, but the tone of pure you-gotta-be-shitting-me in Chelsea's voice broke through her mental guilt-fog.

"That can't be right," Trevor said.

They were both staring in the direction of the lakehouse, so Kayla swayed around to look for herself.

What? The house was fine—

No, it wasn't.

It…wavered. One moment, it was normal, as intact and perfect as when they'd first driven up. The next, it was an insubstantial heat-mirage, a distortion, a storm in the vague shape of a house, with the sky behind it as churning and seething a red as the lake, a sky where a dead-black moon hung like a tumor.

"It doesn't look real," Trevor added. "Like the projection of a house, an illusion, a glitch in a video game. It's not really there."

"But we were *in* it," Chelsea said. "We brought stuff *out* of it!" She brandished the only water bottle any of them had managed to hang onto.

Kayla dropped her gaze to the sundress she'd found in one of the upstairs closets after her shower. Almost cute, she'd thought of it at the time, even if its thin cloth and loose drape displayed every sumptuous jiggle of boob and butt. Now, its hem hung around her thighs in tatters, its floral pattern blotched with stains.

"There's something moving over there, too," Trevor said, shading his eyes. "A car or something on the road… back by where, uh, we were."

Back by where they'd left Andy, Kayla knew he'd meant. Back where they—no, *she*!—had *killed* Andy.

"Yeah, I hear the engine," Chelsea said.

"What if whoever it is finds him?"

"What's left of him, you mean."

Inside Kayla, inside her mind or maybe her soul, the last strand of some strained, frayed thing finally broke. "I *had* to do it!" she screamed, lunging at Chelsea. "I had to, you sneering slut-bitch, I *had* to!"

The sensation of her palm striking Chelsea's face—Chelsea's shocked, outraged, WTF-did-you-call-me face!—was the emotional opposite of the poker meeting Andy's skull. The sound of it, the feel of it…savage fury and joy! This was no girl-fight play-slap; she got her weight behind it, her whole arm, and it was better than sex!

Chelsea, almost knocked off her feet, rebounded with her own surge of fury. "Fat-ass cunt!"

Then it was on, and oh was it ever, tit-punches and crotch-kicks, torn clothes, gouging raking fingernail claws, fistfuls of hair yanked out by the roots, screaming and swearing—

Until a vicious blow sent Kayla reeling back, tripping on her flip-flops, suddenly finding nothing beneath her heels.

Over the edge she went, over and down-down-down, toward the roiling red whirlpool of blood.

***

Silence held a moment atop Bighead Rock.

Chelsea stood bent double, panting, hands on her knees. When she regained her breath, she straightened up, pawed disheveled straggles of hair from her eyes, and looked at her brother, who'd wisely backed *way* the fuck up.

"I had to do it," she told him, with a wide-eyed lunatic stare. "I *had* to!"

Then they were both laughing their asses off.

"If I had to hear her say that too many more times, I would've thrown her off the edge myself," Trevor said. He peered over.

"Do you see her?" asked Chelsea, wincing as she did a quick damage assessment—Kayla had gotten in a few good ones.

"Nope. She's gone."

"Think she's dead?"

"Fuck, yes. Even if she survived the drop, Michael-goddamn-Phelps couldn't swim out of that whirlpool."

"Oh well. Sucks to be her. Skank tore my top and almost

clawed my tit off."

Trevor shrugged out of his shirt. "Here. No sense giving the world a free show."

"Thanks."

"So...now what?" he asked. "Try to find whoever was driving, keep heading for the writer's place, what?"

"The writer's place," Chelsea said. "We're almost there anyway. And I don't know about you, brother-dear, but the farther we are from that...that house-*thing*, the better."

"No arguments here."

They hiked back down the promontory, through the nasty pubic-hair tangles of grass and big spider-beetle anthills, past thickets where the scraggly birds—bastards made Canadian geese look friendly by comparison—nested, and finally rejoined the road.   A short turnoff led to what used to be a small gravel parking lot, empty now except for a couple of broken bicycles, a lone car tire, and the busted remains of a shack where creepy locals once sold dubious snow-cones and lemonade.

Another turnoff led through the woods in the direction of the cabin they'd seen from the height. Parts of a rusted-out chain trailed across it. A weathered sign reading PRIVATE in faded paint tilted askew.

"The writer, huh?" Chelsea said. "Sick horror shit?"

"And Mom thought he must be a serial killer."

"Great."

From somewhere up ahead, they heard music. Not banjos, not even country, just what sounded like an ordinary radio tuned to an ordinary, if distant and static-ridden, station. There was also a distinctive generator-type hum; as Trevor had observed from Bighead Rock, the writer's place did have power.

They emerged onto a stretch of pebbled beach, wavelets lapping and burbling at the shore. It would've been pleasant back when the lake was water; less so when blood and shit slimed the pebbles, the wavelets leaving behind a brownish foamy froth, the burbling sounding like a clogged sewer. Further down was a pile of assorted flotsam and jetsam, including a few large metal drums of the type that might've held oil or industrial waste.

The cabin itself appeared normal enough, but filling the yard were rustic driftwood sculptures of unsettling design. One appeared to be of a nude woman of the curvaceous knockout variety, except her head was that of a broad-horned bull. Another looked crazily like a six-foot-tall dick on legs, bulging nutsack and all. Atop a metal mailbox was one of those whimsical wooden wind-powered whatchamacallits, but the herky-jerky moving figures depicted a burly guy fucking a twitching girl through a hole in her head.

"Starting to think Mom might've been right," Trevor said.

Chelsea nodded. "Yeah, maybe this wasn't the best plan."

Before they could reverse their course, the cabin's screen door banged breezily open and a man emerged, bottle of beer in one hand and a sandwich in the other. He had longish greying hair and a scruff of beard, wore a plain white shirt half-unbuttoned, and had taken two steps toward a picnic table where the radio sat beside a somewhat outdated laptop computer when he saw them.

"Oh," he said, with a sort of mild, affable surprise. "You two must be new here. Hungry? Want a beer? Nice and cold."

***

Kayla didn't scream on the way down. Partly from shock—that bitch!—but mostly from acceptance. She deserved it. After what she'd done to poor Andy, she deserved to have Chelsea damn near throw her off the top of Bighead Rock.

It was a long drop.

A long drop toward churning red horror.

She hit hard.

Ass-first, with a resounding smack. A booty-flop instead of a belly-flop if ever there was one. It felt like the world's biggest spanking, a single slapping wallop of sheeting fire-pain so intense her skin seemed about split wide open.

A crowd of observers, or the America's Funniest Video studio audience, would have winced and voiced ow-noises in unison, before laughing, but in the guilty way people do when they can't help it even though they know that really must smart like a motherfucker.

Which it did.

Kayla had a brief moment of thinking that, should she survive this, her ass was going to be one brilliant shade of scarlet, from cheek to shining cheek.

The impact jarred her bones as if she'd butt-planted onto concrete from five stories up. Her limbs ragdolled. Her neck whiplashed. She wasn't sure, but suspected she actually bounced before splat-splashing into the lake for keeps.

It was warm. *Loathsomely* warm. Not tropical-warm or bathtub-warm, but a humid, fecund, sludgy, body-temperature warm.

Half-stunned, the breath driven out of her lungs, and possibly paralyzed with spine fractures, she sank like a stone. The soupy diarrheal redness immersed and surrounded her body, flowed over her head, swallowing her with a wet, sticky gulp.

And vice versa. She swallowed with a wet, sticky gulp as it flooded her mouth, nose, and throat. Gagging-thick, somehow oily and mealy, the taste awful beyond anything she ever imagined.

She vomited, choked, felt drowned from inside and out. Her bulging eyes saw only dark, seething murk. Her pulse throbbed in her ears. A current catching her; she was drawn and pulled, spun and helpless, swept under.

She'd die. Any second. Any second, she'd die. She'd die and it'd be over and why was it taking so long? Couldn't she just die already?

No. No, she couldn't.

Because there was more than the lake, more than the current and whirlpool. More than drowning. Worse than drowning. Drowning would have been getting off easy. There were things with teeth. Things that each wanted a piece and didn't want to share. Things with tentacles, and she'd seen enough memes about *hentai* to know where this was going.

Agony and violation and she was conscious of every single atrocity...until she suddenly wasn't. Until she suddenly didn't feel the pain of needle-sharp teeth shredding flesh, or of wicked-barbed hooks and tendrils invading her innermost orifices.

Until she suddenly felt small, somehow secure and anonymous. Safety in numbers. Safety as one among many. Safety with a single sucker-foot clinging to a lake-bottom rock, safety with a ridged bivalve shell.

The clam-beds ringed the whirlpool's shallower edges, thousands of them, clustered mussels, anchored and awash in the constant cyclonic current. Their cilia strained tiny particles, filtering out purities, helping keep the lake a thriving unholy ecosystem.

Most of the clams were mindless around her, brainless and soulless. The others, sentient subcarnated damned like herself, pretty much gave up and went mad.

With no eyes, Kayla found sight no longer mattered. Other senses revealed the bloodquatic depths...waving wavering vaginal anemones, ribbons of crimson-black lakegrass, lilypads of veined and quivering flesh...fish with human faces, or human heads, or hands where fins should

be, or other hideous far-from-mermaid combinations...
bullet-shaped cocksquid darting in and out of decaying
sunken carcasses...crawdads snapping their claws at devil-
horned crabs strutting by on long spindly legs...the bulky
behemoth glide of demon-gators...flotsam and jetsam...
ancient shipwrecks...

This was her home now. Her place and her role.

Straining and siphoning six billion gallons of shit,
feeding on and filtering six billion gallons of filth.

Forever.

13

A strange sense of calm descended over June as she reloaded the shotgun with swift, efficient movements that should have seemed utterly foreign to her.

Wouldn't you know, she was a natural after all!

Next, she ran to Brother Lucas. By the looks of it, he'd dealt with the conjoined triplets by grasping one head in each big hand and slamming them together like coconuts. With similar effect—hairy shells cracked, leaking fluid. The third head, dazed and mewling, seemed to be trying to gain control of their shared body, but most of it was inert deadweight.

June stepped closer. The head—that of a boy, maybe eleven or twelve—peered pleadingly at her, red eyes through tangled black hair. His mouth was set crooked, lips stretched by too many teeth on one side. His chin and lower lip quivered. His hand, feebly shaking, reached out in an imploring gesture.

"Don't even think it, you little hellion!" And *crunch* again with the butt of the shotgun, shattering his jaw into pulp and chunks of bone.

He flopped onto his siblings, dead or close enough. Keeping wary tabs on him just in case, June skirted the deformed mess and went to a knee beside Brother Lucas. Six sets of bruised fingermarks, even darker than his dark skin, stood out on his neck, as if the triplets had simultaneously strangled him.

If he'd been killed…

Then his broad chest moved. He was breathing. Shallow and slow, but breathing. A lumpy abrasion by his temple, as well as a smear of blood on a nearby rock, told her he'd smacked his head when they tackled him. His last act before losing consciousness must have been that mighty two-fisted coconut slam.

"Lucas!" She shook him. "Brother Lucas, wake up!"

He groaned. He stirred. His eyelids rose, blinking blearily a few times. "Hunh?" Then, in a flash, she saw his awareness come flooding back. "Shit!"

He sat up in a lunge, grabbing his gun, surveying the scene. The creeker-freak corpses...the missing Gabelmans...his gaze coming to rest on June herself... seeing her as if he'd never truly seen her before.

"Sister June?"

That deep-bass rumble, rolling through her like thunder! Caressing her nerve-endings with firm velvet strokes.

"Yes," she said, sounding steadier than she felt.

"Where are—"

"They took them."

"Shit," he said again.

"You're hurt."

"I'm fine. We need to—mmph!"

The 'mmph!' was a muffled bleat of surprise as she kissed him, as she practically dove on top of him, mashing her lips to his. One arm held the shotgun out to her side, business end angled away. The other curled around the back of his neck. Her tongue darted sure and quick, plunging into his mouth, tasting blood and adrenaline and *yes-God-oh-yes!* Their chests pressed together, impeded by the stupid bulky vests.

"Mmph!" Brother Lucas repeated.

June straddled him without breaking the kiss, grinding her pelvis into his lap. He was heat and strength beneath her, solid muscle, a huge slab of man-meat rock-hard

157

gorgeousness! She writhed, moaning low and urgent in her throat. She could feel him responding, stiffening, swelling!

Delicious sensations kindled hot and slippery within her, and she was ready, so ready! Ready to tear off these damn vests, tear off their clothes, free his erection from its prison, glorious and thick, plum-shaped tip already eagerly oozing! She'd impale herself on it, drive down fast and hard, the splitting stretch of his girth battering her sopping pussy! Filling her with his stiff flesh, with pain and pleasure, agony and ecstasy! Tiresome virginity ripped away, no more spinster's albatross hung around her! Taking him all the way up into her belly, having him seize her hips as she rode him, as he forcefully thrust, as their skin slapped together in sweaty fervor!

He wedged an arm between them and pushed, rearing back, parting their mouths with a noisy wet slurp. "Good God, Sister June, have you lost your mind?"

***

"What?" June panted. "Lost my mind? Have I? Maybe. Who cares? I need you right now, I want you inside me, buried all the way, do it, do it hard, take me, fuck me!"

As the words spilled from her lips, she let go of the back of his neck and shoved her hand to his waist, where she tugged at his belt.

"Sister June!" exclaimed Brother Lucas again, not with the hoped-for surrendering passion but in astonished shock. "This is crazy. Stop that. Get 'hold of yourself, woman!"

"I'd rather get hold of *you*!" Which she did, forsaking the belt to go lower, groping as much of his burgeoning hard-on as her grasp could encompass. Dear Lord, he was big, even bigger than she'd imagined! It'd probably kill her, but what a way to go!

He jumped like she'd tasered him or dumped ice

down his collar. His lower body bucked as if having its own different opinion, the bulge under her palm straining, throbbing as she rubbed.

But then he had her by the upper arms, lifting her off and away, depositing her none-too-gently on the ground beside the puddles of blood and brain-fluids that had leaked from the crushed creek-freak skulls. She plopped onto her backside with an "oof!" and sat there, splay-legged, staring at him while her pulse raced and her thighs trembled.

"Have you lost your mind?" he asked again, already on his feet. "It's the evil getting to you—"

"No! No, it isn't!"

"You're a good, godly—"

"Just fuck me! No one has to know! I won't tell! Or, you can tell if you want, tell the whole world, it doesn't matter, just do it!"

He retreated a step. "Sister, listen to me. You aren't in a right frame of—"

"You want to, you know you do, I felt it!" Her gaze went to the front of his pants, the proof there still bulging, still very obvious. "I know I'm not pretty, but you can do anything, use me, treat me like a dirty whore!"

"These devil-bastards attacked us!" he bellowed, pointing at the creeker corpses. "They killed or captured some of our own, and could come back any second to finish the job! This is not the time or the place for sin and temptation, Sister!"

Temptation…so, did that mean he *was* tempted?

Oh, who was she kidding? It had been an involuntary response, nothing more, not as if a man like him could ever be interested in *her*.

Except, he hadn't actually *said* no, had he?

June burst into tears of hot, hateful shame. She clutched the shotgun, for an instant not sure if she meant to prop it under her chin and end this misery one way, or threaten to

159

shoot Lucas in the kneecap if he didn't end it the other.

She did neither. The weapon steadied her somehow, grounded her. Swiping her eyes with a sleeve, she drew a fortifying breath. "All right," she said. "What do we do? Go back to camp, get help?"

"It'd be too late for the Gabelmans by then, if it isn't already. Were they still alive when those animals dragged them off?"

"She was. I don't know about him. I doubt it, not after a spear to the chest and the old guy ripping out half his throat with that fishhook-on-a-stick. Even if she is alive, though—"

He nodded grimly. "We have to go after them just the same. Besides, you heard what the Crusader said. The commotion, he's probably already on the way with reinforcements."

Dear God, if she *had* gotten her way, that meant others—possibly including her mother and the busybody Shinns—would've arrived to find her and Brother Lucas rutting like beasts amid the slaughtered creekers...

Dear *God*. Her face flamed. She gripped the shotgun tighter.

"Careful, though," Lucas said. "Careful, and quiet. If they got the Gabelmans, they also got the Gabelmans' guns."

***

So here she was, sneaking through the woods like some kind of would-be guerilla ninja soldier, following Brother Lucas—who moved like a magnificent jaguar despite his size and bulk—on a mission to...what?

Rescue Mrs. Gabelman? Who'd probably already been butchered and thrown in the creeker-freaks' cookpot along with choice cuts from her husband. Or who was being ravished by one deformed brute after another, *then* to be butchered and thrown in the cookpot.

Even if they weren't too late for rescue to be an option, June wasn't sure they'd be doing her any favors. The trauma would've shattered her sanity. Saving her, only to have her commit suicide? Saving her, only to have her end up pregnant with some two-headed red-eyed flipper spawn?

What would the Shinns have to say about *that*? Abortion was as bad as suicide, if not worse. Pregnancy was God's gift and God's will; pregnancy from rape was God's silver lining, and so on and so forth. Funny, though…in their many years of picketing and protesting, the saintly Shinns had never so much as taken in a foster kid, let alone adopted, and just perish the thought of raising some special-needs drug-addicted problem child!

A well-beaten path led away from the dammed pool with its fish nets and crawdad traps, but Lucas didn't trust it and June agreed. Too easy for the creekers to ambush them, or to have rigged other traps for larger game. Better to circle around and try to come in from the side. Better to get an idea of what they'd be up against instead of walking smack into the middle of a whole village.

Lucas held up a hand. June stopped. They stood listening, hearing voices and activity from up ahead. The voices sounded human enough, but the language wasn't English, was something guttural and crude. Agitated, too, and angry, accusatory and fearful, as if several arguments were going on. The other noises, the activity noises, were…

…meaty and wet, chopping and tearing.

June suppressed a shudder, thinking she'd been right about the cookpot thing after all.

From elsewhere came a spate of echoing cracks and pops. She might've dismissed them as fireworks, but the instincts pushing her onward knew better. Gunfire. Back in the direction of the lake, back in the direction of the camp where Crusader Markane and the others had been. Where her mother had been!

She looked at Lucas, whose expression was graven and sober as that of a stone idol. He silently shook his head. Whatever was happening, it'd be over before they could get there.

As if to punctuate his sentiment, a distant but thunderous boom rattled the air. She remembered the grenades, nestled in their foam egg-carton arrangement, and winced.

He gestured, and they crept closer to the sounds of arguing and slaughter.

The trees thinned to expose a sort of clearing, with a creek—Bible Creek, upstream from the dam, she supposed—running through the middle. A wretched shanty-town of tents and lean-tos filled the space, looking like the creekers had salvaged and scavenged anything of possible use from whatever'd been left behind at the campground. There were a few durable coolers, a few hammocks and lawn chairs, a small trailer of the sort that could be hitched behind a car.

And there were creeker-freaks, a dozen or more. All of them naked and grimy, red-eyed, black-haired, as malformed and misshapen as the previous ones they'd seen. Adults, old folks, grossly gravid women, feral kids. Some wore decorative ornaments fashioned from junk, some carried clubs and knives and more makeshift weapons.

Several of them were clustered around a mess on the ground, a slick red pile of flesh and entrails and gleaming bones. Clustered around it, and fighting over it, bickering like hyenas, swatting and snapping at each other.

A split-second later, June recognized Mr. Gabelman, and realized that, no, she'd been wrong about the cookpot.

They were eating him raw.

***

Lucas tensed, and June could tell he wanted to charge in guns a'blazing, but he held back and kept watching. She did, too. Calm. Horrified and revolted...but calm. Or in shock. Whichever.

A grubby child with an elongated multi-jointed arm scurried in, snatching a dripping morsel that might've been a kidney. A hunchbacked man and a woman whose pelvis appeared to be wrenched around sideways were negotiating a trade: he held the scooped-out orbs of Mr. Gabelman's eyes, while she clutched a pinkish-red triangular flap of spongy meat...was that his tongue?

Nearby, a youth rocked back and forth on the broad flat footlike pads growing from his hips; he had no legs, black peachfuzz on his chin and his groin, and munched happily on something unmistakably fleshy and tubular. Two little girls squabbled over the empty scrotum, while their—presumably—parents feasted on its contents the way June might've feasted on juicy ripe plums.

And yes, no cookpot in evidence. No campfires or fire of any sort, for that matter. Racks made from lashed-together sticks held slices of fish hung to dry but not smoke. At one edge of the clearing was a midden pile of bones and shells. The overall effect was primitive at best.

Another creeker-freak, a tall man with a frizzy black ZZ-Top beard tapering to his waist, barked an attention-getting glottal cry. His only visible aberration was extra fingers on each hand, making June wonder if he was the father of the girl she'd killed. Given his commanding tone, plus the fact that he alone wore some sort of clothing—a tattered poncho made from one of those silvery mylar waterproof thermal sheets—he must have been some sort of headman or chieftain.

This theory was supported by the way the others left

off their bickering and bartering, turning from the mangled carcass. Blood spattered their bodies, ran from the corners of their mouths as they finished chewing and swallowing whatever parts they'd managed to get.

The chieftain uttered an important-sounding announcement and swept an arm, beckoning. Between the hitch-trailer and the largest tent, an uphill incline of rocky slabs formed a natural stairway, curving out of sight among taller trees.

It was slow going for the less-mobile creekers, including the paddle-footed boy with no legs, but they all filed after the man in the shiny poncho.

"They didn't take his gun," whispered Brother Lucas, indicating a heap of discarded items stripped from the unfortunate Mr. Gabelman.

"Or his vest, not even his shoes," June said.

"Good. I don't want to get stabbed, but I sure as Christmas don't want to get shot. Come on."

With no apparent alternatives to the stairway trail, they had little choice but to follow it, moving as quickly as they dared, but slowly enough as to hopefully not overtake any creekers lagging behind, until they had a better idea of what was in store. For all they knew, fifty more might be waiting at the top of the trail, equally hungry and bent on revenge.

There weren't fifty more, just another four or five, but that hardly mattered in the greater scheme of things. What mattered was the ring of stones around a central pillar, topped with an immense, monstrous skull. What mattered were the skull's great downcurving ram's horns, though no ram on Earth had ever grown so large. Just as no ram on Earth had the fanged jaws of a lion, or a ridge of bony spines. Or disturbingly human, if disturbingly giant, characteristics of nose, cheekbones, brow, and eye sockets.

It was the skull of a demon, an arch-duke, some prince of Hell. Washed up from the unholy lake, perhaps; the ultimate insult to poor desecrated Bible Creek.

And, of course, as they should have expected, as they should have known...on the flat bloodstained altar-slab stone beneath the skull's diabolical hollow gaze, was Mrs. Gabelman.

Bound and gagged, nude and helpless, the picture-perfect pretty little blonde sacrifice.

***

June noticed with a wallop of shock that Mrs. Gabelman's pubic hair was coarse and mouse-brown—the perfect blonde was a dye job! Furthermore, those boobies were fake! They didn't loll toward her armpits, but held their firm upright shape...dollars to donuts, up close, the faint curving scars of pricey surgery would be visible!

Why, that phony little Stepford-bitch! June was also willing to bet that her pearl-white smile resulted from dental work. The cornflower-blue eyes? Probably contact lenses!

And to think, all the times Mrs. Gabelman went on about the evils of make-up, what a shame it was so many girls these days couldn't simply let their natural beauty shine through...

The creeker-freak in the mylar poncho—maybe not a chieftain, but a high priest instead—stood before the looming devil-skull with his arms upraised and extra-fingered hands splayed. Throwing his head back, he loosed a ululation like something from a documentary about remote tribes who'd never had contact with the outside world.

The others chant-grunted in response. The parents who'd eaten Mr. Gabelman's testicles each hoisted one of their daughters up to better see. Their presumed son, the paddle-footed youth, furtively rubbed himself while peeking at the naked sacrifice. Another man, shameless, openly leered as he yanked on the crooked stub jutting from his groin. A woman whose joints all seemed to bend the wrong ways writhed in a jerky, spasmodic, puppet-like dance of frenzy.

Mrs. Gabelman struggled in her bonds, weeping, trying to scream through a gag of knotted cloth. Her own blouse? June thought so.

She heard Brother Lucas's breath hissing through clenched teeth beside her. She could almost hear his hammering pulse, and feel the angry heat radiating from his body. Maybe these savages hadn't harmed Mrs. Gabelman yet, hadn't raped her, or cannibalized her the way they had her poor fool of a husband, but those things could still happen…while sacrifice certainly would.

Or worse.

A chill opened in June's stomach.

"The skull," she whispered. "Do you see—?"

It was beginning to glow from within. A strange, smoky light dawned in the hollow eye sockets and long nostril slits, shone through the jaw's rows of fangs. A jack-o-lantern look, sullen hot orange, but the smell was nothing of pumpkin and candles. The smell was of charred fur and cremation.

Mrs. Gabelman saw it too. She froze in her struggles, bladder voiding in a gush. Urine flooded down the sides of the altar-slab.

"Oh, screw *this* noise," said Brother Lucas.

Then he roared like a berserker and *did* charge in guns a'blazing. His first shots caught the high priest center-mass, nice grouping, one-two-three-four. The priest, who'd just produced a ceremonial-looking dagger, jittered as holes punched into the front of that ridiculous poncho and exited the back in gory maroon sprays. The dagger went flying.

Lucas's second round of shots went not for any of the

creekers but at their hideous god. Bullets struck blue-white sparks from the great downcurved ram's horns. Ricochets chipped and pinged off of bone, peppering the nearest creekers before they'd even started to react.

As for June, she wasn't standing idle. She ran in right behind Lucas, pumping and firing the shotgun as if born and raised to the task. Its blatting thunder counterpointed the pistols' sharp cracks. The man who'd been yanking his knob while leering at Mrs. Gabelman yanked it no more; he hadn't even removed his hand from his groin when the shotgun's blast turned hand and groin alike into so much shredded meat. Or, pulled pork.

Next, she blew the legs out from under the father-figure of the happy creeker family as he turned to run. His knees exploded. The daughter he'd been carrying somersaulted ass over teakettle to the ground, snapping her frail little neck.

A pang of guilt lanced June but was gone just as quick. *Nits make lice*, she told herself, and swung around to serve mommy and sister a similar deadly helping.

***

The demon-skull didn't seem to be taking much damage, so Brother Lucas shifted his attention to the creekers. By then, a few had recovered their wits enough to grab for weapons. They fanned out, circling.

One hurled his club, a clumsy throw with more luck than aim. Lucas raised an arm in a defensive gesture. The sound of it shattering his elbow was audible even above the general screaming pandemonium; Lucas's profane exclamation of pain even more so.

Creek-freaks sprawled or crawled, dead or dying, all around the clearing. The paddle-foot kid with no legs hadn't bothered trying to escape, either knowing it was futile or not caring because June had just mown down his entire family. She socked the barrels of the shotgun under his peach-fuzz chin.

"Goodbye and good riddance, you abomination!" she snarled.

But—*click*—dammit! She had to reload before she could paint the woods with his brains.

The paddle-foot creeker blinked at his surprise reprieve. He didn't waste the opportunity, either. His arms were overdeveloped and powerful, had to be since they did most of the work. He flailed them like an enraged orangutan. One knocked the shotgun from June's grasp. The other walloped into her ribs, driving the breath from her lungs. She thumped to her backside yet again, the impact so jarring she nearly bit off her tongue as her teeth clacked hard together.

Then he was on her, his filthy malformed body at once both flabby and feverishly strong. He bore her to the ground, pinning her with those orangutan arms. His garbled grunts were all hate and fury, needing no translation. Spittle and chunks of his most recent meal splattered her face. She could taste it, salty raw meat, half-chewed uncooked hotdog—

Oh dear Lord.

His last meal? She'd seen him snacking on it, his portion of the Mr. Gabelman buffet. Of all the times and ways to suddenly have a man's cock in her mouth!

Somehow, this further insult to injury irked June beyond reason. She startled the creeker youth by lunging up at him, just as she'd started Brother Lucas when she went for that kiss. Only, this wasn't a kiss…this was her biting his nose, cartilage crunching, blood everywhere.

Biting it off, or most of it anyway, a mangled lump trailing stringers of mucus and skin, as the paddle-foot creeker howled in pain. He rolled sideways. She helped him along with a shoving kick, scrambling to her hands and knees. With a wet *phtuh!,* she spat the bloodied chunk of nose at him. He somehow caught it and…she could hardly believe her eyes…tried to put it back where it belonged.

It wouldn't stay. He gibbered and sobbed, trying again.

June spotted a discarded creeker weapon nearby, a tent peg lashed to a stick to form a short spear. She snatched it up.

"Here, try this!" she said, and drove the point into the ragged nose-hole. The sensation reminded her of jabbing a pencil through the side of a styrofoam cup.

Paddle-foot's howl hit new high notes. June threw her whole weight behind the push, thinking vaguely of some Old Testament tale. Straight into the brain rather than transfixing the temples, straight into the brain, skewering and twisting, until the tent peg's point jarred to a scraping halt against the inside of the back of his skull.

He was dead, and in death she saw again he couldn't have been more than twelve or thirteen. But, the brief pangs of guilt she'd felt over the little girls did not resurface.

A hasty glance showed her Brother Lucas, backed up against the post that held the monstrous skull. Also needing to reload, he fended off club- and spear-wielding creekers with his less-injured arm.

On the altar-slab, the tearful and mewling Mrs. Gabelman had nearly squirmed her abraded wrists free.

But, just as one hand slipped loose, the backward-jointed dancer popped up beside her with the priest's ceremonial knife, and slashed.

14

Her cheek-pouches are empty and her belly is full. The taste of delicious decay lingers on her tongue. Stuffed, sated, and warm, instincts compel her to find a nice den. A cozy burrow where she can curl up and sleep.

Then, later, in the cooler gloaming of dusk, she might venture out in search of others of her kind. A suitable male, perhaps…small but virile…to lure and fuck, bodies rolling together, nipping and hissing…until he spurts his seed into her, and she opens him with her teeth…heat and blood, heat and blood…under the scabrous moon she'll expel slippery, squirming masses of young…and eat them.

No!

This isn't me!

Oh, but it is…it could be.

The old-her may have been the girl who would catch a spider in a paper cup to release it outside. The old-her may have volunteered at the animal shelter and gotten choked up over commercials about abused or neglected pets. The old-her may have considered switching to ethical vegetarianism—except her friends would have given her no end of mockery and torment.

This new-her sees nothing wrong at all with squeezing out a litter of jellybean-sized pink grublike babies and munching them up, still wet with birthing fluids, as they feebly struggle and squeak.

A den, a sleep, a fuck and a kill, and then a richly tender meal…

Do it again the next day, and the day after that, and forever...

Or until a mate-male gets in a lucky shot, or a wombful of young devour her from within, or some predator higher up the infernal food chain makes a meal of her instead, destroying this body, forcing her spirit to subcarnate again into some other form.

She doesn't know how she knows these things that she knows. In her previous life, she'd never so much as imagined a concept such as subcarnation. Yet, the knowledge came to her as cleanly and completely as the knowledge of how to walk on four webbed feet, how to swim and dig, bite and sting.

Really, she's aware that she's gotten a pretty decent deal. It could have been a lot worse. She could've come back as a rot-fly, a urethr-eel, a corpro-lich, a bile-cluster, any of a number of lowly things. This isn't so bad.

The urge to find a den and sleep continues to tug at her, but she resists it. Her thoughts are still human enough to be curious. With an ear tuned for danger, she prowls snuffling along the foundation of the lakehouse.

She seems to recall that, as a general rule, basements aren't common in Florida; something to do with the water table. Yet, with a burrowing rodent's keenly attuned senses, she's sure she detects a void under the house. Not just a crawlspace; a serious, sizable, gaping **void**.

There is, however, also a modest crawlspace, accessed by a padlocked hatch made from sheet plywood. She could gnaw through it in a jiffy, but she doesn't have to. A crumbled crack in the stonework allows her to creep through, aided by the oily slickness of her pelt.

Her ears prick at a soft, whispery, rustly sound. She thinks of wind-stirred leaves and tall grass, though she feels no movement in the air.

Her nose twitches. A strange smell strengthens as she

171

worms through the crevice. It isn't blood, or pus, or shit, or rot—tasty, tasty rot!—but is stormlike and prickly and cold.

Her eyes peer into an oddly lit dimness, purple-tinged, shot with veins of magenta and black in branching pathways. Bright flickers dart along them in sporadic, random sequences.

Nerves. Neurons. Synapses.

She remembers biology classes, images of electrical impulses in brain tissue, and realizes she's invaded the thought-center of some conscious being, and it is very aware of her.

If only she'd heeded her instincts...slept and fucked, birthed and ate.

Instead, thanks to curiosity, she is engulfed.

***

She is part of it now, part of the house, part of the thing pretending to be a house. The entity, not conscious but not unthinking. A nexus, a nerve point, a bridge, a barrier.

The walls are thin here, she understands. The power is strong. Energy? Magic? Cosmic? It doesn't matter. Power is power is power is power.

And perhaps that is why the original transference was possible. The Spatial Merge, even-steven swapsies, six billion gallons of Lake Misquamicus for six billion gallons pumped from the filth-ridden blood seas of the Gulf of Cagliostro. Fresh water in Hell, for a small slice of Hell on Earth.

This spot is one of the anchor points, what remains of Madison Jones' psyche and mind realizes. The rest of her has been engulfed, subsumed and absorbed...but in some tenacious persistence a spark of self stays intact.

Perhaps it is her soul, her immortal soul. Her body is gone—bodies plural, by now. The human original devoured, the lion's share to her killer and the rest to myriad scavengers. Devoured, digested, shat out, devoured again by those maggots and mites even further down the chain; it's the circle, the circle of life—

Haaaaaaa-cienda, mozambique chihuahua!

What's with this Lion King stuff? No place for it here. Circle of life? Not really. Circle of death? Not really that either. Salvation and damnation revolving and interfolding through an eternity of instants, not a circle but fractals within fractals, a Moebius ouroboros origami optical illusion switching in and switching out and remaking itself.

It hurts. There is no true reality. There is no real truth.

The nutria-form into which she subcarnated is also gone now. Dissolved and diffused, without having found a mate to fight and fuck, without spawning any squirming grublike pink litters of crunchy-bleedy soft jellybean offspring to consume. Survival and reproduction; those most basic imperatives are meaningless, let alone anything higher, anything more...art, faith, invention, philosophy, emotion...

Anchor point. One of six. Being of a generation that grew up on Harry Potter, she readily grasps this concept and its importance. **Horcrux much?** *But she doesn't know what, if anything, can or should be done about it.*

Before she can begin to organize more thoughts, a distraction impinges on her awareness. The man who'd visited earlier, the brutish barefoot stranger in overalls, has returned. Not alone.

"I'se tellin' ya, y'ain't gonna hardly believe it," he says to the short, pudgy person limp-trudging along beside him.

Apart from their differences in body size and shape, it's clear they're related, sporting similar features and the same mismatched eyes: one brown, one silver.

Though there's also the fact that the smaller man has a couple of extra heads sprouting from his ribs. He isn't merely carrying them, which had been Madison's first impression; their necks are fused into flab and skin. He cradles them in the crooks of his elbows like a lady with two babies, or a hen sheltering chicks.

The head on his left is that of a ruddy, hearty-looking man whose thick crop of white hair and muttonchops belonged in a Civil War documentary. The other head is a woman's, wrinkled but apple-cheeked, a sweet pie-making granny type with a loose pewter-colored bun. Both heads appear to be snoozing despite the rocking pitch-and-yaw of their host's uneven gait.

"I don't hardly b'leeve it already," this shorter figure says, puffing, hitching at a sagging pair of brown corduroys. He's shirtless, for obvious reasons. He's also barefoot...by which, Madison notices, the lone foot he still has is bare, while he otherwise hobbles along on a stump of gnarled-over callus. "You best not've made me lug Ma and Pa all's the way here for nothin', Lester Riggers, or we'se'll have words."

"Don't be like that, Ronny. Jest wait 'til you gets a gander at Chelsea Carmichael's boobfruits. Finest I ever seen, hand-t'-Lucifer. An' that purty-boy rich-bitch brother of'n hers near shit hisself. They'se goan' be **fun**!"

***

To say that the Riggers are disappointed would be an understatement, Madison thinks, listening in as the four of them—big brother Lester, little brother Ronny, and the heads of Ma and Pa—bicker at each other.

Lester's particularly annoyed by the implication he imagined or made up the whole thing. He gesticulates at the crushed and semen-gunked SUV; if he's making it up, how do they explain this, huh?

Then Ma reckons to Pa that maybe the boy's right, and

if'n he is, if'n any Carmichaels really have come back to the lake, they mebbe ought'a just keep on doin' their jobs... seen as how that's what they've been bein' paid for all these years.

Pa agrees. Caretakin' and housekeepin'.

So, they urge their boys to set to work cleaning up the mess, collecting strewn luggage and scattered groceries. Madison lets her consciousness drift from the scene. She senses the house is pleased, but has better things to do than watch Lester and Ronny chortle over skimpy pairs of panties, miraculously intact tequila bottles, and Andy's surviving stash.

The house. A nexus, an anchor point. One of six. With invisible, intangible, but very real lines stretching between them. Ley lines. Power lines. Thrumming with diabolical magic.

She finds she can move along them. Can travel along them, skimming like a zipline through trees and solid objects. From the lakehouse to a rearing ugly headland of rock jutting above a violent whirlpool—Kayla? Is that one of Kayla's flip-flops abandoned at the edge? Is that Kayla's primal spirit in a new form somewhere far below? **Keep clam and carry on.**

From the headland, Madison moves to a ramshackle shitty-looking skeevy bar that had probably been ramshackle, shitty-looking and skeevy even before all this. In the reddening light as the sun sinks and the lake fumes like a cauldron, patrons of every description from normal to unspeakable move toward the door. Dull discordant music thuds through the walls, accompanied either by singing that makes Chelsea's karaoke efforts sound halfway decent, or the screams of people being slowly skinned alive.

And from there to a spot on the lake's muddy-bloody shore, a spot where some kind of statue or monument has been put up...something weirdly Roman about it...part column, part plinth...topped not with a golden Caesar's eagle but a goat-headed dragon wrought from cold blood-iron...and a sign proclaiming in angular letters: HERE DID THE GREAT GENERAL FAVIUS FIRST SET FOOT AGAIN UPON EARTH! ALL GLORY UNTO HIM, LUCIFER BE PRAISED! Around it are urns and vases, stained altar slabs, braziers and burnt offerings, a crucified baby nailed to a board, a pile of severed heads from which the faces have been stripped.

Then zipping along another line, feeling the thrum of power vibrating every particle of her insubstantial being... passing over a spot in the woods where a recent massacre seems to have taken place, blood and smoke, shards of bone, bodies everywhere...to another lakehouse, older and funkier, sprawling with many additions, far less fancy than the one belonging to the Carmichaels but far more steeped in decades of ordinary sin. Incest and adultery, murder and lies.

Moving on from that house, the lines carry Madison zip-swift through inhospitable 'gator-infested marshlands to a winding inlet where spring-fed streams trickle fresh water into swampy morasses of bile, pus, and blood. Rising here, from a massive root-gnarled hummock, is what she can only think of as a "Tim Burton" tree. Or an "H.P. Lovecraft" tree. Or an "if Tim Burton did a Lovecraft movie" tree. Words like 'eldritch' and 'rugose' squirm through her mind. Its bark is slick and fissured. Its limbs spread and intertwine in unnatural contortions. Veils of damp moss hang like tatters of rotting skin and long tangles of scalped hair from its twisted branches. Deep within the convoluted thickness of the tree's squat, horrible bole, its spongy black heart beats a turgid, squelching rhythm.

15

The blade must've had a razor's edge, or the creeker was stronger than she looked, or both, because Mrs. Gabelman's flesh parted like tissue paper.

One slice, and her throat opened to the bone on a fountain of blood, a Las Vegas Bellagio of blood, a leaping crimson torrent reaching nearly eight feet in the air before pattering down in a wide rain.

"No!" yelled Brother Lucas. Too late.

Also too late, he hurled an empty gun the way they sometimes did in the movies, or those old Superman episodes when the Man of Steel would stand laughing as bullets bounced off his heroic chest, then dodge aside when the pistol came spinning toward him.

The woman whose joints all bent the wrong way, busy shouting or chanting in their caveman language, did not dodge. It didn't matter anyway. The throw went wide.

Mrs. Gabelman's back arched, her body quivered, a look of incredulous horror filled her blue (maybe) eyes, and then she was as dead as the paddle-footed youth. As dead as Mr. Gabelman, and June-had-lost-count members of this deformed, primitive clan.

"Azbunael!" cried the woman, brandishing the knife with a flourish that sent more crimson droplets arcing into the air. ***"AZBUNAEL!!!"***

Whatever it was, it couldn't be good. June, who'd reloaded without even thinking about it, sprang up and fired. Both barrels. Double thunder. Yet a third grisly shower

177

rained down, the woman's torso half blown to pieces.

Got her.

Only…

AZBUNAEL!!!

Too late?

The sullen orange inner glow suffusing the immense demon-skull, turning it into a nightmare mockery of a jack-o-lantern, intensified. It did more than burn brighter; it bonfire *blazed.*

Yes, too late.

A name. Not merely a name, but a Name.

A summoning. A power.

Azbunael was here.

Furnace-hot beams shot from the hollow eye sockets, raving this way and that, used-car-lot spotlights of infernal radiance. Its fanged maw was a churning volcano, a literal hellmouth. Turbulent darkness streamed from its horns, wreathing the terrible visage in shifting black tendrils.

"GIVE ME THE DEAD!"

The voice, from nowhere and everywhere, shook the earth. June fought for her balance, not wanting to land on her backside yet again. She saw Brother Lucas on his knees, cradling his injured arm, his eyes those of a wild stallion trapped in the path of a tornado. She saw the surviving creek-freaks, prostrate in some combination of worship, terror, and exultation.

Those furnace-hot beams fixed on the altar, and Mrs. Gabelman was gone. Poof, just like that. Gone into a whiff of smoke, nothing left but a spill of gritty greyish-white ash. The smoke wafted up, then flowed into the demon's slitted nostrils as if inhaled. And it, too, was gone. Just like that.

Next, the beams swept the clearing, and every creeker corpse got the same treatment. Instant cremation, whiff of smoke swiftly inhaled. Bodies consumed. Souls? Were those smoke-whiffs their souls, also being consumed?

The backwashes of heat passed over June in waves, but did not harm her, did not so much as singe a single hair. She didn't pause to question it. She just ran to Brother Lucas, where he still knelt with that tornado-caught stare. His elbow, struck by that flung club, looked pulverized. He'd sustained a few other wounds, minor stabs and scratches, but the arm was by far the worst.

"Time to go!" she heard herself say, in an absurdly bright, cheerful tone.

"Yeah," he muttered. "Yeah, this shit right here is beyond my pay grade."

Working her shoulder under his other arm, she helped him to his feet. A creeker—male or female or both or neither, she couldn't tell—clawed at her leg; she stomped his/her/its fingers. Another screeched at them and got punted in the chin by Lucas's boot, crushing jawbone like eggshell.

"Let's get out of here," he said.

June couldn't agree more.

They hadn't gone six paces when the earth shook again, Azbunael's dreadful voice with a new demand.

NOW GIVE ME THE LIVING!"

***

At that apocalyptic bellow, the remaining creekers left off trying to reach June and Brother Lucas. They swarmed to the area in front of the glowing-eyed skull instead, vying for position, clamoring, pushing and jostling like ducks vying for tossed scraps of bread. Like concert-goers or game-show audience members, hoping to be chosen and drawn up on stage.

Me me me pick me!, their gabbling cries and eager gestures seemed to say.

The hot beams surveyed the creekers, moving from one

to the next. Azbunael's crown of tendrils writhed, smoky black snakes, seething vines, coiling from the huge ram-horns, lashing the air.

"Quick," urged Lucas.

But, before they'd gone more than another few steps, the heatlamp beams glared over them, rooting them in place as if cementing their feet to the ground. June had an awful moment of feeling examined from within, evaluated, turned inside out, every part of her under a cruel microscope.

What followed was an even worse moment of derision, of feeling sneered at and passed over.

The intensity of the beams' focus fixed on Lucas. He shivered, as if experiencing the similar dissection June had just endured.

In his case, however, the result differed...

"YOU," Azbunael declared. **"YOU WILL DO NICELY."**

"Run," Lucas said. But they couldn't.

Snaky black tendrils of smoke swarmed toward them, twining around Lucas's arms and legs. One brushed June and she flinched. If the draconian eye-beams were hot, these were cold and somehow oily.

"DARE NOT RUN FROM ME! YOU HAVE BEEN CHOSEN, YOU ARE HONORED! FOR THIS BRIEF TIME SHALL I, AZBUNAEL, DUKE OF DUKES, INHABIT YOUR MORTAL FORM!"

"Oh *hell* no!"

In a flash, he was hauled into the air as if he weighed next to nothing. He thrashed against the coils, fought although it must have been agony to his shattered elbow.

"HELL, YES!" The demonic voice boomed soul-killing laughter, reeling him closer, reeling him in.

June brought up the shotgun, thinking to blast one of the smoke-tendril-things. Before she could, more of them whipped toward her, striking the weapon from her grasp.

They snared her by wrists and ankles, and she too was yanked into the air, struggling like a hooked fish on a line.

"NOT SO FAST, WOMAN...I SHALL MAKE THOROUGH USE OF YOU AS WELL!"

The smoke-vine tendrils slammed her down, flat on her back, onto a hard surface. A hard stone surface. The altar slab, where Mrs. Gabelman had lain, where Mrs. Gabelman had wet herself, been throat-slashed in a bloody Bellagio fountain, died, been cremated, and consumed. The stone was sticky with half-boiled blood and urine, gritty with ash.

Brother Lucas, suspended cruciform in mid-air in front of Azbunael's baleful fire-gaze, continued to shout and swear.

"SECURE HER, MY THRALLS!"

Creeker-freaks rushed to do the demon's bidding, binding June spread-eagle across the altar. Crazily, in the midst of everything else, it occurred to her to wonder... could they understand English, or were they hearing the dreadful voice speaking their own devolved grunting tongue? Or was the voice technically 'speaking' any language at all? Was it in their heads, rather than their ears?

"BARE HER TO MY SIGHTS," Azbunael commanded.

She gasped in affront, but the creekers were still just as quick to obey. In a trice, despite the bulky Kevlar vest with its buckles, she was stark birthday-suit naked, her clothes and sensible underwear sliced clean away with crude knives.

Mocking fingers poked and prodded. Someone snickered—

—*as if you deformed wretches are anything to write home about!*—

—and someone else tweaked her tight-puckered nipple-nubs, pinching and twisting.

"ENH, IT'LL DO," said the demon.

Infuriated, a retort burst from her before she could hold

181

her tongue. "Well, up yours, Duke of Earl, or whatever you call yourself!"

"OH, NO, NO, NO," came the reply. *"IT WILL MOST DEFINITELY BE UP YOURS, WOMAN. UP YOURS AS FAR AS 'TWILL GO, AND THEN SOME."*

Again, Azbunael laughed.

So did Brother Lucas, hellfire embers kindling in his eyes.

***

The smoky tendrils lowered him, released him. Lucas stretched, drawing a deep breath. He paused to study his injured elbow, the flesh swollen and spongy around shattered bone, the dark skin made even darker from bruising.

"FIRST THINGS FIRST." Azbunael's words came from Lucas's lips, as well as from the immense skull on its pole. *"IF I'M TO PUT THIS VESSEL THROUGH ITS PACES, I WANT IT IN GOOD CONDITION."*

Lucas's eyes glowed brighter. Flames rushed over him in rippling patterns, sheeting whorls of fire, burning but leaving him miraculously untouched. Better than untouched. Leaving him healed.

And nude.

And glorious.

June, bound to the altar, could only stare.

His clothing, his Kevlar vest, his boots, his weapons… all gone, burned to nothing, sifted away in drifts of ash. His muscular body utterly exposed, utterly unblemished. Flawless from his shining-smooth pate to his toes. Even old scars from altercations years past were gone. He was a majestic mahogany god.

And—had she mentioned?—nude.

Nude and enormous.

So nude. So enormous. Rising stiff and engorged.

Bigger than she'd imagined. Better. Spectacular.

Her mouth went dry.

Understandable; all the moisture in her had gone elsewhere. Oh, she was wet there, down *there*, instantly drenched, her loins surging with a plump floodgate throb.

This was what Azbunael had meant? This was why she'd been stripped and tied spread-eagle to the altar? So that the demon, possessing Brother Lucas, could plunder and defile her?

A needful little whine escaped her throat. She squirmed her hips, flexed her buttocks. Her thighs were already parted wide; she strained to part them wider.

A diabolical knowing smirk crossed Lucas's face. He stroked himself with both hands—he *needed* both hands for the job, to heft such solid length and girth!

Up hers, hadn't the demon said? Up hers as far as it would go, and then some?

Fine, so it might hurt. Fine, so it might split her open, rupture something, kill her. Fine, what a way to go, bring it on!

He strode toward the altar. The creeker-freaks watched avidly from the sidelines.

And maybe it was against Brother Lucas's will, but what of it? He could hardly be held responsible. Nor could she! This was a power beyond their control. Beyond either of them. They couldn't help what was about to happen, couldn't resist, couldn't be blamed! They both were victims!

Lucas—oh, she knew it was really Azbunael, but didn't care—set his big hands on her chest. His hands on her breasts, her bare breasts, such as they were! His palms warm, firm, giving a gentle squeeze. June moaned.

His knowing smirk broadened. He trailed a fingertip over her cheek, over her lips. She could have bitten it, shown defiance, futile though it was. Instead, she hungrily sucked at it, curling her tongue, finding her mouth wasn't so dry after all.

Removing his now-wetted finger from her mouth, he skimmed it lightly down her body, between her breasts, tickling her navel, moving lower. June quivered, buttocks so tense they ached as she tried to tilt herself to meet the teasing caress.

Just a little further…just a little…his fingertip brushing her mound, tracing feather-light along the outer folds of her labia. June thought she'd go insane. Someone else, touching *there*! Someone else, not a doctor, but a real man!

Okay, a demonically-possessed man. Okay, and the circumstances weren't the greatest, splayed on a blood-stained infernal altar with an audience of gibbering cannibal creek-freaks.

But it was finally happening!

In a sudden motion, he slid his saliva-slicked finger over her clitoris and into her vagina, probing inside her. June screamed, hips bucking madly, hurtling toward orgasm. He withdrew his hand a heartbeat before she got there. June screamed again, a sobbing wail. His smirk widened to a leering grin.

"OH, SLUT OF EDEN," chortled the voice of Azbuneal, as he swung Lucas's body onto the slab, erection poised between her legs. *"THIS WILL BE FUN!"*

***

June braced herself. Ready, oh so ready! Let it hurt, let it kill her, she didn't care as long as the deed was finally done! As long as she got to come before she went. It wouldn't take much. The first rough thrust of his entrance should—

"No!" someone shouted. "Oh cripes, he's possessed!"

"Back off!" shouted someone else. "Leave her alone!"

A rattling fusillade shattered the air. Machine-gun

fire, strafing high, shredding treetops on the far side of the clearing from the path. Loud as doomsday, drowning out the continued shouting, the startled outcries from the creek-freaks around the altar. Drowning out June's own cheated shriek as Lucas reared up, eyes blazing, his rigid cock towering above her still-unfucked pussy.

"WHO DARES???" roared Azbuneal's voice from Lucas's mouth as well as from the jaws of the fiery skull, and that was *not* drowned out by the clattering thunder.

June's head snapped to the side, wondering the same thing herself. She looked wildly toward the path and saw two men in Kevlar vests and riot helmets—David and Ramon?

None other.

They raced in, fragging creekers right and left like this was just another violent video game, yelling through the bullet-hail cacophony for Lucas to fight it, fight the demon, God was with him and so were they, yelling to June, "We'll save you, Sister!"

Lucas sprang from the altar-slab, leaping inhumanly high in a powerful flip, landing superhero-style in front of them, then rising to his full height with gauntlets of flame igniting on both fists. He laughed. So did the monstrous skull.

"MORTAL FOOLS! YOU THINK TO STOP ME?!"

"Don't make us hurt you, Brother!" David's hands shook.

"AS IF YOU COULD!"

"Leave him, you hell-beast son of a bitch!" Ramon's hands didn't shake, but his expression through the helmet's clear visor was a mask of horror and sick despair.

Again, Azbuneal laughed. *"I WILL HAVE YOUR HEADS AS TROPHIES AND YOUR SOULS AS TRINKETS!"*

He charged, fire-fisted, flame-eyed.

185

They wouldn't really—

They did. At such close range, they could hardly miss. Brass casings pinged everywhere, a slot machine payoff counterpoint to the deadly lead barrage. Gory lines of holes stitched across Lucas's body, sizzling flesh and steaming blood exploding from dozens of wounds. Face and neck, chest and abdomen, even his magnificent cock—no!—were perforated, shredded, obliterated.

He pitched backwards, hit the ground with a thud, and lay motionless with wisps of smoke curling up from his body. Silence fell, but for the ragged breathing of June and her two young 'saviors.' She didn't think she could speak. She wanted to scream, sob, and curse.

"It's all right, Sister." David took a few hesitant steps toward her while doing his best to avert his gaze from her staked-out nudity. "You're safe now. We're here."

"You killed him," she managed to say without screaming, sobbing, or cursing. "You killed Lucas."

"He wasn't Lucas any more," Ramon said. "A devil got into him."

And almost into *her*, but did they hear her complaining? June bit her lip.

"We…we saw what he was about to…do," David added, moving between the altar and Lucas, partially blocking her view. "Thank God we were in time."

June bit her lip harder, until it bled. In time…they couldn't have been five minutes slower? *Two* minutes?

"Let's get you untied," he went on, "and, um, find you some, uh, clothes, and—"

Behind him, Lucas lunged upright, ripples of flame coursing over his skin, flowing over him in a cauterizing, healing miracle.

Ramon cried a warning, raising his gun, but before he could squeeze off another burst, Lucas punched burning fingers through the small of David's back.

David gasped, a thin little whistling squeak. He shuddered. His eyes met June's, looking confused and surprised.

Lucas yanked, ripping out David's entire spine with a great unzipping series of gristle-pops. The length of vertebrae and nerve-bundles thrashed in his grip like a bloodied bone-ivory snake.

***

Knees buckling, David did a slow accordion collapse that reminded June absurdly of the coyote in all those old cartoons. By craning her neck, she could just see him in a heap beside the altar, ends of ribs poking through his torn flesh like a crown roast.

"David!" Ramon cut loose with the machine gun, peppering Lucas's fire-sheathed form. This time, the flames acted as armor as well as healing, the bullets disintegrating into little showers of sparks upon impact, with no more effect than a kid hitting caps with a stone.

"PREPARE TO FOLLOW HIM!" Azbunael gloated. The smoky tendrils issuing from those great ram's horns undulated in anticipation.

With long strides, Lucas closed the distance between himself and a rapidly backpedaling, still-shooting Ramon. One muscular arm bunched and swung, David's detached spine acting as a fiery bone-whip. It cracked against Ramon's visor, splitting the plexiglas, gashing a charred weal across his face.

As Ramon went down, the spray of bullets went up and askew, some striking the stone altar-slab and missing June by bare inches. Wouldn't it *be* just her luck to get killed now, by one of her own church-group?

"Hey, watch it!" she heard herself say, an indignant blurt as if he'd merely been horsing around with spitballs or paper airplanes.

187

Christine Morgan

The bone-whip lashed a second time, obliterating the machine gun into scraps and shrapnel, obliterating most of Ramon's left hand along with it. He rolled, screaming, scrabbling on the ground in a clumsy and desperate crab-crawl.

Azbunael threw back Lucas's head, fists on hips, erection bobbing tall and proud, in a triumphant bellow of laughter. The skull's maw and sockets blazed brighter than ever, twin cauldrons above a fuming inferno.

"NOW FOR MY TROPHIES…AND THEN FOR MY PRIZE!"

Another stride brought him to Ramon, David's spine stretched between his fists as if he meant to use it as a garrote. Ramon rolled again, something in his right hand, something dark and egg-shaped.

—was that…? was he…? oh no…!—

He pulled the pin with his teeth and lobbed the grenade in a high arc, a Hail Mary if ever there was one. By either God's grace or a cruel fluke of fate, it soared up and over Lucas's head and dropped neatly into one of the skull's blazing eyes.

Nothing but orbit.

"NOOOOOOO!!!" howled Azbunael.

"What—?" June began.

Kaboom.

The immense skull fractured like a plate in a shooting gallery. It blew apart and outward, flying shards of coal-ember bone expanding in a shockwave, the downcurving horns doing ungainly pinwheels. A concussive blast of sooty heat would have swatted June from the altar if not for her bonds; as it was, her ankles nearly snapped and one shoulder creaked almost to dislocation. Every inch of her exposed skin felt sandblasted with fire—especially the sensitive places!

Lucas stopped short and stood still. The flames

188

wreathing his body dwindled and died. For a fleeting moment, his eyes cleared, were his own eyes and aware. They met June's, wild with turbulent emotions.

Then he was a Pompeii statue, perfectly preserved in solid dense-coarse ash.

And *then*, tiny fissures raced in spreading, branching cracks, and he fell apart into crumbling meaningless charcoal chunks.

June realized she was crying. Hardly a surprise. The next thing she realized was that Ramon was still alive, staggering to his feet with the stunned manner of a car wreck survivor. Half his face was laid open, his right hand a mangled mess bristling with slivers of fingerbone, but the wounds had been cauterized and he wasn't bleeding.

He stumbled to the altar. "Sister?"

Crying, she couldn't speak. Ramon nodded in a vague shell-shocked way, as if he understood. As if he possibly could!

"I know," he said. "It's all right. It's over. I'll get you out of here."

Picking up a creeker-freak knife that might've been the same one to slash Mrs. Gabelman's throat, he managed to saw through the ropes and free her.

***

They didn't converse much beyond the basics as they made their way downstream back toward Bible Creek Campground. Both of them were too numbed, too wrapped up in their own reactions.

June's footwear had been removed intact, so she didn't have to go barefoot at least. For other clothing, her options proved extremely limited. The sliced-up pieces of her own garments, strategically knotted, covered her nudity. Toting her shotgun and wearing David's no-longer-needed riot helmet, she supposed she looked like an extra from some deranged post-apocalyptic movie.

Ramon carried David's machine gun slung across his back. As for the rest of David himself, there was no time to do anything but lay him out as peacefully as possible, covering him with the bullet-holed remnants of the high priest's absurd silvery poncho.

As for Brother Lucas…well, not much they could do.

"We can come back for them later," Ramon had said. "Give them a decent burial. But it doesn't much matter. Their souls are with the Lord now."

About that, she had her doubts. She'd seen Azbunael inhale those wisps of essential smoke from Mrs. Gabelman. Which didn't seem fair, didn't seem right. The murdered were meant to go exalted to Heaven, those slain by the forces of evil automatically washed clean of all sins. Even dye-job boob-job vain deceivers. No matter her opinions, did Mrs. Gabelman really deserve an eternity in Hell?

Did her husband? Did David? Did Lucas?

She'd considered searching through the creeker-freak village—even if they didn't have actual clothes, they might have had scavenged blankets or beach towels used for bedding—but decided she didn't want to touch anything else of theirs. Who knew what kind of parasites there could be? Ordinary lice and bedbugs were bad enough.

If any creek-freaks survived, they were hiding or had run for it into the surrounding woods. June kept her gun at the ready just in case. Ramon tried to do the same, but, with the pain from his injuries, it was all he could do to stay on his feet. His face was a mess, sultry good looks ruined. His hand was worse, a July 4th don't-drink-and-firework public service advertisement in the making.

He had told her this much: to his most recent knowledge, Crusader Markane and her mother and the Shinns were all right. Or, had been when he and David followed the sounds of gunfire up the creek.

Up the creek, yes, very apt; they certainly were.

"Brother William, though," Ramon had added, with a shrug. "He and Mr. Shinn were on watch, but nobody's seen him since. He's just gone. Maybe something got him, maybe he ran...no one knows."

As for the other sounds of gunfire, which she and Lucas had heard, Ramon said a bunch of dead people attacked the campground.

"They were zombies, rotting and everything. You could see they used to be ordinary vacationers, in swim suits and hiking shorts, souvenir tee shirts. One, a little kid, was still wearing a mouse-ears hat from Disney World."

According to Ramon, he and David had been on their scouting expedition at the time, but Crusader Markane rallied his remaining troops and made short work of the zombies. Headshots, just like on TV.

"No one was bitten?" asked June, imagining her mother as a shambling corpse.

"No."

"We also heard an explosion."

"That was David and me. We went to the lakeshore. Stupid, but we wanted to see it up close. It's..." He'd shaken his head, unable to elaborate. "Then we saw a mermaid. Only, it wasn't a mermaid. It was a...a lure, a decoy...growing out of the head of this...this *thing*...this monster...like a shark and an alligator and a manta ray all blended together. If David hadn't suggested we each sneak a grenade..."

He'd shuddered, and that was the end of the discussion, until they reached the campground and stopped dead in their tracks.

16

Suspended in darkness, unable to move.

Was this death? Was this being dead?

Being *dead*? How about being *killed*? Being murdered?

By his own supposed girlfriend, of all people. Picking up a fireplace poker, using his skull for a pinata.

After his own supposed best friend hacked off his leg with a butcher knife and tried to flame-broil him! He wondered if he'd broken Trevor's nose, hoping he had.

This was either death or a really good facsimile. He could hear, and think, but none of his other senses seemed to be on the job. Couldn't see, taste or smell, couldn't touch. As if his body wasn't even there anymore.

What if he was in a coma? What if Kayla scrambled his brains so hard he'd never wake up? Or, was he paralyzed?

Paralyzed, comatose, or brain-scrambled would still have been better than having the flesh rot right off his bones, soggy skin peeling, muscles squishing like sponges filled with tepid soup, organs fermenting inside his guts.

How it had hurt!

And now, here he was. Disembodied, or whatever, but here.

Was he still himself? Still Andy? His memories said so. Memories leading up to this doomed Spring Break road trip, memories of the house and the turtle and…

…the sting and bite and oily-acidic residue from that swamp-rat's slick fur…Trevor, with the knife and the torch (weird game of CLUE)…

192

He's trying to save your dumb ass, Chelsea had shouted.

Even if so, then Kayla and the fireplace poker, what the fuck was that? Some kind of well-intentioned mercy killing?

Was he dead? Was he?

He heard a rumbling. And realized he did, in some way, feel…a vibration. An approaching engine. Then he discovered he also could see, if he concentrated.

The scene below him was wide angle, as if shot from above. The stretch of lakeshore road…a glistening tangle of bones wrapped in the clothes he'd been wearing…the broken egg pieces of his cranium.

Flies using him for an airport. Busy maggots churning in the puddles. Some sort of wizened, bald bird perched on his collarbone, darting the thin crochet-hook beak of its vulture-like head into the cavities of his eye sockets and mouth.

He saw dropped water bottles, fruit snacks, the butcher knife, the smoking ashes of a crude fire.

And the source of the rumbling engine noise/vibration: a mongrel franken-pickup, a backwater backwoods A-Team project, post-apocalyptic meets redneck. It was fitted with studded side-panels and nests of barbed wire, a corrugated tin cow-catcher bolted to the front. The truck body was so blotched with rust and mud and primer paint, its original color could be anyone's guess.

The engine idled for an eternity. The windshield and windows were filthy—one of them had been replaced with a patch of tarpaper secured with duct-tape—but there appeared to be two figures in the cab. Conversing in muffled twangy voices.

"—leave'r runnin'?" said one as the driver's door opens. A woman, or a girl; despite the hillbilly twang, her voice was pure honey-soaked honeysuckle.

"Betcherass gon' leave'r runnin," replied the other, a

dude, but there was no honey in his voice at all. It was all banjos and moonshine and home-rolled cigarettes.

The dude, the driver, emerged warily. He was a lean and rangy type, disheveled in jeans and a threadbare flannel, holding a weapon as mongrel as his truck. It resembled a baseball bat embedded with machete blades, topped with a pickaxe and a six-inch iron spike.

"Wut'cher want I sh'd do?" the girl asked.

"Diddle y'self all's I care, just stay put." The rangy dude approached the scene below Andy's disembodied vantage point, chasing off the vulture-bird, disturbing the flies. He prodded the knife with his workboot, kicked a couple of the water bottles, nudged the bones.

Then he looked straight up, somehow making direct eye contact with Andy, and said, "Shee-it, fella, someone sure'as did a numb'r on you!"

***

Andy, if he *was* still Andy, didn't know how any of this was possible. How his body, or at least the steaming bones of it, could be strewn there on the gravel road…while he, some part of himself anyway, watched the scene from this strange above-vantage.

Or how the rangy guy from the frankentruck could apparently see him. And not just see.

"Let's getcha down from there whilst you're still fresh," the guy said, reaching up. "Afore'n the Catch wakes up fer a snack."

His hand, scarred and grimy, rough of knuckle and rougher of nail, seemed to extend in some kind of telescope fish-eye vision, but Andy—*am I still Andy?*—realized it was a trick of whatever had gone so drastically weird with his perspective.

"Wha'cher got, Heck?" called the twangy honeysuckle

voice of the girl.

"Shet up an' stay put like I toldya."

The hand grew huge, oncoming fingers in warped 3-D, cupping around Andy. The sensation was vague, more the notion of a touch than an actual one.

Cupping, gripping, and then...

Unscrewing?

Yes. Twisting, unscrewing him like a lightbulb. Reminding him of a dumb joke he'd thought funny as fuck in fifth grade—what's the difference between a lightbulb and a pregnant lady? you can unscrew a lightbulb!

Andy's view, mostly obscured by the guy's fingers anyway, revolved weirdly, then swung around as he was apparently not just unscrewed but plucked or picked or pulled free. He would have closed his eyes if he could. The spinny no-control reeling vertigo was worse than the time he tried a VR headset while wrecked.

In the midst of it, he saw where the rangy guy—*did she call him Heck? why does that sound familiar?*—removed him from. Woven among the tree branches was a crazy Blair Witch dreamcatcher kind of thing, the size of an umbrella. Bulbous objects dangled from its underside. They resembled teardrops of dried glue, glass, and murky wax all swirled together.

Some were shriveled and empty, deflated balloons. Others were not, and encased within those, Andy was pretty sure he glimpsed the tiny shapes of animals and people, most just floating or suspended there, bugs in amber, bodies in Matrix pods.

Holy shit, *he* was in one of those gluey, glassy, waxy teardrops! His was still clear, not gone dull and murky yet, not punctured open yet so that the 'Catch' could have a 'snack'...

However horrible the spiderlike nightmare images his imagination conjured up, Andy felt sure the reality would be a million times worse. He did *not* want to know.

"There we go," the guy said, holding Andy's lightbulb bubble teardrop whatever in front of his stubble-chinned, yellow-grinned face. Even without the fisheye distortion, it wasn't a great view.

"What is it, Heck?" honey-twanged the girl. She leaned halfway out the passenger window, giving Andy a brief impression of a backwoods goddess with messy yarn-tied pigtails, a thin tank top, and no bra.

Andy suddenly remembered. Heck somebody, Bodie maybe. Drove like Dukes-a-Hazzard when the turtle-monster went for his truck. That was what Lester, the overalled hick, had said at the lakehouse.

"Lucifer's sakes, Lorlinda, setcher ass in that seat!" Heck squinted at Andy, tapping at the surface of his... capsule? Pod? "Aw'right in there, fella? If'n you unnerstan me, give a li'l wiggle or sommat."

Andy wasn't sure how, or if he even could, but he tried. Whatever he did must have worked well enough to satisfy the guy, who nodded, did a kind of victory-shake Andy could've done without, and returned to the vehicle.

As he slid behind the wheel, he tossed Andy to the girl, who handled him deftly and peered in at him. The up-close view of her was *far* preferable to that of her companion.

"Why, he musta just been dis-car-nay-ted," she said. She pinkie-waved and blew a little kiss. "Hiya, sugarbun! Don'choo worry none now. Me an' Heck, we gon' take *good* care of you."

17

The writer—Edgely or Edley or something; he'd mumbled his introduction around a mouthful of sandwich, and they didn't want to be rude by pressing for clarification—made good on his offer of nice cold beer, and soon, Trevor and Chelsea were kicked back in deck chairs, each with a frosty bottle of Collier's in hand.

The afternoon sun stretched lazily, a refreshing breeze picked up. It was pretty nice, actually. Relaxing. Almost idyllic.

If, of course, you could ignore the festering horrible lake. And the blood-shit-rot smell. And the various flyblown buzzing, guttural grunts, inhuman screeching, and whatever else passed for the dulcet tones of 'nature' out here.

Trevor also could have done without having a busted nose, but the beer bottle felt like cool bliss when he held it against his swollen bruises. He eyed the writer's sandwich with a slight stirring of appetite. The bread looked coarse-ground and rustic, the sliced meat a tender juicy-rare pink. Maybe they should have accepted that offer as well.

"Let me finish up and send this email," the writer said, "and we can chat."

"Email?" Chelsea perked up. "Whatsisname, Lester, said you didn't have internet out here."

"Well...Lester's a fine boy and a hard worker, but he's not the brightest crayon in the box, if you take my meaning. Same could be said for a lot of the folks around here. Not so bad, once you get to know them."

His fingers clicked rapidly on the laptop keyboard. The radio played. The generator hummed, though this close it sounded like someone groaning in constant pain.

"There we go. Proofreader, quibbling over whether I wanted 'cunt-kicking' and 'cream-pie' hyphenated or not, for consistency. She's fussy that way."

Chelsea and Trevor exchanged a raised-eyebrows glance and by mutual twin-telepathy decided not to pursue it.

Trevor drained half his beer and exhaled a gusty sigh, not quite a belch. "How do you get Collier's?" he asked instead.

"Oh...arrangements." The writer flapped a hand. "Trade, you know. Some on the other side will pay pretty well for the Bodeans' homebrewed hellshine. They think it's got fountain-of-youth properties, isn't that wacky? As for me, I get by."

"Books?" Chelsea asked.

"And...uh...films. Short independent films. Specialty stuff. Experimental. I'm no big movie-maker, but I've got my audience."

Another exchanged glance proved them in agreement not to pursue that, either...though Trevor had to admit, he was more than a little curious.

As the writer closed his laptop, Chels put on a smile. "So, you have regular contact with the outside world, then? Can you leave if you want to?"

"I don't know about regular. Occasional. But, leave? Why would I want to do that?"

"*Could* you, though?" she pressed.

He mulled it over so long Trevor thought he'd forgotten the question. "I suppose. Yes, there's the quarantine, but there are ways around. Bribes and such."

"Yeah, Lester told us about the barter system," she said. "Let's cut right to it then, mister...if I show you my tits, will you help us get a ride out of this damn place?"

198

Sighing again, Trevor finished his beer.

The writer, who'd been taking a long chilled sip himself, coughed. He set down the bottle and blinked at her. "Excuse me? If you what now?"

"You're not *that* old." Chelsea arched her back and did a wiggle, making the unfettered contents of the borrowed tee shirt dance. "And I bet you don't get many primo college girl tits around here anymore."

"Oh, kiddo." He chuckled, shaking his head. "I'm sure they're very nice and all, but..."

"What, are you into dudes or something?"

"Chels!" Trevor said. His sister, soul of diplomacy.

The writer's chuckle turned into a full laugh. "Didn't I just tell you I make films? I was doing that before AllHell happened and the wall went up. Trust me, I have access to all the 'tits'—" he made air-quotes, "—I need."

***

As Chelsea sputtered, not sure how indignant or offended to be—no one had ever laughed her off like that!—the weirdo horror writer turned his head and called into the cabin.

"Jubblies! Come on out here a minute, sweetheart!"

"If you could see your face," muttered Trevor. "You're so *Mom* right now, it'd make you shit."

She almost smashed her beer bottle over his smirking head, but then the screen door opened and Jubblies appeared, and all either she or her smartmouth brother could do was stare.

Access to all the tits he needed, wasn't that what the writer had said? And here they were.

It wasn't that Jubblies had big ones. It wasn't that Jubblies had great ones, or perky ones, or pillowy ones.

It was that Jubblies had big ones *and* small ones, great ones *and* so-so ones, perky ones *and* pillowy ones. Jubblies was, in fact, entirely made of tits. She was an ambulatory pile of tits.

Tits of every size and shape, from budding puberty bumps to porn-star beachballs to saggy old-lady droopers. In every possible skin tone and several impossible ones… not just albino to ebony, but blue, green, gold, purple… finely scaled, lightly furred, insectile-iridescent…

With, of course, nipples of every hue, type, and description. Broad pale flattish nipples, nubby raspberry nipples, stiff-poking pencil eraser nipples, dark chocolate-kiss nipples, pierced nipples, lactating nipples, nipples with shyly peeking eyes and fluttery eyelashes, nipples unfolding into tiny fragrant flower-petals…

Watching Jubblies cross the deck was like watching a humanoid-shaped bundle of water balloons learning to walk. Her limbs were short and thick stacks, tit-totem-poles. She didn't have hands, but bulbous udders with prehensile teats, fleshy tit-mittens. She didn't even have a head or face, unless buried under the topmost tits; Chelsea wondered if she used those nipple-eyes to see, wondered how she breathed or ate or anything.

"What…the…absolute…fuck..." said Trevor, sounding like someone both slow-motion and underwater. If he hadn't already been sitting down, he probably would have fallen over.

Worst of all, and god-fucking-dammit, Chelsea estimated that at least twenty percent of Jubblies' tits *were* superior to her own set. That did not seem right, or natural, or fair. How was 'quality over quantity' supposed to be a consolation now?

Quan-titty, some inner voice snickered.

"This is Jubblies," the writer said, doing an affectionate fondle followed by a casual boob-honk. "I found her in the lake a few months after AllHell."

"You…found…her…in the lake?" Trevor shook

himself as if catching back up to normal speed.

"Well, not as in swimming; sealed in one of those prison-casks you sometimes see floating around." He gestured down the beach, where some broken metal drums rested amid driftwood and debris. "I'd taken to hauling them ashore to see what was inside. You can find some of the craziest stuff that way, let me tell you. Some nasty stuff, too. Had to put a couple of them down. Others ran for it, or I let them go, or something else nabbed them first. Jubblies, though...I kind of like having her around."

"I bet," Chelsea said. Snidely. God. She *was* turning into their mother.

"It seems she was the favorite concubine to an arch-lord with a serious breast-fetish," he went on, "but the arch-lord's wife got jealous and had her condemned to be cast into the Gulf of Cagliostro. Part of which, then, as you know, ended up here."

"Did she tell you that?" asked Trevor.

"Not in so many words. There's a..." The writer hummed as he mused, gazing absently skyward. "A kind of infernal osmosis, I guess. You pick things up. It comes to you." He shrugged. "You'll see. You'll get used to it."

"We don't *want* to get used to it!" Chelsea snapped. "What we want is to get the hell out of here! So, are you going to help us, or not?"

***

The writer—it was just easier to think of him that way, Trevor decided—seemed actually pretty cool. Weird, but cool. Friendly. Had good taste in beer. Made a decent sandwich. Enjoyed a casual, laid-back lifestyle, spending his time making movies and writing books. With a damn near infinite variety of tits on demand.

A guy could do worse.

Chels wasn't as impressed. Her bulldog determination had shifted from 'spring break at the lake come Hell or high water' to 'getting the fuck out of here asap pronto,' and the writer's disinterest in her offer had struck a real blow to her pride. Trevor knew better than to comment, but really, as sweet a set as Chels had, how could she hope to compete with Beelzeboob?

The writer wasn't, however, unwilling to help. The thing was, he explained, Heck Bodean's mail route didn't keep to a regular schedule. He'd show up when he showed up. When he did, the writer said he'd be happy to put in a word. Until then, though, they might as well take it easy.

Sounded like a plan to Trevor. The day'd seen enough excitement already as far as he was concerned. He needed some time to sort it all out in his head. The checkpoint, the lake, the SUV…Madison disappearing…his sister about to suck his dick…Lester grabbing him by the throat…cutting off Andy's leg…having his nose broken…Kayla losing her shit…yeah, it was a lot.

Seeing how disgruntled Chels was, the writer then suggested they could try asking at Crawdaddy's. "I heard there's a Hock Party set for tonight. Heck normally tends to steer clear of the place unless on business, but he can never resist a good Hock Party."

Despite a powerful hunch he was going to regret it, Trevor asked the inevitable question. And, sure enough, he regretted it.

"Even for this hick shithole," Chelsea said when the writer finished explaining, "that's disgusting!"

The writer shrugged. "Popular, though. People bet on it, and it's a lot less damaging than some of what goes on."

This time, Trev didn't ask, though he kind of wanted to.

"Besides, even if Heck doesn't show, someone there is bound to know how to get in touch with him. Or you might find someone else willing to give you a lift to the wall."

"For a price," Chelsea said.

"Don't worry, kiddo." He tipped his beer bottle at her with an avuncular twinkle in his eye. "You'll be a sensation."

"Hey, sis, maybe we should sign you up for the Hoc—"

"Fuck off."

"Heh." The writer got up. "Well, if you'll excuse me a second, I'd better check the genny and take care of a few things in the studio. Shooting a mutilation scene later."

Chelsea made a face but said nothing.

"Mind if I tag along?" Trev asked. "I'm, uh, interested in..."

"Mutilation?"

"...well, I was gonna say 'film-making'..."

"Either or." The writer clapped him on the shoulder. "Come on. I'll show you around."

While his sister settled into the deck chair for a grumbling sulk, Trevor followed the writer around to the back of the cabin. First stop was a sturdy thick-walled little shed, the source of the generator-type hum they'd noticed upon arrival. Up close, Trevor noticed, the noise was less of a hum and more of a groan. A low, protracted, organic groaning, as of some living thing enduring endless and unendurable pain.

"What's—?"

"Just the genny. Need to refuel." Despite the solidity of the shed's construction, an indifferent padlock hung unlocked. The writer hauled open the stout door, which, along with the thick walls, proved to be more for soundproofing than security.

A rank smell of piss and sour sweat wafted out, along with a strange not-quite-galvanic crackle.

"Electricity?" Trevor raised his voice to be heard through the now-louder miserable groaning.

"Agonicity," the writer said, and flipped on a light.

18

"Sorry," Greg said as the workers lugged them down the slope. "I tried."

"Why didn't you *run?*" Ethriel asked from her wicker prison.

"I wouldn't leave you."

"Noble."

He flexed the fist with the cheese-gratered knuckles. It smarted and stung. "Thanks."

"And dumb."

"Yeah, probably."

"No 'probably' about it."

He kind of had to agree. Not that he would've gotten very far without her anyway, and not that he would've been able to live with himself if he had. Having a guardian angel was one thing. Abandoning her to certain horror to save his own ass? That was something else.

Uh-huh, and just what, smart guy, was abandoning himself to certain horror?

For that, Greg didn't have much of an answer.

Their procession wended through the grape trellises—which really *were* made of bone, Greg saw: femurs and humeruses (humerii?) tied together with some kind of twine he'd like to have believed was rawhide but was probably tendon. The grapes themselves really were jet-black, blacker than black, black and shiny as octopus eyes. Their scent was rich and boozy, as if already fermented on the vine.

"Well," declared the satyr as the procession reached his

lounging couch. "Well. This is…interesting."

The cloud of attendant imps cackled and fawned. The workers presented their prizes, then backed off and obsequiesed themselves.

Greg, rudely dropped, stifled a groan. His shoulders hadn't popped from their sockets, but felt like rubber bands stretched juuuuust to the fringe of the breaking point. He hurt where the shears had gouged him, hurt from the plane crash, hurt all over.

And here he was, in front of an obscenely lolling devil-satyr who smelled of wild musk. Up close, more of his diabolical features were evident, from the stubby horns protruding through his unkempt mane to the deeply-split cloven hooves and a wiry wine-stained goatee.

Also evident, far too evident for Greg's liking, was a huge shaggy sheath resting upon a huge shaggy scrotum… and the purplish tip of something dewy and eager beginning to protrude from that sheath.

Shifting his indolent bulk, he leaned in to peer at Greg with yellow-gold goat-pupiled eyes. They narrowed, squinting first at the sigil branded onto his forehead, and then at the medallion on its strand of beads.

"So," said the satyr. "Who might…you be?"

"Don't tell him any—" Ethriel began,

"Hush!" A hand, which was also cloven, with a deeper than normal split between the middle and ring fingers, the nails thickly hooflike, passed over the basket. "Your. Turn. In due. Time." Pausing for a slow, savory grin, he added, "Sweetmeats."

Still Shatnery, but Shatnery with skin-crawling menace, some weird merging of Shatner and Christopher Walken… unsettling either way.

Ethriel uttered a tremulous cry, something soft and helpless, heartbreaking, not quite a sob. Greg's fists clenched, his cheese-gratered knuckles stinging.

205

The satyr's attention returned to him, narrow goat-pupiled gaze flicking again to the silver medallion.

"Take," he intoned, "that…off."

"No."

"You…defy…me?"

"I'm dumb that way."

"So. I. See. Who…are you?"

"Gregory Nachtwald. My plane—"

Did he imagine it, or did the satyr recoil a bit at the mention of his name?

"The crash. Yes. Unfortunate. Your…business?"

"Greg, don't—" Ethriel tried again, but another pass of that cloven hand quelled her.

"Smuggling," he said. "Drug-running."

"Ahhh." The satyr settled back, gloating. "A criminal."

"Not in the way you think. I bring things down, across the border from Canada. Painkillers, yeah, but mostly medicine. Cancer meds. Insulin. The stuff Big Pharma charges a damn fortune for here because our system is…" He stopped himself, not needing to get on the old soapbox again.

"Fucked," the satyr finished for him.

As strange as it'd been to hear that word from Ethriel, it was way worse hearing it from this guy.

"Deliciously so," the satyr added, licking his lips, casting a sly sidelong glance at the basket. "So. Deliciously."

***

"Who are you?" Greg asked, not sure why he felt emboldened. Was it that flinch when the satyr heard his name? The narrowing eyes and frown about the medallion he'd refused to remove—an issue the satyr hadn't pressed—or the seared sigil?

"I…am called…Zilch. That…will do…for here."

An expansive gesture took in the valley, the winery and vineyards, the abject workers and capering imps. "Lord... of...all I survey."

"It's nice," Greg said. Which wasn't entirely sarcasm; comparatively speaking, it *was*, in a torture-gimp slave-labor-camp sort of way.

Whether the scarred, mutilated workers would agree was another matter. Now he'd had a chance to look at them, he could tell they must've been typical tourists once. What tatters and rags they wore beneath the barbed-wire head wrappings and broad-brimmed hats still showed the faded patterns of gaudy tropical shirts and theme park logos, the remnants of swim trunks and cargo shorts. Formerly pudgy bodies, formerly sunburned skin...tightened now, toned and weathered from their labors.

None, he saw, were women, and that stirred further unease in the pit of his stomach. The men ranged from college-age to retired—wasn't Florida's unofficial motto something about the newly wed and nearly dead?—but where were their girlfriends, their wives? Their families? No kids in view, either.

He wasn't sure he wanted to think about that. Wasn't sure he really needed to.

"So, now what?" he asked Zilch.

"Are you...in such...a hurry?" Spreading his arms, the satyr gestured again, magnanimously. "Why not...relax? Be...comfortable. Try some...wine."

"I'll pass. We'd rather just keep going."

"Going? But that...cannot be. You...are mine now. My...guests. You. Brought me. An...angel."

"Hey, she's *my* angel," Greg said. "My personal guardian angel."

Why did it seem like they were both bluffing their butts off? What could he possibly have to bluff *with*?

"I could," said Zilch, "have my...minions...drain your

blood, crush…the juices…from your flesh…and mix it. Into the vats. A. Rare. Vintage. Indeed."

So why, Greg wondered but was smart enough not to ask, hadn't they done it already? They'd captured him and Ethriel readily enough. What was stopping them? Was there one of those loopholes in play somehow? Fine print?

"You don't want to do that," he said. Bluff, bluff, bluff. Sound confident. Not cocky, not daring, but confident. Confident and calm. As if he had something up his sleeve.

"No. I do. Not. I would…rather…have you…serve me…willingly."

At this, he heard a faint, startled gasp from inside the basket. And a flat little *thwap!* sound, as of an angel smacking herself in the forehead.

"Serve you?"

"I. Could use. A. Skilled. Warlock."

He'd never been much of a gambler, but in his line of work, a poker face was always a plus. Drawing himself as straight as his aches would allow, while also aiming for nonchalant, he folded his arms and said, "I'm listening."

"As you. Have seen." Zilch did the lord-of-all-I-survey sweep again. "I. Do well here. I…thrive."

Greg nodded.

"But I have…competition."

"That's usually the way of things, yeah. Another vineyard?"

"No. Hellshine. The Bodeans. Distill it. Sell it. To… locals…but. Across…the wall. As well. To the…outside."

"Sneaky," he said. It didn't take much of an educated guess to know what 'hellshine' must be, though why anybody beyond the wall would buy it was another matter. He couldn't imagine much coming out of here being very good for normal people, healthwise or otherwise.

"So. Serve…me. Oathbind…yourself…to me. Ruin. Them. And I…will…reward you…greatly."

Ethriel whirred with bee-in-a-bottle agitation, but didn't try to speak. She didn't have to. The word alone—*oathbind*—was enough.

***

"Nice try, pal, but no dice," Greg said. "Strictly freelance."

The response came automatically, one used on the infrequent occasions he'd been offered a more permanent arrangement by a supplier or distributor. Too often, their fingers dipped into a bunch of other pies beyond prescription medicine, and he had no interest in running the bad stuff. No coke, no meth, no heroin.

Or the dubious stuff. No weapons. No exotic endangered animal parts. Let alone, people parts. Someone shows up with a kidney on ice in a cooler, obtained who-knows-how? Yeah, no thanks. For that matter, he wasn't big on entire animals or people, either.

He might like Jason Statham movies as much as the next guy, but his transporter rules were on the stricter side. When he did move live cargo, it tended to be reuniting a lost or stolen pet with its person, helping someone escape an abusive situation, bringing remorseful runaways home. That kind of thing. The more do-gooder kind of thing.

Maybe it still didn't make him anything like a hero, but it let him feel okay about himself. Maybe no hero, maybe even a criminal as Zilch had said—fine, forget the maybe, but the laws could be more hurtful and stupid than they were worth. Maybe, technically, a vigilante of sorts, though that sounded a lot more romantic than his life tended to get. Just, not a villain. Not a bad guy.

And what was this run of thought as he stood here damn near literally dealing with a devil?

Greg shook some sense back into his head. Angels and devils, bat-winged imps, maimed tourists all around him…

and he was philosophizing over his morality scores?

"If," said Zilch, steepling his cloven hoof-nailed fingers, "you will…not. Then. We. Have a. Problem."

"This is where you threaten me," Greg said. Continuing to bluff his ass off, playing cards of random value in a high-stakes game to which he didn't know the rules. "But you'd rather not."

"An…unbound…warlock…of unknown…abilities..." The satyr drew a deep breath, goatish nostrils flaring.

For some reason, Greg didn't like that deep, sniffing inhale, didn't like it at all. What if Zilch could smell his, uh, warlockiness? What did that even mean in the first place? He recognized the word, of course. Male version of a witch, if he had it right, but it didn't give him much to go on.

"You've got a nice setup here," Greg said. His mind autofilled, *be a real shame if something...happened to it,* then wondered if he watched too many movies. "Even with competition, you don't want to take unnecessary risks."

"Unless. There is. The. Potential. Of immeasurable. Gain." Another sly goat-pupiled glance slid toward the basket.

"No dice," Greg repeated. "The angel's mine. You want her, you've got to go through me."

Shit on toast, he *did* watch too many movies.

He heard the dainty little smack of Ethriel facepalming again.

Of greater concern was the vicious gleam of Zilch's widening grin.

Exposing *teeth.* Yellowed, croggled, strong-looking teeth. *Sharp* teeth. Did goats have sharp teeth?

"Since you…insist," Zilch said,

The workers, armed with shears and pronged rakes, fanned out into a cinematic fight-scene circle, ready to come at him one by one or in choreographed groups. If he was lucky (or unlucky?) Zilch would order them to take him alive—

Instead, Zilch was up from his couch in a sudden bound, hind-hooves thudding the earth.

Despite his obesity and lolling indolence, the satyr moved fast. Damned fast. Although half Greg's height, Zilch had more than triple the width and weight and girth. His stance was part sumo wrestler, part billy-goats-gruff. The horns, for all they might've been stubby, even blunted, looked plenty capable of goring and gouging tender human flesh.

The lowering of his head put those stubby horns at Greg's groin level. And, hooves digging divots, kicking up sprays of dirt, Zilch charged.

***

"Hey!" Greg leap-twisted aside, no Statham move this time but a wild attempt at matador improv.

Buffeted by the nearness of Zilch's rushing bulk, blasted by that rank and musky goatish smell, he did not stick the landing. Far from it. Overbalancing, windmilling his arms, he went headfirst into one of the grape-stomping vats with a pungent, inky-black splat.

A single mouthful, gulped accidentally, and he felt drunker than he ever had in his entire life. The world spun woozily as he righted himself. He clung to the vat's edges, gasping, mushy grape-pulp pasted to his clothes and skin.

"Or," Zilch said, "I could. Trample. You. Under. My. own. Hooves."

The satyr leaped. Higher than it seemed his bulk should allow, with an impressive moment of hang-time affording all within eyeshot a vivid view of his shaggy undercarriage. More than just the purplish tip of what Greg had regretted noticing earlier now protruded from its furry sheath, by now also more than dewy, and more than eager as well. The word 'rampant' sprang to mind and he wished it hadn't.

As Zilch descended, Greg scrambled out of the way, slipping on crushed grapes, splashing in juice, morbidly sure his own squeezings were about to join the batch after all.

A. Rare. Vintage. Indeed. Unbound Warlock wine. Bottle it up!

Something snapped like a blown circuit. Silvery sparks flashed above Greg's eyes. His face tingled. He felt as if he'd been hit in the forehead with an electric fly swatter.

There was a brief, brilliant flare from everywhere and nowhere. The stomping-vat flipped like a tiddlywink, dousing the area with black wine and grapemash.

It took Greg a stunned moment to realize Zilch hadn't flattened him. Hadn't even touched him, as it happened. He'd been hurled one way, the satyr the other. The encircling ring of workers had been knocked off their feet. The imps that hadn't dropped dazed from the sky veered in crazy, disoriented spirals.

Ethriel!

He looked, expecting to see his guardian angel rising from her shattered prison, a fierce vengeful phoenix of heavenly light, haloed in righteousness and ready to unleash divine wrath. Expecting to hear a soaring choir of unearthly voices, golden harps, trilling horns.

Instead, he saw the wicker basket, its makeshift plywood lid still lashed into place, tipped over sideways, jostle-rolling back and forth in herkyjerky frustrated arcs. He heard Ethriel swearing and struggling within, kicking and clawing. The effect was not unlike that of an angry kitten caught in a laundry hamper.

If not Ethriel, then…?

The sigil on his brow blazed silver fire. The medallion on his chest seemed to vibrate with energy. Power suffused him, filled him, overflowed. He felt as if he could do anything, anything!

Okay, for a start, could he get up?

He got up. Stood tall and straight, his previous aching injuries mere distant memories. Spilled wine sluiced from him, rinsing clean away.

If this was warlockery, it scared him shitless.

Some of the workers ran at him, brandishing their pronged rakes and shears. Greg shouted a word in a language he didn't understand. No. Not a word, but a Word. At once, the weapons they held ignited in brilliant magnesium flames. The workers, clearly no strangers to pain, nonetheless shrieked intolerable agony. They tried to cast down the white-hot implements and couldn't.

Then the crisscrossing skeins of barbed wire enwrapping their heads lit up, simultaneously sizzling and contracting. It was steaks on an overheated griddle, hard sear and scorched hair. It was the proverbial hot knife through soft butter, wires digging in, cutting laser-like, slicing into skin and bone.

Had he thought they were already shrieking in intolerable agony? It had been nothing compared to this, as they flailed and jerked like people in the grips of full-blown seizures.

The frenzied death-dance continued until their heads fell apart into numerous irregular wedge-shaped smoking pieces. Even then, their bodies continued to convulse and jitter.

Had *he* done that???

Yes. Yes, he had.

***

Greg surveyed the twitching carnage, the smoldering rake-handles and sunhats and shears. A conflict demolition derby was going on in his mind. Yeah, they'd been trying to kill him…yeah, they were mutilated demon-minions…but they were still *people*!

213

Ordinary (once), innocent (presumably), human people. Tourists. Vacationers. Old guys wanting to play some golf. Young guys wanting to see some bikini action. Middle-aged guys wanting to go fishing, while maybe also wanting to see some bikini action.

Postcards. Margaritas. Souvenirs. Theme parks. All-you-can-eat buffets. They'd had families. Girlfriends. Wives. Kids. Grandkids.

And now, because of him, their brains were oozing out like wedges of freshly-sliced brie cheese.

He was going to faint. He was going to puke.

He better do neither, because the trouble was far from over.

Across from him, Zilch likewise took in the damage. His tail flipped fitfully up and down. He shifted his rotund weight uneasily on his cloven hooves. The earlier purplish, dewy evidence of excitement had retracted into its hairy sheath, the shaggy scrotum drawn defensively tight between his thighs.

The satyr lifted his narrow goat-pupiled gaze to Greg's. If amused condescension tinged with wariness had been in those eyes before, a seething mixture of hate and fear ruled there now.

Tough-talk lines from a dozen movies jockeyed for position in Greg's mind, but he didn't trust himself to try and voice any of them. In his current state, poker face no longer applied. His own eyes probably showed a mix of horror, revulsion, and confusion.

Yes, he had done this…though he had no clue how. Or if he'd be able to do it again. If he could bring himself to do it again.

The surviving workers had retreated, not quite cowering among the wine-presses and vats. Most, after witnessing what happened to their companions, had dropped their shears and rakes. A few seemed to be tugging at the barbed wire wrapping their heads. That had to hurt; in many places, scarred skin and crusted scabs had grown over the metal barbs.

The imps had done more than retreat. The imps had scattered, frantic chittering flocks darting into the vineyard, hiding amid grape-laden bone trellises.

"Ethriel?" Greg called. His voice was not the strongest, but steadier than he'd expected—given he'd been expecting a shaky childish squeak at best, he'd take the uncertain throat-tightness.

The wicker basket had stopped its kitten-in-a-hamper jostling. A pang of icy dread pierced his soul in the forever it took her to answer.

"I'm here. I'm all right."

The icy dread melted. Although his mind still reeled from what he'd done, he felt most of his equilibrium return. He hadn't lost her. Hadn't driven faster than his guardian angel could fly.

Custos Viatorum, he thought, for no real reason. He gripped his medallion briefly between thumb and foreknuckle in the familiar gesture and sure would have liked a few minutes to chat with his grandmother. His grandmother with her weird garden, and her close-mouthedness about the grandfather he'd never known.

Nachtwald, he thought next, recalling Zilch's reaction to the name, recalling various murmurings and whisperings over the years. *Night wood,* it meant, or *night forest.*

Not now.

"Can you get out?" he asked instead.

"There's some kind of spell-lock. I can't break it."

Greg looked at Zilch. "Let her go."

The satyr's lips curled back in a sneer. "Or you…will… destroy…me?"

"What makes you think I won't do that anyway?"

Again, Zilch's nostrils flared as he inhaled a deep,

sniffing breath. "You," he said, "may...be. A. Warlock. But you. Have. Some. Sense…of. Honor."

"What, and I'm supposed to believe *you* do?" Greg laughed, then stifled it quickly because it was a lunatic's laugh. "How about this, then? Oathbind yourself to *me*, and we'll talk."

Ethriel sputtered in shock. Zilch looked offended to the point of fussy dowager outrage. If he'd worn pearls, he would've clutched them.

"That. Is. *Not*. How. It. Works!"

***

"Too bad," Greg said. The lunatic laugh escaped before he could stifle it that time, and he didn't really care. He felt drunk, doubly drunk, drunk on power as much as on black-grape wine.

And Zilch? Zilch was afraid! Afraid of *him*! They might've both been bluffing their butts off, but wouldn't you know, Greg turned out to be holding pocket aces! Or something. His head spun with a not-unpleasant dizziness. The sigil upon his brow pulsated, silver fire in time with his heartbeat.

He looked at the basket in which Ethriel was imprisoned. No. He Looked at it, just as his earlier word had been a Word. He Looked, and he Saw the spell-threads, strings of dark magic like crude goat-hair macrame, weaving in and out of the wicker and around the plywood in a complex pattern of knotwork.

Okay, then.

Extending a hand, he pointed at the basket and made a sharp scissor-snip motion with his fingers. A crisp spark shot up his arm. The spell-threads parted as if cut by invisible blades. The knotwork pattern unraveled into disarray.

"No!" shouted Zilch. "You…cannot!"

"Can, will, and did," Greg said.

A bubble of scintillating heavenly-choir light swelled, streaming through the gaps again in porcupine quills. The basket exploded into wicker confetti. Now Ethriel did rise up, an iridescent phoenix, a shining sylph, tiny but beautiful.

This had gotten epic in a hurry. Never mind Disney classics; they were into Avengers territory, with him as a really unlikely and underdressed Dr. Strange. He needed a cape.

His angel flitted to her customary spot by his shoulder, and together they regarded the cringing satyr.

"Wait," Zilch said, lifting cloven-fingered hands. "Let us…negotiate."

Greg tilted his head, glancing at Ethriel from the corner of his eye. Her expression was anything but cherubic. Hadn't angels carved a bloody swath across Egypt, slaughtering firstborns? You didn't want to piss off an angel. Even a cute little minor-league member of the *Custos Viatorum.*

"We could," he said to Zilch. "Or…"

He curled both fists. If the previous sensation had been of invisible scissor-blades sprouting from the ends of his fingers, this was somewhere between invisible Wolverine claws and scythes. A shimmering glow wove into being around him, Ethriel's doing, a protective armor. Not a cape, but pretty damn cool.

A scatter of goat-pellets shot from beneath Zilch's fear-flippy tail. The satyr turned to run, but barely made it to the first rank of trellises before Greg slashed at the air. Another surge of power blazed hot on his brow. The unseen blades met brief resistance and went through it unhindered.

Slice-slice! Right and left, carving an X. Gaping wounds split Zilch's hairy hide on two vicious diagonals. A bleating scream gave way almost instantly to a gruesome gurgle. His body fell apart into quivering fleshy chunks, wine-dark fluid gushing, greasy suet bubbling.

"Or," Greg continued, "we could scrag your shaggy ass."

Every last imp took to the sky, fleeing in a wheeling bat-winged starling flock. The remaining workers threw themselves flat, pressing their barbed wire faces into the dirt, *grinding* their barbed wire faces into the dirt, groveling so hard it hurt just to see.

"Boo-yah!" Ethriel swooped up and over in a giddy victory loop. She twirled to high-five Greg, then planted a celebratory smooch on the end of his nose—*mwah*! The sensation was champagne poured into a crystal flute stuffed with cotton candy, sweet and sparkling, effervescent, a heady kick. "Take *that*, forces of evil! That's what happens when you fuck with a blessed Nachtwald!"

"Uh, yeah, hey," Greg said, rubbing his nose. "About that..."

She windchimed a rueful giggle. "In front of me the whole time and I didn't even think to check. Must be why your grandmother gave you the amulet in the first place. Once she realized what kind of family she'd married into, no wonder she took up charms of faith and white magic. You've got it all!"

***

"You're going to have to slow down and explain," he said.

"What's to explain?" She mimicked a rough Hagrid-voice. "Yer a warlock, Greg'ry."

"I barely know what that *means*!"

"Look around! Look what you did!" Ethriel indicated the pile of big meaty jigsaw pieces formerly known as Zilch. "You have the Nachtwald bloodline's power—gift, talent, curse, whatever you want to call it—but you're also, thanks to your grandma, protected by the other side. I bet she knew. I bet she saw it in you. Dormant in your dad, probably, and your aunt and cousins. Not so dormant in you. She tried to guard you against it, and it worked...until

218

you came here. This was the catalyst. It woke your power. Uriel's pinfeathers! How did I miss it? Maybe the wine. Did you swallow?"

"Did I...what?" He blinked. *There* was a question unexpected and befuddling to his sodden brain.

"The wine! It happened after you tripped into the vat, remember? Some must've gotten into your mouth."

He nodded, still tasting it, like the ghosts of the dregs of every cask or bottle throughout human history. The saintly and the sinful, sacred wine from monasteries and churches, swilled wine from decadent orgies.

"Some, yeah, a little. Potent stuff. Makes tequila seem tame."

"It's one of the symbolic fundamentals," Ethriel said. "Eating or drinking. Like with the fae, or...or Idunn's apples...or Persephone and the pomegranate...or communion."

"Wait. Wait, wait, wait." He signaled for a time-out. "I'm confused. I'm drunk as fuck. I just chopped a William Shatner goat-devil into pieces with invisible magic swords. I need to get my shit together before any of this is going to make sense."

"Okay. Good point. This isn't the best place to do it, either. We should move on. Keep traveling, gain some distance. We don't want to be here when Zilch comes back."

"Huh? We scragged—"

"He's a demon. He was subcarnated in that form, but—"

"Stop. Too much. Later."

"Right." She hovered in his face, cupping his cheeks in her tiny palms, her limpid anime-eyes peering anxiously into his. "How do you feel?"

"Drunk as fuck," he repeated. "High on power. Half out of my mind. Fairly freaked. Not sure if I'm going to faint, or puke, or what. I killed a bunch of people just now, and that is a far cry from normal."

"Normal doesn't apply. Can you walk? Are you hurt?"

Greg took as much of a mental inventory and roll-call as he could. The injuries from the plane crash were almost a far and faded memory. The spot where he'd been gouged by shears felt tender, but was no longer bleeding. "Good to go," he said. "Or, as good as I'm gonna be, until I sober up."

She guided him past the groveling workers—some of whom had really gotten serious about the face-grinding; smears of blood muddied the ground, curls of scraped-off skin lay crumpled like peeled decals—and through the vineyard, leaving Zilch's winery behind. Each purposeful step in the right direction felt like an improvement. Nobody followed them, unless stealthy imps kept tabs from on high. Or unless the flowers with their multifaceted fly-eye centers transmitted whatever they saw, botanical spy-cams, why not?

They climbed the shallow slope up from the valley, toward a stand of trees that looked far more Florida-ordinary (Flordinary?) than the utero-melon grove, though Greg suspected he was going to be hesitant about accepting anything on appearances for a long, long time.

"What you did back there," Ethriel said, in a way that, for her, seemed oddly hesitant, "when you wouldn't run, wouldn't leave me even though I told you to..."

"I know." He sighed, recalling their earlier conversation. "Dumb."

"Yeah, probably."

"No 'probably' about it."

"*And* noble."

"Really?"

"Really."

"Do I get another celestial star?"

She smooched him again, sweet cotton candy and effervescent champagne. "*All* the celestial stars. Thank you."

19

This whole place was bullshit. The whole idea of coming here had been bullshit. Her parents were bullshit, her (dead) friends were bullshit, this writer weirdo was bullshit, ambulatory tit-women were bullshit, and even her brother was turning out to be bullshit.

Chelsea had had enough. Forget it, okay? Fuck it, okay? Game-fucking-over. She wanted to be at some trendy beach hotspot instead, with happy hour appetizers and frozen rum-a-rita concoctions. She wanted live music, guys buying her drinks, maybe a threesome with a couple of hunky fratboys.

But what was she doing instead?

Trudging around to the back of the weirdo writer's cabin to see what he and Trevor were up to, because they were sure as shit taking their time. For all she knew, Trevor might have become an involuntary movie star—mutilation scene, wasn't that what the writer had said? Okay, maybe he was bullshit and maybe deserved it, but he was still her brother, and as bad as it was being stuck in this infernal shithole, it'd be worse to be stuck in this infernal shithole alone.

The agonized wailing from the shed did *not* help. She dashed toward the open door, then stopped as she heard Trev's voice, raised to converse above the volume of those tortured cries.

"—arms and legs off?"

"Supposedly, it's easier to take care of them this way,"

the writer replied. "Keeps them from trying to go anywhere, makes them lighter weight to move around, and so on."

"Freaky."

"I'm told the fellow who perfected the technique would also perform a lobotomy, scramble the brains so they don't know what's happening to them, but that won't work for this. Well, it'd probably *work*; even a mindless grub feels *some* pain, but it'd be much less efficient."

Chelsea crept to the edge of the doorway and peeked in. A single lightbulb dimly illuminated the shed's interior, its walls lined with shelves of tools and paint cans and assorted junk. In one corner squatted a generator that could've come straight from Home Depot, except for modifications like a witch doctor and a mad scientist had gone crazy together. Sporadic yellow-black sparks crackled along wires leading from the generator to a metal and sinew skullcap clamped to the head of...

...of a naked, filthy, spasming torso in an elevated wooden trough. A thirty-something man's torso, fit gone slack, tan gone pale, unwashed junk bobbling atop bushy pubes, castaway-style hair and beard. Ugly gnarls of scar tissue at shoulders and hips showed where his limbs had been removed, stitched-shut eyelids drooped over sunken hollows where his eyes had once been.

In addition to the wire-snaky metal and sinew skullcap affair, several needles pierced his flesh...serrated alligator clips pinched his scabbed and blood-crusted nipples as well as his ears, nose, tongue, and lips...a rash of tiny blistering welts covered most of his skin...

"So, his pain is what juices the genny?" Trevor asked. "That's what runs your fridge and your lights and everything? The more he suffers, the more energy he gives off?"

"Pretty much." The writer took an old coffee can from one of the cluttered shelves, popped the lid, and dumped a measure of its contents—vivid diablo-orange stinging ants—over the torso's belly. They immediately dug in, raising more angry welts.

The groaning wails spiked to sheer screams. He jerked and jolted like an epileptic in the trough. Piss squirt-dribbled from his dick into a strategically-placed bucket below. The yellow-black sparks intensified, snapping louder, sputtering brighter.

Trevor only flinched a little, his tone more fascinated than repulsed. "When Lester said he could hook us up, at the lakehouse...he meant installing one of these?"

"Oh, sure. Agonicity adaptors can be fitted to about any appliance. Can charge batteries, too. Comes in handy."

"I bet. Where do you get the, uh, materials?"

The writer re-lidded and replaced the ant can. "Outsiders, mostly. Tourists, trespassers. Or, sometimes, people just sacrifice their own."

***

Energy through torture, pain-power! Suffering human batteries as a renewable resource, and what would the liberal agenda make of that? No more coal and oil, not even wind farms and solar panels...never mind going green, how about going agonicity red?

"Awesome," Trevor said. "Sincerely, too cool."

The way the dude's torso bucked and jerked was hilarious. So were his inarticulate cries, the way wrinkled folds of eyelids sagged where eyes used to be, and the way his dick and balls flopped around.

Totally helpless and vulnerable, too. He had to have gone bugfuck insane after being hooked up to this generator gizmo for who-knew-how-long, yet was still with it enough to feel whatever new abuse got inflicted.

Hell, maybe after a while he'd grown to like it. Late-onset masochism, why not? When the only sensation in your whole world was pain, wouldn't you develop a taste for it sooner or later?

Best of all, though, were the four scarred-over stumps, looking like the tied-off ends of pork roasts. The job maybe hadn't been done at any surgical professional level, but was far less amateurish than the hack-and-slash Trevor had attempted on Andy's leg with the butcher knife.

What had been used here? An ax? A chainsaw? He imagined the steely whir of a circular saw blade being lowered, the first hot misting spray of blood as it cut, the grinding chug through meat and shuddering screech hitting bone—

For some bizarre reason, it turned him on. Even more than seeing Jubblies in all her bountiful boobedness. Sure, there was something to be said about being able to tittyfuck for days, but compared to the mental image of a severed limb smacking the floor in a crimson arterial shower…

Memories rushed into his mind out of nowhere: a desperate childhood crush on a hot babysitter who'd lost her arm at the elbow after a motorcycle accident, the time the new gardener tried to dislodge a rock from the lawnmower's spinning underside without turning it off first, the ex-Marine male underwear model with a high-tech cyberleg from mid-thigh down, Jessica Lange's AHS Freakshow GILF strapping on her wooden legs sexier than some women donned stockings, the Evil Dead guy's hammy over-acting as he cut off his own hand, a wheelchair-bound redhead he'd seen in passing at a train station whose tender pink stumps unexpectedly guest-starred in his wank-sessions for weeks after…

Well, shit. Of all the times to discover he had a fetish. A sick one, at that. An amputation fetish. Great.

Trevor forced himself to look away from the torso in the trough, willing his burgeoning erection to settle down and wondering if being turned on like this made him some kind of sociopath. "What, uh, what did you do with the rest of him? His, uh, dismembered bits?"

"Ah, the Riggers boys took those as their fee for hooking it all up," the writer said, fiddling with switches on the generator. "The eyes went to one of the warlocks, I forget who. Nothing much goes to waste around here, I can tell you."

Obvious follow-ups came to mind but he dismissed them, thinking in particular of the tasty sandwich he'd enjoyed on the deck, packed with juicy slices of deli-fresh meat. Probably best not to ask. Probably, he didn't want to know.

It'd been good, though. Tangy and flavorful.

They left the shed, the writer pausing long enough to hook the padlock's arm through the clasp, not bothering to actually lock it, just hold the door closed and muffle some of the noise.

Another outbuilding—a long, low, windowless prefab of the sort Trev associated with 'temporary' classrooms at public schools—sat further back behind the cabin. Its interior was a chaos of cameras, mikes, lighting, backdrops, furniture, costume racks, equipment, and props. Anything from sex-dungeon to evil asylum, from torture chamber to sitcom suburb, could be thrown together.

"And here," said the writer, beaming with pride, "is where the magic happens."

***

Her brother was getting *way* too into this sick shit.

What happened to leaving? Finding a ride out of here? Sayonara, fucked-up Lake Misquamicus!

Instead, Trevor had spent the past couple of hours— hours!—in the writer's movie studio. Watching. Helping. Making 'magic' happen.

The fact that most of the 'magic' happened by way of special effects wasn't a whole lot of consolation. Chelsea knew sick shit when she saw it, and this was some sick, sick shit.

Special effects way too realistic, even. Okay, the bodies weren't actually alive, but they bled, but they twitched and flinched, but they struggled. Maybe they didn't feel pain, as opposed to that poor doomed torso dude hooked up to the generator, but it sure looked like they did. Sounded like they did.

"You mean, you don't use real people?" Trevor had asked. Crestfallen Doge, such disappoint, very letdown, wow.

The writer, weird old bastard though he may have been, seemed a little shocked by that. "Of course not. I do movies, not snuff films."

Then they'd gotten into a long discussion on the differences between Homunculi, Golems, Manikins, and Chelsea didn't know or care what the fuck else. As with the idea of sexbots, there was just something extra creepy about it…creating these artificial men and women— mostly women, duh—to film being raped and tortured and mutilated…and murdered…in extremely vivid, lifelike detail…

And there, in the thick of it, her brother. Who hadn't been content on the sidelines for long, or behind the camera. Who'd volunteered to play dress-up and get his hands dirty.

Really dirty.

"The hatchet's good, but what about a hacksaw?" he suggested at one point. "Instead of a single hack-chop, cutting her hand off nice and slow?"

"We can try both," the writer said. "See which works better."

Not wanting her to feel left out, they offered Chelsea the chance to join in. Put on a psycho mask, a slutty nun's habit or Silent Hill nurse's outfit, a werewolf costume, whatever she liked. There were plenty of tools to choose from. Scalpels, machetes, whips, branding irons...not to mention enough dildos, nipple clamps, butt plugs, and strap-ons to stock a sex shop.

"Yeah *no*," Chelsea said. "What about going to the bar? Seeing if anyone there will give us a ride to the nearest checkpoint? The plan, Trevor? Remember?"

"I know, I know, but why the big rush?"

"Why the big rush...?"

"We've got all week. Isn't as if Kayla, Andy, and Madison are going to complain."

"Because they're *dead*, hel*lo*! And our house isn't a house, and a giant turtle raped our car, and this whole place is not right!"

"But you have to admit, it's sure not boring. Beats the shit out of yet another same old Spring Break."

"Are you enjoying yourself, Trev? Is that it? Having fun helping this sick fuck carve up girls?"

"Fake girls!" he and the sick fuck said together, as, behind them knelt a chained redhead, freckled and naked, with both arms secured to a bloodstained, blade-marked butcher's block.

Something in her expression must have let Trevor know Chelsea was at her absolute push-your-luck limit, because he made with a dramatic long-suffering sigh and handed the hacksaw to the writer.

"Okay, okay," he said. "We'll go over to the bar, see what's what, see if we can make some arrangements. Okay?"

"Okay. Yes. Good. Great."

She waited with undisguised foot-tapping impatience as he changed back to regular clothes, said his goodbyes to the writer, thanked him again for the sandwiches and beer, and thought of all the times their mother had nearly lost her

227

shit when dawdling drag-asses failed to appreciate that a reservation didn't mean showing up whenever the hell you felt like it.

Finally, though, they were on their way, walking in the slaughterhouse furnace glow of a horrible sunset.

"Christ on a yo-yo, Chels," Trevor said. "You need to relax. We're on vacation."

20

"I'm Lorlinda," the girl said, still holding Andy in front of her face. "Lorlinda Bodean. This's my cousin, Heck. Well, we calls each other cousin but it's a tetch more complercated than that. His momma and mine're sisters whose own daddy was like as not their grandpa…an' as for our own daddies, no way t' tell really; so yeah, complercated like I said."

"Pope's nuts, Lorlinda, you got to give him the whole blessin' geneology just t' say hi?" Heck put in.

"I'se tryin' t' be sociable! We don't often get no-one new t' talk to!"

"Yeah, well, whatever." He drove on, the frankentruck rumbling over gravel with lakeside hellgrowth crowding in on both sides.

"Don't mind him none." Lorlinda smiled in at Andy. "You'se lucky we happen'd by whens we did. Catch would'a made a meal outta you fer sure."

Andy tried, with what limited gestures he seemed capable of in the strange encapsulated ball, to indicate his gratitude. Whatever might be next, it had to be better than ending up dinner. Lorlinda seemed friendly enough, not to mention gorgeous. Things certainly could have been be worse.

"Aww, ain'tchoo sweet!" She blew him another kiss, then giggled. "Kinda cute, too."

Heck snorted and muttered under his breath.

"Wish you could talk in there an' tell me yer name," Lorlinda went on. "Bet you gots a lots o' questions."

Andy did his best to nod emphatically, indicating himself and doing a stupid mime-in-a-box routine he immediately regrets, but hoped would convey his meaning.

"Wonderin' about what you'se stuck in?"

Again, he nodded.

"Well, it's hard t' explain since I don't know the science an' all, but, when your physercal body ended up all dead-like, your spirit-part—y'know, soul—normally would'a gone inta some other critter. Onlies, you died right under the Catch's tree, so, instead, you ended up caught in her web. Kind of cocooned, t' save for later, until the Catch hungried up. She'd pop her fangs in there an' drink you like a Capri Sun."

"After which," Heck said, "you'd spend a thousand years or so in the Catch's guts bein' digested, and after that, prob'ly turn into a chitin-mite on her carapace or somethin'."

"Here, lemme show you." Lorlinda rotated and lifted Andy with one hand while folding down the passenger side sunvisor. It was cracked and split and mended with duct tape, and when she slid open a little panel, the mirror revealed was grimy. She wiped a clean-ish patch with her thumb, then held him up to it.

He peered through fisheye distortion and murky glass, and yeah, it was like being a bug in amber…a coin-machine novelty in one of those plastic bubble-capsules…inside a lightbulb or snowglobe or Christmas ornament bauble… immersed or suspended in some semi-solid substance. He could move, sort of, but with a thick gelatinous resistance that made him think of old Mythbusters episodes where the guy tried to swim in syrup or cornstarch glop.

It *was* him, though. A miniature maybe two-inch-high version of himself. Not looking dead or even injured, no mangled skull or gory rotted leg, just regular Andy, the same as when he'd woken up that morning.

Naked. Shit. Totally bareass in all his scrawny, gangly

lack of glory. He blushed and did the awkward knee-tuck and arm-cross. Not that it really mattered when he was the size of a toy; she'd need a magnifying glass or microscope to see anything. But still.

Lorlinda laughed. It wasn't a mean-girl laugh in the slightest. "Now don'tchoo fret none on my account, sugar. I'se seen nekkid men a'plenty, b'leeve you me."

"Ain't that the truth," Heck said.

"Don't mind him none, neither." She turned the bauble around again and leaned confidingly close as if to share a secret just between her and Andy, despite Heck sitting right beside her. "He's jist the jealous type 'cause he's been tryin' t' get inta my pants since I'se ten years old."

***

"I ain't not been tryin' t' get inta yer pants since you was ten!" Heck Bodean protested. "That is a lie, a stone-cold lie!"

"Thirteen, then," Lorlinda said.

"Damn right. I ain't no pedder-file!"

"Well saw-*reee*!" She did an extravagant eyeroll, then winked at Andy. "I never let him, though. Promised my momma I wouldn't."

"Your momma's a 'shine-addled idjit," Heck grumbled.

"So's yours."

"Mebbe so, but she din't go tellin' me wheres I could an' couldn't stick m'dick."

During this enlightening chat, the frankentruck continued navigating the rough and rutted backroads. The ground had gotten swampier, the tires splashing through puddles like open wounds or rumbling over crude log bridges. Horned mosquitoes the size of hummingbirds buzzed the windows, sometimes splatting in red smears. Sullen embers, presumably fireflies, floated and bloated in the humid shadows. A twenty-foot-long leech/snake thing with a lamprey's suckermouth reared up, slimy body cobra-swaying, pinwheel eyes swirling Futurama Hypno-Toad style.

They passed derelict shacks up on stilts, a few clearly still occupied despite their condition. Laundry hung limp from clotheslines, washtubs and washboards nearby. An elderly couple rocked in tandem in creaky bentwood rockers out on a creaky plank porch. The man puffed at an actual corncob pipe. The woman held what was either a possum, or the world's ugliest cat, in her lap.

It reminded Andy of someplace, and after a moment, he got it it…the start of the Pirates of the Caribbean ride, cruising through the serene bayou before flume-dropping into yo-ho-yo-ho caverns.

Except, he was pretty sure none of the Disney parks featured a pack of droopy-diapered mutant cyclops kids with misshapen heads playing by the side of the road, or a female version of Jabba the Hutt lolling grotesquely obese and flab-breasted in a scum-coated oily pool, or brawny creatures with tusked bristling boar-snouts grunting as they snuffle-rooted through the torn-open cavities of eviscerated corpses.

"Almost there," Heck said, voice and expression grim, as if bracing for an unpleasant task. "You take in his groceries, while I—"

"I sure as Satan will *not!*"

"Cross and bless it, Lorlinda—"

"Nuh-unh, no way. I'se tole you what happened last time."

"Well, you think *I* wanna see him like that? He gets worse when it's me, you know it's true."

"Too bad. He's *your* brother."

"He might be yours, too."

"I don't give a saint's fart. *You* take him his heaven-sent groceries."

"Aw, c'mon, Lor," he wheedled.

They arrived at an overgrown yard strewn with rusted

and busted redneck detritus—car parts, machinery, farm equipment, appliances, scrap lumber, old tires. At the center of it sat a swaybacked trailer that might've been new in the 70's and hadn't aged well.

"I'mma wait right here," she said firmly. "Or you best plans on findin' another gal t' take t' the Hock Parties from now on."

Heck heaved a monumental sigh, turned off the engine, and got out. Going around to the back of the truck, he began unlatching cargo compartments.

"It's fer Zeke," Lorlinda told Andy. "Heck near to idolized him when's they was growin' up, but he ain't never been the same after AllHell's. Lives out here alone, a real ree-cluse, like."

Arms laden with bags and boxes, Heck made his way up the trailer's rickety steps to bang on the door with his boot toe.

"See, that Roman general feller, the one what come out of the lake that day? Bent poor Zeke over a pool table an' popped his ass-cherry in front of all'n sundry." She glanced at the trailer. "Way I hears it, they say he got a hard-on while the general was plowin' his back forty, and was so 'shamed he ain't hardly showed his face since't."

It was probably just as well Andy couldn't talk, since he had no idea what he would have said.

Lorlinda, meanwhile, giggled. "Is it bad I kinda wish I'd been there t' see it? Why, the very idear gets me wetter'n rainy season!"

***

Yeah, definitely for the best he couldn't talk.

"In fact," Lorlinda went on, her giggle turning wicked, "I wouldn't mind none doin' somethin' about it righ' now. Heck did say I could diddle m'self for all he cared. Sounds

233

a fine plan t'me, dontcha think? An' you, sugar, you c'n help!"

Help? Andy was the size of a LEGO mini-fig in a plastic bubble, how the hell was he supposed to—

A moment later, he understood, as Lorlinda lowered him into her lap. With one thumb, she hiked aside the frayed crotch of her cut-offs, revealing no panties and a plump little pussy fringed with soft, fleecy curls.

She was pretty wet, all right, Andy saw. Saw in great detail. Saw in extreme close-up as two fingers parted her labia. Moist folds, the sweet pinkness of a strawberry shake, pouted like tender petals.

"Unless'n you erbject?" she asked, briefly lifting him again to peer in, cute brow creased with worry. "I wouldn't want ter take advantage."

Andy indicated by every pantomime at his disposal that he didn't object.

Lorlinda beamed. "Ain't you a darlin!" She kissed the pod, and licked it, running her tongue over its surface, slicking it with saliva. Then she lowered it again and slid its lubed smooth roundness along her sweet pink cleft.

He'd had some pretty weird experiences, usually while wrecked, but this one took the cake. It reminded him of an x-rated version of those cartoons where someone got shrunk to microscopic size and went on an inside tour of someone else's anatomy…Futurama had done that one, and the crazy frizzy-haired chick with the schoolbus…only those hadn't been nearly so…gynecological.

Slippery flesh parted around the pod's clear, glassy curve as Lorlinda glided the pod up and down in slow strokes, feather-light alternating with firmer pressure, teasing herself with occasional circlings of her rosebud clit.

"Oooh, sugar," she sighed, slouching in the passenger seat with hips tilted and thighs wide. "Oooh, that feels niiiice!"

Andy himself couldn't feel much of anything, except for a vague warmth, and the rocking-rolling motion. He didn't care. This was crazy and he loved it, was fascinated by watching the flex and clasp of her quivering tissues enfolding the pod. He was in a submersible, exploring strange oceans. He was in a bubble-domed spaceship, cruising the mysteries of a swirling pink nebula.

Cooing and crooning in pleasure, Lorlinda picked up the pace with her peculiar sex-toy. She eased it partway inside, drew it back out, rolled it directly over her clit—the nub of nerve-endings was fully Andy's size, and he wished he could touch it…though, in a way, he was.

His limited, gelatinous ability to move allowed him to finally wrap a hand around his hard-on. Minuscule by comparison, maybe, but to him it felt like the biggest and stiffest he'd ever achieved.

The other hand, he pushed against the pod wall's inside curve, so that it at least looked as if he were massaging that giant clitoris. Lorlinda's gasps and quickening breath added to the illusion of active participation.

"I'm a'gonna cum, sugar," she panted. "Feels so good, gonna…oh yeah…here it is…here we…ooooooohh!"

Her hips bucked. Sweet, wet pinkness convulsed around him. Her clit pulsed like a huge heart. He had a moment to wonder if the pod would hold, or if it'd give way, if she'd crush him flat, the submersible imploding…and didn't care about that, either. This was the epicenter of an orgasmic earthquake and he would ride it out if it killed him.

At the height of her climax, she sank the pod fully into her vaginal canal, and Andy was immersed in sudden red-veined throbbing darkness. Lorlinda's ecstatic cries, now somewhat muffled, hit a crescendo before trailing off into a long, low, satisfied moan.

"Oh, sugar," she said huskily. "Oh, that was deee-vine."

***

A split-second later, Lorlinda shrieked, vaulting upright with a lunge that shot Andy's pod out of her like a squeezed watermelon seed, or those videos of strippers popping ping-pong balls from their pussies.

The next thing he knew, he was wobbling and rolling around on the floor of the frankentruck's passenger side footwell, amid empty beer cans and cigarette packs and road-litter.

Meanwhile, Lorlinda was hollering out the window, letting Heck have it up one side and down the other.

"—be mindin' yer own bizn's, not creepin' up fer a peek, spyn' on me when I'se practic'ly yer sister! An' put that sorry excuse fer a dingus away, Heck Bodean, yer disgustin', ain't nobody wanna see ya floggin' the bishop right out in public!"

"Well, saint's sakes, what about what *you* was doin'?" Heck yelled back. "Right out in public y'self, even!"

"That's differnt! I was here in the truck where's no one was lookin'! No one 'cept *you*, ya pervert!"

"It's *my* truck!"

The harangues continued as Andy tried to more-or-less orient himself. His pod, smeared with copious vaginal secretions, had also picked up a sticky coating of dirt, grit, and tobacco. Visibility was, to say the least, somewhat obscured.

Which, he decided, was not so bad…he couldn't exactly put his sorry excuse for a dingus away, but no one had seen him flogging the bishop…

"I'se *sawry*, awright?" Heck finally said. "C'n we jist drop it a'ready? Eve's tits, ya ain't gotta be s' blessed tetchy."

"I ain't no such thing," huffed Lorlinda. She leaned down into the footwell. "Sugarbun, where you at?"

"Sure you din't lose him up there? He ain't stuck?"

"Think I would know!"

"As if; pro'lly got the Port Miami Tunnel in yer pants."

"Which you'll sure as Satan never find out!" A bit of shuffling and rummaging later, she went, "aha!" and brought Andy's pod up from the debris, then tutted when she saw the state of it. "Need t' rinse y' off, sugar. Heck, lemme have one o' them waters."

A sluicing from a water bottle and a brisk toweling with a scrap of cloth later, and visibility was restored. Lorlinda smiled and blew him another kiss. Andy did his best to wave, wondering how badly he was blushing.

"Zeke's not so well, in case ya care," Heck said as he started the engine. "Seems t' b'lieve a storm's brewin', hurricane or some other big disaster, worse'n we ever seen."

"What could be worse'n AllHell?" scoffed Lorlinda. "He's outta his head anyways."

"I guess. Worried 'bout him, though. He looks bad. Real bad."

"He din't look good t' start with."

"What I'm sayin'. Mebbe we should stay, keep an eye on him."

"Cross-an'-bless that," she said. "You come back if'n you want, but take me home first."

Heck turned to look at the trailer, which remained shut up tight. Zeke had not emerged despite the shouting, must just be hunkered down with his groceries. Exhaling, Heck put them in gear. "Later," he said. "Still got a load o' 'shine t' deliver, and I don' wanna miss the Hock Party."

As he retraced the road's winding course, past swamp-shacks on stilts, the snuffling boar-creatures, the diapered cyclops kids, and other scenic backwoods backwater sights, Lorlinda idly toyed with Andy's pod, dandling it along her neck and cleavage.

"So, you two goin' steady now?" asked Heck, dripping sarcasm.

"Don' listen to him none, sugar. I tol' you, he's jist jealous."

What Andy wanted was to ask about this Hock Party; it was the second time it'd been mentioned. Pantomime and charades were not going to cut it, though.

Soon, they were to the main lake road again, following the shoreline's curve past a huge ugly rearing boulder, then a beach and parking lot, then more woods with occasional branching-off gravel driveways.

"Well, baptize me," said Heck, amused. "Lookee here. Found us some hitchhikers!"

The truck rumbled to a stop, and there stood Chelsea and Trevor Carmichael.

21

"I…" June began, then just gave up. There were no words. Well, there were words, but not words she felt like wasting on this scene.

Signs of the undead massacre Ramon had described were indeed in evidence, headshot and gutshot rotting corpses strewn hither and yon. But, there by the firepit, sat her mother and the Shinns as if they hadn't a care in the world. Chatting, relaxing, and making s'mores. Making goddamn *s'mores*!

Worse yet, another vehicle was parked near the Holy Roller, some sort of cross between a military ATV and a souped-up golf cart…and its obvious driver, none other than the female guard from Checkpoint Gabriel, leaned casually against one of the picnic tables, drinking beers with Crusader Markane. It was what's-her-name, Sanchez or whatever. Their posture, body language, and laughter suggested they were getting along *very* well.

"What is this?" cried Ramon. "Are you serious?"

Five heads snapped around to look at them. Five faces displayed astonishment, and no wonder. Ramon looked like someone had put him through a meat grinder followed by a barbecue; June could only imagine the sight she herself made, in her apocalyptic wasteland couture, wild-eyed, toting her shotgun.

Margaret Goldsmith clapped a palm to her bosom. "My God, June!" Bits of graham cracker flew from her chocolate-smudged mouth.

239

Moments later, June and Ramon were at the center of a circle, being bombarded by questions, everyone talking at once until Crusader Markane raised his voice in a stern call for silence. His gaze swept over them, past them, back to them.

"Where are the others?" he asked.

"Dead," Ramon said, and burst into tears. "Dead, man, they're all dead, and..." He held out the Fourth of July ruins of his hand. "I'm a wreck, and you're here having a... having a party?!"

"Dead?" Markane shook his head in disbelief. "Brother Lucas?"

"Dead!" June shouted. "Dead and gone, possessed, slaughtered, taken to Hell! Him and the Gabelmans and David too! While you're kicking back drinking *beer!* Making *s'mores*! And what's *she* doing here?"

Then everyone was talking at once again, protests and denials, accusations, queries, demands. How did it happen, were they sure they were dead? Even Brother Lucas? Maybe they were mistaken. June's mother wanted to know what in the *world* she thought she was *doing*, going around dressed like that. Mrs. Shinn couldn't believe it, not the Gabelmans, such a goodly pious couple, not David, such a nice boy, so polite. What about Brother William, had they seen him? He didn't seem like a man who'd up and desert his post. Creek-freaks? What were creek-freaks? A demon's skull? Brother Lucas almost did *what* to Sister June?

Oh and at that piece of news, didn't her mother nearly faint on the spot! Then recovered, and muttered something under her breath—what? Something about too bad not getting a taste of big black cock after all must be so disappointed? *What?!?*

Before June could confront her—maybe she'd misheard or imagined, but she didn't think so!—Ramon passed out from the shock and pain of his injuries. It broke the chaos a second time, giving Crusader Markane another chance to restore order.

Shoving aside bags of chips and hot-dog buns, they slung Ramon's unconscious body onto one of the picnic tables. First aid kits were fetched from the footlockers, though as far as she knew, most standard store-bought first aid kits didn't routinely include syringes of morphine.

The female guard—Corporal Garcia, not Sanchez, though Markane referred to her far too companionably as 'Sister Anna'—proved an adequate combat medic. Soon, Ramon was, if not resting comfortably, at least drugged to the gills, gooped with ointment, and so swaddled in gauze he resembled the Invisible Man.

"He needs a hospital," Mrs. Shinn said.

"Or a miracle," Mr. Shinn added.

"Oh, yeah, let's pray for him!" June didn't even try to hide her sarcasm. "Worked so well for Mrs. Gabelman, didn't it? You fucking idiots!"

***

"June Esther *Goldsmith*!" gasped her mother.

Yes, thank you, tell the whole world what you saddled me with as a middle name, why don't you? Which you only did anyway in hopes of currying favor with your great-aunt, the old bat, and did she reward us in her will like you wanted? Ha!

The Shinns overlapped each other. "There is no call for such lang—"/"Don't you speak to my hus—"

Shut up, oh shut up, you pompous windbags, and what happened to all that previous grumbling about libtards and lesbians and feminazis once this bitch Garcia rolled in? No, you were too busy congratulating yourselves on being mighty zombie slayers and making goddamn *s'mores*!

"Now's not the time to lose your faith—"

241

And *you*, Markane, this was *your* stupid idea in the first place, bringing us here like it was nothing more than leafleting the shopping center parking lot! Now Lucas is dead, three times the man you'll ever be, and you're swilling beers with your precious 'Sister Anna' and haven't even bothered to ask if I'm okay, so fuck you too!

Dear Lord, she was going to scream. She thought of the shotgun, how she'd handled it with such natural ease and skill. How, for a little while there, she'd felt kind of badass, a tough chick, a warrior. But now, here she was again, just the same plain June *Esther* Goldsmith, dried-up virgin old maid, in this ridiculous outfit of rags and scraps!

Clenching her fists, she spun away before any more of her thoughts went spewing from her mouth. Or before she just unslung the shotgun and let it do the talking, a few thunderous final expletives to end this fucked-up day.

"Okay, look," Garcia said, as if *she* were the one to get things back on track and under control. "You've all been through a lot today. Everyone's under a lot of stress. But let's not fall apart."

Markane agreed as if this were some brilliant jewel of wisdom. "Yes, yes of course. More than ever, we must stick together. What's important is keeping everyone safe. It may be too late for the others, but the rest of us are alive… though Ramon needs immediate help. Anna, where is the nearest hospital?"

"Too far."

"Local doctor?"

Her scoffing snort was answer enough.

"Can't you call in a helicopter?" asked Mr. Shinn. "Evac us?"

"Not from here. Maybe back at Gabriel, though I don't know how long it would take."

"Well, there's got to be something!" shrilled Mrs. Shinn.

"We did get a transmission shortly after you came in.

A special op of some kind, a military convoy, top brass planning to go through over at Nazareth. They're bound to have a medical team with them. A mobile surgical unit, if we're lucky. Either way, it'll be better than we can do with a first aid kit." Garcia paused, and June didn't have to turn to know she was giving Markane a wry look. "Wherever you got those, which, I'm guessing, is the same place you got the rest of your..."

"Faith," he replied, no doubt with a wry look of his own. "Armed and armored with faith, Sister."

"In the form of grenades and bulletproof vests."

"The Lord provides."

"Yeah. How about the Lord provides another beer while we load your people up and get this show on the road?"

"You heard her," Markane said. "Grab only what you need. Don't bother striking camp."

"But, the tents, the brand-new gear—" protested Mr. Shinn.

"You heard *me,* Brother. Unless you'd rather stay, keep an eye on things here, until—"

"No, no, you're right, don't bother, grab only what we need."

June felt a familiar not-quite-pinching grip take her arm, just above the elbow. "Come along, Junie," her mother said, in a tone of forced brightness...then added, in a hiss, "And, for God's sake, put some clothes on!"

22

The prototype was, in form, no crude manlike brute such as those geas-bound to Favius. No, this was a mighty-thewed brother of Adonis, the strong-man power-fantasy sculpted ideal.

It measured fully twelve feet tall, meticulously molded of pure Georgia-sourced clay. Absurd amounts of detail had gone into its fashioning. Its face was a god's in repose, chiseled of jaw, cleft of chin, noble of brow. They'd even given it the semblance of hair, eyes, and teeth.

"We want him to look good," one of the designers had said, when Favius asked why this was deemed necessary. "We want our nation's enemies not only afraid, but jealous, intimidated, and impressed."

Favius also pointed out that the visual definition of musculature had no effect on a Golem's abilities. Strictly speaking, it did not *need* 'pecs' and 'six-pack abs' and the rest. Strictly speaking, its mighty chest had no need of nipples, its washboard belly no need of a navel.

"We want him to be anatomically correct," another of the designers had said, and shown Favius a marathon of manly-man movies to prove the point. Superheroes and action heroes, even 'historical' epics quite a far cry from his actual memories of Rome, Egypt, and Greece.

Anatomically correct, yet they'd given the Golem a phallus to make war-elephants and Grand Dukes insecure.

Trying once more, in the interest of accuracy, Favius explained how, in his era, depictions of Priapus were meant as a joke, the enormous swinging cock for comedic effect. This, too, fell on deaf ears.

At that, he'd shrugged and left them to do as they willed. Let it not be said he hadn't made an effort to help. The generals and senators wanted a massively-endowed Ameri-Golem, a massively-endowed Ameri-Golem they got. So it was and so let it be.

After all, what were *friends* for?

Friends.

As if Favius wouldn't have peeled the skin from their bodies and rolled the resulting rawness of flayed meat in coarse salt until every nerve ending screamed with white-hot fire! As if he wouldn't have tortured them, slaughtered them, lain waste to their entire families!

The whispers in his mind, the whispers of the lake, grew ever-clearer with each mile. A familiar home-sense suffused him, as if sinking into a heated bath of fresh infant's blood—a pleasure he had been denied, accommodating though his 'captors' were...but Favius did not begrudge them; he'd rarely been able to afford it on his salary to begin with. The bath-houses of Hell did not run cheap.

Some of the soldiers had the occasional temerity to grumble, impatient with the convoy's progress. Which apparently was, by their modern standards, both slow and uncomfortable.

Hah! They should have tried it when a day's travel was set by a marching legion! Let them feel the hard stones through their sandals, the sun hot on their helms. Let them breathe road-dust, carrying not only their gear but possessions and provisions upon their backs!

Were he their commander, he'd have had them all whipped. And perhaps taught them the true meaning of decimation into the bargain.

Instead, he rode and said nothing, turning his thoughts

ahead to what would come next. To when his work would really begin.

During his educational 'captivity,' he'd been afforded many opportunities to study maps of what had once been Lake Misquamicus. He knew the locations of the six checkpoints, and the course of the wall. He saw regular reports, including infrequent correspondence. The gangly youth, Spot, seemed to have taken well to his role as Favius's thrall, clearly glad for the chance to wield power for a change.

He knew also that which was not shown on any map, saving the one in his head...of the six anchor-points, holding fast and firm, sunk to the bedrock like talons deep into bone, lines of dark magic strung taut between them.

To have one suddenly vanish, snuffed out in a single violent heartbeat, came as a very unexpected and nasty shock.

***

They'd crossed at Checkpoint Nazareth, of the six the largest, the most militaristic and secure. It was also the closest to the spot where Favius had been taken 'captive,' as well as where he'd come ashore, and fairly near to the public house called Crawdaddy's where his sworn thrall remained stationed.

Nazareth would make a most formidable fortress. The others might need work, especially with one of the anchor-points eliminated. He had not anticipated that possibility. Would the rest hold? Would the magic be sufficient? A more powerful ritual than he'd planned might be required to attain his glorious ultimate goal.

His palm itched for the worn leather hilt of his gladius. Its blade thirsted for hot, fresh blood. The three Golems sat quiescent, obedient, waiting. And their new brother, the Ameri-Golem, would soon bear the Mark, bringing a semblance of life to its dense clay flesh.

Here, though he could not see from within this windowless transport, was the road where officers of the local constabulary had met such quick but gruesome ends. Here was the place he had made his 'surrender.'

"Lots of activity at the roadhouse," a scout driver reported over the internal radios. "Think they've got a live band tonight, or what?"

Soldiers laughed. Some suggested perhaps it was well-drinks on special, bottomless hellshine and spicy wings. Some speculated with lewd jokes about wet tee-shirt contests, it being well-known the transformations undergone by many locals as well as certain denizens who'd emerged from the lake.

Although none said outright, the hopeful undercurrent ran strong that, when their initial mission was finished, there might be an opportunity to stop on back by Crawdaddy's for hearty entertainment. Wine and women, ah yes, things never did change.

First things first, though. First to the lake itself, the brimming redblack blood-filth edge, the stretch of beach. Favius thrilled to feel a dark surge of power and purpose. He was eager to behold with his own eyes the shrine that had been raised, the offerings left as token and tribute.

He had done well his duty, served well his Luciferic lord, but now came the true test.

At the shore, the convoy rumbled to a halt, each vehicle taking its assigned position. Unlikely as it was they'd fall under attack, a defensive perimeter was only simple sense. The bivouacking began. Finally, still under guard, flanked by his handlers, Favius was allowed to emerge and breathe deeply of the reeking corruption.

How he had missed it! And, the surroundings, how they had changed! The flora and fauna twisted, enmonstered, deformed! Such magnificence! And the column! A monument...a monument in *his* honor, topped with a Mephistopoleon dragon! Awestruck humility left him choked up as he read the inscribed words:

HERE DID THE GREAT GENERAL FAVIUS FIRST SET FOOT AGAIN UPON EARTH! ALL GLORY UNTO HIM, LUCIFER BE PRAISED!

Oh, he was not worthy, would never be, would ever and forever strive to become so!

His handlers, the scientist and the specialist, had not been here in person before. They seemed in like measures excited and terrified, marveling over each spectacle, but never straying far from Favius. Not, he suspected, for his security so much as for their own. As if he, once again in his element, could safeguard and protect and render them immune from harm.

Most eager of all—aside from Favius, who kept his eagerness well-hidden—were the general and senator who'd spearheaded Operation Ameri-Golem. Their people scurried about as diligently as the bivouacking soldiers, setting up a large pavilion, the cameras, the agonicity-adapted uplinks, and all that would be needed to broadcast this moment of patriotic achievement to a proud nation and an intimidated world. This would be the photo op of all photo ops, their political ambitions secured. Favius wondered if they'd yet worked out between them which should be President and which V.P., the electoral outcome no doubt to be clinched by this day's dramatic event.

Hail Caesar. Yea verily, hail Caesar.

23

A man in riot-gear trudged up the road. Blood, ichor, and a host of unknowable/unspeakable substances splattered him head to foot in caked smears and drying clots.

He'd had to fight his way through, his machine gun long since out of ammo. Only four rounds remained in his sidearm, four held in reserve, for the worst-case scenario.

This was it, the home stretch. After years of guilt and not-knowing, after so many futile attempts, so much deception. Now, finally, as the end of a gravel driveway came into view, he might find out, one way or another.

Even so, his feet slowed instead of breaking into a desperate run.

What if he got there and found nothing, no one?

What if he got there and found...something?

He wasn't sure which would be worse. At least if there were...remains...at least then he'd *know*. He'd have what the therapists liked to call 'closure.'

Closure, great. Closure and a lifetime to live with himself.

It was *his* fault they'd been here. He'd never be able to get past that stark, simple truth.

His fault.

Oh, he could go on about how she had overreacted, flown off the handle, run away to the lake without hearing his side and giving him a chance to explain...

But that was bullshit.

He stopped by the mailbox, shedding his riot helmet. The meta-church decal pasted on the side was all but indistinguishable, stained with gore. Sweat plastered his greying hair to his scalp. The face revealed could have—and probably had—been likened to a careworn George Clooney.

The padded gloves went next, then the Kevlar vest. Risky, dangerous, even stupid, since he knew all too well what kinds of creatures now inhabited the lakeside woods. Hadn't he shot enough of them already along the way?

Bill, known most recently as Brother William, was not about to go up to the house dressed like a SWAT team. He piled his gear by the base of the mailbox post, useless machine gun included. The sidearm, he tucked into his waistband, letting his shirt cover it.

He opened the mailbox, half-expecting to see it crammed with every imploring letter he'd sent by way of the military's supposed program. Or for it to be full of nesting rodents, spiderwebs, dead birds. Or worse.

Instead, it was empty.

Not even a yellowed scrap of paper or dried leaf.

That...was a good sign, right? Suggesting someone checked it regularly?

Why, then, did his feet still drag, heavy with dread and apprehension, as he continued up the drive?

The house came into view, the same ramshackle hippie-hideaway he'd hated from the first moment he saw it. From *before* he saw it, if he was being honest. From as soon as he'd realized, looking at the map, that when Sharon said 'remote,' she meant fucking *remote*.

Now, here he was again, and it was no longer just fucking *remote*...it was fucking *remote* in the middle of a government-quarantined Hell-zone.

And he was alone. He'd deserted his post, ditched the rest of the church group without a second thought, as soon as he had the opportunity. It had only been a ruse in the first place, a last-ditch effort to get inside the wall.

He had no guilt left over to squander on worrying about

them. Those people weren't his friends. He didn't share their faith—doubted some of them even truly possessed any; Markane had always given him a shifty con-artist vibe, the Shinns just wanted excuses to be shitty in the name of righteousness, and who knew what was really going on in the Goldsmith women's heads.

No, all his guilt, all his existence, all his anything, revolved around his family. His wife, his children, and the happiness he'd stupidly thrown away because he'd begun feeling old and bored.

To think, he'd felt old back *then*...

Well, at least here and now, he was anything but bored.

***

The view, which had always been impressive no matter how he felt about the lakehouse or location, unfolded before him.

It was still impressive, though in a different and horrible way. The sky was fire, the lake blood, the setting sun a baleful demon's eye. The dock, where he'd taught Billy to fish and Sherri to do cannonballs, was a dark slash in the red and blazing burnt-orange.

Seeing a familiar minivan parked under the carport made his heart squeeze in his chest. It looked as if it hadn't been driven in a long time. In years. As if it hadn't been driven at all since it got here.

In a deep corner of his mind, he'd clung to an unspoken hope that Sharon and the kids had gotten out, even if they'd gone somewhere else, started new lives under new names. That hope died now in a bubbling hiss like acid.

He started to turn toward the house, to face the music as it were, to find out once and for all, when he noticed a silhouetted figure standing at the end of the dock, watching the fiery sunset.

A figure he'd recognize anywhere.

A figure he'd stupidly thought he was tired of, bored with. Because she had a mature, aging body with stretch marks and imperfections. Because it wasn't as trim and tight and young and fresh a body as that of their giggling vapid air-head of a nineteen-year-old babysitter.

Sharon.

The reek of the lake assailed him, but he did his best to ignore it as he stepped onto the dock planking and began slowly walking toward the shape of his wife.

Sharon. The woman he'd married, the mother of his children, the love of his life.

Whom he'd betrayed and cheated on like any of a million other selfish, horny, mid-life crisis stupid bastards.

Just as he tried to ignore the lake's abominable stench, Bill tried to ignore the loathsome slurping noise it made as thick wavelets sloshed against the shore. He tried to ignore the way the protruding tops of rocks in the shallows looked like heads in a festering cauldron of blood. He tried to ignore the huge, twisted mockeries of waterbugs skating on the surface, and the ominous swells and fin-breaks of whatever cruised beneath it.

He tried to ignore all these things, but wasn't terribly successful.

Keeping his eyes on the prize, so to speak, helped. Sharon didn't turn, although he was sure she heard his footfalls. She simply stood there, watching the sunset. Looking ample and curvaceous, better than he remembered.

Was she wearing a swim cap and bathing suit? She couldn't be thinking of *swimming* in that stuff, could she? That stuff like an open sewer combined with autopsy room runoff?

Bill hesitated, more scared than he'd ever been, but managed to clear his dry throat enough to speak.

"...Sharon?"

"Hi, Bill," she said, still without turning. Unsurprised. Neutral. Not angry, not happy. Just neutral.

He took another couple of faltering steps, thinking something about her was different after all. He'd certainly never seen that bathing suit before. More like a bodysuit, really, sleek and form-fitting, patterned like snakeskin or intricate serpentine tattoos. It clung so seamlessly, she might have been naked...

Was she wearing a swim cap?

Or...had she...what? Shaved and tattooed her head?

She finally did turn, the blaze-orange light limning her like liquid fire.

Time stopped as he stared, a circuit blown in his mind.

It *was* Sharon, he *knew* that; her underlying features as familiar as when he'd last seen her, as familiar as the photographs he'd brooded over since she'd left. She didn't appear to have aged a day, unlike the toll the years had taken on his own countenance.

Sharon, and yes, she was utterly naked. Her breasts hung full and slightly sagging, hips rounded, thighs thick.

Utterly hairless as well, lacking even eyebrows, her smooth scalp bald...

And not just her scalp.

***

He looked; of course he looked, how could he not?

Below the soft curve of her stretch-marked tummy, where once had been a demure tuft of bush, the bare mound of her pubis plumped brazenly, its enticing crease seeming to glisten.

An erection so sudden and hard it was painful surged in his pants. Bill felt dizzied from redirected blood flow... dizzied by a headrushing lust he hadn't experienced since that first regrettable night with Brittney.

This was his *wife*, standing here mother-naked in the sunset!

"Sharon," he said again, dragging his gaze upward... or trying to. He stalled at her breasts, at their large pebbly nipples, puckered and jutting.

And what he'd thought a snakeskin-patterned bodysuit or tattoos...

Wasn't.

It was her own skin, finely dusted with delicate scales.

Lines of them swept from the crown of her head, curling down the sides of her neck. The scales splayed out across her collarbones and shoulderblades in branching designs, running the length of her sternum and spine. They gloved her hands like embroidered lace, braceleted her wrists, twined up her arms, coiled weaving tendrils around her legs.

Thin ridges of scales replaced her eyebrows. Tiny ones overlapped in supple patterns on her lips, curving sinuously as she smiled.

"Sharon?" His voice shook, barely sounded like his own.

"Bill," she repeated.

"What's happened to you?"

"You wanted to see me in Hell. Here I am."

"Oh, God..."

She shook her head. "God? No, not here."

"The...the kids?"

"They're fine. They missed you, at first."

"I...I've missed them too...I've missed you..."

"Did you?" Sharon licked her lips. "Then prove it."

Had her quick-flicking tongue been *forked*?

He decided he didn't care. An intoxicating scene, milky and minty, like crème de menthe, like crushed peppermint leaves, like mint-chip ice cream, slipped into his nose and he no longer noticed the smell of the lake.

There was so much he should say, so much he needed to say. To apologize. To explain. To beg her forgiveness. To tell her he'd made the biggest mistake of his life, and was ready to do anything for a second chance,

But he couldn't say any of those things, because she stepped up to him, pressing her lush body against his, melting and molding it against his, covering his mouth with a crème de menthe kiss.

Bill groaned helplessly, low in his throat. His arms went around her, his palms skimming the cool, delicate texture of her scale-patterned skin. Cool, yes, she felt cool, wonderfully cool in the sweltering humidity. Her pelvis pushed firmly into his, not shying away from his evident arousal but rubbing it with that slick, glistening bald mound. He grabbed her voluptuous ass in both hands, grinding his hips, already about to spurt in his pants…God, she felt good!

God? No, not here.

Her tongue—and yes, it was forked, and yes, he didn't care—darted and flicked, tasting, teasing. She pulled at his shirt, not bothering with buttons, simply trying to yank the whole thing up and over and off.

The motion dislodged the gun from his waistband. It clunked to the dock, interrupting the moment. Sharon glanced down at the weapon, then glanced at Bill, her expression the one she'd always used when he bought some new power tool or expensive gadget for a pursuit that never seemed to pan out, yet another unfinished project in the making or lost-interest hobby.

*And just what do you think you're going to do with **that**?* her wifely look asked. *Who do you think you're fooling, anyway?*

Sheepishly, he stammered the start of a feeble excuse, but a sweep of her fine-scaled foot slid the weapon off the dock. It vanished into the red lake with a sinking splash.

Then she was kissing him again, pulling at his shirt again. At his pants. And he was helping her, fumbling and struggling, trying to get undressed without falling over.

***

His hiking boots, well-laced, were the problem, tangling his pants at the ankles. The result wasn't a fall, more of a half-controlled collapse.

The next thing he knew he was flat on his back on the dock, the weathered planks coarse beneath his bare buttocks. Sharon straddled him, lips still locked to his, one cool hand cupping the nape of his neck while the other curled around his aching-stiff cock.

He worked his fingers between her legs, plunged them into a slick, clasping channel of moist, minty ambrosia. A stunned corner of his mind couldn't believe this was happening...right here in the infernal sunset-glare, right here in the open...that same stunned corner of his mind was aware of, in his peripheral vision, things surfacing to watch...hideous, inhuman things...ridge-backed eels with leering men's faces...huge catfish whose sharklike maws were ringed with writhing tentacles instead of whiskers... malformed hermit crabs using partially-flensed skulls for their shells...

The rest of his mind wasn't aware of anything other than frenzied urgency. Sharon undulated atop him, the flexible tunnel-walls of her pussy seeming to work like a boa constrictor swallowing its prey whole, only the prey was his fingers...his entire hand...he was fisting her up to the wrist, then halfway up his forearm, and she rocked and moaned as her mint-scented oils dripped from his elbow...

She released his arm with a slurping squelch, reared back, and impaled herself on his cock. All the way to the root. Balls deep. Balls deep and then some, it seemed like, as if now she were trying to swallow him whole that way. Ecstatic cries burst from his throat. She rode him fast and hard, with wild abandon, and Bill thrust fervently to meet each squishy downward stroke. Her back arched, her hips rolled. She screamed at the blazing sky. He filled both hands to overflowing with her bountiful breasts, thumbing her nipples like doorbells.

"Don't you come yet, don't you dare!" Sharon shouted. "Don't you dare until I'm ready!"

Another inarticulate cry was the best he could manage. He didn't know if he was promising agreement or pleading that he could make no promises. All he did know was the delicious rhythmic squeezes convulsing around his shaft, and a slippery wet fleshiness engulfing his cockhead, and gush after gush of oily-cool fluids flooding his groin and thighs. It tingled, crème de menthe, peppermint, wintergreen, freshness and chill, zing and thrill—

And he was coming, fuck yes, coming with a firehose's pressure, pumping what felt like gallons of scalding-hot seed up deep into her coolness. His head slammed the dock planks with a clunk as solid and loud as the gun had made when it fell; he saw starbursts and spinning dark whorls; his cry this time was so primal and loud its echoes rolled across the lake.

Sharon matched his cry, shuddering, something releasing within her. Another gushing flood drenched his loins. She'd never been what the porn sites called a 'squirter' before, and wasn't now; this was far beyond squirting, this was the deluge, this was animals two by two and build an Ark!

The world went momentarily grey and quiet, his senses going briefly on break. He felt numb, drained, and spent. He couldn't have moved if he wanted to, could only loll on the planking, wrung out like a dishrag, and wonder if he was still breathing. He must have been, chest probably heaving and gasping, body trembling as nerve endings sputter-jittered, but he was only conscious of a suffusing, cool-tingling, wintermint sensation spreading through him.

His head rolled limply on his neck. He blinked at an upside-down panorama of the dock leading to shore, his wife's family's lakehouse bathed in hellish sunset light, and...

...and two small figures, one wearing a Ninja Turtles tee-shirt, the other with hair clumped up into half a dozen uneven pigtails.

"Hi, Daddy," they chorused.

***

Consciousness returned in a slow reverse-dissolve, leaving Bill unsure when he'd lost it in the first place. Or how. Or if any of this had happened/was really happening.

—Sharon as a voluptuous nude crème de menthe snakewoman, fucking his brains out in front of God and everybody?—

God? No, not here.

—including whatever those monstrous things in the bloodwater had been—

—and the kids—

The kids!

Bill jolted fully awake, only to find himself no less disoriented. The world still seemed upside-down, his brain dizzy, his body sticky and drained.

He'd seen them, hadn't he? Billy and little Sherri?

Little. Still so little.

That couldn't be right. They'd been eight and almost-six when Sharon brought them to the lake...years ago... they should've been...

He peered quizzically at what wasn't the upside-down view of the dock and house anymore, but was instead an upside-down view of a room. A room he recognized: faux-wood paneling, shag carpet, macrame hangings, 1970's kitsch. The spacious family/rumpus room at the rear of the lakehouse, musty with the ghosts of long-ago marijuana and cigarette smoke steeped into old upholstery, doors opening onto a covered back deck facing the woods.

Standing in front of him, also upside-down, were his children. Billy in a Ninja Turtles tee-shirt—and what was he wearing around his neck? a skull? Sherri with her hair in crazy pigtails, beaming the same gap-toothed smile he remembered, her face peppered with tiny scabs and bruises as if she'd been scratching too hard at bug bites.

"Billy..." Bill said. There was something about the boy's eyes, too, something dark and weird and not-right. "Sherri?"

She giggled, turning around and bending way over so she was looking at him through the triangle of her legs, which made her look almost rightside-up from his skewed perspective. "Hi, Daddy," she said again, chipper as ever.

So many questions, too many questions; he didn't know where to begin.

It dawned on him that he *was* upside-down, suspended as if from one of those funky fitness machines, which explained the state of his head. He craned his neck—it creaked, ouch—to try and look at himself, to get a sense of this increasingly peculiar situation.

One: it wasn't a fitness machine, it was a big wooden X, with him secured to it at ankles, waist, and wrists.

Two: naked. Entirely naked now, boots and tangled pants gone.

All parents had those awkward moments when the kids might walk in on what was best left to grown-ups behind closed doors; he and Sharon had never been overly uptight and prudish about it, but...

This was a bit much.

This, and what they'd been doing on the dock! With

not just fish-monsters leering from the lake, but, within full sight of Billy and Sherri!

Now, here he was strapped head-down to a big wooden X with his sticky dick hanging out, while his daughter giggled and his son regarded him in a kind of cool but curious detachment.

"I..." he said. "I…ugh. Where's your mother? Why am I…what's going on?"

"Mommy's busy," Sherri said, somersaulting the rest of the way over and kicking her feet.

"You…you both look just the same."

"You don't," said Billy. "You're *old*."

"It's been..."

"A long time. We know. We've been *here*."

"How come you're not any—?"

"She wouldn't let us." The boy's eyes were *black*, solid black except for eerie gold pupils.

"Maybe now she will." Sherri rolled onto her tummy. "Once she's got new babies, maybe she'll let us grow up."

"Babies?"

Gold-pupiled black though they were, Billy rolled his eyes. "We saw what you were doing. We're not stupid."

"Silly Daddy."

"Wait." Bill tried to gather his thoughts. "Get me down from here and find me some clothes, and we can—"

"Silly, silly Daddy," Sherri repeated, sing-song.

"You're not the boss of us anymore," Billy said. "Not anymore."

***

"I'm your *father*!" Going for stern, only sounding confused. No wonder; he *was*! The entire insane scenario, his children talking to him that way…

"Not any-mo-oore," chanted Sherri. "Not any-mo-oore!"

Billy folded his arms under the skull on his chest. "This is all your fault. We didn't want to come here. We didn't want to stay here. The 'lectricity went out, and everything got gross—"

"The lake went all ucky!"

"—bunches of devils and monsters and bad people—"

"No other kids to play with!"

"There were some at first," said Billy. "But not so much now."

"I didn't want you to come here either!" Bill cried. "I begged your mother to bring you home!"

Sherri glowered. "You made Mommy sad-mad."

"I didn't mean to—"

Another eye-roll; Billy may not have aged outwardly, but he had teenage attitude down pat. "Oh, yeah, like it was on accident."

"You put your weener-neener in Brittney's hoo-hah and then she couldn't babysit us no more."

"Did you make new kids with her?"

"Stop it! Both of you stop this right now!"

"Did you marry her, too?"

"I'm still married to your mother!"

"Only 'cause she couldn't d'vorce you from Hell."

"No...no, that's not true, we would have worked things out. I'm here now, aren't I? I came to find you! You don't know how sorry I was, how sorry I am, how much I missed you! We can leave this awful place, be together again, be a family again!"

"We can't *leave*," Billy sneered.

"You said you didn't like it here. Don't you want to go home? To our old house? Our real house?"

"Can we get a puppy?" asked Sherri.

"A puppy, a kitty, whatever you like, sweetheart! Just get Daddy down from this contraption, and—"

They looked at each other, the way they used to when

261

he'd negotiate some sort of deal—if you put away all your toys, we can go to Chuck E. Cheese for lunch.

"There'd be other kids to play with," Sherri said.

"There'd be school, too, though," Billy replied.

"Oh…yeah."

"Plus, there's the soldiers and stuff."

"Just…go get your mother," Bill said. "Let Mommy and Daddy talk this over."

"I *tol'* you, Mommy's *busy!*"

"Besides," said Billy, moving briefly out of Bill's line of sight and returning with a dented old classic little red wagon in tow, "she said it was our turn."

A jumble of items filled the wagon; upside-down with the blood rushed to his head, Bill couldn't immediately identify everything. Toys, office supplies, kitchen implements…electronic odds and ends…what looked like Halloween decorations…parts of those science experiment kits Billy had always been so into—build your own remote controlled robot! power your radio with a potato! junior chemistry set!

Office supplies? Kitchen implements? Electronic odds and ends?

"What's all that for?" Bill asked. Feeling nervous, which was crazy.

These were his *children*! Fine, maybe he was strapped naked and upside-down to a big wooden X, but…

…and was that a vegetable peeler? and those prongs to poke into the ends of a corn on the cob? and a stapler and a staple remover, and an X-acto knife…

…which his son, wearing a studious frown, was laying out on a folding TV tray table with the precision of a surgical prep nurse…

…and what was with the cauldron? The witchy hat and robe? The bowl of what appeared to be coarse salt mixed with bone dust, dried blood, and ashes?

...while his daughter, doing a sing-song chant—was that Latin?—set up a ring of dollies and stuffed animals and lit a greasy yellow-black candle in front of each...

"Are you supposed to be playing with matches?!?"

They ignored him. Bill struggled, but the straps held firm. Nervousness had given way to genuine fear.

And fear, very quickly, gave way to **PAIN**.

***

Sharon hummed as she worked, listening to the screams and laughter from the family room. So nice to hear the children spending some quality time with their father!

After this long, and with everything else going on, a visit from her estranged husband was about the last surprise she'd expected.

Maybe it wasn't much in the greater scheme of things... which, honestly, it wasn't, when stacked up against an angel and a new warlock among them, the return of the Carmichaels, Azbunael's destruction, and of course the most momentous portent of all—

Ecce, novum princeps de inferno, novus rex terrae!

—but, on a personal level, quite the surprise indeed. To cast the divinations and see Bill's name come up, unmistakable, plain as day? She'd hardly been able to believe it, yet, there it was.

And there, soon enough, he'd been as well.

Bill, her own Bill, in the flesh. A bit older, and showing it; whatever rejuvenating effects banging a nineteen-year-old may have had, they'd worn off and been replaced by encompassing guilt.

In a way, it was kind of touching, his half-mad obsession, his desperation. In another way, it was annoying as fuck. As if he could simply show up here, after what he'd done, and expect to be welcomed back with open arms?

She chuckled. Poor choice of words, given the way she'd greeted him out on the dock. Open arms, open mouth, open legs, open everything. He certainly hadn't objected, despite the changes she'd undergone over the years. If anything, he'd seemed to like it.

Not the best fuck of her life, perhaps, and he'd blown his load a bit earlier than she might've preferred. Still, she'd had fun. Riding him brazenly, feeling him helpless beneath her, letting every past sin of her family's property and history fuel the act.

Best of all, it had gotten the job done.

There was a plastic kiddie wading pool in one of the outbuildings, along with several bags of sand from the sandbox Bill had kept saying he was going to build… first for Billy, then for Sherri…but, as with so many of his flash-in-the-pan hobbies or lost-interest projects, he'd never done more than buy a bunch of tools and materials.

She went into the converted pantry/root cellar her uncles had referred to as 'the greenhouse,' complete with drip faucets and full-spectrum bulbs. Their amateur attempts at horticulture had been middling successes at best, nothing remaining but brittle stalks and even brittler leaves.

Clearing a space in the center of the floor, Sharon filled the kiddie pool with sand, placed the lamps around it, and fussed until all was arranged to her satisfaction. Once connected to the house's agonicity generator—she wasn't going to feel nearly so bad about the power source now; this would be much better than using some camper or tourist—the lights shed a steady clean white glow very different from the reddish haze passing for sunshine.

The sand was clean and dry, warm and smooth, ready. She wouldn't have minded curling up for a nice basking nap, but still had too much to do. Dinner wasn't going to prepare itself, both kids would probably need baths after they finished with Bill, neighbors were bound to be dropping by to share the latest news—

Sharon smiled, eager to share her own latest news.

Her palms skimmed over the curve of her belly, already rounder than it had been scant hours ago. Rounder, but firmer. Six eggs? Ten? Even more? She wouldn't know for sure until she clutched, another few days at least.

Then, of course, she'd have to see how many survived the hatching and the initial vicious melee. Although the prospect grieved a mother's heart, well, sometimes it was necessary. The ones who made it would be the strongest, fierce and tenacious, clever. They would need to be, to thrive in the new kingdom almost upon them.

Ecce, novum princeps de inferno, novus rex terrae!

24

All was arranged. The Ameri-Golem in its inert majesty lay upon a platform ceremonially draped in red-white-and-blue bunting. For the sake of televised modesty, it had been fitted with a stars-and-stripes loincloth, though the rest of its chiseled and sculpted build was on display. A camera team even now panned slowly up and down the length of the muscular body.

Thing, Hulk, and Juggernaut looked cruder than ever by comparison, but jealousy lurked nowhere in the nature of Golems. The three stood sentinel against the scenic, seething backdrop of the lake, their slitted eyes dimly crimson.

Favius, splendid in his Hell-forged armor, stood with them. He smiled inwardly to imagine himself on millions of screens, millions of mortals watching, witnessing the tormented living faces stitched into his skin.

"Ratings gold," someone said, and if Favius wasn't fully sure what it meant, he got the gist. Gold was gold, after all, needing little other explanation.

The general and the senator took turns giving speeches, being interviewed. Favius himself was not so favored, but both of his handlers made statements. So did some of the occultists and technicians brought along to take care of the ceremonial trappings. Behind them, apprentices and interns fussed busily with various items: black wax candles, lines of salt, car batteries arranged at the points of a pentacle, cages containing live chickens, portable computers, vials of harvested virgin's blood.

Where they'd obtained that last, Favius would've liked to know. But, as with sacrificial infants, his captors' hospitality extended only so far.

"...unprecedented combination of science and sorcery..."

"...next and most decisive step in the arms race..."

"...new avenues of sustainable energy..."

"...defend this great country from enemies both foreign and domestic..."

On and on they went, until, at last, it was time. Soldiers at attention, dignitaries taking their seats, programs being initiated, a low chant commencing. Favius felt, for a moment, a flash of what he'd heard described as 'stage fright' when every eye—human or camera glass or hellish onlooker—fixed upon him as he stepped into position.

This was it. They had done as instructed, each detail to exact specifications. How they wanted their obedient, unstoppable super-soldier! Favius could taste the greedlust, the warlust, the hunger.

Three lake-pebbles, water-worn flattish stones carefully chosen, clicked together in his palm. Each had been etched with ancient glyphs, symbols he knew but did not know, symbols sent to him in mind-whispers. LIFE, meant the first. SERVITUDE, the second. Upon the third, BREATH.

Yes, this was it. This was it, now or never.

They'd swallowed every line he'd fed them, every lie he'd told.

With his thumb, Favius drove the LIFE-glyph stone into the center of the Ameri-Golem's magnificent 'six-pack.' The designers who'd lectured him about the importance of looking good and being anatomically correct were not in attendance, but, wherever they were, he knew they must be bleating in protest.

SERVITUDE, he buried deep in the Ameri-Golem's flawless brow. Around him, consternation stirred, for none of this had been in the script. The rest of it—the candles and chanting and batteries and blood—were mere window dressing. All he needed were these stones, and the Golem itself.

And the nearness to Hell, the lake's potent magic, the anchor points and lines of infernal power.

BREATH went into the magnificent chest, squarely between the 'pecs' with their absurd man-nipples. As the disrupted audience looked to one another in a baffled query-clamor of uncertainty, Favius spat a wad of saliva into each thumb-hole, then smeared the clay back together with the heel of his hand.

"I, Favius, am your Master," he announced, his Voice like the striking of a great iron bell. "Rise, and obey!"

The Ameri-Golem shuddered, drawing in a gasp. Its eyes flew open, no simple crimson slits but shining starbursts of red, white, and blue. As it sprang up, in its manly perfection, Favius hoped the cameras had gotten good close-ups.

Then the killing began.

***

"You tricked us!"

This, from the senator of a nation whose very founding documents mentioned truths held self-evident?

Favius removed the man's face with a practiced slice-and-peel—some skills, even let go a while unpracticed, were never forgotten. He supposed this was what they meant by 'like riding a bike.'

On a similar subject of sudden epiphany, he finally understood several overheard references to a Captain Obvious. Who was not, it would seem, some officer of the military he merely hadn't met.

Gibbering and screaming, the senator fell to his knees

and clutched at the raw-meat seeping tissue of fatty muscle and tendon now covering the front of his skull. He'd been a well-groomed man but also well-fed, tending toward jowliness; if chosen to be added to the physiognomical quiltwork of Favius's skin, it might fit baggily as a loose sock.

Being that Favius was also fairly well out of blank canvas space for such adornments, he would probably have no use of the face, but old habits died hard. He planned to claim more than a few trophies this glorious day!

The general, for instance…

The general had not come to the party unarmed. His first shot rang against Favius's breastplate, barely nicking the Hell-forged alloy of iron and bronze, the impact little more than a flung stone. For his second shot, he aimed higher, but Favius deflected it with a deft wrist-turn, sparks flying as the bullet glanced off the gladius's blade.

Peace-bonded, as if a plastic zip-tie would matter? They might as well have used twine. The trusty weapon sang its death-song, whistling through air, cleaving flesh, chopping bone. Two soldiers dropped, one slashed crotch to gullet, the other gullet to crotch, entrails unraveling, intestines spilling shit.

Then no one was between Favius and the general. Around them were gunfire and terror and screams, the Golems bludgeoning a brutal swath, stomping and crushing, wreaking ruthless havoc.

"Traitor!" shouted the general.

Favius thought *that* was rich. Traitor, indeed.

A third shot nicked his neck; a graze, Favius had cut himself worse shaving. His gladius took the general's hand at the wrist, gun and all. Boggling in disbelief at the spurting stump, the general staggered backward as if trying to flee, and bumped into a twelve-foot-tall, solid, immovable mass.

In a stars-and-stripes loincloth.

"Remove his head intact," ordered Favius, deciding the face-trophy could wait, "and place it atop the monument spike."

"No! No, you're ours, you're American, we made you—!"

—crackle-TWIST-crackle-POP—

Off it came, with accompanying grisly shower. Still shouting, but silent without helpful connecting bronchial passages to air from lungs to vocal cords. The Ameri-Golem dutifully carried its prize toward the monument, where a tall spike jutted up from the Mephistopolean dragon.

Favius himself wouldn't have been able to reach up there unaided, but it proved no problem for the towering specimen. Up went the detached head, mouth mutely gawping and raving. Down came the head, windpipe onto the spike, with a wet noise best rendered as *gliiittch-gurgle!*

"Soldiers!" bellowed Favius, leaping onto the bunting-bedecked platform where the Ameri-Golem had lain. "Golems, stand down! Soldiers, hear me!"

Both of his handlers, he saw, had survived. So had a few of the camera people, for whom filming seemed to take precedence over their very lives.

"Hear me," he repeated, when the firing stopped and he had their full attention. "Join me. Serve my cause. Serve my lord, serve the Morning Star. Become warriors of Hell, and reap its eternal, decadent rewards!"

They didn't all take him up on it, but those who didn't were swiftly dealt with by those who did. A fervor fell over them, a beautiful madness. There followed such scenes of atrocity as to make archangels weep…and when it was finished, Favius had his own army.

Hulk and Juggernaut brought him his handlers, forcing them to kneel at his feet. The specialist looked up, tearfully. "I thought we were friends."

With another practiced slice-and-peel, off went his face.

25

It was hate at first sight.

Hate at first sight, squared.

Trevor and Heck. Chelsea and Lorlinda.

Instant, immediate, bone-deep hate at first sight.

Andy had never been gladder to be so inconspicuous. His pod was snuggled deep into Lorlinda's cleavage, as if the last thing she wanted was for anyone else to know about him, and neither she nor Heck mentioned it.

Not that there was a lot of talking during the drive to Crawdaddy's. Hate on first sight aside, business was business. Trev promised money, Chels flashed her tits, and Heck agreed to drive them to the nearest checkpoint. But only after, he informed them, he'd delivered his load of hellshine and stayed for the Hock Party.

Even Chelsea's offer of a blowjob didn't sway him. An offer Andy suspected she'd made more out of an opportunity to piss off Trevor and Lorlinda in a two-fer than from any interest in Heck. The relationship between the Carmichael twins seemed…on the tense side, Andy thought.

They said they'd been visiting the writer, who recommended Heck. They didn't say much else.

They sure didn't say anything about Kayla. Andy had a brief pang of guilt over his experience with Lorlinda—did that count as cheating on his girlfriend, even if he'd only been a passive sex-toy? or did his agreeing to it make him just as culpable?—but then was all, oh wait. Kayla had cracked his head open with a fireplace poker. If that wasn't

271

a decisive break-up, he couldn't imagine what was.

He did wonder what had happened to her, though. Did she end up like Madison, dragged off and devoured by monsters? Had they left her with this writer guy, whoever he was? Little was said about him, either; the Bodeans merely acknowledged the remark like, well, yeah, that's cool.

The frankentruck's cab was packed, Lorlinda scootched way over against Heck, Chelsea beside her although they were both practically hissing, and Trevor by the passenger door.

Somehow, the idea of the twins sitting on the spot where Lorlinda had done what she'd done made Andy grin, then twinge another guilt-pang and oh-wait again. They were his friends, or had been, but they were also the people who'd brought him here, let him get bitten by a toxic acid rat, cut off his leg, tried to burn the stump, and then left him for dead under the Catch's tree.

So much for friendship and loyalty. Fuck that. Andy might not have been Heck's biggest fan, but if he had to choose sides, it would be Bodean over Carmichael all the way. He'd had enough of a glimpse to determine Trevor's nose was indeed good and broken, both eyes nearly lost in puffy bruises, and it gave him a fierce sense of take-that satisfaction.

The truck slowed. "What's this cherub-shit?" Heck said, breaking the hate-squared silence. "Ain't never seen so much traffic, not jist fer no Hock Party."

"Sumpin' else must be goin' on," said Lorlinda. "Sumpin' big. Been quite a day 'round here. Was even a plane crash earlier on t'other side of the lake, so's I heard."

Andy couldn't see anything except boobs and harsh red sunlight filtering through her thin tank top, but he could *feel* the snide rich-bitch sneering coming off Chelsea in waves. The promised ride to the checkpoint had to be all that kept her from mocking their twangy hillbilly speech the way she'd mocked the overalls dude who dropped by the lakehouse.

He could hear, though: a few other engines (including some that might've been boat outboard motors), the rough babble of voices, an occasional barking laugh, an occasional hoot or yee-haw, casual swearing, and a general hum of excitement. It sounded like a typical crowded payday weekend night at some redneck bar, where the waitresses might coyote-ugly dance on the bartop in cowboy boots, the band would play from behind chickenwire to ward off thrown bottles, and six fights would break out before closing time.

***

There seemed to be a degree of agitation in the air as well as excitement. Sumpin' big, Lorlinda had surmised, and Andy agreed.

Snatches of conversation flowed through the rolled-down windows as Heck prowled for parking. Overheard phrases included *military convoy, the guv'mint mebbe?, ter'rist attack, gen'rull, out ter git us,* and *let 'em try 'cause we'll fuck 'em t' Hell an' back*...plus what sounded like a trio of mad crones doomsday-screeching in Latin or some shit. *Ekkay terrasaurus rex?*

"What's going on?" Trevor asked.

"Bless'd if'n I know," Heck said. He maneuvered, parked, and everyone piled out.

Lorlinda kindly nudged Andy's pod higher in her cleavage, enabling him to peek over the neckline of her tank top. The scene was much as he'd envisioned, but with added elements. Elements that could've come straight out of Hell-themed episodes of South Park or Ugly Americans. Redneckimus Bosch. Jethro's Inferno. And listen to him, wasted stoner in a pod, being all literary and art-appreciation! His professors never would've believed it.

Some of these dudes and dudettes had horns. Tails.

273

Long split toothy 'gator muzzles. Tentacles. Most wore jeans or regular attire; some were decked out in cultist robes. Many had weapons; open carry was clearly very popular. He saw a multi-titted bearded lady with five or six maniacal half-werewolf pups on leashes, and a headless guy with clustered eyeballs on stalks wavering around out of the stump of his neck.

He also, in the course of their progress toward the roadhouse, heard enough to get the gross gist of what a Hock Party was. Worst of all…

"Twenny bucks on ya t'night, Lorlinda hon! Don't'choo let me down!"

"I'se so fulla lung-butter I'se c'n barely t' breathe. They best start this thang soon afore'n I ace-fixee-ate!"

"Careful, Lorlie…Maisy-Sue's still sore about you taking it last time!"

"Maisy-Sue can kiss my bee-hind!" Lorlinda crowed, with a hearty slap to the behind in question, and people cheered.

"You *compete* in this shitshow?" Chelsea boggled.

"Spitshow," Trevor corrected.

"Compete, nothin'," said Heck. "Lorlinda here's the reigning champeen."

A lot of things had freaked and horrified Andy since passing through Area 666, but this…his honeysuckle backwoods goddess defiled…making herself a willing target for a phlegm and snot shower, a loogie barrage courtesy of these tooth-missing tobacco-chawing hicks… this was more than he could bear!

He found himself in the fetal position at the bottom of his pod, trying not to puke. Lorlinda, during a lull in which Heck ventured into the roadhouse searching for someone called 'Spot' and Chelsea and Trevor took in the ambiance, fished him out.

"You okay in there, sugar?"

Sunset was fading toward a rusty maroon twilight, but plenty of illumination was provided by torches and lines of glowing green eyeballs like Christmas lights, and drifting spheres of crackling red energy. Huge pots bubbled over bonfires, making Andy not want to know what a crab-and-crawdad boil consisted of here. Beer and hellshine were being liberally guzzled, various substances smoked or otherwise consumed. Two pig-faced men with corkscrew pig-dicks busily throat-fucked a flabby couch-sized eel-woman with a head at each end.

Was he okay in there?

No, not really, no.

"I'se'll find somewheres safe t' put ya before'n I go on," she assured him, then giggled. "S'pose, since as how I usually go nekkid, I c'd tuck y' back—"

Heck appeared at her side, grabbing her elbow. "We'se leavin'."

"What? Heck, we jist got—"

"Don' care. We'se leavin'. Move yer caboose."

"Pearly gates, why?"

"Talked ter Spot. Smarmy li'l fuck more fulla hisself than usual, an' no wonder…turns out, yeah, military convoy went by a while ago."

Lorlinda gaped. "*Is* it ter'rists? Or the guv'mint really gonna wipe us out? Eee-radicate us with a nuke or sommat?"

Heck grimly shook his head. "It's that general," he said. "The centurion, that Favius fella. He's back. He's back, an' Spot says he's here t' stay."

"What 'bout them two?" Lorlinda said as Heck towed her by the elbow toward the parking lot.

Not far away, an uncomfortable reunion of sorts was occurring, the Carmichael twins having bumped into their overall-wearing pal Lester Riggers in the crowd. Lester, jovial as could be with a companionable hand clamped neck-breakingly firm around Trevor and Chelsea's necks,

275

seemed to be introducing them to a short chubby dude with the living heads of two elderly people cradled in his arms.

"Ask me if'n I give a fried fuck," Heck said.

"You had a deal. An' th' Hock Party—"

"Ain't'choo been lissenin'? We done had that plane crash earlier, there been gunshots an' explosions 'round the lake all damn day, omens and pree-monitions…Spot also said an angel—not a fallen; a hand-t'-Heaven *angel*—took down that goaty bastard Zilch out t' th' winery—"

"Well, but that's a good thing!" Lorlinda argued. "Perv tryin' t' cut in on our business—"

"An *angel*, Lorlinda! Don'choo know what that means? An' someone done blew up the skull over t' Bible Creek, an'—" He jerked a thumb in the direction of three old woman, straggle-haired and ratty-robed, cackling around a cauldron; the crones Andy had heard earlier, no doubt. "—an' the Wyrds been all 'new prince of Hell, new king on Earth'…means a Reckonin', tha'ss what it means!"

"Like, End Times?"

"Could be."

"Mebbe they *is* gonna nuke us!"

"Wouldn't put it past 'em none, but I sure as Satan don' wanna be here t' find out. So, kindly, getcher ass in gear, or do I hafta—?"

"Awright, I'se goin'!" She quit resisting his tug, picked up her pace. "But if'n it turns out t' be nothin', you owe me what I woulda won t'night."

"Fine, fine," said Heck, barely paying attention. He swore as they reached the frankentruck, hemmed in on all sides by pickups and motorcycles and modified mongrel mash-ups of all description, parked with little in the way of rhyme or reason.

As he seemed to be speculating whose rides he could bump aside or drive over while causing the least damage— to his reputation and person more than to any of the other

276

vehicles; plenty of them already looked like they'd been on the receiving end of some unwanted foreplay from Ol' Hornyshell—Lorlinda lifted Andy's pod up to her face again.

Glad though he was to not have to see her participate in the Hock Party, it distressed him to see her anxious and scared. He wished there was something he could do to reassure her; instead, she seemed to be trying to reassure him.

"I tol' you before, me an' Heck, we'd take good care of you," she said. "That Favius fella, th' one he mentioned? Same one as messed up Zeke. Spot—nasty kiss-ass ginger shithead what runs Crawdy's now—swore hisself t' Favius an' Lucifer that first AllHell day an' been makin' the most of it ever since. If it is true th' general's comin' back, Spot gonna be jist insuff'r—"

From further down the lakeshore, the a Voice rang through the twilight, the words indecipherable at this distance but the Voice itself resonant with power and might, like the striking of a great iron bell.

It froze everyone at Crawdy's, all heads turning. Then the dusk erupted with noise and light, a serious rocket's red glare/bombs bursting in air warzone heavy munitions thunderstorm…followed by screams of mortal terror and face-peeling agony.

Nobody spoke or moved, until the three crones flung their wizened claw-hands wildly in the air. "*Ecce, novum princeps de inferno, novus rex terrae!*" they cried. "Behold, a new prince of Hell, a new king on Earth! Hail, Lucifer! Hail, Favius! The Second Coming!"

As dramatic proclamations went, Andy thought it lost a bit of oomph when someone said, "Heh, 'coming,'" and a wave of juvenile snickers swept the crowd.

26

Some defiant spirit of who-gives-a-shit stubbornness made June refuse. "I'm fine," she said. "No use putting on anything else that might just get torn up or covered with blood."

"Hmf! Suit yourself then, but don't say I didn't warn you, and don't run complaining to me when people say you look like a homeless meth-head stripper!"

"Let them." June patted her shotgun. "Just let them."

Everyone scrambled around, grabbing weapons and provisions. Mr. Shinn made sure to grab the marshmallows, chocolate bars, and graham crackers, as well as a bundle of toasting forks; evidently the greedy son of a bitch hadn't yet had his fill of goddamn s'mores.

It turned out, June learned as they threw things more or less randomly into the back of the Holy Roller, that 'Sister Anna' and her counterpart back at the checkpoint had heard the initial gunshots and grenades. So she...and wasn't it simply saintly of her? So Samaritan!...had decided to ride in to see if they were okay.

Yes, very saintly, very Samaritan indeed. Got her in all good and chummy with Crusader Markane, too. He'd still barely acknowledged, let alone noticed, June since her action-heroic return.

With the Gabelmans, Lucas, David, and Brother William all gone, there was plenty of room for the rest of them to spread out in the bus, even if the unconscious and wounded Ramon took up a whole middle row. Markane drove. Somehow, maybe because she carried one, June snagged the shotgun seat.

Garcia—*Sister Annn-na!* her mind jeered in mocking falsetto—rode ahead on her military ATV/golf-cart, leading the way. Their headlights cut the muggy gloom, a misty miasma simmering up from the lake as the sun sank and the skies darkened toward the color of dried blood. It seemed risky, those bright beams slashing ahead, but predators could just as easily be drawn by the sounds of the engines… and it'd be far riskier trying these roads without them.

In the back, her mother and Mrs. Shinn at least went through the motions of pretending to attend to Ramon; neither of them knew jack squat about nursing or medicine except what they'd seen on television medical dramas. Mr. Shinn 'kept watch' from the rear windows.

If he ate all the chocolate…

The local wildlife, not exactly scarce during the day, sure seemed ready to become more active at night. A creature like a fifteen-foot-long ferret with multiple legs scurried out directly in front of Garcia. June thought (hoped? maybe a little) she would hit it and flip the ATV and be dragged off screaming into the underbrush before any of them could do anything, but Garcia steered one-handed and fired her sidearm with the other and blew its brains to oatmeal, veering neatly around the crumpling body.

"Nice," Markane said, possibly not knowing it was aloud.

The Holy Roller bumped as its tires made roadkill treadmarks across the ferret-pede's carcass.

"Careful!" Mrs. Shinn scolded. "We've got a hurt boy back here, did you forget?"

"Thank you, Sister."

On they went, around the lake, seeing more indescribable horrors. Trees, and things in the trees, and things under the trees, watched them pass. Ominous shapes heaved and wallowed. The dusk echoed with not-quite-animal noises: honks and roars, hoots, screeches, weird bellows, dinosaur sounds. And not-quite-human noises: chanting, sobbing, laughter, guttural groaning.

A few cabins and lakehouses looked almost normal, with lit windows and activity, people tending grills on their decks, soaking in hot tubs. Others looked anything but normal, haunted or abandoned, rundown nightmares.

Ahead, and suddenly very close, a fusillade of gunfire rattled the air. There were screams, and explosions. They'd found the military convoy, now arranged in a military camp, but the war appeared to be going on within its perimeter. Soldier against soldier, soldier against civilian…scattered battles of murder and brutality, cannibalism, and rape…

…hulking grey slablike monsters…

…and an imposing figure in Hell-forged Roman armor.

***

Garcia hit the brakes. Her ATV slewed sideways. Markane almost plowed right into it, but by then Garcia was off and running toward the nearest injured soldier.

Bringing the bus to a jarring halt, Markane ordered, "Stay here!" and sprang out to go after her, leaving his door wide open and key in the ignition.

"This is bad," said Mrs. Shinn. "We should just go, don't you think? I think we should just go."

"Junie, drive," her mother said.

Drive? Or jump into the fray? Crusader Markane was going to get himself killed, over his precious 'Sister Anna'…could she save him? Could she save them both? Or should she do what her mother and the Shinns so vociferously clamored? Drive like the very bat out of Hell, before anybody opened fire on them?

She vaulted across the center console, into the driver's

seat—warmed by Markane's body heat, as close as she was ever likely to get!—and yanked the door shut, then stared hectically at the unfamiliar, complicated controls.

"Oh, my Lord!" shrieked her mother and Mrs. Shinn.

June looked up in time to see one of the hulking grey slablike monsters—*It's a Golem*, she thought, astounded—swing the huge grey club of its fist. One second, Crusader Markane was there, caught in mid-stride. The next, he wasn't. The Golem's haymaker sent some limp twisted dishrag of a starfish cartwheeling through the air, where it splattered against a military transport truck like a bug hitting a windshield.

Yelling in Spanish, Garcia drilled several bullet holes in the vicinity of where a living being's heart might have been. Too late to help Markane, and about as effective as blowing soap bubbles; the Golem merely lumbered around as if to see who'd shot it.

Garcia fired again. This time to the face, and this time as she backpedaled like crazy. Her heels hit another soldier, not injured but dead, and she fell. Before she could get up, the Golem stomped one massive foot onto her belly, pulverizing her pelvis, causing internal organs to jettison out of her mouth like toothpaste from a tube.

A stinging smack hit the back of June's head. "Drive, you numpty, drive!" cried her mother.

"Ahhh!" shouted June, shoving the lever into what she hoped was a useful gear and flooring it.

The Holy Roller leaped forward, straight at the Golem. It met the oncoming bus with a punch, which did not flip the vehicle like in the movies but stopped them dead with a squealing crunch of metal. A big pale blur went WHOOMP in her face as the airbag deployed, slamming her into her seat instead of fracturing her sternum on the steering wheel.

For a moment, she just slumped there, dazed, head spinning. None of them had bothered with seatbelts; Ramon rolled to the floor with a thump, her mother and the Shinns were tossed around like beanbag dolls.

Movement in her peripheral vision caught her eye. June turned her head and saw the Golem's crimson eyeslits peering in at her through the driver's side window. She hit the auto-lock button; fat lot of help that would be but oh well. They were going nowhere.

Or…they were going somewhere…as the Golem effortlessly hefted the church bus over its head. June braced for the throw, the crush and crumple and impact of landing. Maybe into the lake, Hell's vileness seeping in through every vent and crevice as they sank, giving anyone who'd survived that far the chance between drowning in blood and shit or being eaten alive.

But the Golem did not throw the bus. The Golem carried the bus, carried it through the battle's aftermath to the platform where the figure in Roman-style armor stood. Three other Golems, two as featureless and slablike as this one, the third such a piece of Michelangelo perfection she worried she'd gotten a concussion, formed a guard around him, while the remaining soldiers had fallen into formation.

***

Were those *faces*? Living, contorted, tormented *faces*? Sewn into his *skin*?

Yes, they were.

With a few freshly-peeled ones dangling like scalps from his belt, and bodies with bare-fleshed wet red skulls at his feet. His armor glinted red-gold light, his sword was a line of blood and fire.

The Golem plunked the Holy Roller to the ground, hard enough to rattle what remained of its suspension and pop all four hubcaps off the tires. The driver's side door, which had been locked but also bent by the devastating punch, popped open with a grinding metallic squeal.

She seized the shotgun and leveled the barrels at the Golem's head, though the deep pocks Garcia's rounds had left in the clay with no discernible adverse effects didn't bode well even for a load of buckshot. Still, when it reached in here for her, it was gonna get a point-blank rebuff.

It didn't reach in. It stepped aside. Like it was making room for her to get out of her own volition.

Having little other choice, June did. Shotgun first.

She felt far more stupid than badass, surrounded by soldiers and much bigger badder guns…and Golems, who'd already demonstrated they could snap her like a twig… under the intense stare of the man in the Roman armor.

If she shot *him*…?

Sure, June, that'd work.

What the fuck, blaze of glory.

KA-BLAM!

The bodybuilder male-model Golem, wearing a stars-and-stripes loincloth, interposed itself between them. Thick ripples spread across its chest, absorbing the blast. Before June could try again, another Golem plucked the shotgun from her hands, bent it into a pretzel, and dropped it in the dirt.

"Who are you, woman?" the armored man asked. He seemed more intrigued than angry, maybe amused, and it pissed her off all the more.

"Who are *you*?" she countered.

"Favius. First Conscript of…never mind. A long story." He surveyed the totaled bus, its front end a mangled accordion hissing steam and leaking oil. "This chariot of yours bears church-signs. Are you warriors of God, come to fight the forces of evil?"

Strike the maybe; he was definitely amused. So were his human troops, though the Golems showed no reaction.

"We're idiots of God," June said. "Or we were. Who

cares? What difference does it make? Go ahead and kill us! I'm going to die a dried-up virgin anyway, might as well get it over with already! It's been a shitty enough day."

Favius tilted his head. "You're a virgin?"

"Sure, rub it in, insult to injury, sad sack old maid can't *give* it away, can't even get ravished by demons, anybody else want to laugh?" She rounded accusingly on the smirking soldiers.

"*June!* What are you *doing*?" shrieked her mother from within the bus. "Are you out of your mind?"

She was getting that question a lot lately, and was really damn tired of it. Partly because she was pretty sure by now it was true. Down to the final few fraying threads of her sanity, at any rate.

"June," said Favius. "Named for Juno, queen of the gods."

"Named because that's the month I was born," she replied tartly. "I'm no queen."

"Would you like to be?"

She strafed him with a narrow laser-hot sarcastic glare. "Oh, very funny. Me, a queen, yeah, right."

"Strong and fearless, willful and tenacious, a savage spirit. Why not? You could be."

"Uh-huh, and whose? Queen of *what*?"

"Mine, and of this."

Her mind did that record-scratch sound effect.

"I speak in earnest," he said. "Not in jest, not a trick."

June stared. "You're serious."

"Unholy consummation with a virgin bride would further strengthen the magic. One who is mortal, and fallen from faith as well? Indeed, I am."

Those final few fraying threads of her sanity…

"By what Great Sin will you prove your worth?"

With a slow turn of her head, she looked from Favius to the bus, then to Favius again. "How about matricide?"

284

27

They'd hiked for hours.

Or, rather, Greg had hiked, with Ethriel flitting along at his shoulder.

Undisturbed. Unmolested. Nothing and no one, denizen or damned, natural or unnatural, wanted to tangle with an angel and warlock. Word must have somehow gotten around. It made him uncomfortable, but he wasn't going to complain.

The further they got from the lake, the more normal the landscape became...but, the more nervous Ethriel seemed to become.

"What is it?" he asked when they paused for a rest. "What's wrong?"

"Not sure," she replied, her frown fitful. "Something. Something's changing. Something's happening."

"Are we getting too far for the magic? You said—"

They were within sight, or within fleeting glimpses through the trees at least, of the wall...grey slabs of concrete and cinderblock, topped with spikes and loops of barbed wire (his favorite!) rose in stark silhouette against the baleful sky as sunset bled into dusk. How close they were to a checkpoint, an exit, he had no idea. But, if the wall itself marked a border...

"I don't think that's it," Ethriel said.

"Maybe we should stop."

"Stop and what? We have to get you to safety."

"Yeah, but...I don't want you to disappear. I don't want to lose you."

"Awww."

"I'm serious."

She downcast her gaze. "I know."

"Ethriel—"

"Look at it this way, though. I may physically fade out of this realm, but you won't lose me. Guardian angel, remember? We're stuck with each other, at least until you pass the medallion on to someone else." Flicking a glance up at his forehead, she amended, "Even then, we might still be connected. There's been some pretty unprecedented mojo going on."

"I guess," he said, with a heavy reluctance, feeling weirdly like they were having the let's-just-stay-friends part of a post-dumping conversation.

"Anyway, that isn't what's bugging me. The balances of power are…shifting. Someone…something…is…"

Her voice trailed off. Her head tipped back in a cloud of shimmering hair, eyes rolling until only the opalescent whites showed.

"Ethriel?"

As her gossamer dragonfly wings stilled, she dropped from the air. Greg caught her, surprised by her solidity, by the living weight and heat of her small body and the satiny texture of her skin.

"Ethriel! Don't do this to me, don't check out on me now!"

She lolled in his arms, eyelids weakly fluttering. A whisper-rush of words issued from her lips.

"*Ecce, novum princeps de inferno, novus rex terrae.*"

"What?" He didn't speak Latin. Something about an inferno? Didn't 'rex' mean 'king,' like in T-rex?

"Behold…" she sighed, then went limp. Pale tendrils, like wisps of cool steam, spiraled upward. They smelled of sweet cotton candy and champagne.

"No, no, no," Greg said. "You're not leaving me alone

out here. I wouldn't leave you. Dumb and noble, remember?'"

Had he been surprised before by the weight and solidity of her? He was stricken now, stricken and dismayed, to feel her turning lighter and less substantial in his grasp.

Damn it, he was supposed to be a warlock; wasn't there something he could *do*?

Her eyelids fluttered again. She peered up at him, hazily, as if seeing him from very far away. Her little hand rose to press a gentle touch to his cheek. "Go," she breathed. "Go, Greg. I'll...find you."

"Screw that!" He pulled the strand of beads from around his neck. Petrified wood, mother-of-pearl, polished smooth, parts of once-living things. The silver medallion glimmered eerily in the shadowed twilight, a liquid shine twisting this way and that. Sigil on one side, words on the other.

"Here," he said, settling it onto her chest. "I'm giving you this. Passing it on. It's yours. *You're* yours, your own guardian angel now. You're free."

With a soft sigh, Ethriel faded...dissolved into mist and light and nothingness in his grasp...and was gone. Amulet and all. Just...

Just gone.

***

Greg dropped to his knees. His eyes stung with unshed tears, his throat choked with unvoiced sobs. Soon, he knew, he would shed them and voice them, and once that began, it would be a maelstrom that might never stop.

Wasn't fair, come so far, been through so much!

To have her simply vanish, whiff out with no reason... no one he could blame, no one upon whom he could at least try to make himself feel better by wreaking revenge...

What was he supposed to do? Go on by himself? Reach the wall, find a gate, return to the real world? To his real life? To the process and hassle of trying to explain what had happened, not only to his friends and family but to his customers, business associates, and the authorities? He'd have a hell of a time, so to speak, dealing with the insurance company, too.

But, what else was there? He didn't have a whole lot of choice. He was still alive, was still here. Ethriel wouldn't want him to sit and have a crybaby pity party. How dare he, when she'd been the one to pay the ultimate price? When she'd done her *job*, above and beyond the call of duty?

Custos Viatorum, protector of travelers, his guardian angel. She'd kept him safe, under some pretty extreme circumstances that no doubt fell outside the usual arrangements. He owed it to her to stay safe, to keep going. To not let her time and effort, and sacrifice, go to waste.

Okay.

With a deep, hitch-sniffly snuffle of breath and a quick wipe of the eyes, he got his shit more or less together and stood up. The wall wasn't far; if he followed it, he would find a checkpoint eventually. Or another way across. If guards gave him any hassle, well, he'd deal with it somehow.

Best to get moving before night fell and full dark—

ECCE, NOVUM PRINCEPS DE INFERNO, NOVUS REX TERRAE!

Greg was on the ground again without knowing what had hit him. His ears rang. His head spun. He sank his fingers into the earth to have something to hold onto. A shockwave, a thunderclap, some incredible wallop of power out of nowhere…an infernal bomb, a magical nuke…even this far from ground zero, it flattened him.

Crimson pillars of fire shot into the sky, spearing high through the dusky darkness from various points around the lake. They met at apex maybe a mile or so up and blossomed into a seething infernal supernova, spreading horrible light in a rippling aurora.

"Oh, shit," Greg said. Didn't have to be a warlock, trained or otherwise, to know this could not be good.

The aurora—Aurora Diabolicus, he dubbed it in his mind—flared wide and fanned out, and flowed downward in a sheeting curve like a liquid glaze of burning oil and blood covering the outside of an immense glass bowl. He watched its nearest edge pass overhead and descend in a coursing, wavering hellfire curtain.

"Oh, *shit!*"

Scrambling back onto his feet, he sprinted for the wall. Which was also changing...growing...building and piling upon itself like vertical lava...hot molten scarlet and cooling, congealing dead-black...rising to meet the descending curtain of hellish light.

He wasn't going to make it.

All those too-many-movies he'd watched made him try anyway. Indiana Jones time, Will Smith time, the portal closing, the gap narrowing, a final balls-out all-out desperate race to shoot through at the last possible skin-of-your-teeth second...

He wasn't going to make it. Even if he did reach the deadly barriers before they merged, what then? Jump? Climb? The wall had been prison-yard high to start with, topped by those loops of barbed wire; it was sixty feet or more now, bristling with obsidian spikes and spires. Towers formed. Citadels. Battlements.

It made Mordor look like Legoland.

Yet here he went, still running right at it.

***

Sulfurous yellow smoke roiled from immense iron cauldrons atop gargoyle-guarded parapets. The outlines of sinister war-machines appeared, catapults and ballistae, siege engines.

And down came the Aurora Diabolicus in its rippling, sheeting, terrible hellfire curtain of light.

Run, right. Jump. Climb. Leap tall buildings at a single bound. Maybe if he'd had more to go on than raw instinct and half-assed intuition…*sheesh, Nachtwald, some warlock you are.*

"Greg! Take my hands!"

The voice was no longer silvery windchimes but a brilliance of crystal and steel, no longer accompanied by the harmonious tones of a heavenly choir but by Wrath-of-God battle cries of a legion of archangels.

He tripped, nearly plowed full on his face. As much by reflex as anything, he grasped the proffered hands reaching toward him from within a dazzle of bright clarity and pure white clouds.

Not tiny hands; full-sized ones, pale as milk but opalescent, touched by shifting sheens of cerulean, lavender, blush-pink, and gold. They closed around his with righteous strength, the grip sure, and Greg looked up into a familiar, yet different, face.

Ethriel had tripled in size, her shimmering wings now diamond-lightning flarebursts crackling from her back, her sylphlike form armored in gold. Her features were stronger, and fiercer, yet largely the same. Her anime eyes shone like twin stars.

"Hold on!" she called, and…

…and lifted him right off the ground.

Greg yelled aloud in surprise, suddenly weightless, suddenly airborne. He held on, though, you bet, held on as if his very life and soul depended on it, which wasn't an exaggeration.

Never drive faster than your Guardian Angel can fly… he needn't have worried…no car in the world could have kept up…neither would his Cessna…a fighter jet might have had trouble. She sped toward the wall so fast he expected sonic booms in their wake, the air parting in a slicing wind tunnel slipstream.

"This might hurt!" Ethriel warned him. "It's going to be close!"

He shouldn't have been able to hear her over the buffeting wind-whistle of their rapid passage. But, with so many laws of nature, physics, and sanity already on hiatus, he wasn't about to quibble.

The looming wall, the descending aurora…the swiftly dwindling gap…and it was Indiana Jones as the portcullis dropped after all, Will Smith trying to escape the alien ship, a frantic double-or-nothing.

He felt a single hard squeeze in the center of his head, as if a mental fist clenched down on a stress ball. The sigil on his brow gave a blazing, blinding flash, and he could have sworn the aurora's hellfire curtain recoiled, retracted the way greasy water did from a drop of dish soap.

There was a sonic boom then, or sensation akin to one, and a ringing vibration inside him as if his bones had been turned into tuning forks.

There was also turbulence, he and Ethriel thrown tumbling around like sneakers in a clothes dryer, tied together by the laces. *Whump-ba-bump-ba-bump,* battering into each other, into the sides of the drum, kicking the dryer door open, ejecting the linked pair of sneakers onto the laundry room floor.

Or, onto the slightly marshy Florida soil. Second crash landing of the day, this one without even involving a plane.

"Oof," he groaned. "Did we make it? Are we dead?"

No one answered.

Greg rolled over and sat up. He saw the rearing nightmare edifice of the transformed wall, the aurora's eerie bubble above it seeming to encompass the entire perimeter.

He was on the outside of it, a good sixty yards clear. Under an otherwise normal evening sky.

He was also alone, though his hands were still closed tightly around...a strand of beads, petrified wood and mother-of-pearl, from which hung a silver medallion. Sigil on one side, inscription on the other—

Wait.

Loophole-looker. Rules lawyer. I knew it. Laughing, he put the amulet back on, ready to resume his travels.

28

The Golems opened the sides of the Holy Roller as easily as someone opening a tin of sardines. They extracted the panicking passengers, bruised and bloodied from having been tossed around in the crash.

"June! June Esther Goldsmith, whatever you think you're doing—"

"Gag her," June said.

A resourceful soldier obliged. Silence was golden, duct tape was silver. Above the muffling strip of it, Margaret Goldsmith's cheeks puffed, nostrils flaring, eyes bulging. She didn't fight, just kept staring incredulous shocked daggers at her daughter as other soldiers suspended her by bound wrists from a stout metal gantry and trundled it into position between the platform and the lake.

The Shinns were likewise gagged, unceremoniously manacled, and chained to a post. Ramon—still unconscious, but, amazingly, still alive—was also hauled out.

"This youth," said Favius speculatively, running his fingertips along Ramon's hairline and jawline, and the cauterized weal where the spine-whip had split his face. "This youth destroyed a major relic, the skull of an arch-duke."

"He lobbed a grenade into its eye socket," June said.

"Impressive. Such a deed marks the soul like a badge. I should like to claim his face, damaged though it is, and eat his yet-beating heart."

She shrugged. "Feel free."

"Perhaps later." He looked at her, with a slow, hungry smile. "We have better and more momentous business to attend to."

A considerable crowd was gathering, not just from the military convoy but a steady stream of what must have been locals. Denizens and Damned. Some looked as twisted as the creeker-freaks, or worse. Some looked perfectly normal. Some were in no way even nearly human. But they gathered, their mood an equally strange mix of somber solemnity and eager anticipation.

"Was lookin' forward t' a nice juicy Hock Party, though," someone remarked.

"Aw, we c'n has Hock Parties any dang time," someone else replied. "How oft'n we get t' see a new king, queen, *and* a matricide? This right here, this gon' be *special!*"

Special.

Margaret Goldsmith hung by the wrists from the gantry hook, her outraged expression above the duct tape gag continuing to berate June—*how could you, how dare you, after everything I've done for you, ungrateful little bitch, stupid cow, shameless hussy, look at this, look at you, didn't I tell you to put some clothes on? ready to whore yourself to this infernal brute, no wonder you never found a husband, probably would have ended up living with me, mooching off me for the rest of your life*—almost by telepathy in lieu of speech.

"Bread and circuses," Favius said. "Give them a memorable show."

June hadn't expected such an audience. Or camera crews.

Well, her mother always had enjoyed being the center of attention. Let's see how she enjoyed being stripped naked, humiliated in front of everyone with her baggy old body and loose, wrinkled skin! Drooping tits, cottage cheese ass, varicose veins, sparse grey pubic tufts like the pelt of a mangy rat!

294

How did she enjoy it? Not, it appeared, very much. The derisive hoots and mocking whistles were very like those June had heard countless times before, but these weren't directed at her, and now she found them meanly satisfying.

It wouldn't be enough simply to kill her, no. That just wouldn't do. A slit throat or a headshot would be far too quick, far too dull, far too merciful. When you were preparing to commit a Great Sin, it was go big or go home. Something blasphemous, something ruthless and cruel, something fitting…

She thought of the fish-gaff the creek-freak had used on Mr. Gabelman, wishing she had one of those. Then a diabolical lightbulb went off above her head and she rummaged in the back of the Holy Roller until she found what she was looking for.

"What is that?" inquired Favius. "A miniature pitchfork with but two tines?"

"A marshmallow fork," she said. "But I'm not going to use it to make goddamn *s'mores*."

***

No, instead, she stabbed it up between her mother's legs, into the old cunt's old cunt as far as it would go!

Margaret screamed through the duct tape, bucking and thrashing, trying to kick, but June had the Golems hold her by the ankles. Blood trickled, surprise post-menopausal visit from the cardinal, as they said…are you there, God? It's me, Margaret!

June laughed aloud, laughed savagely as she jabbed the fork deeper. The tines skewered the cervix and pierced through into the womb, in sharp mimicry of a coathanger abortion—for the benefit of the Shinns, so sanctimonious with all their clinic protests!—and the trickle of blood became what the feminine hygiene product commercials would call 'heavy flow.'

Into the womb, yes! More than matricide, more than mother-killing, an utter renunciation of the very cradle of life! Into the soft, dark, pear-shaped uterus. Into that musty, long-empty nursery from which June herself, and only she, had been born. No brothers, no sisters. No sons to become doctors or lawyers and make lots of money, no pretty daughters who'd marry doctors or lawyers and make adorable grandchildren.

Only her. Only one. Only plain-jane-Junie-June. Never a pride to her parents, never allowed to forget. Always a disappointment, always reminded.

Well, but look at her now!

The tines of the marshmallow fork were not simple smooth prongs. They had small flared barbs on the ends, like arrowheads, the intention being to keep a roasting marshmallow from sliding off into the fire. But they served equally well to dig into the uterine walls, to hook and snag at the tissue.

From trickle to 'heavy flow' to a torrent, a thick crimson waterfall, pattering the earth, dousing June's arm as she twisted the implement. Twisted, and pulled. A slow, steady, wrenching pull, accompanied by deep ripping sounds and a velcro-like sensation of separation and *give*.

Margaret had either stopped screaming or hit notes so high only dogs and bats would hear, but her thrashing struggles went into frenzied overdrive…to the point that even the Golems, strong as they were, strong enough to crumple a church-bus like a ball of tinfoil, had a hard time holding on. More blood rained from her bound wrists; she'd nearly degloved one hand already, the skin bunched in sloppy, floppy folds. Both of her shoulders dislocated with meaty wet pops. With the weight of her body dragging downward, a bizarre elongation occurred, torso seeming to stretch away from her arms on putty-flesh.

Before matters progressed to spontaneous drawing-and-quartering, June gave the fork another good hard twisting pull, yanking the motherly part of her mother inside-out. It was prolapse and then some, entire reproductive evisceration, a slippery tangle of gynecological offal—uterus, cervix, vaginal walls, fallopian tubes trailing after with ovaries attached like tin cans tied to a wedding car's bumper, the whole works a purplish-grey squiddy mess suddenly pendulous and swinging free.

All that with a marshmallow fork!

June uttered a wild banshee cry and spun toward the Shinns, brandishing the bloodied implement. "Where's your goddamn s'mores now?"

They cowered, weeping and wetting themselves like preschoolers. Several of the crowd, and even some soldiers who'd recently been furiously engaging in their own acts of atrocity, took respectful steps back as June continued turning.

People had never looked at her like that before.

Men had never looked at her like that before.

"Daaa-aaa-amn," said whoever'd earlier bemoaned missing the Hock Party, in a low, awed tone.

"Din't I tell yer?" replied his companion. "Din't I jist tell yer?"

"That," added a college-age guy who was probably quite the hottie when not a busted-nose, puffy-eyed mess, "was hardcore. Hard-fucking-*core.*"

The shapely girl next to him, who had seemed shellshocked and aghast before, regarded June with a mixture of fear, respect, and envy. "Shiiiiiiit," she breathed.

"I know, right?" said the guy. "Wishing we'd brought Mom?"

"Kind of..."

"So, we'll just have to persuade her and Dad to visit us at the lakehouse."

***

June completed her turn, facing the gantry. The Golems had released their hold on Margaret Goldsmith's dangling, trembling body and moved deferentially aside.

Using the tine-end of the fork, clotted with gore, she forced her mother's chin upward. Margaret's eyelids struggled weakly open. Her pain-filmed gaze wavered before fixing on June. Then it cleared into a piercing glare of pure, venomous loathing.

She could have ripped off the duct tape and given the old bitch a chance at last words, but why set herself up to be belittled and insulted yet again? Instead, she rammed the fork straight up, through the flabby chin undershelf, tacking her mother's hateful tongue to the roof of her mouth before sinking the tines up into the sinuses. A brief resistance of orbital bone later, and both eyeballs were speared from below like martini olives.

Then she let go of the handle, and simply stood watching until the final gurgling shudder, the gushing release of bladder and bowels, and the limp droop of deadweight.

There.

Done.

There arose a spontaneous thunder of cheers and applause, the crowd going wild, hoots and hollers and yee-haws, gunshot salutes fired into the sky.

A hand settled onto June's shoulder. A large hand, callused and strong, but with the tender face of a neonatal fetus stitched into center of the palm. She felt its barely-formed little features scrunch and squirm against her skin.

It should have been revolting.

Should have been. Wasn't.

"Magnificent," Favius said, the word an intimate growl close to her ear, the heat of his breath a wash of steam on her throat.

"A great enough sin?"

"Verily."

"A memorable enough show?"

He indicated the celebratory crowd. "Tell me they will soon forget this day."

"I doubt it."

"Nor shall you. Nor shall I. Nor shall any who witness and survive."

She shivered all the way to her marrow. Something intangible at the very core of herself seemed to curl, to cocoon itself and die and change, and be reborn with an unfurling of membranous black wings.

Favius's other hand settled upon her other shoulder. The fetus-face there also scrunched and squirmed, as if seeking to suckle.

Should have been revolting. Wasn't. Was darkly, damningly exciting.

He did not have claws, but his thumbnails were inhumanly thick, ragged, and sharp, and sliced through the knotted tatters of her makeshift top as easily as blades. June flinched as her breasts in their insignificance fell bared to the world, bracing herself for the inevitable snickers, the inevitable shame.

No one snickered. No one dared. Favius slid his hands down, palms pressed snug to her chest. The tiny, squirming faces sought…found…latched on. She gasped at the strange dual nursing suction, her nipples suddenly more sensitive than they'd ever been in her life.

Then his arms were around her, crushing her to the hard contours of his Hell-forged Roman armor. His mouth covered hers in a forceful, bruising kiss that tasted of fire and murder and blood.

The crowd, already gone wild, went absolutely nuts.

Ecce, novum princeps de inferno, novus rex terrae!

He swept her up, shredding the rest of her clothes in the

process, and lowered her roughly onto the bunting-draped platform beneath torchlight and television cameras. June clutched at his back, clawed at his shoulders, savaged with her teeth his lips and his hot, plundering tongue.

Ecce, novum princeps de inferno, novus rex terrae!

She remembered some long-ago middle-school English teacher telling the class that you could easily determine a Shakespearean comedy from a tragedy because the former always ended with a wedding and the latter always ended with the stage strewn with corpses.

Which was this? Both? Neither? Did she care? Did it matter?

No.

What mattered was…

ECCE, NOVUM PRINCEPS DE INFERNO, NOVUS REX TERRAE!

And behold, so did Favius, former First Conscript, become a new prince of Hell and a new king on Earth, claiming his queen and his kingdom with a violent, victorious thrust.

AUTHOR'S NOTE

How in the Hell, so to speak, did this happen? There I was, just a struggling fangirl nobody, contributing my ramblings to The Horror Fiction Review back when it was still a stapled-paper 'zine…when, out of nowhere, I got a response from Edward Lee, thanking me for the good reviews.

Edward-freakin'-LEE! The man himself, the king of extreme horror, my literary idol, thanking ME! The Mephistopolis is my favorite setting ever, such a great blend of mythologies, funny and gross and so vivid and visceral … I love his other stuff too, but the Mephistopolis seized an immediate forever-place in my twisted heart.

Next I knew, we were corresponding, and we met at a couple of cons, and he gave positive feedback on one of my more messed-up stories ("The Defiled" in *Splatterlands*) and was so kind and supportive that I decided to try an impertinent request.

I'd written a hardboiled/noir-type story called "Matt Brimstone, P.I.," about a 1930s detective who ends up in Hell after he's killed by a demoness disguised as a lounge singer. The characters were originally part of an ongoing storyline in an online roleplaying game, and I used the Mephistopolis as background inspiration.

So, I asked Lee if he'd mind if I submitted Matt's story to an anthology call. He granted permission. It was accepted and published. Eventually, so were its connected follow-ups, "Torch Songs in Purgatory" and "One Less Fury."

303

And, well, when you give a mouse a cookie … flash forward a few years, after he's been sending me books, giving more feedback, even putting me to work proofreading for him and being an all-around great guy … I took the big plunge and really went for it.

See, he'd done this book called *Lucifer's Lottery*, in which Satan's forces steal a freshwater lake from our world and replace it with the contents of a reservoir from Hell. If you haven't read it … well, then you probably wouldn't be reading this anyway, so, nevermind!

What most captivated me was what might happen around that lake afterward, the effects it would have on the environment and ecosystem and locals, how the rest of the world would react. I wrote to Lee and begged pretty-please to be allowed to play with his toys not just a little, but bigtime, by doing a sequel.

Once again, he generously (even, perhaps, gleefully) granted permission. His only stipulation was that he wanted a cameo. I may have gone a bit beyond 'cameo.' In fact, as is my usual wont, I ended up having way too much fun with the whole damn thing. It's total shameless Edward Lee fanfic throughout, riddled with references to not just the Infernal series but many others of his books.

And I had this whole lake to play with! A whole cast of characters to torment in horrible, horrible ways! The opportunity to kick out the stops and just go gloriously nuts! I could even, in a blatant grab for illegitimate backdoor roundabout canon-adjacency, sneakily connect my own Spermjackers From Hell with the Infernal universe.

Then, just to add to the madness, I got this notion to try writing the entire thing in 666-word increments. Really, I did! It posed a challenge at times, but ultimately worked surprisingly well. Yes, it's silly. Yes, it's gimmicky as fuck. Even this afterword is 666 words. When you're going to Hell anyway, at some point it becomes go big or go home.

Speaking of home, in real life, I'm a twice-married, twice-divorced, twice-cancer-survivor, with a grown daughter who once did a book report on City Infernal and sold her own first horror story at age fourteen (yay parenting skills!). I live in Portland, Oregon with a roomie and three cats. I read, I write, I edit, I review, I work nights in a residential psych facility. In what remains of my free time, I enjoy cooking and baking and crafts. You know, nice normal fiftyish-frump-old-lady type stuff. Nothing WEIRD. Honest.

— *Christine Morgan*

deadite
press

"Header" Edward Lee - In the dark backwoods, where law enforcement doesn't dare tread, there exists a special type of revenge. Something so awful that it is only whispered about. Something so terrible that few believe it is real. Stewart Cummings is a government agent whose life is going to Hell. His wife is ill and to pay for her medication he turns to bootlegging. But things will get much worse when bodies begin showing up in his sleepy small town. Victims of an act known only as "a Header."

"Punk Rock Ghost Story" David Agranoff - In the summer of 1982, legendary Indianapolis hardcore band, The Fuckers, became the victim of a mysterious tragedy. They returned home without their vocalist and the band disappeared. A single record sought by collectors, a band nearly forgotten, and an urban legend passed from punk to punk. What happened to The Fuckers on that tour? Why was their singer never seen again? No one has been able to say. Until now…

"Zombies and Shit" Carlton Mellick III - Twenty people wake to find themselves in a boarded-up building in the middle of the zombie wasteland. They soon discover they have been chosen as contestants on a popular reality show called Zombie Survival. Each contestant is given a backpack of supplies and a unique weapon. Their goal: be the first to make it through the zombie-plagued city to the pick-up zone alive. But because there's only one seat available on the helicopter, the contestants not only have to fight against the hordes of the living dead, they must also fight each other.

"The Book of a Thousand Sins" Wrath James White - Welcome to a world of Zombie nymphomaniacs, psychopathic deities, voodoo surgery, and murderous priests. Where mutilation sex clubs are in vogue and torture machines are sex toys. No one makes it out alive – not even God himself.
"If Wrath James White doesn't make you cringe, you must be riding in the wrong end of a hearse."
    -Jack Ketchum

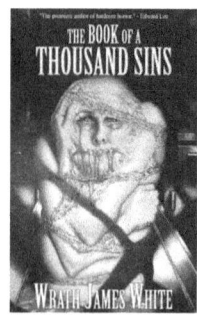

"Like Porno for Psychos" Wrath James White - From a world-ending orgy to home liposuction. From the hidden desires of politicians to a woman with a fetish for lions. This is a place where necrophilia, self-mutilation, and murder are all roads to love. Like Porno for Psychos collects the most extreme erotic horror from the celebrated hardcore horror master. Wrath James White is your guide through sex, death, and the darkest desires of the heart.

"Bigfoot Crank Stomp" Erik Williams - Bigfoot is real and he's addicted to meth! It should have been so easy. Get in, kill everyone, and take all the money and drugs. That was Russell and Mickey's plan. But the drug den they were raiding in the middle of the woods holds a dark secret chained up in the basement. A beast filled with rage and methamphetamine and tonight it will break loose. Nothing can stop Bigfoot's drug-fueled rampage and before the sun rises there is going to be a lot of dead cops and junkies.

"Survivor" J.F. Gonzalez - Lisa was looking forward to spending time alone with her husband. Instead, it becomes a nightmare when her husband is arrested and Lisa is kidnapped. But the kidnappers aren't asking for ransom. They're going to make her a star-in a snuff film.. They plan to torture and murder her as graphically and brutally as possible, and to capture it all on film. If they have their way, Lisa's death will be truly horrifying...but even more horrifying is what Lisa will do to survive...

"Genital Grinder" Ryan Harding - *"Think you're hardcore? Think again. If you've handled everything Edward Lee, Wrath James White, and Bryan Smith have thrown at you, then put on your rubber parka, spread some plastic across the floor, and get ready for Ryan Harding, the unsung master of hardcore horror. Abandon all hope, ye who enter here. Harding's work is like an acid bath, and pain has never been so sweet."*
- Brian Keene

AVAILABLE FROM AMAZON.COM